# Eyes of Green

*Book One of the Eyes of Green Saga*

Lucy Novacek

Cover design: Lucy Novacek
Editing: Self-edited.
ISBN: 9798270696641
Printed by Amazon KDP
First edition, 2025

For updates and upcoming releases, follow @Lucy.Novacek on Instagram.

For my mum, Allison —

for always being my rock, my calm, and my constant.


And for my little boy —

the brightest light in every chapter of my life.

# Chapter One

Emmeline Trevelyn had always been good at leaving quietly. She'd perfected it in small ways as a child — slipping out of crowded village gatherings before questions started, slipping away from the too-curious eyes of neighbours who saw everything. But this move felt different. It was not a small slip; it was a full, deliberate exit from a life that had grown too heavy for her to carry.

She needed a fresh start.

This early Sunday morning just as the dawn light was pale and tentative, slowly melting away the mist that clung to the hedgerows. Emmy sat on the edge of the bus seat as the bus jerked as the engine started; her fingers tapping nervously against her knee. She knew this was the right thing to do. A whole fresh start. She had chosen this new town carefully, almost methodically. Far enough from her childhood village that her parents wouldn't worry about surprise visits, but not so far that she felt she had disappeared completely. Here, she would be just another newcomer, another young woman seeking a fresh start. It was exactly what she needed.

It was not long before the bus had made its short journey to the train station. Emmeline thanked the bus driver for helping her lift off her heavy suitcase and bag. "Hope you enjoy your trip Emmy, I bet your parents attempted to talk you out of it?".

Emmy smiled, and nodded as she adjusted her bag strap, "they still are – but it's time I found my place in the world again". The bus driver gave a comforting tap on Emmy's shoulder as she started to walk up the steep road to the train station.

Mixed emotions flooded Emmy's mind like a whirlwind. She knew deep down she had to do this; it had been two years. The memories in her parents' home were thick as dust from her childhood. There was the night she'd cried herself to sleep after her first heartbreak, the afternoons spent curled up with novels that smelled like old libraries, the whispered phone calls to friends and sneaking out to meet them.

But there was also the newer layer — the silence that followed her after that night out two years ago, the one she barely spoke of even to herself. The way her mother hovered now, her father's protective glances that landed heavy as wool. Emmy had learned to smile, to assure them she was fine, to pour tea and change the subject. But she knew they worried — she saw it in every drawn line on her mother's face.

As the train pulled up; Emmy took one last deep breath and glanced back at the quiet station. Half expecting a cavalry of family with their final pleas to persuade her to stay, that things will get better. Her parents had slowly come round to the idea and told her she can do this just this morning. Agreeing this is good for her. This will be the making of her. She will be fine. Emmy had asked her parents to let her do the journey alone; that she would be afraid she would back down and change her mind if she had to witness their sad faces left behind. Reluctantly, her parents agreed.

The train carriage rattled gently as it wound its way through the soft curves of the English countryside. Emmy watched the fields roll past in long, green waves punctuated by early yellow daffodils and budding hedgerows. Her reflection wavered faintly in the window: big dark eyes, honey-gold skin, her long black curls pulled into a loose bun that refused to stay tidy.

She touched her reflection absentmindedly, tracing the edge of her cheek. Her mother's words drifted back, as they so often did when she was alone: "Your curls are your crown, Emmeline. Don't ever let anyone make you feel small for them." Emmy had grown up learning to treat her hair like a living thing — carefully twisting, braiding, oiling. In her childhood village, she had sometimes felt like a bright smudge in a sea of fair faces. But here on the train, she felt quietly anonymous. And for now, that felt like freedom to her. A much-desired freedom.

The rocking of the carriage lulled her into a gentle daze. She tried reading, a novel she'd tucked in her lap, but her mind kept drifting. Memories floated up uninvited: the last phone call with her parents, her father's soft plea that she reconsiders moving so far away; her mother's measured calm, masking an ache that mirrored Emmy's own.

She remembered the night she decided to leave. The moonlight on her bedroom floor, her suitcase gaping open, her heart a tight knot of fear and determination. She could not keep living as the girl who had survived a bad relationship — the girl whispered about, pitied, watched too closely at the grocer's and at church. She needed a place where no one knew her, where she might simply be Miss Trevelyn, a new teacher with bright eyes and a quiet voice.

A few hours rolled by when Emmy's thoughts were jolted back to the present when the conductor's voice announced: "Next stop, Stonebridge Hollow Station." Emmy gathered her bag, tucking her book away. The train pulled in with a slow sigh. She stepped onto the small platform, the air carrying the smell of damp stone and freshly turned earth.

She paused for a moment, savouring the strange quiet — no one waiting, no familiar faces pressing in. Just space.

A single taxi idled at the curb. The driver, a middle-aged man with wind-rough cheeks and a bright blue knit cap, leaned out. "Miss Trevelyn?" he called.

"Yes — that's me," she said, shifting her suitcase toward him.

"Hop in. You're going to the square, right?"

She nodded, climbing into the back. The seats smelled faintly of vanilla air freshener and engine oil.

As they pulled away from the station, Emmy watched the small houses slip past — ivy-tangled fences, crooked chimneys, gardens brimming with early blooms. In places, narrow lanes dipped into shallow valleys, lined with low dry-stone walls. The town felt stitched together by memory rather than design, each corner suggesting lives lived slowly, deliberately.

The driver glanced at her in the rear-view mirror. "New in town?" he asked, his accent rounded and warm.

"Yes," she replied softly. "I'm going to be teaching at the primary school."

"Ah! They'll be lucky to have you. It's a good place here. Folks mostly mind their own, but they'll warm up to you once they see your kind."

She smiled faintly. "I hope so."

"You from London, then?"

"No. A little town outside Bath," she answered. "But... it was time for a change."

He nodded knowingly, tapping the steering wheel in a gentle rhythm. "Sometimes a change is exactly what a person needs. You'll see. This place has a way of making you slow down, breathe different."

They passed a row of old oaks, their branches still bare but promising green soon. Farther along, she caught a glimpse of a pond reflecting the pale sky, a lone swan gliding across like a secret. Emmy felt her chest soften a little at the sight. Just past a row of trees they turned onto the narrow high street. The driver eased to a stop at the edge of the village green. Emmy paid him and stepped out, the morning light catching on her curls. She paused, rolling her suitcase to the side, and took her first full breath in her new home.

The green stretched before her like a soft quilt, bordered by a row of brick and stone shops. Hanging baskets brimmed with bright petunias and trailing ivy, and an elderly man in a wax jacket fed crumbs to a pair of stubborn pigeons on a nearby bench.

She watched them for a moment, grounding herself in the ordinariness of it all.

She shifted her gaze to the shop signs, reading each one with curiosity: Aubrey's Book Shop, with its gold lettering so carefully painted it looked like it belonged in another century; Pearson's Bakery, with a chalkboard boasting the best scones in the county; a florist spilling bright blooms onto the pavement. The simple beauty of it tugged at something inside her, a small but stubborn hope.

She brushed a stray curl from her face, feeling her golden honey-brown skin warm under the growing sun. Her features — the slender nose, the big dark eyes, the full lips — reflected her mixed heritage in a delicate balancing act. She carried her mother's softness in her smile, and her father's gentle seriousness in her gaze. The curls were her mother's gift, worn proudly, a small rebellion against the world's attempts to smooth her down.

Rolling her suitcase carefully over the uneven paving stones, Emmy made her way toward her new flat above Aubrey's. The staircase leading to the flat entrance was narrow and steep, its wooden steps worn smooth by countless tenants. A small brass plaque reading Private Residence glinted faintly. Emmy ran her fingers across it, feeling the little ridges, before unlocking the door with a key Mr. Aubrey had sent in a neat brown envelope the previous week.

Inside, the flat smelled of old paper and lavender polish. The morning light filtered through wide sash windows, illuminating floating dust motes that looked like tiny dancers. A pale green armchair waited by the window, and a battered bookshelf lined the far wall, filled with dog-eared novels left behind by other wanderers like her.

She set her suitcase down and exhaled a slow breath she hadn't realized she'd been holding.

Emmy wandered to the window and looked out over the green. From here, she could see the curve of the high street, the bakery's striped awning, and the old church steeple standing watch in the distance. Children ran circles around each other in bright coats, laughter rising up toward her window. Emmy leaned her forehead against the glass for a moment, letting the warmth soak in.

Taking a deep breath; Emmy stood with her hands on her hips, staring at the boxes piled in uneven towers across the living room floor which she had delivered by a courier the previous day. The flat was small, but charming in its own unpolished way. The floorboards were worn smooth with age, and the plastered walls bowed slightly as though leaning in to keep her company. She let out a slow breath. This was it. This was home now.

She crouched down and tore the tape from the nearest box, the sound loud in the stillness. Books spilled into her lap, their spines bent from years of being thumbed through. She stacked them along the shelf one by one, arranging them without thinking: the well-loved novels first, then the ones she had always meant to read but never had the time for. By the time she finished, the once-bare shelf looked alive, weighted with a story of its own.

Her next box was lighter, filled with small keepsakes she had wrapped in crumpled tissue. She unwrapped a porcelain trinket dish her grandmother once gave her; the glaze chipped on one side but still gleaming softly in the light. Emmy placed it carefully on the narrow hallway table and smiled faintly. These little things mattered, she thought. They were proof that she belonged here.

The wardrobe took longer. Emmy carried her clothes in armfuls, hanging them with care. She smoothed each blouse, each skirt, letting her fingers linger over the fabric as if that act alone could steady her nerves. She caught sight of herself in the mirror fixed inside the door: her curls loose from the humidity, her face flushed with the effort of lifting. For a moment, her reflection looked like a stranger. She tilted her head, tucked a curl behind her ear, and forced a small smile.

By late afternoon, she had found the courage to open the box she had been avoiding. Old papers, notebooks, a few photographs she hadn't looked at in years. She sifted through them slowly. A scrap of handwriting from her mother, tucked between folded pages. She pressed it to her chest, eyes closing briefly before she placed it in the drawer beside her bed. Safe. Out of sight, but close.

In the kitchen, she set about lining the cupboards. The clink of her mismatched mugs filled the silence, a comforting rhythm. She placed the yellow one on the end—her favourite, though the glaze was cracked at the handle—and felt her chest ease a little at the sight of it. She unwrapped the small tin of loose tea she'd packed last minute, inhaling the earthy scent. It reminded her of calm mornings, of routine. Perhaps she could find that here too.

By the time the sun had begun to sink, the flat was changing shape. A woven throw softened the sofa. The small rug she had rolled beneath her arm during the move now spread across the wooden floor, warm against her bare feet. On the mantel, photographs leaned together like quiet witnesses of her past: her mother in a sunlit garden, Emmy as a child, her arms full of a kitten that had long since grown old.

She placed her plant on the windowsill—a trailing ivy, stubborn and green, its leaves curling toward the glass. It looked too small for the wide sill, but Emmy liked the way it reached, as if determined to claim its place in the new space, just as she was.

At last, Emmy sank into the chair she had pulled by the window. She curled her legs beneath her and let her gaze drift outside. The village square lay hushed below, the cobbled street gleaming faintly in the dimming light. The bookshop sign swayed gently in the breeze, its painted letters catching the last of the day. Somewhere in the distance a bell tolled the hour, slow and certain.

She closed her eyes briefly, the ache of the day settling into her shoulders. It wasn't perfect—not yet. The paint was peeling in places, the floor creaked when she crossed it, and the air still carried the faint must of an empty space. But it was hers now. A place to begin again.

Emmy wrapped the throw tighter around her shoulders, breathed in the mingled scents of old books, wood, and her own perfume settling into the room, and whispered softly to herself, "Home."

Her fingers hovered over to a framed photograph of her family: her mother in a bright headwrap, laughing, her father with his quiet eyes, and Emmy standing in front, her curls a wild halo. She touched her mother's face in the glass, feeling the echo of warmth and the sharp pull of loss.

She placed the photo on her bedside table and glanced at her phone. No new messages yet, but she knew they would come. They always did.

Emmy moved to make tea — a soft chamomile blend, her mother's favourite for calming nerves. The kettle hissed in the small kitchen, pulling her from her reverie. She poured it slowly, watching the pale-yellow swirl fill the mug.

When it was ready, she carried it to the window again. Outside, she saw a young woman walking a terrier, nodding politely to an older man who tipped his hat in return. A postman coasted by on a bright red bicycle, whistling a jaunty tune she didn't recognize. The entire town seemed to move in gentle loops, a quiet dance that felt both alien and comforting.

For the first time in a long while, Emmy let herself breathe fully. Here, she wouldn't be the girl everyone pitied or whispered about. Here, she might simply be Miss Trevelyn — a new teacher who loved wildflowers and lost villages and the soft hush of morning tea.

She sipped, her eyes drifting to the curve of the street below, where the sign for Aubrey's Book shop gleamed gently in the sunlight.

* * *

Later that afternoon, Emmy finally decided to explore. The itch to move, to learn every corner of this new place, was too strong to ignore. She tucked her curls beneath a wool beret and slipped on her softest scarf — a deep burgundy her mother had once described as "a hug in a colour."

Down on the green, she let herself wander. She paused at the florist first, her eyes sweeping over the crowded buckets of tulips and daffodils. A young girl with freckles and a bright yellow apron was arranging roses in a basket by the door.

"Lovely day for it," Emmy said shyly.

The girl grinned. "Perfect for daffs. They make the whole shop smell like spring."

Emmy bought a small bunch and tucked them into her satchel, the scent following her as she moved on.

She peered into Aubrey's Book shop, heart stuttering a little. The shop's sign — that soft gold lettering curling like ivy

— seemed to promise stories both old and waiting to be told. Through the window, she saw narrow wooden shelves stacked to the ceiling and an old brass till. In one corner sat a faded armchair, its cushion dented from many readers who had curled up and lost themselves among the pages.

A bell tinkled lightly as she stepped inside. The scent of paper and ink washed over her at once, familiar and comforting as a childhood blanket.

A tall man with wispy grey hair and reading glasses perched on the tip of his nose looked up from behind the counter. Mr. Aubrey, she presumed.

"Good afternoon," he said warmly, folding a newspaper and rising to greet her.

"Good afternoon," Emmy replied, smiling. "I'm... just browsing today. I live just upstairs, actually."

His eyes twinkled. "Ah, the new tenant. We've been expecting you. Welcome to Stonebridge Hollow."

"Thank you. It's... it's lovely here."

"Do you like old books, Miss—?"

"Trevelyn," she supplied. "Emmeline Trevelyn. But I go by Emmy."

"Emmy. A fine name. You'll fit right in, I suspect." He gestured broadly at the shelves. "Feel free to wander. If you need help finding anything — or if you want to discuss the secret life of badgers or the original meaning of certain medieval curses — just holler."

Emmy laughed, the sound light and surprised even to her own ears. "Thank you. I think I will."

She drifted from shelf to shelf, running her fingers along spines stamped in gold leaf, others with brittle paper jackets. History sections lured her in first: volumes on Tudor politics, on village folklore, on local churches and vanished hamlets. Each title felt like a small invitation to slip away from herself and step into another time.

She pulled out a thin volume titled The Lost Villages of England and flipped it open. On the inside cover, a handwritten note in looping ink read:

*Some places vanish in silence. Others, with a scream. And some, simply wait to be remembered.*

A small shiver rippled up her spine. She tucked the book under her arm before she could second-guess herself.

Back at the counter, Mr. Aubrey wrapped it in brown paper and tied it with a thin green string. Emmy paid, holding the parcel like something fragile.

As she left, the bell tinkled again, and she found herself smiling up at the sign before stepping onto the pavement.

She wandered further down the high street next, stopping outside Pearson's Bakery. The scent of sugar and warm bread wrapped around her like an embrace. Inside, a short, broad-shouldered woman with a flour-dusted apron was laughing heartily with an older gentleman nursing a takeaway tea.

Emmy pushed open the door cautiously.

"Hello, love!" the woman called out immediately. "You're new! I never forget a face."

Emmy blushed faintly. "Yes — Emmy. I've just moved into the flat above Aubrey's."

"Ah! We've been wondering when we'd see you. I'm Margaret Pearson. Call me Mags." She leaned forward conspiratorially. "If you don't leave here with at least two pastries, I'll consider it a personal failure."

Emmy laughed, her cheeks warming. "In that case, I'd better take three, to be safe."

They both chuckled. Emmy pointed to a tray of custard tarts and a loaf of poppy seed bread.

"Good choices!" Mags declared, expertly bagging them up. "First one's on the house, mind you. Consider it a 'welcome to the village' gift."

"That's so kind," Emmy said softly, touched despite herself.

She left the bakery feeling oddly light, a tiny warmth unfurling in her chest.

On her way back toward the green, she stopped to watch a pair of children playing marbles near the fountain. One of them paused to squint up at her.

"Are you the new teacher?" the boy called.

"Yes, I am," Emmy said, smiling.

"Cool! I bet you can't beat me at marbles though," he bragged, puffing out his chest.

She laughed, promising she'd try another day, and moved on before she was challenged into a match she'd surely lose.

When she reached her flat again, the sun was beginning to dip, the sky streaked with soft lilacs and warm amber. She climbed the stairs slowly, each creak of wood echoing in the stillness. Inside, she placed her new treasures on the kitchen table and unpacked them one by one.

She filled a vase with the daffodils from the florist, arranging them by the window where they caught the last light of the day. The pastries went onto a small plate, their sugary tops glistening like jewels.

Finally, she sat down with her wrapped book from Aubrey's, carefully untying the string. She opened to the first page, tracing the handwritten note once more.

*Some places vanish in silence. Others, with a scream. And some, simply wait to be remembered.*

She read it aloud softly, the words curling through the room like smoke.

Outside, the quiet deepened, broken only by the occasional bark of a dog or the distant creak of a shop shutter closing.

Emmy leaned her head back against the chair and closed her eyes. She felt the hum of the day settle in her bones — the kindness of strangers, the delicate excitement of the unknown, the heady blend of fear and relief that comes with starting again.

Her phone buzzed on the table. She picked it up, smiling when she saw the name.

Mum calling.

She answered, her mother's soft, steady voice instantly filling her ear.

"How's my girl?"

Emmy's throat tightened. "I'm okay, Mum. The village is beautiful. I think I might actually like it here."

Her mother paused, and Emmy could picture her in the kitchen back home, dish towel slung over one shoulder, eyes fixed on a patch of afternoon sky.

"Good," her mother finally said. "You deserve somewhere that feels safe, Emmeline."

They spoke for a while longer — small things, garden updates, her father's latest crossword victory. When they finally hung up, Emmy held the phone to her chest for a moment, breathing in the soft afterglow of connection.

She stood then, moving slowly to close the curtains. The village lights flickered below, warm and scattered like fallen stars. She stood there for a long moment, her fingers brushing the heavy fabric, her mind echoing with her mother's words.

Tomorrow would bring the school, the new colleagues, the children's wide-eyed curiosity. Tomorrow would bring the beginning of her new life in earnest.

But tonight was just hers.

She turned away from the window, pausing to glance at her reflection. Her curls had escaped their knot again, framing her face like an unruly crown. She reached up and tucked them back, smiling faintly at the woman looking back.

Emmy Trevelyn. Not a survivor tonight. Just a woman with a new book, a flat full of flowers, and the quiet possibility of belonging.

# Chapter Two

The morning sun rose early, filtering into Emmy's flat in warm, slanting rays that fell across her face. She woke slowly, disoriented at first, until she remembered where she was. The soft clatter of the street below — a delivery lorry reversing, someone calling good morning to a neighbour — all gently reminded her she wasn't in her parents' house, or her old shared flat, but here.

Stonebridge Hollow.

Emmy yawned and stretched beneath the quilt, her golden honey-toned skin catching the light. She glanced at her phone: 6:48 a.m. Plenty of time before she needed to be at the school.

She shuffled into the kitchen; her long curls twisted into a loose braid that spilled over her shoulder like black silk. As she set the kettle to boil, she let her eyes wander over the new details of her flat — the chipped enamel sink, the little bunch of daffodils from the day before, the framed print of an old railway station she'd found at a market years ago. It all felt tenderly borrowed, like wearing someone else's favourite cardigan.

While she waited for the water in the kettle to boil, she started making her packed lunch — cheese and chutney sandwich, apple slices, and a biscuit. She'd even tucked in a small note to herself: "You're doing fine. Just breathe." It was silly, but her therapist had once suggested writing affirmations. Emmy hadn't believed it would help, but she found herself clinging to them on mornings like this.

She poured her tea, strong and almost syrupy black, just how her grandmother had taught her. As she sipped, she checked her messages. A new one from her father appeared: "Good luck today, Emmeline. Mum and I are so proud of you. Let us know how it goes. We love you."

A lump rose in her throat.

I will. Love you both, she typed back, though the words felt too small to hold all that she felt.

She finished her tea slowly, letting the warmth bloom in her chest. Then she dressed carefully — a soft cream blouse with tiny embroidered wildflowers on the collar, a navy pleated skirt that brushed her calves, and her favourite flat leather shoes. She pinned her curls back with a few clips but left most of them cascading down her back in soft, inky waves.

Before she left, she stood in front of the mirror. Her big, warm brown eyes seemed even larger against her delicate features today, her full lips pressed together in a small, determined line. She looked, she thought, like someone about to step into a new life.

She grabbed her bag, double-checked for her planner and pen case, and finally headed out into the early morning.

Outside, the village felt different than it had the day before. There was a hum of anticipation in the air, the gentle busyness of people starting their routines. A milkman unloaded glass bottles onto doorsteps. A postwoman in a bright orange vest sorted letters at the back of her van.

Emmy paused near Aubrey's shop to glance up at her window. The daffodils glowed in the morning light, nodding gently as if encouraging her onward.

She turned and started toward the school.

The walk wasn't far — ten minutes along the winding main road, past Pearson's Bakery and the florist, then turning left near the war memorial where red poppy wreaths still clung from November. Along the way, Emmy let her eyes wander: a dog walker coaxing a stubborn spaniel; an elderly man in a flat cap whistling as he swept his front step; a young mother struggling with a pram and two fidgeting toddlers.

As she passed the bakery, Mags spotted her through the window and tapped the glass excitedly. Emmy waved back, smiling at the sight of her cheer.

Beyond the square, a narrow street wound between cottages, their windowsills crowded with geraniums and lavender. Emmy followed it slowly, brushing her fingers against the rough stone wall as she passed. A cat darted across her path, vanishing into the shadow of a gate left ajar. She smiled faintly and continued, letting her steps carry her until the bustle of the centre was behind her.

The lane bent toward a cluster of trees where the village seemed to thin out. Here, the air felt cooler, the hush of leaves mingling with the distant sound of a stream. Emmy paused, adjusting the strap of her bag on her shoulder, her gaze tracing the quiet road ahead.

A solitary figure emerged from the shade ahead, tall and composed, moving with a steadiness that set him apart from the bustle she had just left behind. His coat was dark, his hair a sweep of black touched faintly by the sun, and as he glanced to the side for the briefest moment, the sharp gleam of green in his eyes caught her unprepared. Emmy's breath stilled, though she could not have said why—he did not look at her, did not hesitate, only continued on, his steps quiet against the worn stones.

She realised only once he had passed from view that she was still standing there, clutching the strap of her bag as though it anchored her. A few children raced passed her from behind her, laughter echoing, but the sound felt far away. With a small shake of her head, Emmy forced herself to move again, telling herself it was nothing—just a stranger. Still, as she continued on her route to work; the memory of those eyes lingered, bright and impossible to ignore.

Soon, the school came into view — a charming, red-bricked Edwardian building with ivy curling up around the arched windows. The small front lawn was neatly trimmed, dotted with daisy clumps that refused to be mowed down completely. A carved wooden sign out front read: Stonebridge Hollow Church of England Primary School — Founded 1903.

A low, wrought-iron gate marked the entrance. Emmy paused just outside it, drawing in a long breath. The last time she'd stood outside a new workplace like this; she'd been filled with a quiet dread. Today felt different, like she was on the edge of something gentle but important.

As she pushed open the gate, she noticed a blackbird hop across the lawn, pecking at worms. A good omen, she decided.

Inside the small reception hall, a kind faced woman with a tidy blonde bob and bright cardigan greeted her warmly.

"You must be Miss Trevelyn!" she said, her voice cheerful and sweet. "I'm Avril, the office manager. We're so excited to have you."

Emmy felt a rush of relief at the genuine welcome. "Thank you, Avril. I'm really excited to be here."

Avril led her toward the staffroom, chatting as they walked.

"The children have been buzzing about the 'new teacher.' You'll have Year Four. Lovely group. Slightly obsessed with dinosaurs at the moment, but otherwise angels."

Emmy laughed. "I can work with dinosaurs."

Avril paused outside a set of double doors. "Here we are. Everyone's inside for morning briefing. Shall I announce you?"

Emmy's stomach fluttered, but she nodded.

Avril pushed open the doors, revealing a cozy room filled with mismatched mugs, a battered kettle, and a circle of teachers hunched over notebooks or stirring tea. A faded cork board displayed staff birthdays and half-torn holiday flyers.

"Morning, everyone!" Avril called, stepping aside. "This is Miss Trevelyn — Emmeline. She's joining us to teach Year Four. Emmeline, please, come in."

Emmy stepped forward, heart thumping.

"Please, call me Emmy," she said quickly, smiling a little too brightly. "Only my mum calls me Emmeline when I'm in trouble."

A ripple of laughter spread across the room, instantly melting some of her tension.

A little round man with close-cropped hair stood and offered a hand. "John Everly, headteacher. Welcome to our little circus."

Emmy shook his hand firmly. "Thank you. I'm thrilled to join."

Next to him, a tall, curvy woman with a floral dress and wild copper curls rose and waved. "June Townsend, Year Six.

If you need tea or a biscuit or a shoulder to cry on, I'm your woman."

Beside her, a slight man in a checked waistcoat lifted his mug in salute. "Arun Bhatt. Year Three. I collect stray footballs and answer endless dinosaur questions."

A few more introductions followed: Maria from Reception, who claimed to be "perpetually sticky" from glitter projects; Sophia, who taught Year One and kept an emergency chocolate drawer; and Mrs. Agnes Flemming, the music teacher, who hummed even when she wasn't aware of it.

Emmy sat down beside June, who immediately passed her a steaming cup of tea and a bourbon biscuit.

"Settling in okay?" June asked, eyes kind behind her large glasses.

Emmy nodded. "So far, everyone has been wonderful. And the village... it feels like home already, somehow."

June tilted her head, studying her. "You know, you have that air about you — like you've lived three lives already. Not in a bad way. Just... layers."

Emmy swallowed, unsure how to respond.

Before she could answer, John Everly cleared his throat. "Alright, folks. Quick run-down for today..."

He listed assembly times, a reminder about World Book Day costumes next week, and a heads-up that the photocopier was, once again, eating paper like a starved goat. Emmy listened, jotting small notes in her planner even though her mind buzzed with anticipation.

When the meeting ended, June slipped her arm through Emmy's. "Come on, I'll show you your classroom before the horde descends."

* * *

The Year Four classroom was at the end of a bright corridor decorated with watercolour rainbows and wobbly felt animal cutouts. Emmy paused outside the door, taking in the little sign: Miss Trevelyn, Year Four.

June opened the door with a dramatic flourish. "Behold!"

The room was spacious and warm, sunlight spilling in through tall sash windows. Along the far wall, a long display board awaited her touch, still bare except for a bright border reading Our Learning Adventure! Small desks formed a loose horseshoe shape, facing a whiteboard that looked new and gleaming.

A bookshelf in the corner already boasted an impressive collection: Roald Dahl, Michael Morpurgo, stacks of well-thumbed non-fiction on sharks and volcanoes. A small aquarium, currently empty, sat beneath the windowsill with a note: New fish arriving soon!

"It's perfect," Emmy whispered.

June patted her shoulder. "You'll make it yours in no time. The kids are curious, sweet, and prone to worshipping anyone who can draw a half-decent dragon."

Emmy smiled, imagining her new charges arriving in a blur of energy and questions.

June glanced at her watch. "Ten minutes to the bell. Need help setting up?"

Emmy shook her head. "I think I'll just... breathe it in for a moment."

June nodded, squeezed her arm, and left.

Alone, Emmy walked around the room slowly, trailing her fingers along the desks. She imagined each seat occupied — a shy boy who always finishes first and checks his answers three times, a chatterbox girl who volunteers even when she doesn't know the answer, a dreamy artist who forgets to put her pen cap back on.

She opened the supply cupboard and found a small tin of colourful stickers labelled Miss Trevelyn's Stars. She held them, smiling softly.

As the first bell rang in the corridor, she set the tin carefully on her desk and straightened her skirt. Her heart thundered in her ears, but underneath the nerves was a quiet, certain warmth.

This was why she had come.

Children's voices rose in the corridor like an excited flock of birds. Emmy took one last deep breath, brushed her fingers down her blouse, and opened the door wide.

One by one, they filed in — some timid, some bursting with chatter, a few wide-eyed and silent. A girl with bright red ribbons in her braids paused to study Emmy, then gave her an approving grin. A tall boy with scuffed knees examined the new teacher's shoes as though judging her sporting potential.

"Good morning!" Emmy said, her voice carrying across the room. A hush fell. "I'm Miss Trevelyn. Some of you might know me as the 'new teacher.' But you can call me Miss Trevelyn — no nicknames yet, please!"

A ripple of giggles broke out. Emmy continued with a smile, "I thought we could start today by getting to know each other a little bit. I promise I won't make you write an essay on what you did this weekend... unless you want to!"

Hands shot up immediately. Emmy called on a few — one boy had gone fishing with his grandfather, a girl had been to a gymnastics competition, another had visited her cousin's farm and seen baby goats. Each story brought a different sparkle to the room, and Emmy felt her shoulders ease as she listened.

Once they had settled, she introduced the day's activities — spelling in the morning, a reading circle before lunch, and an art project in the afternoon. The children groaned at the mention of spelling, but she coaxed them into good spirits with promises of stickers and a secret drawing time if they tried their best.

During the spelling test, Emmy walked among the desks, peeking over shoulders and giving gentle encouragement. She paused by a boy in the back row who hesitated over the word "friend."

"You're nearly there," she whispered. "Just think of 'fri' like Friday — the best day of the week."

He beamed and wrote it down confidently.

They moved on to reading, gathering in a loose circle on the big classroom rug. Emmy read aloud from a classic children's book, her voice softening in all the right places and rising with gentle excitement during each adventure. Every so often, a child gasped or clapped a hand to their mouth.

As they listened, Emmy studied their faces: how open they were, how easily they surrendered to wonder. She remembered being that age, lying on her stomach in her childhood room, devouring books late into the night despite her mother's protests.

At lunch, she sat at her desk, munching her cheese and chutney sandwich. The classroom buzzed with leftover energy — some children stayed in to finish drawings, while others argued about the best Pokémon. Emmy watched them, touched by their small dramas and alliances.

Outside, she could see the playground through the tall windows: hopscotch chalk lines, a group playing tag near the old oak, a football rolling dangerously close to a flowerbed.

Halfway through her lunch, June popped her head in. "Fancy a wander outside? I could do with some fresh air before I brave the Year Six poetry recitals."

Emmy hesitated, then nodded eagerly. She followed June out to the staff garden — a small enclosed patch behind the building, shielded from view by hedges.

A robin hopped along the low stone wall, eyeing them curiously. June pulled a crust of bread from her pocket and crumbled it, tossing pieces onto the wall.

"He comes every day now," June said softly. "Cheeky thing. I think he expects a full meal deal."

Emmy smiled, watching the robin peck at the crumbs. The bird's tiny movements were delicate and determined, its orange breast glowing like a small flame.

June leaned against the wall and glanced sideways at Emmy. "So what brought you over to Stonebridge Hollow? Have you brought anyone special along with you?"

The question caught Emmy off guard. She picked at her sandwich wrapper, avoiding June's eyes.

"A new adventure was much needed and this opportunity came up...But no, just me. I mean, I was with someone. A while ago," Emmy admitted slowly. "It ended badly."

June's expression softened. "I'm sorry, love. You don't have to tell me anything you don't want to."

Emmy hesitated, her eyes drifting to the robin again. She took a deep breath, feeling the damp spring air fill her lungs.

"It's okay, I just want to find my feet here and blend in," she said finally.

June laid a hand gently on Emmy's arm. "Well, you're safe here. Everyone is lovely, and if you ever feel like talking — or not talking — I'll be here with tea and biscuits."

A long silence settled between them, not uncomfortable but heavy with unspoken understanding. Emmy looked out at the robin, feeling something uncoil in her chest, a small knot of nerves that loosened just a little.

The bell rang in the distance, breaking the moment. June gave her a quick squeeze and stood. "Duty calls! Year Six awaits."

Emmy stood too, brushing crumbs from her skirt. "Thanks, June."

"Anytime, love."

Back inside, she found her students already trickling in, chatting loudly and comparing packed lunches. She greeted them with a grin, her voice stronger than she felt inside.

Their art project that afternoon involved creating "dream landscapes" using pastels and scraps of tissue paper. Emmy set out baskets of materials on each table and explained, "Imagine

31

a place where you feel calm, or happy, or brave. It can be real or imaginary. Use any colours you like — there's no wrong way to do this."

The room soon filled with the gentle scrape of pastels and the soft rip of tissue. Emmy moved among them, crouching to look at their work: a boy's galaxy full of silver stars, a girl's secret garden with talking rabbits, another's underwater castle guarded by mermaids.

She found herself absorbed, pausing to help a shy boy choose the right shade of blue for his sky, or showing a girl how to blend two colours with her fingertip.

Time slipped by until Emmy realized it was nearly 3pm. She tidied up with the children, laughing as they raced to see who could stack the most chairs.

Once the last bell rang, children began to collect coats and water bottles, shouting goodbyes as they left. Emmy stood at the door, smiling and answering every farewell.

When the classroom finally emptied, she slumped into her chair, her energy spent but her heart light. She glanced at the day's spelling tests and art pieces piled on her desk and decided they could wait until tomorrow.

As she packed her bag, her phone buzzed. A new message from her father: "How was your first proper day? Mum wants all the details when you call tonight!"

She smiled softly, typing back: "It was wonderful. I'll call after dinner. Tell her not to worry — I survived the spelling gauntlet."

She left the school slowly, watching the late afternoon sun dip behind the low rooftops. A few parents still lingered at the gate, chatting with each other while their children clambered around the nearby bench.

At the high street, she stopped to admire the display outside the florist: buckets of tulips and narcissi, sprigs of eucalyptus in a crate. She picked up a small bunch of pale-yellow tulips and carried them back toward Aubrey's.

She could see Mags through the bakery window again, arranging buns in the display case. Mags waved her rolling pin triumphantly, and Emmy waved her tulips in reply.

Inside Aubrey's, Emmy paused near the entrance. The old oak counter glowed softly under the late light, and the faint scent of old paper and dried lavender hung in the air.

She stepped further in and trailed her fingers along the spines of books as she moved toward the stairs. A thick book on medieval folklore caught her eye, and she pulled it out briefly, weighing its heft in her hand.

A small note fell from between the pages and landed on the floor. She bent to pick it up and read the words scrawled in elegant script: "Some histories aren't written. They live, waiting for the right eyes."

A shiver passed through her. She slid the note back into the book and carefully replaced it on the shelf.

Upstairs, she unlocked her flat and carried the tulips into the kitchen, placing them in an old glass jug on the counter. She let her bag slide to the floor and turned on the kettle, listening to its rising hiss.

She thought of the children's dream landscapes, the robin with his expectant stare, June's hand on her arm, and her father's message waiting for her call.

The evening stretched ahead, soft and unknown. She poured her tea, carried it to the window, and sat cross-legged in the armchair. Outside, a robin darted between rooftops, its tiny shape almost lost in the vast sky.

Emmy traced the rim of her mug and let her eyes drift to the woods beyond the village. Somehow, even with all she didn't know, she felt a pulse of belonging here — like she had landed where she needed to be.

As she sipped, her thoughts finally settled. A small smile played at the corners of her lips. Tomorrow would come with its own challenges, but tonight, she could let herself simply be.

# Chapter 3

Emmy woke early the next morning to the gentle patter of rain against her window, a soothing hush that seemed to hush the whole world. She lay still for a few minutes, listening, her breath slow and even. The room was painted in pale dawn light, her curtains shifting softly with each draft that crept in.

When she finally rose, she moved through her flat quietly, as if not to disturb the lingering peace. She brewed tea first — a strong English breakfast with a dash of honey — and stood barefoot in the kitchen while the kettle steamed. The tulips she'd bought yesterday nodded gently in their jug, delicate heads brushing each other as though sharing secrets.

While her tea steeped, she checked her phone. A message from her father, sent late last night: "Call us tomorrow, love. Mum's excited to hear your voice. She says she dreamt of you walking in a garden." Emmy smiled, her chest tightening at the image of her mother sitting up in bed, eyes wide with some sudden, inexplicable knowing.

She texted back quickly: "I will. Tell her I had a great day yesterday. Settling in slowly."

After showering, Emmy pulled on a soft lilac jumper and a knee-length navy skirt, pairing it with thick tights and her favourite black boots. Her curls, damp and springy, she twisted into a loose braid over one shoulder. She studied herself in the mirror briefly — the gentle curve of her golden honey skin, the strong shape of her brows, the fullness of her lips that she had inherited from her mother. Her large, dark eyes watched her thoughtfully.

There were days she saw more of her mother's heritage in her face, days when she saw her father's lighter features peeking through. She had always felt like a blending of two worlds, a bridge that sometimes wobbled under her own feet. But here, away from the curious whispers of her childhood town, she felt more herself.

Downstairs, Aubrey's was still closed when she slipped past. She paused to peer in through the small leaded windows, admiring the way the morning light touched the rows of spines and dust motes floating in the hush. Outside, the street was still waking up. A few early risers hurried under umbrellas, and Mags at the bakery across the street could be seen through the steamy glass, arranging a tray of scones with practiced grace.

Emmy ducked her head and stepped out, her breath catching in the damp air. The walk to school felt slower today, her steps more thoughtful, each puddle a small mirror that caught the grey sky above.

At school, the children arrived draped in raincoats and carrying plastic bags over their bookbags, dripping on the tiled floors as they stomped into the hall. Emmy welcomed them at her classroom door, offering bright smiles and quiet encouragement.

"Morning, Miss Trevelyn!" called out Thomas, holding his rain-splattered spelling book like a trophy.

"Good morning, Thomas," Emmy laughed. "That spelling book looks like it went on an adventure of its own!"

Once the school bell rung to signal the start of the day; Emmy waited until the children were settled and guided them into morning activities — arithmetic exercises first. Small groups solving puzzles using coloured counters. Emmy moved among them, offering hints or a gentle nudge when someone hesitated. She loved seeing them light up when something finally clicked, their small faces brightening as if someone had lit a lantern inside them.

After arithmetic, they began work on a shared reading project. Emmy handed out excerpts from different folk tales and watched as they leaned over the pages, their fingers tracing lines, their lips moving silently as they read. She felt a surge of warmth at their enthusiasm, a sense of quiet pride that she had found her way here, to this small corner of the world where stories still felt alive.

During break, she joined June in the staffroom. The robin made another appearance at the window, pecking for crumbs. June, as always, had come prepared with a biscuit or two.

"You spoil him," Emmy teased, nodding at the bird.

"He deserves it. A loyal friend," June replied, tossing a few crumbs out the window. Then she turned to Emmy, studying her face with a curious tilt of her head.

"You seem... different today," June remarked. "Lighter. Almost as if you've started to settle into your own routine."

Emmy smiled and then shrugged, not quite ready to put words to her shifting feelings.

June offered a gentle smile. "Well, for what it's worth, you're doing beautifully."

The remainder of the school day had Emmy guiding her students through a science lesson about habitats. They drew diagrams of ponds and woods, chattering about ducks and frogs and imagining secret fox dens beneath the roots of ancient oaks.

The last bell of the school day echoed down the corridors, thin and metallic, and then was followed by the rush of children's laughter spilling into the playground. Emmy leaned against the doorframe of her classroom, watching her pupils scatter. Small hands clutched lunchboxes, scarves trailed in the wind, and voices carried into the pale March sky. Their energy seemed boundless, a stark contrast to the heaviness she sometimes felt as the building emptied and quiet crept back in.

She tidied the last stack of exercise books into her satchel, clicked off the lamps, and pulled her coat tighter around her shoulders. A faint chill lingered even though spring was stirring at the edges of the season. Emmy paused at the gate, deciding whether to return to the bookshop flat or to walk a little, to stretch her legs and her thoughts before retreating to her small, half-furnished rooms.

The lane beside the school dipped away from the high street, lined with hawthorn hedges and narrow enough for little more than a cart in years gone by. Emmy followed it almost without thinking, drawn by the promise of trees beyond. She hadn't yet explored this side of the village but with the light lingering faintly and nothing urgent pulling her back, she let curiosity guide her.

The lane opened onto woodland. Tall oaks and beeches arched overhead, their bare branches crisscrossing like black lace against the late-afternoon sky. The path was soft beneath her boots, springy with moss and last year's leaves. The silence here was a different kind of quiet than the empty classroom — not lonely, but watchful. A blackbird darted across the path, wings flashing, and the smell of damp earth rose with every step she took deeper into the trees.

It reminded her of childhood walks, of days when she and her mother would escape the town and find some trail to wander, her small hand tucked inside a larger one. She remembered the sense of being safely enclosed, wrapped in something older than time. That same feeling brushed her now, though she also felt the prickle of being somewhere unfamiliar.

She passed a cluster of early snowdrops, their delicate bells nodding, and bent to touch one, the petals cool as porcelain. Somewhere above, a branch cracked with the shifting weight of a rook. Emmy straightened and carried on, her senses sharpening. The path meandered, narrowing, then widened again, weaving her further from the known edges of the village.

After a time, the trees thinned, and through a veil of branches she glimpsed the shimmer of water. A lake. Her pace quickened, the sight tugging at her with unexpected eagerness. She had always been drawn to water — rivers, ponds, even the smallest pools after rain. They held a stillness, a way of catching the light that made the world feel altered.

The ground dipped, opening into a hollow where the lake spread wide and quiet, its surface glassy except for the slow ripples of birds. Swans. Their white bodies drifted like pieces of cloud broken loose, their necks curved into graceful arcs.

Emmy stopped at the tree line, breath catching. The scene was too perfect, too composed, like a painting she had stumbled into.

And then she saw him.

On the far side of the lake stood a figure. A man. He was tall, his shoulders straight beneath a dark coat that moved faintly with the breeze. He did not move with the restless energy of someone out for a stroll, nor with the awkward pauses of someone waiting. He was still — deeply, wholly still — as if the world had slowed around him.

He watched the swans. One hand slipped into his pocket while the other scattered crumbs with absent precision. The birds edged closer, as though they knew him.

Emmy's pulse quickened. She hadn't expected anyone else here. Something about the way he stood unsettled her: not threatening, but other. He belonged in the scene as much as the birds and water, and yet he seemed set apart, a presence woven through with strangeness.

The distance was too great to make out details clearly, but as he turned slightly toward the water, she glimpsed the sharpness of his profile, the line of a jaw that might have been carved from stone. A lock of dark hair fell across his brow. And then — when a shaft of light broke through cloud and touched him — she saw his eyes.

Green. Startling, luminous in the fading light. The sight made her chest tighten, as though she had stumbled upon something private.

She ducked back behind a tree, breath uneven. She hadn't meant to spy, hadn't meant to intrude. But curiosity anchored her. She peered again, careful, hidden.

The man crouched at the edge of the bank. His hand extended, steady, scattering the last of the crumbs into the ripples. The swans bent their necks to feed, the water breaking in rings around them. For a moment, something softened in his face — not quite a smile, but a loosening, a glimpse of warmth held close.

It struck her with force: he looked lonely. Not in the ordinary sense of someone who dines alone or passes unnoticed in a crowd, but with the gravity of solitude that had stretched across years.

She could have stepped out then. She could have called a greeting, or simply walked openly along the bank and pretended she hadn't noticed him. But something restrained her. Instinct, perhaps. Or the quiet certainty that if she broke the moment, it would vanish like mist.

So she stayed where she was, heart racing, rooted by both fascination and unease.

At last, the man straightened. His coat flared slightly as he turned, his gaze sweeping the far shore. Emmy pressed herself to the bark, heat rising to her face. She told herself he couldn't possibly see her — the trees shielded her — but she still felt the uncanny sense of being observed.

But instead of leaving, he reached into his coat. From within, he drew a leather-bound book, its edges worn smooth with use, and a slim length of charcoal, already blackened at his fingers. He lowered himself onto a flat stone near the bank, the water lapping just inches away, and opened the book across his knee.

Emmy held her breath.

He began to sketch. Slow, deliberate strokes, his hand moving with the sureness of someone long practiced. His gaze lifted often to the swans, then to the reeds, then back to the page, adjusting, correcting, shading. She could almost imagine the faint rasp of charcoal against paper. The stillness of him was different now — not distant, but alive with intent. Every movement carried a quiet urgency, a desire to capture the fragile perfection before it shifted and was lost.

The swans obliged him by lingering, their bodies luminous against the water. He traced their forms, head bent in concentration, green eyes flickering upward then narrowing as he bent closer to his work. Emmy noticed how wholly absorbed he became. Nothing around him seemed to exist but the scene before him and the marks he made.

A strange ache stirred in her chest. She had known artists before — classmates, friends — but none with this kind of focus, this gravity that made the ordinary moment feel monumental. Even at a distance, she could sense the intensity with which he pursued the lines, the careful patience as if one false stroke might shatter everything.

Minutes passed. She dared not move, dared not breathe too loudly. She should have turned away, left him to his solitude, but her eyes refused to release the sight.

There was something profoundly human in it — and yet something untouchable, as though he were not merely sketching swans on a village lake, but conjuring memory itself onto the page.

The light deepened. The faintest smile touched his lips when one swan curved its neck just so, echoing the line he had already drawn. He caught it quickly, his charcoal darting across the page with sudden speed, then slowing again as he shaded the water's ripple.

Minutes passed. She dared not move, dared not breathe too loudly. She should have turned away, left him to his solitude, but her eyes refused to release the sight.

She could almost see what appeared on the page: the slender curve of the swans' necks, the mirrored bodies rippling across the lake, the tangle of reeds like strokes of ink. His hand paused, then shaded carefully, smudging with the side of his finger, softening the water's texture. He caught the delicate sweep of a wing lifting, the arch of a reflection, the restless stir of wind across the surface. Every mark he made carried precision, as though he had done this a thousand times and still treated each stroke as if it mattered.

There was something profoundly human in it — and yet something untouchable, as though he were not merely sketching swans on a village lake, but conjuring memory itself onto the page.

The light deepened. The faintest smile touched his lips when one swan curved its neck just so, echoing the line he had already drawn. He caught it quickly, his charcoal darting across the page with sudden speed, then slowing again as he shaded the water's ripple. Emmy's heart thudded.

This was not simply a pastime. It was devotion.

Her pulse quickened with the thought that she should leave — and yet, her feet betrayed her. Almost without deciding, she stepped out from the shelter of the trees. The faint crack of a twig under her boot made her flinch, but the man did not startle. His head lifted slowly, his green eyes finding her at once.

Emmy froze.

For the briefest second she thought of retreating, of pretending she had only been passing. But his gaze held hers with a calm that made lies feel impossible.

"I'm sorry," she said quickly, her voice thinner than she meant. "I didn't mean to interrupt. I was just—walking. I didn't realise anyone was here."

The man regarded her for a moment longer before he closed the sketchbook with quiet finality. A faint smudge of charcoal marked the side of his hand.

"You needn't apologise," he said. His voice was low, even, carrying strangely across the water. "These woods belong to no one."

The words settled between them, though Emmy felt they were not entirely true. Something in his tone suggested claim, as though he belonged more to this place than she ever could.

She gestured faintly toward the lake. "You... draw beautifully. The swans. I could see from the trees."

His gaze flickered — not quite surprise, not quite displeasure. Slowly, he set the sketchbook on his knee again but did not reopen it.

"They make willing subjects," he replied, glancing toward the birds still drifting near. "They return here, season after season."

Emmy nodded, her hands twisting together in her coat pockets. She felt foolish, standing there like a trespasser, yet something about his steadiness anchored her.

"I should let you get back to it," she murmured.

But still she did not move.

The man inclined his head, almost a dismissal, almost a bow. "As you wish."

For a breath longer, their eyes held — his green, clear and unreadable; hers searching, unsettled. Then Emmy stepped back, her boots whispering over the leaves, retreating into the trees.

When at last the lake lay hidden again behind trunks and branches, she let out the breath she hadn't realised she was holding. Her heart still beat too fast, her cheeks too warm.

She had spoken to him. To the man by the lake.

And though the exchange had been brief, the image of him bent over his sketchbook, eyes intent, hands stained with charcoal, lodged itself inside her like something that would not be dislodged.

When she finally turned, retracing her steps up through the trees, the light had shifted into evening. The sky deepened, and the branches overhead seemed heavier, drawing her back toward the familiarity of the village.

Yet the image clung to her — a man in solitude, swans gathering near, eyes the colour of something untamed. She could not shake it, nor explain why it pressed so strongly into her memory.

By the time she reached the bookshop's narrow doorway, breath quick from the hill, she told herself she had imagined half of it. She was tired, new to this place, overwhelmed by the rush of new names and faces and duties.

And yet, when she closed the door behind her and leaned against it in the dim quiet of her flat, she saw again the green of his eyes, bright against the lake, impossible to dismiss.

Upstairs in her flat, she made tea and settled into her armchair, a blanket tucked over her knees. She called her parents then, her father answering on the second ring.

"Emmy! How's our bright star doing today?" his voice boomed through the speaker.

She laughed, warmth blooming in her chest. "Hi, Dad. I survived another day."

"Is that so? And the children? Any new adventures?"

She told him about the pond diagrams, the spelling corrections, the shy boy who finally dared to read aloud. Her mother's voice chimed in occasionally, asking small, gentle questions. Emmy could hear her mother's breathing, slower now, each word chosen carefully.

When she finally hung up, Emmy felt a tender ache in her heart, like missing a favourite song just as it starts to play. She stood at the window, watching the village below, the last of the evening light softening everything it touched.

She didn't know how long she stood there, but when she finally turned away, she felt steadier somehow — her parents' voices an echo she carried forward.

She cleaned up the kitchen, set out clothes for the next day, and finally climbed into bed. As she lay there, she listened to the gentle sigh of the wind beyond her window. The night shifted softly, an owl's distant call echoing in the dark. Emmy closed her eyes and finally let sleep take her, the lines of the day blurring into dreams.

Emmy woke the next morning feeling refreshed. Sunlight spilled across her duvet in long golden lines, warming the room in soft patches. For a few disoriented seconds, she thought she was still back in her childhood bedroom, the pale wallpaper with its small floral print, the hum of her mother moving about downstairs. But as she sat up, the now-familiar shape of her flat unfolded around her: the narrow bookshelf crammed with dog-eared paperbacks, the worn armchair by the window, the gentle creak of the floorboards under her feet.

She moved through her morning in a comfortable rhythm — tea first, then a quick shower, her curls pinned back today with a simple tortoiseshell clip. She selected a pale cream blouse that set off her golden honey skin and a soft green cardigan that complemented her dark hair. As she leaned toward the mirror, she noted again the bright, alert shape of her eyes — so wide and expressive they often betrayed her thoughts before she could catch them. Her lips, naturally full, were curved faintly today, as though she carried a private joke just for herself.

After a quick breakfast of buttered toast and honey, Emmy pulled on her boots and grabbed her bag. On her way out, she paused at the bookshelf to slip The Lost Villages of England into her tote. She didn't know why she felt the urge to carry it — maybe a quiet wish for something familiar to hold during the day.

Downstairs, the narrow lane was waking up. Mags was sweeping the bakery steps, calling a cheerful good morning to a passing postman. Across the street, Mrs. Hargreaves from the flower shop arranged buckets of tulips and ranunculus, bright little flags of spring that made Emmy pause to admire them.

"Morning, love!" Mrs. Hargreaves called. "You look as fresh as a daisy today."

Emmy laughed lightly, feeling her cheeks warm. "Thank you," she called back, waving before heading off toward the school.

At the corner, she saw the town's old iron lampposts lined like quiet sentinels along the pavement. They looked as though they belonged to a different century, and Emmy often imagined them coming alive at night, whispering secrets to each other as the fog rolled in from the fields.

She arrived at school a few minutes before the gates opened. A hush still hung over the playground, the wet tarmac glistening under the morning sun. The early warmth made everything smell alive — earth and grass and the faint sweet scent drifting from the bakery down the road. Emmy leaned on the fence, watching two magpies chase each other across the sky.

Inside, the staffroom buzzed with its usual soft chaos. Arun Bhatt was already rummaging through the biscuit tin, Agnes Flemming scribbled notes on a clipboard while humming under her breath, and June Townsend recounted a story about her cat getting stuck behind the boiler at 2 a.m.

"Morning, Emmy," June called, her head lifting. "Your hair looks lovely today. You look like you've stepped out of a hairdressers salon."

Emmy flushed at the compliment, her fingers instinctively twisting a loose curl. "Thank you. I think it's just the humidity today working in my favour for once."

Arun popped up from the tin, brandishing a custard cream. "The children better brace themselves today — I'm feeling especially chaotic."

"That's what they would like to hear," Emmy teased. She loved these morning moments, the easy jokes and gentle rhythms before the day's real work began.

She glanced out the window, catching a glimpse of the field beyond the hedge. A few stray birds darted across the grass, and the trees beyond trembled in the gentle breeze. She found her thoughts wandering to the woods — the mossy paths, the quiet pond. She could almost hear the hush of the water, the secretive rustle of something unseen just beyond the hedgerows.

The bell rang, and Emmy rose, gathering her books.

"Good luck out there," June called after her, raising her mug in a small salute.

Emmy's classroom buzzed as she entered. Children dashed to their hooks, dropping bags, swapping stories about breakfast or a new sticker collection.

"Miss Trevelyn, can I show you my rock collection at lunch?" piped up Isla, her freckled face alight with excitement.

"Of course," Emmy replied. "But only if you promise not to start a geological excavation in the cloakroom."

The girl giggled, giving Emmy a mock-serious salute before running off to her desk.

They began with a reading session — today, a short passage from Charlotte's Web, which Emmy read aloud while pacing slowly at the front. The children sat cross-legged, eyes wide and spellbound. Emmy loved seeing their faces shift and glow with each twist of the story, each quiet line that made them gasp or giggle.

Next came a math activity involving paper shapes and measuring lengths. Emmy moved between desks, guiding them with patient encouragement, offering small high-fives when they solved a tricky part. She admired their resilience — how they stumbled, frowned, then picked up their pencils and kept going.

By the time lunch arrived, she felt buoyed by a gentle kind of pride. She ate her sandwich at her desk, scribbling notes for an upcoming art project. When Isla arrived with her rocks — smooth grey stones, a chunk of quartz, and something she insisted was a dinosaur tooth — Emmy listened with genuine interest, nodding along as if she were an expert palaeontologist.

"These are incredible, Isla. You should write labels for them — make a mini museum for the class," Emmy suggested.

Isla's eyes went wide with delight. "Really?!"

"Really," Emmy confirmed. "We can work on it together tomorrow."


When the final bell rang, the children filed out in a clamour of farewells and tangled jumpers. Emmy stayed behind to tidy up, wiping stray glue from the tables and reordering the paper stacks.

Emmy glanced at the clock, her heart pinching with a familiar ache. She finished her last task, packed up her bag, and locked the classroom door behind her.

Outside, the sky had turned a soft apricot at the edges, fading into a dusky lavender above. She paused at the gate, taking a slow breath. In this light, the village looked almost magical — the roof tiles glinting like fish scales, the winding alleys like hidden veins leading somewhere secret.

She took the long route home, turning down a narrow lane that skirted the fields. Along the way, she paused to watch the cows grazing lazily beyond the hedgerow, their soft eyes and rhythmic chewing strangely comforting. She ran her fingers along the rough stone wall, feeling the warmth still held from the afternoon sun.

As she neared her building, she could hear the faint clink of crockery from Aubrey's kitchen below, the low hum of someone sweeping. The scent of lavender and old paper drifted from the open window, welcoming her back.

She slipped inside and climbed the stairs slowly. Once in her flat, she set her bag down and dropped her keys into the little clay dish by the door. She made tea — chamomile this time — and settled into her armchair, pulling a knitted blanket over her lap.

She called her parents then, and this time her mother answered.

"Emmy, my darling," her mother breathed, her voice a gentle melody even through the crackling line.

"Hi, Mum," Emmy said softly, her throat tightening as she heard the warmth and fragility woven together.

They talked about the garden back home, the tulips just beginning to open, the robin that had started nesting in the old pear tree. Her mother asked if Emmy had unpacked everything yet, if she was eating enough vegetables, if she remembered to wear her scarf on damp early mornings.

Emmy reassured her, adding small, bright details she knew her mother loved — the bakery's scones, the children's tiny victories, the laughter echoing through the classroom halls.

When they finally said goodbye, Emmy sat quietly for a moment, the phone still warm in her hand. The last glow of daylight had faded, leaving the room washed in a soft, silvery hue.

She rose to light a candle on the windowsill, its flame trembling in the gentle draft. Outside, the early moon climbed above the rooftops, casting pale light across the uneven stones and chimney stacks. Emmy leaned her forehead against the glass, watching her breath fog briefly with each exhale.

She pulled her blanket tighter around her shoulders and returned to her armchair. Picking up The Lost Villages of England, she opened to the page with the note again. She traced the words with her fingertip, as though they might reveal something more if she pressed hard enough.

She didn't know what she was looking for — a sign, an answer, a simple thread to pull — but she felt a tiny pull inside her, as if someone had tugged lightly on her sleeve from the other side of a crowded room.

Emmy closed the book at last, setting it carefully on the table beside her. The candle flickered, painting long shadows on the walls.

She leaned back, listening to the hush of the evening and the steady echo of her own heartbeat. She closed her eyes and let her breathing slow, the last threads of thought drifting away like birds toward the dusk.

# Chapter Four

The next morning arrived draped in gentle mist, the kind that softened the rooftops and curled around the hedgerows as though the whole town was wrapped in a quiet sigh. Emmy rose before her alarm, blinking in the pale half-light that edged around her curtains.

She dressed slowly, her mind half-drifting — cream jumper today, paired with a soft patterned skirt that reminded her of old tapestries. She brushed her hair carefully, pulling the curls into a loose low ponytail, leaving a few tendrils to frame her face. In the mirror, she paused. Her skin glowed a warm honey, the early light giving her features a softened glow. Her dark curls, now a little frizzed from the damp air, framed her wide eyes and full lips.

She thought of her mother, who always used to fuss over her hair on damp mornings. "Your hair is a crown, Emmeline. A wild, glorious crown." She felt a pang, sharp and tender all at once, but she pressed it down, breathing slowly.

After buttering two slices of toast — one with strawberry jam, one with honey — she scribbled a quick note on a sticky pad for herself: Pick up milk. Call Dad. She tucked it into her coat pocket before heading out.

The town lay half-awake as she walked. A woman in a red headscarf shuffled out to sweep her steps, and a delivery lorry rumbled past Aubrey's bookshop, unloading boxes marked second-hand treasures. Emmy paused, peering through the glass. Aubrey's windows were stacked with teetering towers of novels, old gardening manuals, and the occasional globe or pottery vase.

She made her way to school at a leisurely pace, enjoying the hush that seemed to hang over the village before the full rush of the day.

At the school gates, she found June balancing a tray of paper tulips and small jars of paint, her cheeks already pink with the morning breeze.

"You look like a woman on a mission," Emmy called.

June startled and then grinned. "Ah! My co-conspirator. We're transforming the Year Six hallway into a 'spring meadow.' Whether or not it looks like one is another question."

Emmy offered to carry some of the jars, and together they crossed the playground. As they went, children ran past in a blur of bright coats and backpacks, voices high and bubbling with anticipation.

Inside the staffroom, the kettle was already gurgling. Arun Bhatt sat perched on a windowsill, one leg drawn up like a thoughtful stork, reading a copy of The Guardian.

"Morning, ladies," he said without looking up. "Guess what headline made me spill my tea this morning?"

"Surprise me," June said, sliding her tray onto the table.

"Apparently, a woman in Essex found a Roman coin in her garden and thought it was a toy," he said, shaking his head. "I mean, imagine tossing a bit of history into the rubbish."

"Roman coin, you say?" Emmy said, her fingers pausing over the teabags.

Arun looked up, surprised. "Ah, our resident historian is intrigued!"

Emmy laughed softly. "Well, it's a strange find, that's all."

June, meanwhile, had begun recounting her latest dating mishap — a man who claimed to be a poet but turned out to write only haikus about his cat.

"Three whole evenings," June declared, wagging a paint-streaked finger. "Three haikus about tuna breath and sofa scratches."

Emmy burst into giggles, nearly splashing her tea.

The morning's laughter followed her into class. Her Year Four students were ready with their questions — a small forest of hands rose the moment she stepped inside.

"Miss Trevelyn, what's for art today?"

"Miss Trevelyn, can we write stories about dragons?"

"Miss Trevelyn, my hamster escaped last night and ate my homework!"

She did her best to answer each one, her voice warm but firm. Emmy loved how they trusted her with their bright, unstoppable thoughts.

During a creative writing session, she walked between desks, reading over shoulders. She paused beside Isla, who was sketching a castle on her exercise book margin.

"That's beautiful," Emmy whispered. "Who lives there?"

"A knight who wants to be a baker instead," Isla replied with perfect seriousness.

Emmy chuckled. "I'd read that story."

At lunch, Emmy sat with June and Arun Bhatt under a broad oak tree near the playground. The children zoomed around them in chaotic loops. June had brought two robin-friendly seed cakes today, breaking off pieces to scatter under the benches.

"One of these days they'll start following you home," Emmy teased.

"I wouldn't mind," June said, watching a robin hop forward bravely. "At least robins don't make bad haikus."

Arun snorted tea through his nose at that, nearly dropping his sandwich. Emmy felt her chest warm at the easy companionship, the small ways they all cared for each other.

They spoke of small town gossip, local events, and the latest child to claim to have seen a fox in the bins. But when the children drifted back toward their classes; Arun Bhatt stood, dusting crumbs from his knees. "Right then. Off to teach the great recorder symphony of 4B. Wish me luck."

June gave him a pitying look. "The brave, the foolish, and the musically tortured."

The rest of the afternoon swept by in a gentle rush of lessons and laughter. Emmy helped Isla write the first lines of her knight-baker story and coached Ellis through a tricky math puzzle. When the final bell rang, she stayed late again to tidy.

Her phone buzzed with a message from her father. "Hope you're resting enough. Mum worries. We both miss you."

She pressed her thumb to the screen, then typed back: "I miss you too. I'll call tonight."

Outside, the sky had shifted to a soft apricot glow. Emmy pulled her coat closer, pausing at the gates. Her thoughts drifted toward the woods and the peculiar calm that seemed to hover around the lake she visited.

She took the longer route home again; her footsteps slow and thoughtful.

At the bakery, she stopped to buy a small loaf of seeded bread for supper. Mags gave her a conspiratorial wink. "You're looking dreamy today, love. Someone put a spell on you?"

Emmy laughed, though her cheeks warmed. "Just a long day, that's all."

Outside, she caught sight of the church spire glinting against the evening sky. For a moment she stood there, her mind drifting backward — to her mother humming in the kitchen, her father reading aloud from old poetry books, her teenage years where everything felt small and safe, even if a bit stifling.

And then, to that single night she never spoke of — a cold room, a familiar hand. The memories flashed like lightning: quick, harsh, gone in an instant but leaving her shaken to the bone. She inhaled sharply, pressing the loaf of bread against her chest like an anchor.

This is a new chapter, she reminded herself. A new place. New air.

She took the last few steps toward her building. The stairs creaked as she climbed, and she paused on the landing to catch her breath, feeling the warmth of her body slowly return.

Inside her flat, the quiet embraced her like an old friend. She set the bread on the kitchen counter, arranged her books neatly on the side table, and finally sat down by the window with her tea. The golden hour light bathed the walls, turning everything into soft gold and rose.

She reached for The Lost Villages of England again, her fingers lingering on the page where she'd last tucked that cryptic note.

Her phone buzzed again, snapping her back. It was her father.

"Hi, Dad," she said, her voice gentler than she meant.

"Emmeline, sweetheart," he replied, his voice instantly warm and lined with concern. "You sound tired today."

"I'm alright. Just a long day at school. The kids had a lot of energy."

There was a small silence, then he cleared his throat. "Are you eating well? Sleeping enough? You know, you can always come home."

"I know, Dad. But... I think I need this. I need to be here, to figure things out on my own."

"I understand," he said, though Emmy could hear the worry woven into every word. "We just... we just miss you."

"I miss you too. I'll visit soon, I promise."

They spoke a few minutes more — about spring flowers, about a neighbour's new dog, about nothing and everything at once — before Emmy hung up and set the phone aside.

She stayed in her seat long after the screen went dark, her thoughts drifting.

* * *

The next morning, Emmy got up early again and had decided to take the long route to the school. She set up her classroom slowly, carefully arranging the new reading corner with a plush rug and beanbags. She tacked up student artwork on the wall — bright splashes of dragons, sunflowers, imaginary animals — each piece like a window into a child's secret world.

In the staffroom, she shared a quiet coffee with June, who was already hunched over a lesson plan.

"You're in early," June said, arching an eyebrow.

"Needed some quiet time before the stampede," Emmy replied with a small smile.

June regarded her for a long moment, then gave a knowing nod. "You're settling in. I can tell."

"I think so," Emmy said softly. "Though I still feel like I'm... I don't know. Waiting for something."

"That's not always a bad thing," June said. "Sometimes waiting gives you space to listen to yourself. To breathe."

Emmy looked down at her mug, tracing the edge with her thumb. "Did you always want to be a teacher?" she asked, surprising herself with the question.

June chuckled. "I wanted to be a marine biologist, actually. But I got seasick on a ferry once and decided to spare the whales my dramatics."

Emmy burst out laughing, the sound echoing off the staffroom walls.

"Teaching found me instead," June continued, her voice softer now. "Sometimes the right path isn't the one you plan. It's the one that feels like coming home, even if it scares you a bit."

Emmy nodded, her laughter fading into a thoughtful hush.


The rest of the morning flowed by in a familiar rhythm. During art, Emmy guided the children in making collages of their imaginary gardens. At break, she played hopscotch with a small group of girls, her skirt swishing as she jumped between chalky squares.

Later, she stayed after class to help Isla gather up her scattered drawings.

"Miss Trevelyn," Isla asked shyly, "do you have a garden?"

Emmy paused. "I don't, not here. But I think gardens can be anywhere. Even in your mind. Or on a piece of paper."

Isla looked thoughtful. "I think I'd plant strawberries everywhere."

"An excellent choice," Emmy said, tapping Isla's nose lightly.

By the time Emmy finally locked up her classroom, the sun was sinking behind the schoolyard oak, turning the sky a bruised purple. She walked home slowly, her bag heavy with lesson plans and stray glitter.

# Chapter Five

The next morning at the school gates, Emmy paused to greet the children who were huddled beneath oversized hoods and plastic ponchos. They waved and called out cheerful greetings, as though rain were nothing more than an added adventure.

Inside, the corridors smelled of damp wool and floor polish. Emmy set her bag down in her classroom, then made her way to the staffroom. She found June already at the kettle, her hair pinned up in a neat twist, glasses perched low on her nose as she thumbed through the morning paper.

"Morning," Emmy said, shaking her umbrella out gently in the doorway.

June looked up, her mouth curving into a sly smile. "Good morning. You look like a proper water nymph today."

Emmy snorted. "I nearly ended up in the canal on the way here. I think the ducks were worried about me."

June laughed, passing her a mug of steaming tea. "Here. Revive yourself."

Arun Bhatt walked in then, juggling a stack of photocopied worksheets and a half-eaten apple.

"Watch out," he warned playfully, "the Year Three pirates have staged a mutiny in the art supply cupboard."

June rolled her eyes. "I told you to hide the glitter. That stuff is basically currency to them."

Emmy took a grateful sip of her tea, the warmth cutting through the morning chill.

They settled into their usual chatter: discussing lesson plans, trading stories about overly enthusiastic parents, debating whether the custard creams in the staff tin were stale or simply "aged to perfection."

When the bell rang, Emmy returned to her classroom to find the children buzzing with leftover rain energy. Little voices rose like a flock of sparrows, each one eager to share some small drama from the morning commute.

"Miss Trevelyn! I saw a snail as big as my fist!"

"Miss, my socks got soaked and now they squelch!"

Emmy laughed and knelt down beside them. "Alright, let's make a deal. Whoever has the squelchiest socks gets first pick at story time today."

They cheered, instantly distracted, and she guided them into their seats for morning registration.

The lessons passed in a soft, rhythmic blur. During numeracy, she watched Isla count on her fingers, her brow furrowed with deep concentration, and gently guided her to see the pattern. In literacy, they read a folk tale about a fisherman and a talking heron, and Emmy found herself swept into the story right alongside them.

When lunchtime finally arrived, Emmy slipped into the staffroom to find June feeding the robin again. They sat together; their sandwiches unwrapped on their laps. June's was filled with egg mayo, and she wrinkled her nose at it with mock disgust.

"I only eat this because it's easy," June confessed. "If it were up to me, I'd live off Victoria sponge and crisps."

Emmy chuckled, biting into her own cheese and chutney sandwich.

June's gaze shifted, sharp but kind. "You know, you don't talk much about your life before you came here."

Emmy hesitated, chewing slowly. "No... I suppose I don't."

"Were you with someone?" June asked softly. "Before all this?"

Emmy's breath caught slightly. She looked down at her sandwich, her fingers tightening on the crust.

"There was someone," she said finally. "But... it wasn't what I thought. And it ended badly."

June didn't push, just nodded, her eyes gentle. "I get it. We all have ghosts, love."

They sat in silence for a moment, the robin hopping between their feet.

Then June brightened suddenly. "Well, at least now you've got a fresh start. And maybe... new stories waiting."

Emmy smiled faintly, her eyes drifting to the window where the rain had begun again in a gentle drizzle, each drop threading silver lines against the glass.

The afternoon passed with the same gentle rhythm as the rain outside. Emmy helped her class design small paper kites for their upcoming art display. She moved between the tables, kneeling beside each child, listening as they debated whether dragons or birds made better kite shapes.

"Mine is going to be a phoenix!" announced Thomas proudly, waving his orange and red tissue paper.

"That's wonderful," Emmy encouraged, smoothing a stray curl from her forehead. "What will rise from its ashes?"

He paused, tongue poking from the corner of his mouth. "Umm… snacks?"

Emmy burst into laughter so sudden she had to steady herself on the table edge.

By the end of the day, the classroom looked as though a rainbow had exploded: scraps of tissue paper drifted like petals across the floor, and every child had at least two glue streaks in their hair. Emmy surveyed the chaos, shaking her head with fond exasperation.

Once the children were gone and the corridor noise had faded to occasional echoing voices, Emmy stayed behind to tidy. She stacked the half-finished kites neatly, rinsed glue pots, and gently coaxed a stray crayon from under the bookshelf.

Outside, the sky was a pale wash of lavender and soft grey, the rain reduced to a light mist that clung to the hedgerows and softened the outlines of the distant fields.

Emmy paused by the window, watching as a fox trotted across the far end of the playground, sleek and self-possessed, its red coat a bright streak against the wet grass. She sighed, collected her bag, and switched off the classroom lights.

On her way out, she stopped by the staffroom to say goodbye to June.

"You're heading straight home?" June asked, folding away a stack of worksheets.

Emmy hesitated. "I thought I might stop by Aubrey's on my way back. Maybe pick up that new folklore book Mrs. Ellis mentioned."

June's eyes sparkled with mischief. "And maybe go for a walk and bump into a certain mysterious gentleman again?"

Emmy flushed. "June!"

"I'm only saying what we're all thinking," June teased, waving her hand airily. "Go on, live a little."

Emmy laughed despite her embarrassment, waved goodbye, and stepped out into the evening.

* * *

70

The air was cool and smelled faintly of wet earth and chimney smoke as she walked. The lamplights flickered to life one by one, casting small golden pools on the damp cobblestones. The town felt suspended between waking and dreaming, each house window glowing warmly, voices and clinks of crockery drifting into the street.

At Aubrey's, the bell above the door gave its usual soft chime. Mr Aubrey looked up from a small pile of new arrivals.

"Ah! There she is," he greeted Emmy. "I put a folklore book aside for you."

Emmy approached the counter, running her fingers along the spines of books as she passed. The scent of paper and ink always grounded her, as though each shelf held a thousand doorways to other lives.

"Thank you," Emmy said, accepting the book and flipping through its pages. Illustrations of harvest festivals, old village songs, and half-forgotten seasonal rites unfolded beneath her fingers.

Mr Aubrey leaned closer. "You know, a man came in earlier asking about that same book."

Emmy looked up sharply. "Really?"

Mr Aubrey gave a knowing smile. "Tall, dark hair, quiet voice. He didn't seem disappointed that it was gone, though. Said he'd find something else to occupy him."

Emmy's stomach gave a small, inexplicable flutter.

After paying, she tucked the book into her satchel and stepped back into the street, her mind echoing with Mr. Aubrey's words. She set off slowly, her feet carrying her almost of their own accord toward the woodland edge rather than straight home.

The forest loomed in the dusky light, the trunks appearing almost silver beneath the moon's first glow. Emmy paused at the entrance, her heart pattering like a startled bird.

She took a hesitant step forward. Then another.

The moss softened her footfalls, and the damp air curled around her like a cloak. A lone owl called somewhere overhead, and tiny droplets clung to her hair. Beneath the canopy of ash and oak, the village seemed far away - Emmy's boots sank softly into the earth as she followed the narrow track, her breath clouding faintly in the cool air.

She slowed when she caught sight of movement through the trees ahead — not the usual twitch of a squirrel or deer, but a taller figure. A man, bent slightly at the waist, pulling a branch free from the undergrowth. Beside him, a handful of chickens pecked and fussed through the fallen leaves, their feathers mottled russet and white, their clucking oddly companionable. The sight of them — so out of place in the middle of the woods — made her stop and smile before she realized she was staring.

The man straightened. He was tall, shoulders broad beneath a dark shirt rolled to the elbows. His hair, black, caught the weak sunlight in threads. He carried the branch easily in one hand, like it weighed almost nothing. At his feet, one of the hens fluttered noisily, indignant at being disturbed.

"You've got chickens out here?" Emmy called before she could think better of it. Her voice seemed louder than it should in the quiet wood, and her cheeks warmed.

The man turned toward her. His eyes — startlingly green, as if they belonged more to spring than autumn — fixed on her for a long moment. He didn't smile right away, though something softened in his expression when he looked at her.

"They follow me," he said at last, his voice low, even. "Though I suspect it's less loyalty than greed. They're convinced I carry feed in my pockets."

Emmy let out a laugh, a little too quickly, but genuine. "Well, they look happy enough. I didn't expect to find chickens in the middle of the forest."

"It isn't the middle," he said, tilting his head slightly. He dropped the branch onto a neat pile at his side, brushing bark dust from his palm. "This is my land."

"Oh." She blinked, her smile faltering just enough to show her embarrassment. "I didn't realize. I thought it was just... open woods."

He studied her a moment, then shook his head lightly. "No harm done. It's a large stretch, and most people walk through it without knowing. You're welcome, although, I believe we have already met?"

The words came with a trace of old-world formality, something that felt too careful, too deliberate for such a simple exchange.

"Yes, by the lake, I'm Emmy," she said after a pause, tucking a curl behind her ear. "I've just moved into the area. I'm the new school teacher."

He seemed to weigh her name on his tongue before replying. "Roman." He looked at her as though he was weighing up his thoughts, "Would Emmy be short for...?"

"Emmeline. But only my parents tend to call me by that".

Roman's gaze lingered on her a moment longer before he bent again to gather another fallen branch. One of the chickens strutted between them as though to break the silence, and Emmy found herself smiling once more — though this time at the strangeness of it all: meeting a man in the woods, his flock clucking around him like loyal little guardians.

"I hope I'm not intruding," she said quickly, feeling a sudden urge to retreat.

Roman shook his head, taking a cautious step closer. "Not at all. I was just tidying some of the old branches. They fall fast this time of year."

Emmy glanced at the pile. "It looks like hard work."

He gave a faint smile. "It keeps me occupied."

She hesitated, her hands twisting around the strap of her satchel. "I, um... I was on my way home from the bookshop and thought... I don't know. I thought I'd walk a little further."

One of the chickens – plumper than the rest, with glossy black feathers – strutter closer to her boots, cocking it's head as if measuring her up.

"She's braver than the others," Emmy remarked, crouching slightly though careful not to touch. "Or just nosier."

Roman glanced up from his task, the faintest curve at the corner of his mouth. "That one causes more trouble than she's worth".

"Does she have a name?"

He paused, "She's Henrietta," Roman said, nodding at the hen. "She believes she owns the entire estate."

"Estate?"

Roman picked up the last of the branches he had been stacking, and smiled slightly, "would you like to see the orchard?" Roman tilted his head towards the trail ahead.

They walked together toward the orchard, the path weaving through narrow clearings where moonlight pooled in silver patches. As they approached the garden wall, the sound of clucking and soft rustling drifted toward them. The chickens, true to Roman's word, followed behind in a state of cheerful chaos — chasing each other towards the rows of vegetable beds, scratching at the damp soil, and occasionally flaring their wings dramatically. Henrietta hopped onto a low stone ledge, surveying them like a queen addressing her court.

Emmy laughed, her breath misting in the cool air. "She looks like she might launch a coup at any moment."

Roman chuckled. "I wouldn't put it past her."

They wandered between the rows; Emmy occasionally pausing to lean down and stroke a curious chicken's feather or examine the small green shoots poking bravely from the soil. She looked up at Roman once, catching a rare softness in his eyes as he watched her.

"You've built something wonderful here," she said quietly. "It feels... alive."

Roman glanced at the orchard trees beyond the fence, their branches stirring slightly in the breeze. "It's been a long labour of love," he said, his voice low. "I suppose it's grown up around me rather than because of me."

Emmy tilted her head, studying him. "That's a poetic way of putting it."

He looked at her then, truly looked, as though weighing words carefully before choosing each one. "You see more than most, Miss Emmy."

She felt warmth rush to her face, and she turned her attention quickly back to the chickens, unable to hold his gaze.

As they walked around the orchard, Emmy glanced over at Roman, curiosity flickering across her face. "When you said the orchard grew up around you… you sounded almost as if you meant it literally."

Roman let out a quiet breath, his eyes briefly drifting to the moonlit treetops before returning to her. "Perhaps it did, in a way. Places like this… they become part of a person. They hold memories, shape habits. You spend enough time with the trees and the soil, and you start to feel as though you've always belonged to them."

Emmy tilted her head, studying him intently. "That's a beautiful way to put it. You speak like someone out of a book of old poems."

A small, almost shy smile touched Roman's lips. "I've always found words to be... comforting. They linger longer than people do, sometimes."

She hesitated, her hand brushing against a low branch as they passed beneath it. "Do you write? Poems, I mean?"

Roman looked at her, surprised, his green eyes catching a shard of moonlight. "I did, once. A long time ago."

"Why did you stop?"

His gaze softened, drifting past her shoulder to some invisible point in the darkened orchard. "Some things feel easier to put away, rather than carry. But perhaps that's cowardice."

Emmy's steps slowed slightly. "Or perhaps it's just... protecting yourself," she offered, her voice gentle.

He looked at her then, really looked, as if seeing beneath her surface. There was a moment — small but sharp — where something unspoken hovered between them.

They walked on, the ground soft beneath their feet, the lantern's fixed to the stoned walls glowing around them like a quiet secret.

"You seem to know this place so intimately," she murmured. "I can't imagine what it must be like to watch the seasons change year after year in the same orchard."

Roman's shoulders shifted, his expression distant but not closed. "Each season has its ghosts. But also its small rebirths. The orchard is a reminder that nothing is ever truly gone, only transformed."

Emmy shivered lightly, though she wasn't cold. "That's... a comforting thought."

"It's the only way I've found to keep moving forward," Roman replied, his voice low.

She glanced at him, her eyes softening. "You sound like someone who's lost a lot."

Roman's steps slowed for a heartbeat. Then he looked at her again, and for a brief second, she saw the weight behind his careful composure — a grief buried so deep it had grown into something else entirely.

He offered her a small, sad smile. "And yet here I am, surrounded by chickens plotting their next insurrection."

Emmy laughed, the sound bouncing lightly off the orchard walls. She reached out instinctively and touched his forearm, the gesture both playful and tender. "I suppose even grief can't survive a hen named Henrietta."

Roman let out a low chuckle, and when their eyes met again, there was a warmth that neither of them quite knew how to name.

They continued through the orchard, Roman occasionally pointing out small details — a mossy patch beneath an apple tree where rabbits often hid, a row of wild violets that had crept in over the years. Emmy asked about each plant, each stone, as if she wanted to memorize every thread in this quiet tapestry of his life.

At one point, she paused, lightly brushing her fingers over the twisted bark of a pear tree. "It feels like you've poured yourself into this place," she said softly. "Almost as though it's breathing because of you."

Roman stood beside her, close enough that she could feel the warmth radiating from his skin. "Perhaps it's the other way around," he said. "Perhaps it's kept me breathing."

A silence fell then, filled with the faint shuffle of the chickens settling in for the night and the distant call of an owl.

When they began the walk back through the woods, Emmy felt the strange urge to keep asking questions, to learn every corner of this hidden life he seemed to carry like an old key in his pocket.

"Do you ever feel lonely here?" she asked, her voice tentative.

Roman's gaze drifted upward to the moonlight snagged in the high branches. "Sometimes," he admitted. "But solitude isn't always loneliness. Sometimes it's... a kind of quiet freedom."

Emmy let that settle in the air between them. Then, surprising herself, she reached out and lightly brushed her fingertips against his hand.

Roman looked down at her hand, his own fingers twitching as if they didn't know whether to grasp hers or let the moment pass. Finally, he allowed their hands to touch fully, his long fingers curling gently around hers, careful, as though holding something precious and fragile.

They walked like that for several slow steps, their joined hands swinging slightly.

Emmy felt her heart thrum beneath her ribs, the warmth of his touch seeping into her, rooting her feet to the damp woodland path.

"Thank you," she whispered.

Roman turned to her, his eyes searching her face as if trying to memorize every contour, every fleeting expression. "For what?" he asked softly.

"For not letting me walk alone," she replied, her voice small but steady.

He smiled then — a real, unguarded smile that seemed to chase the last shadows from his eyes. "You should never have to."

They continued slowly, each step echoing with the gentle promise that neither of them dared to speak aloud just yet.

At the edge of the woods, when Emmy turned toward the town, she glanced back one last time. Roman stood still, half in shadow, half in late evening sunset — a figure out of some ancient tale, waiting at the threshold between the wild and the civilized world.

She held his gaze for a moment longer before she turned and made her way home, her thoughts swirling with images of orchard ghosts, sunset smiles, and the quiet warmth of a hand that had felt like an anchor in the dark.

# Chapter Six

Monday dawned bright and tentative, a pale wash of gold creeping across Emmy's ceiling as she stirred awake. She lay still for a moment, listening to the faint hum of town life below — a delivery lorry backing into the alley, a doorbell chiming in the bakery, the hush of an early bicycle passing.

She pressed her cheek deeper into her pillow, trying to catch the fading edges of her dream. It was the orchard again — she could almost smell the sweet tang of blossom and hear the low rustle of chicken feathers in the grass. Roman had been there, though his face had been a blur in the morning fog of her mind. She sat up slowly, shaking off the shiver of memory, and swung her legs over the edge of the bed.

After a quick shower, she dressed in a sage green blouse tucked into a navy pleated skirt, her curls pinned back to keep them from springing wild around her face. She studied her reflection in the small hallway mirror: her golden honey skin gleamed in the soft morning light, her wide, curious brown eyes framed by thick lashes. Her full lips, usually so quick to form a warm smile for her students, felt more hesitant today.

She forced a small grin at herself. "Come on, Emmy," she whispered. "Monday waits for no one."

Grabbing her bag and the marked spelling tests she'd worked through late into Sunday night, she descended the narrow stairs to her front door.

The walk to the school was gentle and familiar now, lined with budding hedgerows and hanging baskets bursting with trailing lobelia. She passed Mrs. Lyle outside the grocer's, who waved her over and pressed a brown paper bag into her hands.

"Apricots," Mrs. Lyle said firmly. "We over-ordered, and they'll spoil before the week's end. You young people need your vitamins."

Emmy laughed. "Thank you. I'll make good use of them."

By the time she reached the school gates, the playground had filled with its usual orchestra of sound — children squealing, balls bouncing off walls, skipping ropes slapping the ground. She waved at a knot of Year Four students playing tag and they immediately surrounded her, peppering her with updates: someone had lost a tooth, another had learned a new cartwheel, and one proudly presented a daisy chain now missing half its blooms.

Inside, the corridors smelled of pencil shavings, glue sticks, and that familiar scent of books warmed slightly by the old radiators. Emmy slipped into the staffroom, setting her bag on a chair near the window. The sunlight glanced off the kettle, illuminating the comforting clutter of mugs and biscuit tins.

June sat with her feet propped on another chair, a robin perched boldly on the ledge outside the window. She broke off pieces of a granola bar, tossing them to the bird as it tilted its head curiously.

"Well, good morning, Miss Sunrise," June called without turning.

Emmy laughed, slipping into the seat beside her. "Feeding your spies again, I see."

"They deserve breakfast too," June said with mock indignation, flicking another crumb outside.

Arun Bhatt sauntered in, rubbing sleep from his eyes. "If I didn't know better, I'd say you two start the day far too chipper."

"It's just the coffee fumes and bird gossip," Emmy teased.

Arun smirked, "Right. I'll just... see if there's any actual tea left in this sorry kettle."

June chuckled, dabbing her eyes dramatically. "Go on then, you coward."

The bell rang overhead, pulling them all back to their feet. Emmy stood, adjusted her blouse, and took a steadying breath.

In her classroom, the children were already waiting, many perched on the edge of their seats. As she greeted them, she felt that familiar surge of calm — teaching was her anchor, the place where her warmth shone brightest.

"Good morning, everyone!"

"Good morning, Miss Trevelyn!" they chorused.

She launched into spelling first, using silly rhymes and a small stuffed owl named Oliver to keep their attention. They moved on to a lesson about habitats next. Emmy had prepared a large poster of a pond scene, complete with cut-out frogs, dragonflies, and a single paper heron looming over the water.

By mid-morning, the children were buzzing. Emmy sent them out to the playground, watching as they spilled onto the tarmac, screaming and giggling. She stayed behind, tidying the art supplies from their morning project.

A knock at the door startled her. She turned to see June leaning in, a mischievous twinkle in her eye.

"Care for a walk to the bakery during lunch?"

Emmy hesitated. "I should probably catch up on marking..."

June shook her head. "Nonsense. Fresh air and pastry solve most problems."

With a laugh, Emmy agreed.

They strolled down the lane together at lunch, their steps unhurried. The bakery's sign — Pearson's Bakery — swung gently above the door, its paint faded by years of sun. Inside, the scent of warm sugar and fresh bread curled around them, and Emmy felt her shoulders drop an inch.

June ordered her usual lemon tart, while Emmy chose a raspberry Danish. As they waited, they talked about everything and nothing: the mischief of Year Six, the new display in Aubrey's window, the best local footpaths for spotting wildflowers.

When they stepped back into the sunlight, June turned to her, her pastry box cradled like treasure. "I know I tease, but truly — you seem brighter lately."

Emmy tilted her head. "Brighter?"

June nodded. "Something's shifted. Maybe it's the town growing on you, maybe it's just spring waking us all up. But I see it."

Emmy felt heat rise to her cheeks, but she didn't look away. "I think... I think I'm just starting to breathe again."

June grinned, tapping Emmy lightly on the shoulder with her pastry box. "That's all I want to hear."

They wandered back slowly, pausing to admire the tulips outside a neighbour's fence and to listen to a blackbird's song echoing off the low stone walls. When they arrived at the school gate, Emmy felt lighter than she had in years.

The afternoon passed in a warm blur. The children had music, where they attempted to play a simple melody on recorders with varying degrees of success, and then art, where Emmy introduced them to watercolours. By the time the last bell rang, most of the students had smudges of blue and green on their sleeves and broad smiles on their faces.

Emmy tidied in a trance of contentment, humming a soft tune under her breath. As she gathered the leftover paint pots, she thought again of the orchard and Roman's steady presence, his eyes that seemed to hold unspoken seasons.

After finishing up, she returned to the staffroom. June was already there; her hair loosened from its earlier tidy bun. She looked up with a weary smile.

"I think your recorder lesson might have ruptured my last nerve," June groaned, stretching her arms.

Emmy laughed. "I promise, no more recorders for at least a month."

June held out her pinky. "Swear it."

Emmy solemnly hooked her pinky with June's, the two of them dissolving into giggles.

Once she had gathered her belongings, Emmy left the school and made her way down the narrow lane toward home. The soft evening air wrapped around her like a shawl. She paused to answer a call from her father, his voice warm but concerned on the other end.

"How's my girl doing?"

Emmy smiled, shifting her shopping bag. "I'm good, Dad. Really. The children are wonderful, and the town... it's starting to feel like home."

"You're eating properly? Not just pastries?"

She laughed. "I promise. Mrs. Lyle keeps me stocked with fruit. I've got apricots this week."

A pause. "And you're still safe? No... trouble?"

The tremor in his voice pulled at her. She took a slow breath. "I'm safe, Dad. Truly."

"Your mother worries," he said, softer now.

"I know. Tell her I'm okay. I'll call her tomorrow."

They chatted a little longer — small stories about the garden back home, a new stray cat that had begun visiting their porch. Emmy promised to visit soon, though she wasn't sure when.

As she reached her flat, she looked up at the golden square of her window glowing against the deepening sky. She climbed the stairs, her steps slower than usual, as if reluctant to let the evening end.

Inside, she placed her apricots on the counter and unpacked her school bag, carefully stacking the day's drawings and lesson notes. She moved about her small kitchen, humming, setting the kettle to boil for a cup of mint tea.

After dinner, Emmy found herself restless. She had tried reading, but her mind wandered; she had tried tidying, but she simply moved objects from one place to another without purpose. The gentle hum of evening beyond her window seemed to pull at her like a thread.

Finally, she slipped on a light cardigan and stepped out into the hallway. The stairs creaked familiarly under her feet as she descended into the soft glow of the street lamps outside. The air was cool and smelled faintly of lilacs and damp stone.

Aubrey's shop below was long since closed, the books in the window standing like quiet sentinels beneath the warm gold of the shop light left on overnight. Emmy paused to peer at a new display — a collection of poetry books with pale covers, carefully arranged around a small vase of dried lavender. She felt her lips curve into a smile.

She turned and began to walk, following no path in particular. The town at this hour felt like an intimate secret: the hush of distant voices from open windows, the occasional barking of a dog echoing off brick, the flicker of a television screen briefly visible through parted curtains.

Her feet led her past Pearson's bakery, now dark and quiet. The sweet scent of baked goods lingered, weaving through the night air like a memory. She thought of June and her pastry box cradled like treasure, and her laugh that rose in bright bursts whenever they walked together.

She passed by the small town green, its benches empty, the flower beds freshly watered and shimmering under the street lamps. Emmy paused at the low iron fence bordering the green, resting her hands on the cool metal.

Her mind drifted to her conversation with her father earlier. His worry always carried an undertow of guilt in her chest. She knew he feared for her safety after what had happened, that terrible night she had only spoken of in half-formed fragments.

Sometimes, when she closed her eyes, she could still feel the trembling in her own bones, the shadow of a voice in her ear. She hadn't shared every detail with her parents — she hadn't wanted them to bear the full weight of it — but they had known enough to understand the depth of her need to leave.

And so she had come here. To start again. To remember how to breathe.

Emmy drew in a long breath, the cool air settling into her lungs like a gentle hand.

After a while, she continued her wandering. Her steps carried her past small cottages with ivy climbing their walls, their gardens tangled and wild, yet clearly loved. The moon hung low and full, throwing pale light across the cobblestones, illuminating the delicate motion of leaves above her.

She thought of Roman — of his quiet steadiness, of the way his eyes seemed to hold something older than they should. She recalled

89

the moment at the pond when he fed the ducks, the way his hands moved with a kind of reverence.

There was something there she could not name, a thread she felt tugging at her, though she did not understand where it might lead.

When she finally turned back toward home, it was well past ten. The town had settled into its deeper hush, the last few windows darkening one by one.

Inside her flat, she slipped off her shoes and padded to the window, looking down at the empty street. A single moth flitted against the glass, its wings pale as parchment. Emmy watched it for a while, her mind a quiet tangle of questions she was not yet ready to ask out loud.

She read for a little while longer, but sleep tugged insistently at her. When she finally crawled into bed, she drifted off quickly, her last waking thought the image of Roman's gentle hands scattering grain for the chickens, like an old ritual half-remembered from a story.

* * *

Morning brought the clatter of a bin lorry and the shriek of a gull outside her window. Emmy groaned, burying her face into the pillow before dragging herself upright. She glanced at her phone — two missed calls from her mother and a text from her father reminding her to wear a coat because "the spring sunshine lies."

She called them back while she boiled water for tea. Her mother answered quickly, her voice bright but taut around the edges.

"Emmeline! I was beginning to think you'd vanished off into the woods!"

"I'm here, Mum. Sorry, I just went for a walk last night and switched my phone off."

A pause. "Out alone? In the dark?"

Emmy pinched the bridge of her nose, exhaling slowly. "Mum, it's a safe town. I promise. And I stayed on the main paths."

Another pause, a small sigh from the other end. "I know. I just... I worry. You know that."

"I know." Emmy softened her voice. "But I'm careful. Really."

They talked a little longer — her mother asked after the school, the children, whether she'd made new friends yet. Emmy mentioned June and Arun Bhatt, describing their good-natured teasing and shared lunches at Pearson's Bakery.

Her mother listened, occasionally humming a small "hmm" of approval. When they finally said goodbye, Emmy could still feel the thin thread of her mother's anxiety stretching across the miles between them.

She sat for a moment at her small table, stirring her tea absently. She wanted to tell her mother about Roman — about the strange feeling she got when talking to him, like stepping into a storybook or brushing against a hidden door. But she knew better than to offer up that mystery to her mother's protective instincts.

At school, Emmy found herself buoyed by the children's chatter and the comfortable rhythms of the day. She helped them design papier-mâché insects for an upcoming science project, the room soon filled with flapping dragonfly wings and bright ladybird shells.

"Miss Trevelyn, does a ladybird get scared if you shout at it?" asked Jonah, wide-eyed, a streak of blue paint across his forehead.

She laughed, kneeling beside his desk. "I imagine it might be startled, but it would fly away before you could explain."

Jonah considered this solemnly, then returned to gluing spots on his insect with renewed concentration.

During lunch, Emmy escaped to the courtyard with her sandwich and a handful of apricots from Mrs. Lyle. June found her there, balancing her own salad container precariously on her knees.

"You're a creature of habit, Emmy," June teased, gesturing at the apricots.

"Better than biscuits every day," Emmy retorted, popping one into her mouth.

June leaned back, her eyes half-closed against the bright sky. "True. Though biscuits have a certain... emotional value."

They shared a laugh, the kind that left Emmy feeling unexpectedly light.

After a moment, June turned to her, curiosity glinting in her gaze. "Tell me something true."

Emmy blinked. "What do you mean?"

"Anything. Something no one here knows."

Emmy hesitated. The town felt like a small, safe pond she was still learning to swim in. But June had that kind of patient warmth that made secrets feel less heavy.

"I used to sing," Emmy said finally. "Not professionally — just at church. Or around the house."

June's eyebrows shot up. "You? Our quietly humming, gentle Emmy? I can't imagine you belting a hymn."

Emmy laughed, heat rising to her cheeks. "I wasn't that loud. My mum said it was the only time I seemed completely free."

June's expression softened. "That's beautiful. Do you still sing?"

"Not really. Not since..." She trailed off, fingers curling into her lap.

June reached over and squeezed her wrist gently. "Maybe you will again. When you're ready."

They sat in silence a little longer, listening to the distant sound of children playing football on the lower field, the rhythmic thump of a ball against the fence.

Later that afternoon, Emmy's Year Four class presented their papier-mâché insects to the rest of the school. Emmy watched proudly as each child held up their creation, some shyly mumbling explanations, others practically leaping off the small stage with excitement.

When it was over and the children were herded back to their classrooms, Emmy stayed behind to help sweep up stray scraps of tissue paper and stray googly eyes.

"Don't stay too long, love," called Arun Bhatt as he passed with a box of sports equipment balanced on his hip. "You'll turn into a permanent fixture in this hall."

93

Emmy laughed. "I'll try to avoid becoming modern art."

Once the last child had been collected, she slipped out into the corridor. She paused by the display of last term's art projects, her eyes lingering on a collage of wildflowers one student had created. The bright splashes of pink and yellow reminded her of the orchard.

As she gathered her things, her phone buzzed again — another call from her father. She answered quickly, stepping into a quiet corner of the corridor.

"Hi, Dad," she said, breathless from her surprise.

"Emmy! I just wanted to make sure you got home safe yesterday. Your mum worries more than usual when you don't call."

"I know. I meant to, but I went for a walk and lost track of time. I promise, I'm fine."

A pause. "You sound... different. Happier."

Emmy leaned against the wall, staring at the floor tiles. "I think I am. I feel... free here."

"That's all we ever wanted for you," he said quietly.

They chatted for a few more minutes, trading small stories about the cat back home and the new vegetable patch her father was tending. When they hung up, Emmy stood there for a moment longer, the echo of her father's voice folding gently around her.

By the time she left the school, the sun was beginning its slow slide toward the horizon. The sky above was painted with streaks of coral and soft purple, like watercolours blending in a basin.

Emmy walked home slowly, stopping to admire the tulips outside Pearson's and to watch a pair of pigeons jostle for crumbs near the lamppost. She carried her school bag over one shoulder and a small bag of leftover art supplies in the other, her curls bouncing lightly with each step.

When she reached her building, she paused outside Aubrey's again. Mr. Aubrey was inside rearranging a display of antique maps. She knocked lightly on the glass, and he looked up, smiling and beckoning her in.

Inside, the familiar smell of old paper and polished wood washed over her. She set her bag down by the front counter and wandered to the shelf near the back, where local histories and folklore books stood in neat rows.

"Looking for something specific today, Miss Trevelyn?" Mr. Aubrey asked, peering over his spectacles.

"Just browsing," Emmy said with a small smile. "I thought I might pick up something to keep me company tonight."

"Ah," he said knowingly, tapping a finger against the edge of the counter. "A book is often the best company one can keep."

She finally selected a slender volume on ancient British gardens and paid, tucking it into her bag. Mr. Aubrey insisted on adding a small bookmark — a pressed violet laminated into a strip of pale paper.

"For luck," he said with a wink.

Emmy stepped back onto the street, her new book snug against her side. She climbed the stairs to her flat, unlocking the door and stepping into the warmth of her small, carefully arranged space.

She placed the book on her coffee table and moved into the kitchen, washing her hands and starting a small pot of vegetable stew. As it simmered, she put on a record — a gentle, winding instrumental piece she had found in a charity shop one time.

While the music filled the flat, she sat on the floor with her back against the armchair, paging through the garden book. The photographs were lush and overgrown, each caption hinting at histories buried beneath petals and moss.

Her mind kept drifting to Roman — his orchard, the quiet way he regarded the world. She wondered what stories he might tell if she asked the right questions.

After dinner, she cleaned up carefully, humming softly to herself. The habit of singing, though quiet and almost hidden now, sometimes slipped through when she thought no one was listening.

She moved to her window, leaning on the sill and looking out at the street below. The town felt like a soft heartbeat beneath her feet — gentle, steady, alive.

A thought came to her then, sudden and bright: I am not the same girl who fled in the night, trembling and lost.

She touched her hand to her cheek, feeling the warmth of her own skin, the way her curls framed her face, the softness at the corner of her mouth. She was Emmy — teacher, reader, friend, daughter, perhaps even singer again someday.

She stayed there for a long while, until the stars blinked into view one by one and the moon rose, wide and watchful above the rooftops.

When she finally turned away, she felt something inside her shift — like a door opening onto a garden she had long forgotten. As she climbed into bed, her thoughts threaded quietly through the orchard paths, the echoes of a robin's trill, and the hush of a voice she hoped to hear again soon.

# Chapter Seven

The last lesson ended with the soft rustle a classroom makes when attention loosens. Emmy capped the board pens, tapped a stack of worksheets straight, and let her palm rest a moment on the cool windowsill. Outside, late afternoon leaned across the playground and laid a pale shine over the faded hopscotch squares. It wasn't entirely quiet—somewhere a trolley rattled, a chair leg squeaked next door—but the day had exhaled. She felt the room's warmth on her forearms and the faint chalk-dust dryness at the back of her throat.

She slid the remaining reading books into their tub, dropped a rubber into the ceramic pot, and took her cardigan from the chair. No ceremony—just the small rightness of finishing things. She switched off the main lights, left the corner lamp glowing for the caretaker, and pulled the classroom door gently to behind her.

The corridor received her with its usual hush. Display boards kept their bright faces; stapled borders marched in tidy lines. From farther down came the click of a kettle and a laugh that was too big for the hour; here only Emmy's footsteps moved, soft on the lino. She locked the classroom, checked the handle twice, and tucked her keys into her pocket. The air smelled of paper, polish, and the faint tang of disinfectant losing its argument with time.

At the end of the corridor she pushed through the fire door and into the side path where the air felt thin and new. Stonebridge

Hollow gathered itself around the school in gentle edges—the low wall with its flecked paint, the hedge keeping its shape out of stubbornness, the view that opened when you reached the corner. Emmy breathed it in. Across the road a boy balanced on a curb with the absorbed seriousness of a tightrope walker; an older woman steered a shopping trolley that had seen cleaner seasons; under the bench, pigeons conducted a complicated negotiation and reached no conclusion at all.

She took the familiar left that slid her away from the centre and toward fields. No slow morning routine, no catalogue of weather— just the hour that belonged to her because she had stepped into it. Past the post box (still faintly red-fingered if you posted in rain), past the cottage where the geraniums refused to admit the month had turned, she let the lane draw her between hedges. The sound of the village thinned into birds and the far, contented machinery of a farm. Evening light angled along the hawthorn, flashing on slick leaf-backs.

The first rows of the orchard appeared to her right—tidy as handwriting, shadows running neat beneath the branches. A few windfalls lay in the verge, bruised and sweet-smelling. Emmy's pace slowed without decision. She hadn't planned a route; she rarely did at this hour. Paths chose themselves if you let them.

The lane dipped where the river ran like a pale ribbon behind the trees. At the usual gap in the hedge—the one locals used when they didn't feel like the long way round—she slipped through, brushing her sleeve against the hawthorn's polite disapproval. Gravel gave underfoot, then the kinder press of grass. The orchard fell away on her right; the low, clean light off the water lifted her gaze ahead.

She didn't intend to go far. The day had been ordinary and good, but she felt that thinness under her ribs that came after too much bright talk. The river kept a steadier attention; it asked less and returned more. She followed the cart track skirting the trees until it bent; reeds raised their dark heads like notes on a staff.

Movement caught her eye around the curve.

Roman.

Roman was knee-deep in the shallows, sleeves rolled to the elbow. In his arms, pressed carefully against his chest, was a cygnet. Grey, downy, with wings flailing in frantic little jerks. A loop of reed had tangled round one wing. Roman's hands moved steady, patient, coaxing the reed loose.

The parent swans were close. Two white shapes like carved marble, necks held rigid. One turned sharply and hissed at Emmy, a sound that cut through the quiet. Its wings lifted a fraction, sharp as warning blades.

Emmy froze.

Roman didn't look up immediately. His attention stayed on the cygnet. Only when the reed loosened free did he raise his head.

"They're protective," he said, his voice calm, pitched to settle. "More so now, with me handling their young. And you appeared suddenly."

"I didn't mean to," Emmy said quickly.

"You didn't frighten them. They frighten themselves."

He lowered the cygnet to the water. It paddled back to its mother, who curved her neck over it and guided it out toward calmer water. The hissing eased. The three white shapes drifted off, whole again.

Roman straightened, brushing his wet hands on his trousers. His boots were dark to the ankle. "Forgiven," he said quietly, the faintest wryness touching his mouth. "Or tolerated."

Emmy let out her breath. "Tolerated is generous. Swans don't usually hand that out."

"True," he agreed. His gaze stayed on the water a moment longer, then returned to her.

"Is this part of your land?" she asked, nodding toward the river and the reed beds.

"Part of it," he said simply.

"I thought so. It feels… different somehow. Kept."

His eyes softened. "I try not to let it run to ruin. The river rewards attention."

"You make it sound alive," she said.

"It is alive," he replied, matter-of-fact. "Same as the orchard. Same as the woods. You notice when they're well, and when they're not."

Emmy smiled. "You sound like one of my pupils talking about their pets."

That earned her a look—half amused, half thoughtful. "Perhaps your pupils are right."

For a while they stood without speaking, the hush between them companionable. Emmy found herself watching the way the breeze caught at his hair, the patience in the set of his shoulders.

At last she said, "Would your map allow company? Just a little further."

He tilted his head, studying her face, then gave a single nod. "To the first turning."

They left the riverbank for the narrow footpath. Hawthorn scratched at their sleeves until the way widened enough for them to walk side by side. Fallen leaves crunched underfoot, the orchard rows stretching orderly to the right, while to the left the river murmured unseen, following them like a second voice.

"You really do seem to know every inch of this land," Emmy said after a while.

Roman's gaze stayed ahead. "I've walked it often enough. The ground remembers who pays attention."

"You make it sound like it has a memory of its own."

"It does," he said without hesitation. "Neglect it, and it answers back."

"You mean weeds and thistles?" she asked lightly.

"I mean everything. Floods. Sickness in the trees. Paths that vanish because no one cares to use them."

Emmy smiled. "You do realise you sound exactly like one of my pupils talking about their hamsters? 'If I don't clean the cage, it sulks. If I forget the lettuce, it won't look at me.'"

That drew an amused flicker from him. "Then perhaps they've understood something most grown men forget."

She tilted her head. "Do you talk to the trees as well, then?"

"Sometimes."

"Do they answer?"

"Not quickly."

Emmy laughed, and the sound surprised her with how easily it came. "Neither do children. I spend all day coaxing sentences out of them. It's like pulling teeth with some."

"Perhaps branches and children aren't so different," Roman said.

"Only one of them throws paint at you," she countered, and he gave her the smallest, genuine smile.

They walked on, and she noticed the dark patches drying on his trousers where the water had reached. "Your boots must be soaked," she said.

"They've survived worse."

"You should have changed before wading in like that."

"The swan didn't leave me time to fetch other shoes."

Emmy shook her head, smiling. "You make it sound as if you're their personal lifeguard."

"I wouldn't go that far." He glanced sideways at her. "Though I imagine you've had to rescue more than one child from a puddle deeper than expected."

"Countless times. Shoes, socks, dignity—all lost to muddy water. I'd have had half the parents at my door if I let them wade in like you did."

"Fortunately, the swans don't send complaints."

She laughed again, warmth bubbling in her chest.

They reached the low stone bridge. It rose only to her thigh, lichen feathering its edges. Emmy set her palms on the cool parapet and leaned forward, watching the water press against the stone.

"It feels hidden here," she said softly. "Like a place that doesn't care who owns it."

Roman rested his hand on the stone, almost as though in greeting. "The bridge has stood longer than anyone who crosses it. It doesn't need ownership. Only care."

"You notice everything," she said, turning toward him. "Do you just… keep it all in your head?"

"Most of it."

"And the rest?"

He hesitated before replying, "I write it down. Small things. A gate that drags. A row of trees that's late to fruit. Where the riverbank slips more each year."

"That sounds more like a diary than notes," Emmy teased.

A faint smile touched his mouth. "Then perhaps it is."

"You surprise me, Roman."

His eyes shifted to hers. "How so?"

"You have a lot of awareness and appreciation for what is around you…" She paused, searching. "Attentive. I wasn't expecting that."

His expression barely changed, but she caught the flicker beneath. "I'm only someone who lives here."

"That's not the whole truth," Emmy said gently. Then, to soften it: "But it's enough for tonight."

The silence that followed wasn't uncomfortable. The river went on writing itself beneath the bridge.

A sudden splash upriver made her start; a fish leapt, sending rings across the current. Emmy leaned over to follow it, her hands tightening on the parapet. "One of my pupils insists he saw a pike in this river," she said. "A monster, as long as his arm. Do you think that's true?"

"Pike grow large," Roman allowed. "Children grow larger stories."

"Meaning no?"

"Meaning perhaps," he said, and the corner of his mouth tipped upward.

Emmy chuckled. "That's not an answer my class would accept."

"Then they're wiser than most."

The light was thinning now, the first chill creeping under her cardigan. Roman's gaze dropped briefly to her hands on the stone, fingers flushed pink from the cold.

"You should head back before it's dark," he said. Not dismissal—concern.

"Walk me to the hedge?" she asked.

He nodded once. "To the hedge."

They retraced the path, hawthorn brushing less sharply now that they knew how to move through it. Their shoulders brushed once in the narrowing, and neither remarked on it.

"You're quieter than I expected, too," Emmy said after a while.

Roman raised an eyebrow. "You thought me talkative?"

"I thought…" She smiled to herself. "I don't know. Perhaps I imagined you would avoid words altogether. But you choose them carefully. That's rarer than you'd think."

"It's easier to listen," he said.

"And yet here you are, speaking."

His green eyes flicked to her. "Perhaps you ask better questions than most."

They reached the gap in the hedge, the lane visible beyond. Emmy paused, reluctant to step away just yet.

"I'm glad I came," she said quietly.

Roman inclined his head, eyes steady on hers. "So am I."

Her smile lingered as she stepped into the lane. When she glanced back, he was still there, one hand resting lightly on the hawthorn as though steadying the evening.

# Chapter Eight

**Romans perspective:**

Roman rose before dawn, as he always did. The habit had long outlasted any practical reason — it was simply woven into his bones now, the way old trees knew to reach for the sun even in winter.

He sat for a moment on the edge of his bed, fingers brushing the linen sheets. The silence of the manor pressed softly around him, broken only by the occasional creak of the old floorboards settling beneath the weight of centuries.

Outside, the first thin light of morning threaded through the trees, touching the gardens with a hesitant grey glow. Roman drew a deep breath, feeling the coolness of the air on his skin, and stood.

His room remained much as it had been for decades — heavy oak furniture, an iron-framed bed, thick woven blankets. He had replaced things over time, of course, but always with an eye for age and craft, objects that felt timeless rather than new. A small photograph of a young woman in a stiff, high-necked gown sat on the mantle — the only remnant of a life so long gone it often felt like a story he'd once read rather than a memory.

Roman dressed without hurry, pulling on dark trousers and a white linen shirt, sleeves rolled to the elbows. His hair, black and slightly curled at the ends, flopped into his eyes until he pushed it back. In the mirror, he caught sight of himself — those same green eyes, the same careful line of his jaw. Unchanging, no matter the years.

In the kitchen, he moved like a quiet ritual. He ground coffee beans by hand, the rhythmic motion soothing. He set water to boil on the stove, sliced a piece of sourdough he had baked the previous day, and brought out fresh eggs collected from the hens.

He worked deftly, the eggs cracking into the pan with a satisfying hiss. While they cooked, he cut ripe tomatoes from the windowsill basket and sprinkled them with sea salt and rosemary. He arranged everything on a plate with a simplicity that bordered on art.

Roman carried his breakfast to the large wooden table in the orangery, where light spilled through tall glass panes. Ivy curled along the frames, and the walled garden beyond was still heavy with dew. He ate in silence, savouring each bite as though it might be the last — not out of fear, but out of a reverence for small pleasures he had learned over centuries to cherish.

After he finished, he rose to tend to the garden. The lemon tree, planted by his mother when he was still a boy, demanded particular care. He checked its leaves, ran his thumb along the bark, whispered in low tones that no one else would hear. He moved on to the vegetable beds next, inspecting carrots, beets, and rows of cabbages.

The chickens clucked noisily as he scattered feed, jostling each other in a flurry of wings and feathers. One particularly bold hen hopped onto the edge of the trough, pecking impatiently at his hand until he chuckled and dropped her an extra handful.

When the sun was fully above the trees, he took a long walk across the estate. Paths twisted between flower beds and old oaks, past the pond where dragonflies skimmed the glassy surface and water lilies bloomed in pale pinks and whites. Over the years, ducks and swans had come and gone, their descendants returning faithfully each spring. Frogs croaked from the pond's shaded edges, their voices a low symphony.

Roman stopped at the pier, running his fingers along the weathered wood. It was here he sometimes sat in the evenings, watching the moon drift across the water, feeling the passage of time in each ripple and gust of wind.

After tending to a few broken fence posts along the orchard's edge, he returned inside to the room he jokingly called his "museum."

Stacks of journals lined the walls, alongside shelves stuffed with old coins, pocket watches, pressed flowers, and books with cracked spines. Artifacts from his past lives — letters from acquaintances long dead, small paintings from artists who had never seen fame in their lifetime, a delicate lace handkerchief from a lost love.

He picked up an old wooden toy horse, its paint faded, and turned it over in his hands. His thumb found a groove where it had been repaired once, so long ago he barely remembered the moment. Carefully, he set it back on the shelf beside a French cavalry sabre and a delicate cameo brooch.

These objects were his silent witnesses, each one a chapter of the same endless story. Over the years, he had donated some items anonymously or sold them under assumed names, sometimes to fund restorations on the estate or simply to see them appreciated rather than locked away.

He closed the door gently behind him, feeling the room's hush settle like a shroud.

Later in the afternoon, he prepared bread dough, kneading it on the wide marble counter until it felt elastic beneath his hands. Flour dusted his forearms and dark hair fell forward again, making him pause to brush it aside with the back of his wrist.

He set the dough to rise and glanced out the kitchen window. The sun had shifted, painting the orchard in dappled gold. He felt the itch to move — a desire not to run, exactly, but to observe, to slip into the world beyond his trees without ever really joining it.

So he washed up, traded his apron for a dark wool coat, and set out on foot.

The town felt familiar and foreign all at once. He stayed on the edges — down narrow side lanes, across hidden paths lined with hawthorn and ivy. He liked these half-forgotten shortcuts, the places no one thought to look.

At the edge of a small green, he paused. From a distance, he saw children skipping rope, a dog chasing a ball across the lawn. Near the bookshop, a group of teenagers sprawled on the steps, passing a bag of crisps between them and shouting half-formed dares at each other.

Then, through a break in the crowd, he saw her.

Emmy.

She stood near a display window of a florist, her face tilted slightly as she examined a pot of small violets. Her curls framed her face like a dark halo, catching the late sun and shimmering with hints of blue-black. Her skin, that warm honey gold, looked almost luminous in the fading light.

He watched as she tucked a stray curl behind her ear, her fingers delicate and quick. A small, thoughtful crease appeared between her brows as she read the label on a card stuck into the soil of the violets.

Roman felt something shift in his chest. It wasn't the violent, fiery rush of youth, nor the distant ache of old heartbreak. It was quieter — a soft, insistent pull, like the first notes of a familiar song drifting in through an open window.

He stepped back into the shadows of the alley, careful to remain unseen. He did not want to frighten her, did not want to appear as a phantom slipping between moments.

As he stood there, he found himself studying the lines of her shoulders, the gentle arch of her neck. In a single movement, she turned and smiled at an elderly woman shuffling past with a walking stick. Emmy bent slightly to adjust the woman's shopping bag, then stood, nodding warmly.

Roman felt the echo of that kindness ripple across the space between them. He wondered what she saw when she looked at the world — if she noticed the tiny cracks in the pavement, the bird nests under eaves, the way ivy climbed brick walls like a secret.

He turned away reluctantly, moving deeper into the alley. His feet carried him past the edges of the green, around the corner by the grocer's, through the back path behind the bakery. The air there smelled of sugar and yeast, a comfort so steady it felt like a heartbeat.

In the window of Aubrey's bookshop, he glimpsed a new display: an arrangement of classic novels and pressed flowers, with a small handwritten sign that read "Stories that outlast us." Roman felt a half-smile tug at his mouth.

He slipped back toward the woods as the last light waned, carrying a handful of fresh mushrooms he had gathered from a hidden grove on the way. When he reached the manor, the chickens were already perched in their coop, feathers fluffed against the cool air.

Roman washed the mushrooms at the kitchen sink, the running water a soft accompaniment to the evening crickets beyond the window. He set a pot of stew to simmer on the stove, tossing in onions, carrots, garlic, and herbs plucked earlier that morning.

The quiet deepened around him, the manor settling into its nocturnal sighs. Roman lit a single candle at the long dining table but chose to eat standing by the window instead, gazing out at the moonlit orchard.

Between each slow mouthful, his mind drifted back to Emmy's face, to the softness in her eyes, the gentle curl of her smile. He did not know when she had begun to inhabit his thoughts so fully. It was not his intention to invite anyone into the stillness of his life, not again.

But there she was — like a thread of morning light winding through a shuttered room.

When his plate was clean, he set it aside and padded softly through the halls. In the library, he pulled out one of his older journals, fingers hesitating at the frayed leather cover. He flipped through entries written in a dozen different scripts, in languages that no longer found a place on most lips.

He paused at a page dated over a hundred years ago — an entry about a woman he had once loved, a woman with quick laughter and restless hands who had left him for a life more ordinary than he could ever offer.

Roman closed the journal carefully, pressing his palm to the cover as if to still the old ghosts inside. Then he returned it to its place on the shelf and stood a long moment in the hush of the room, feeling the pulse of time move all around him.

At last, he moved to the window. Beyond the orchard, the moonlight picked out silver streaks on the pond, where frogs occasionally croaked in the reeds. A fox trotted across the far edge of the lawn, tail sweeping like a paintbrush.

Roman leaned his forehead against the cool glass and let out a long, quiet breath.

"Emmeline," he whispered, testing her full name on his tongue as though it were a prayer.

He knew he could not — should not — let her step closer into the labyrinth of his life. But even as he told himself this, he felt the hush between them growing smaller, as if the world itself were slowly drawing them into orbit.

He pushed away from the window, extinguished the candle, and began his slow walk through the halls, checking each room in a routine so ingrained it felt like breathing. As he moved, he felt the faint warmth of her presence echoing inside him — a warmth he had not permitted himself in decades.

When he finally returned to his bedroom, he undressed and lay atop the blankets, listening to the soft night sounds beyond the manor walls. The house held its secrets like an old friend, bearing witness to each silent confession, each quiet longing.

Roman closed his eyes and let his mind drift. Tomorrow, he knew, he might see her again. And whether he admitted it aloud or not, part of him was already waiting.

# Chapter 9

Emmy hadn't intended to spend the Saturday afternoon wandering. She'd meant to mark exercise books, tidy the flat, maybe even finally call her father back. But by the time lunch was over, the quiet had become unbearable — the sort of heavy silence that seemed to press in from the walls.

She grabbed her coat and left without much thought, letting her feet decide the direction.

The main square was busy, the usual weekend crowd spilling in and out of the market stalls. Children darted between clusters of neighbours, clutching paper bags of sweets, while older couples lingered at the greengrocer's, debating apples over gossip. Emmy skirted the edges, weaving through side streets she hadn't walked in some time, until the hum of chatter gave way to something softer.

She ended up on one of the back lanes that ran parallel to the stream — a narrow track lined with uneven stone walls and hedgerows thick with the first signs of spring. Moss softened the stones, and little bursts of snowdrops peeked up through the grass, fragile but stubborn.

She walked slowly, breathing in the damp, earthy air. It was here, away from the busier roads, that she felt her thoughts settle.

Halfway along the track, she spotted him.

Roman sat on a low stone wall near the bend, his back partially to her, a sketchbook open on his lap. His posture was relaxed but intent, one elbow braced against his knee as his hand moved with deliberate strokes across the page. The early afternoon light caught in his dark hair, bringing out a subtle sheen, and she noticed the faint smudge of charcoal on his forearm.

She hesitated. For a moment, she considered turning back, not wanting to intrude. But curiosity — and something she couldn't quite name — kept her rooted.

She watched quietly, noting the way his hand paused between lines, as though listening for what the paper wanted next. He wasn't just drawing; he was studying. Recording. Preserving.

"You're very focused," she said softly.

Roman turned his head slightly, his green eyes lifting to meet hers. For a moment, surprise flickered there, followed by the faintest curve of a smile. "Emmy."

She stepped closer, hands stuffed into the pockets of her coat. "I didn't mean to interrupt."

"You didn't," he said, closing the book halfway, though not completely.

She tilted her head, peering at the page. "What are you drawing?"

Roman hesitated, then turned the book toward her. It was the bend in the lane, captured with bold, confident lines — the moss-covered stones, the tangle of branches overhead, the delicate scatter of flowers at the path's edge.

"It's beautiful," she said honestly.

"It's ordinary," he replied.

"Maybe," she said, "but you make it look worth noticing."

His lips quirked at that, though he didn't comment.

Emmy gestured toward the sketchbook. "Do you always draw like this? Out here, I mean."

"When I can. Quiet places hold more truth than busy ones."

"That sounds very poetic," she teased lightly.

He smirked faintly. "Maybe I've read too many books."

There was a pause, comfortable this time, as a breeze stirred the branches above. Emmy perched on the wall beside him, leaving a respectful gap between them. For a while, they sat in companionable silence, listening to the distant sound of the brook and the occasional caw of a crow overhead.

Roman closed his book at last, tucking the charcoal stick neatly into its spine. "You walk this way often?"

"Sometimes," she said. "When I need to clear my head."

He studied her for a moment. "You needed to clear it today?"

She gave a small shrug. "It's been a long week."

"Do you like it? Teaching?"

She blinked, surprised by the directness of the question. "I do. Most days, anyway. It feels like… I don't know. Like I'm making a difference, even if it's small."

Roman nodded slowly. "There's honour in work like that. More than most people realise."

She tilted her head, curious. "And what about you? What do you do besides draw and walk quiet lanes? Rescue wildlife? Keep mysterious orchards?"

His mouth curved into the faintest suggestion of a smile. "I keep the house in order. Maintain the grounds. Sometimes I read, sometimes I travel… though not far these days."

"That's not much of an answer."

He glanced at her, something knowing in his expression. "I've found people rarely want the whole truth when they ask simple questions."

She frowned slightly. "I'd like to think I do."

"Perhaps," he said softly, and she couldn't tell whether it was approval or deflection.

"Would you ever show me more of your drawings?" she asked after a pause.

"Maybe."

"'Maybe'?"

Roman stood smoothly, brushing off his coat. "If the moment felt right."

"That's the second time you've said that," Emmy said, standing as well. "You seem to live a lot by the 'right moment.'"

"It's how you avoid regret."

"And does that work for you?"

For the first time, he didn't answer.

"Walk with me," he said instead.

She hesitated only for a moment before nodding. "Alright."


They followed the lane toward the edge of the village, the path narrowing as it dipped toward the stream. Roman walked at an unhurried pace, matching hers, and they fell into conversation that meandered as naturally as the path itself.

"Why did you come here?" he asked at one point.

Emmy blinked at the question. "The village?"

He nodded.

She hesitated, weighing her answer. "I needed a change."

Roman glanced at her. "From what?"

Her throat tightened slightly. "A place that no longer felt like home."

He didn't press, and she was grateful.

The lane eventually opened onto a small cobbled square, tucked between a cluster of older buildings. Emmy didn't recognise it — a quieter corner of the village, far from the bustle of the main market. At its centre stood a little café with mismatched tables outside, its sign swinging gently in the breeze.

"Coffee?" Roman asked, nodding toward it.

Emmy hesitated, then smiled. "Sure".

Inside, the café was warm and faintly fragrant with roasted beans and sugar. They found a small table near the window, the kind that invited leaning elbows and long, easy conversations.

Roman ordered for them — black coffee for himself, a latte for her — and when the drinks arrived, they sat in a quiet that felt companionable rather than awkward.

Emmy traced the rim of her cup with her finger. "You don't talk much about yourself."

Roman arched a brow. "Neither do you."

She laughed softly. "Touché."

"Do you miss where you came from?" he asked.

Emmy thought for a moment. "Sometimes. But missing it doesn't mean I want to go back."

Roman studied her, his fingers absently tracing the rim of his mug. "You sound like someone who's had to start over."

Her laugh was soft, but without humour. "You make it sound like I've done it more than once."

"Haven't you?"

She met his gaze, surprised by the weight of the question. For a moment, she considered telling him more — about the night she left, about the things she hadn't said even to June. But the words stuck in her throat.

"Maybe I'll tell you one day," she said lightly, deflecting.

Roman's eyes lingered on her for a moment before he nodded. "Then I'll wait for that day."

They spoke of safer things instead — books they liked, places in the village she hadn't yet explored, the merits of the café's cinnamon buns (which, Roman informed her gravely, were "best on Tuesdays"). He listened more than he spoke, but when he did, his words carried weight, carefully chosen.

By the time they finished their drinks, the light outside had deepened to gold, and Emmy felt a strange reluctance to leave.

"Thank you," she said as they stood, pulling her coat tighter. "For… this."

Roman inclined his head slightly. "It was nothing."

"It didn't feel like nothing," she said before she could stop herself.

For a moment, his eyes met hers, unreadable but steady. "Then I'm glad," he said simply.

The café door swung shut behind them, muting the gentle hum of conversation and the hiss of the espresso machine. Outside, the air had cooled, and the cobbled square seemed washed in gold, the kind of light that softened even the harshest corners of the old stone buildings.

Roman glanced toward the far end of the square, where the narrow lanes funnelled back toward the village heart. "Do you need to head straight back?"

"Not yet," Emmy said, surprising herself. "I don't really want to go home yet."

He nodded as though he understood completely. "Then walk with me a little longer."

They took the long way back, skirting the quieter lanes. The streets were nearly empty now, the market stalls closed and the last few stragglers heading home with their bags and baskets. Emmy wrapped her coat tighter against the chill breeze and kept her pace slow, unhurried.

Roman seemed perfectly comfortable in silence, but she wasn't ready to let the conversation end. "You didn't grow up here, did you?" she asked.

"No."

"Where then?"

He hesitated — just long enough for her to notice — before answering. "A long way from here. In a very different time."

She frowned at that. "Different time?"

Roman gave a faint, almost amused smile. "You don't ever feel that? Like you've stepped out of one world into another? Some places make you feel that way."

She let out a quiet laugh. "That's very cryptic."

"Some things are better that way."

Emmy glanced at him sidelong. "You really do enjoy being mysterious, don't you?"

His smile deepened, and let out a low laugh but he didn't answer.

They walked until the village gave way to the start of the lanes that led toward the fields. Emmy paused at the edge of a low stone wall, resting her hands against it. Beyond, the fields stretched out in gentle dips and rises, the evening light turning them almost bronze.

"I used to imagine I'd live somewhere like this," she said quietly. "When I was little. I thought it would be... I don't know. A place where life couldn't touch me."

Roman leaned against the wall beside her. "And has it been that?"

She thought for a moment, picking at a loose thread on her sleeve. "It's been safe. Which is more than I could say about where I was before."

There was a stillness between them then, not awkward, but heavy. Roman didn't press her to explain, but his silence felt like an invitation — a quiet acknowledgement that he would listen if she wanted to give more.

"I don't talk about it," Emmy said finally, her voice barely above a whisper.

"You don't have to," Roman replied, his tone steady, grounding.

She let out a breath she hadn't realised she'd been holding. "Do you ever wish you could go back? To who you were before everything changed?"

Roman didn't answer immediately. "No," he said at last. "But I wish I'd understood what it would cost."

The words sank between them like stones in water. Emmy studied his profile, wondering what kind of past left a man speaking like that.

The wind picked up, rustling through the hedgerows and carrying with it the faint smell of rain. Emmy tilted her head back, watching as clouds began to creep in from the west, dulling the glow of the fading sun.

"We should head back," Roman said. "It'll rain soon."

They turned toward the path, walking side by side once more. The conversation drifted to safer ground — books again, the best places in the village for coffee, her students' most ridiculous spelling mistakes — but Emmy felt the weight of what had gone unsaid lingering between them.

At the fork where the lane split toward the square, Roman stopped. "Wait," he said, reaching into his coat.

He pulled out his sketchbook, flipping past several pages before tearing one free. It was the drawing from earlier — the bend in the lane, captured with bold, deliberate strokes. He held it out to her.

"For you."

Emmy blinked. "Really? I thought you didn't share your drawings."

"I don't," he said simply. "But this one felt like it should be yours."

She took it carefully, fingers brushing his for the briefest moment. "Thank you," she said, meaning it more than she expected.

Roman gave a small nod. "Goodnight, Emmy."

"Goodnight, Roman."

She watched him turn back toward the fields before heading in the opposite direction, the folded sketch tucked carefully inside her coat.

By the time she reached her flat, the first drops of rain had begun to fall, tapping softly against the window as she stood inside, still holding the drawing like it was something rare.

# Chapter 10

The last bell of the day echoed faintly down the corridor, and with it came a wave of soft, chaotic energy — the kind that marked the true end of a school day. Doors opened and slammed; children's voices carried in fragments ("…but I was first!" "Miss, can I show you what I drew?"), and the steady patter of little feet faded toward the playground as parents began their patient herding.

Emmy leaned against the edge of her classroom desk, glancing over the rows of bright displays and half-open exercise books. The quiet that followed was one she hadn't yet learned to love — the kind that made her painfully aware of how loud the day had been.

"You survived," came a familiar voice from the doorway.

June leaned casually against the frame, her hair pulled up into a loose bun that had mostly escaped its pins. She still had her lanyard around her neck, though it was dangling at an angle as if even it was ready to go home.

Emmy laughed softly. "It was touch and go around two o'clock. You missed the great glue-stick disaster of Year Four."

June stepped inside, her shoes clicking lightly against the worn floorboards. "Please tell me no one tried to eat it."

"No," Emmy said with a dramatic sigh, "but we came close. Turns out, if you give them group work and leave glue unattended, you get one actual project and three very elaborate sculptures of… well, I'm not sure what."

June chuckled, perching on the edge of a nearby table. "One day I want to walk into a classroom at 3:15 and not feel like I'm stepping onto the aftermath of a battlefield."

"Good luck with that," Emmy said, picking up a stray pen and tucking it into a mug on her desk.

June studied her for a moment. "You're getting the hang of it, though. I remember my first term — I barely made it out alive. You look almost serene."

"Serene is a strong word," Emmy replied. "But… I think I'm starting to find my rhythm."

"Good." June paused. "It suits you, you know."

Emmy glanced up. "What does?"

"Being here. This place. The kids. Even the chaos. You seem… I don't know. Settled."

Emmy blinked at that. The word settled felt strange, too big for her just yet. But she didn't disagree.

"Do you want to walk out together?" June asked, hopping off the table.

"Yeah," Emmy said, grabbing her coat and bag. "I could do with some fresh air."

They left the classroom side by side, the corridor now mostly empty except for a few stragglers in the staffroom. Arun Bhatt waved a lazy goodbye on his way out, juggling a stack of marking and what looked suspiciously like a Tupperware of biscuits.

Outside, the cool air carried the faint smell of damp grass and chalk dust. The playground was nearly empty now, save for one or two children dragging their feet toward the gate and a mother corralling a toddler into a pushchair. The sky had begun its slow drift toward evening, a soft blush of gold creeping into the pale blue.

"So," June said as they reached the gate, "what do you do after work? I mean, other than become a recluse in that little flat above the bookshop."

Emmy raised an eyebrow. "You make me sound mysterious."

"Don't flatter yourself," June teased. "I just can't work out if you're one of those people who thrives in the quiet or one of those who's hiding from it."

Emmy smiled faintly. "Maybe a bit of both."

"Spoken like someone who's going to make me buy the first round at The Crown one night."

"The Crown?"

"The pub, Emmy," June said, mock-exasperated. "The only one worth bothering with in this village. We'll go sometime. You can experience the full joy of lukewarm ale and village gossip."

Emmy laughed. "Sounds… educational."

"Exactly."

They turned onto the lane that led toward the square. The houses they passed were bathed in the softening light, their gardens buzzing faintly with the early evening hum of bees. Emmy noticed a cat sprawled on a windowsill, tail flicking lazily as it tracked something invisible in the air.

"It's strange," Emmy said after a moment. "I thought it would feel harder than this. Starting over."

June glanced at her. "It still might. But you've done the hardest part. You came."

The words landed heavier than Emmy expected. She didn't answer, just tucked her hands deeper into her coat pockets.

June didn't press, and Emmy was grateful for it.

"Anyway," June said after a moment, brightening her tone, "you know the real reason I wanted to walk with you?"

"Go on."

"I saw you last weekend," June said casually, though there was a glint of amusement in her eye.

Emmy blinked. "Saw me?"

"Don't play coy," June said. "You were walking out near the old square. With someone tall. Dark hair. Bit of a broody poet look going on."

Heat crept into Emmy's cheeks before she could stop it. "Oh. That."

"That," June repeated, grinning. "Who is he? And don't say 'just someone I met.' I've been teaching long enough to spot a non-answer when I hear one."

Emmy shook her head, laughing softly. "His name's Roman. He lives out near the woods. That's all I know."

"And yet," June said, "you know enough to walk quiet country lanes with him. Interesting."

"It's nothing like that," Emmy protested, though she wasn't sure who she was trying to convince.

June let it drop, though the smirk didn't leave her face. "Fine. But if you're going to become the leading lady in some moody period drama, at least let me be your sounding board."

"I'll keep that in mind," Emmy said dryly.

They reached the square, where the bakery's sign swayed gently in the breeze and Aubrey's bookshop glowed faintly under the soft light of its front lamps. The village felt different at this hour — quieter, but not asleep.

"Do you want to grab a coffee?" June asked. "Or are you heading straight up?"

Emmy considered. "I think I'll walk a bit. Clear my head before I hole up for the evening."

"Suit yourself," June said, looping her arm through Emmy's briefly in a quick squeeze. "Don't be a stranger, Trevelyn. And don't let Mr. Tall-Dark-and-Broody be your only source of company, alright?"

Emmy rolled her eyes, smiling. "Goodnight, June."

"Goodnight."

June peeled off toward the bakery, and Emmy lingered in the square for a moment, letting the stillness settle.

Emmy lingered at the edge of the square longer than she meant to, watching the shifting colours of the sky as the first hints of evening crept in. She wasn't ready to climb the narrow stairs to her flat just yet. Not when the air felt this soft and the streets this quiet.

So she turned, almost on instinct, toward the lane that wound out of the village.

The further she walked, the less the world felt like it belonged to anyone else. The cobbled edges gave way to packed earth, the houses to hedgerows. Somewhere beyond the fields, a blackbird sang, its notes sharp and clean in the stillness.

She didn't hear him at first.

"Miss Trevelyn."

The voice carried lightly on the breeze, low but unmistakable.

Emmy stopped, heart giving an involuntary jump. Roman stood a little further along the lane, leaning against a weathered gate that led onto an overgrown footpath. He was dressed simply, his coat unbuttoned, sleeves pushed up as though he'd been working before pausing here.

"Roman," she said, more surprised than she sounded. "You're everywhere these days."

"Only where the lanes are quiet," he replied.

She walked toward him, closing the gap at a measured pace. "Do you always wait by gates until someone walks by, or am I just lucky?"

"Perhaps a bit of both."

There was a flicker of amusement in his expression, subtle but enough to disarm her slightly.

They fell into step as they started down the path beyond the gate, neither of them acknowledging the decision to walk together. It just happened, as natural as breathing.

The hedgerows leaned close here, making the lane feel almost like a tunnel of green. Patches of sunlight cut through the leaves, dappling the ground in shifting shapes.

"You seemed... elsewhere," Roman said after a time, glancing at her.

"I had a long day," Emmy replied. "June and I walked out together. She thinks I'm settling in."

"Are you?"

She thought for a moment. "I think so. It feels less like I'm on borrowed time now. More like I actually live here."

Roman nodded slightly, as though the answer pleased him.

"Do you like it?" she asked.

"Living here?"

"Yes."

He considered the question longer than seemed necessary. "I like that it doesn't ask much of me."

"That's a very evasive answer."

"I'm a very evasive person."

She smiled despite herself. "I'm starting to notice."

They reached a break in the hedgerows where the fields opened wide, a stretch of soft green rolling toward the horizon. Roman slowed, resting his hand on the top of the gatepost as if weighing whether to turn back.

"Do you ever miss where you came from?" she asked before she could stop herself.

Roman didn't look at her when he answered. "Sometimes."

"Then why stay here?"

He glanced at her then, his expression unreadable. "Some places keep their hold on you, even when you've outgrown them."

There was a quiet heaviness in the way he said it — like he wasn't talking about the village at all.

"You talk like you've been here forever," she said, trying to lighten the mood.

"Perhaps I have," he replied, and she couldn't tell if it was a joke.

They walked on in silence for a while, the conversation hanging between them like an unfinished thought. Emmy felt her curiosity tugging at her, sharper now than it had been before.

"You're hard to read," she said instead.

"Good."

"Good?"

"It means I'm doing something right."

The words were half-teasing, but they landed differently, a strange mix of charm and deflection.

They didn't go straight back toward the square. Instead, Roman led her down a side lane she hadn't walked before, the kind that felt like it belonged to an older map — narrow, uneven, hemmed in by leaning hedgerows that seemed to close the world off behind them.

Emmy slowed when a splash of colour caught her eye: a weathered noticeboard nailed to a post, its peeling paint just about holding together. Among the faded leaflets and local adverts, a newer poster stood out — bright lettering framed by garlands of painted flowers.

"Spring Festival," she read aloud. "Two weeks from now."

Roman had stopped beside her, hands tucked into his coat pockets. He glanced at the poster, his expression unreadable.

"You don't seem impressed," Emmy said lightly, glancing at him.

He let out a breath that might have been a laugh, though it held no real amusement. "They've been holding it for centuries. Different names. Same intent."

That caught her off guard. "Centuries?"

Roman gave a small shrug, still looking at the poster. "People like to believe their traditions are new. They rarely are."

There was something in his tone — a quiet disapproval, maybe even bitterness.

"You sound like you don't think much of it," she said, studying his face.

"I think festivals make people feel like they belong. Even if it's only for a day."

"That's not such a bad thing."

"No," he admitted. "It isn't."

Emmy hesitated, then turned to him. "Would you... like to go? ...With me?"

The words came out before she could stop them, and she was suddenly very aware of how bold they sounded.

Roman turned to her, and for a moment she thought she saw something flicker in his expression — surprise? Amusement? Something else entirely?

"I don't think that would be wise," he said at last.

"Why not?"

He didn't answer right away. His gaze shifted toward the darkening path ahead, as though the hedgerows had suddenly become deeply interesting.

"Emmy," he said finally, his voice softer than before, "we should stop spending time together like this."

The words landed like a stone in her chest. "Why?"

"Because it's not good for you."

She blinked at him, incredulous. "Not good for me?"

He nodded once, still not meeting her eyes. "You came here for a fresh start. To build a life. To meet people who can give you that — someone nice. Someone... uncomplicated."

Emmy stared at him. "You make it sound like you're incapable of being those things."

Roman's mouth twitched in what might have been a smile, but it didn't reach his eyes. "I'm not uncomplicated. And I'm certainly not nice."

She folded her arms, squaring her shoulders. "That's not what I've seen."

"That's because," he said, his tone dipping just slightly, "you don't know me."

"Then let me."

The words came out before she could think them through, firm and certain.

Roman finally met her gaze, and for a long moment, neither of them spoke.

"I've been enjoying spending time with you," Emmy said quietly. "If you think I haven't, you're wrong."

His jaw tightened. Whatever he wanted to say, he swallowed it back, letting the silence stretch between them until it almost hurt.

Finally, he said, "You should go home, Emmy. Before the rain sets in."

And just like that, the conversation was over.

They walked back toward the square in silence, their earlier ease replaced by something heavier, unspoken but undeniable.

When they reached the gate to the square, Roman stopped. "Goodnight," he said softly, almost reluctantly.

138

Emmy wanted to say more — to push again — but the words stuck. So she nodded. "Goodnight."

She climbed the stairs to her flat in a daze, her mind replaying every word of the conversation. Though she'd promised herself she wouldn't, she found herself hoping — desperately — that he'd change his mind.

# Chapter 11

### Roman's POV: Returning Home

The manor greeted him in silence, as it always did.

Roman stepped inside, pushing the heavy oak door closed behind him. The air smelled of cedar and dust, faintly sweet with the lingering scent of the orchard that crept through an open window somewhere in the back of the house. It was a comforting sort of stillness — the kind that came from walls that had seen too much and spoken too little.

He shrugged off his coat and draped it across the chair by the entryway. The hall felt cavernous in the half-light, its familiar shadows stretching up the old wood panelling. His hand brushed the banister as he passed, feeling the grooves worn by centuries of touch — his touch.

But his mind wasn't in the present.

"Then let me."

Her voice echoed as if she were standing behind him. He could still see her face, the way her eyes had lit with something stubborn, something unafraid.

Roman crossed into the drawing room and lit the candle on the mantelpiece. The match hissed, the small flame bending in the draft before it steadied. He stared at it longer than he meant to, caught in the hypnotic flicker.

"I've been enjoying spending time with you. If you think I haven't, you're wrong."

He sat heavily in the armchair by the empty hearth, resting his elbows on his knees. How long had it been since someone had spoken to him like that? Not as a shadow in the woods. Not as the quiet recluse at the edge of the village. But as a man.

He shouldn't have let it happen. Shouldn't have lingered with her in the lanes, shouldn't have let her voice burrow under his skin like this.

He knew how this ended.

It always ended the same.

Roman stood abruptly, crossing to the sideboard. He poured a measure of brandy into a glass, swirling the amber liquid. He took one slow sip, feeling the burn travel down his throat, before setting it aside untouched.

His reflection caught in the tall mirror above the mantel — green eyes, black hair that still curled at the ends, the same face he'd seen for lifetimes. He'd buried entire generations, and yet the mirror never changed.

Not for him.

Roman raked a hand through his hair, shaking the thought away. He needed rest, not another night staring at flames and listening to ghosts.

He climbed the stairs to his room. Each creak of the floorboards was familiar — a rhythm that had followed him since boyhood. His bedroom was simple, deliberately untouched by the centuries beyond the door: a heavy four-poster bed, a dresser, a single bookshelf.

He undressed slowly, leaving his clothes draped across the chair by the window. For a moment, he stood in front of the mirror on the dresser. The man staring back at him was ageless, unmarked by time.

And yet his eyes looked tired.

He blew out the candle and lay in the cool bed.

Sleep took him slowly, pulling him under like deep water.

The dream came, as it always did…

Smoke.

It clung to his throat, bitter and sharp. The air was damp with rain, but inside the cottage it felt dry, burning.

"Roman, don't—"

Her voice.

He couldn't see her face, but the sound of her tore through him. He reached for her, but the shadows between them stretched, warped, like oil across water.

The door. His hands were slick on the iron latch — rain? Blood? He shoved it open and stepped into a place that wasn't a cottage at all.

Walls pulsed with carved sigils, glowing faintly. Candles burned in strange colours — green, white, flickering unnaturally. The air tasted of honey and iron, cloying.

And there she was.

Not the woman he loved.

Someone else.

"Take me," he heard himself say. His voice sounded stretched, unfamiliar. "Not her. Take me."

Her smile widened, revealing teeth too sharp for a human mouth.

And then — light.

White-hot, blinding. It seared his skin, burned through his bones. He tried to scream, but the wind swallowed it, tearing the world to ash.

The bed.

His mother's hands on his face, cool against his burning skin. Her tears splashing his cheeks.

"Roman. Roman, please."

He tried to speak, but his tongue felt heavy, his body unresponsive.

His father. His sister. A priest murmuring last rites.

The faces swirled, bled together, then dissolved.

The stables.

The sharp tang of hay, the wet slap of hooves on mud.

"Easy," he said, reaching for the bridle of the nervous

mare.

Then thunder cracked like a whip, and the world

exploded.

Pain.

Bones snapping. Hooves crushing his chest. The air gone

from his lungs.

Then — nothing.

When his eyes opened, the pain was gone.

His body unbroken.

The horses watching him with wide, frightened eyes.

Time fractured.

A dinner table.

His mother, older now. His father, frail, then gone.

A grave dug in frozen ground.

A tavern. The music louder than the laughter, a woman

singing in a tongue long dead.

War.

The mud thick with blood, the stench of death choking

him.

Friends. Lovers. Brothers.

All of them dying.

All of them leaving him behind.

Faces.

Hundreds. Thousands.

Young. Old. Laughing. Crying.

All of them fading.

Until only one remained.


Emmy.

She stood in the orchard, sunlight catching in her dark
curls, her golden skin glowing like warmth itself. She smiled
at him.

He stepped toward her, but the ground stretched,
dragging her further away.

"Don't," she said.

Her voice was hers — soft, breaking.

Then it wasn't.

But her voice wasn't hers.

It was the voice of someone long since gone.

"You don't know what you are."

"You don't know what you ask for."

The orchard blackened. The sky split with white-hot
light.

And then nothing.


Roman woke with a start.

Moonlight pooled through the window, silvering the edges of the room. His skin was damp with sweat, his breath shallow, his heart pounding a rhythm too fast for the stillness around him.

He sat up slowly, elbows on his knees, pressing his palms into his eyes.

It was always the same.

The pain. The loss.

But tonight, Emmy had been there.

Not just as herself, but stitched into everything — the lovers, the family, the faces of those long gone.

He raked a hand through his hair, trying to shake the image of her smile, her voice, from his mind.

Stay away from her, he told himself.

It was the only way to protect her.

But even as he said it, he knew it was already too late.

# Chapter 12

By Thursday, the village felt like it was humming.

It started small — paper flyers on lampposts, bright splashes of colour against the grey metal, announcing dates and times in looping script. Then came the bunting: long strings of fabric triangles stretched across the main streets, swaying gently in the early spring breeze. And now, as Emmy walked toward the school gates, she saw the festival taking shape in earnest.

Stalls were popping up in the square, each a wooden skeleton draped in tarps and half-finished signs: Mulled cider, Handcrafted jewellery, Local honey. The air carried a medley of scents — woodsmoke, cinnamon, fresh-cut greenery — faint hints of what the weekend would bring.

She adjusted the strap of her satchel and smiled faintly as she passed Aubrey's bookshop. A ladder leaned against the side of the building, Aubrey himself perched halfway up it, fiddling with a string of paper lanterns.

"Morning, Emmy!" he called, his voice gravelly with the cheer of someone who enjoyed having a project. "Spring Festival's coming along, eh? Whole place will be unrecognisable by Saturday."

"It's looking wonderful already," Emmy replied, pausing at the foot of the ladder. "Need a hand?"

"Kind offer, but I've got it. You're off to school — don't let me make you late!"

She waved and continued on, though she couldn't help glancing over her shoulder. Aubrey's little shop looked like something out of a postcard, the lanterns casting gentle shadows over the dark wood of the facade.

The children were just as restless as the village. Her Year Fours couldn't seem to focus on fractions, their minds clearly elsewhere.

"Miss, will there be fireworks?" one of them blurted out as she collected their worksheets.

"Not this time," Emmy said, smiling. "But I hear there'll be live music."

"And dancing!" another added, bouncing in her seat.

"And the puppet show," chimed a third. "My dad said he's taking me!"

Their chatter carried on through the morning, a steady undercurrent even as Emmy steered them through reading comprehension and spelling. She didn't mind. It was infectious — their excitement, their anticipation.

At lunch, she found June already in the staffroom, leaning back in one of the mismatched chairs with her shoes kicked off.

"Feel that?" June said, gesturing vaguely toward the open window. "It's in the air. The whole place has gone festival-mad."

"I think half the class spent maths imagining what they'll eat this weekend," Emmy replied, pouring herself a cup of tea from the chipped pot by the kettle.

"Priorities," June said, grinning. "To be fair, I'm not far off. Margot's doing her famous lemon tarts again. I'd sell my soul for one of those."

Emmy smiled faintly and took the seat opposite her.

June studied her for a moment. "You've been quiet this week."

"Have I?"

"Mm." June sipped her tea. "Usually you're all chirpy, even when the kids drive you to the brink. Something's on your mind."

Emmy hesitated. She could say it — she could tell June about the last walk with Roman, about the sting of his words. But she didn't. Instead, she said, "Just… thinking about the weekend, I suppose."

June arched an eyebrow. "Hoping a certain tall, dark stranger will make an appearance?"

149

Emmy felt heat rise to her cheeks. "June—"

"What? You can't blame me for being curious."

"I hardly know him," Emmy protested, staring down into her tea.

"Mm-hm." June smirked knowingly. "And yet you look like someone who wants to."

Emmy rolled her eyes, but she couldn't deny the truth in it.

"Anyway," June said, leaning forward conspiratorially, "we're going to The Crown tonight. A little pre-festival drink to unwind. You should come."

"The pub?"

"Yes, Emmy. The pub. You can't live above a bookshop your whole life."

"I've been here for two months."

"And already developing hermit tendencies." June grinned. "Seriously, come. It's nothing fancy. Bit of bad wine, a lot of gossip. Just what you need."

Emmy hesitated. "I… might."

"No might about it. I'll text you later. We'll lure you out somehow."

Emmy laughed softly. "You're relentless."

"Exactly why I'm so good at getting people to do things," June said smugly.

She reached into her bag and pulled out her phone, scrolling briefly before adding, "Oh, and do you want to hear what my darling menace of a cat did this morning?"

Emmy raised her brows. "Do I?"

"He brought me a 'gift.' A half-dead blackbird. Left it on my bed like he'd just solved the village famine. I nearly had a heart attack before breakfast."

Emmy winced sympathetically. "That's... thoughtful?"

"Thoughtful," June said dryly. "The little monster nearly destroyed my duvet in the process. Spent ten minutes chasing him with a towel like some sort of slapstick routine."

Emmy chuckled, shaking her head. "You should write about your mornings. They sound eventful."

"Tragic comedy, more like. Anyway, I got the poor thing back out into the garden. Hopefully it survived. If not, well — at least the cat thinks I appreciated his effort."

"Sounds like a handful."

"Oh, absolutely. But he's good company. Better than some men I've known."

They both laughed, and the conversation shifted back to the festival, June animatedly describing which stalls she'd beeline for first, which cider was worth drinking, and her firm plan to convince Emmy to try one of the dancing workshops.

They spent the rest of lunch swapping plans for the weekend, June insisting Emmy should join her and a few others at one of the cider stalls. Emmy agreed, though the idea of wandering the festival alone tugged at her — the thought of maybe, just maybe, running into Roman.

On the walk home that evening, Emmy slowed her pace, letting herself take in the transformation of the village. The square was unrecognisable now — not just bunting and lanterns, but chalkboards advertising live folk music and storytelling for children. Volunteers were stringing fresh garlands of ivy and wildflowers between the lampposts, the greenery bright against the stone buildings.

A trio of musicians tuned their instruments outside The Crown, the low twang of a fiddle drifting on the breeze. Someone laughed — a deep, hearty sound — as a keg was rolled toward a makeshift bar.

The festival wasn't even here yet, and already the village felt alive in a way Emmy hadn't seen before.

And yet, beneath all that colour and sound, her thoughts drifted inevitably back to him.

Roman.

She hadn't seen him since that night in the lane. Since he'd told her, so carefully, that they shouldn't spend time together. She didn't know what she expected — to bump into him in the square? To catch sight of him in the orchard?

But the absence gnawed at her all the same.

By the time she climbed the stairs to her flat, the last of the daylight was fading. She pushed open the door and was greeted by the familiar scent of old wood and books, faintly sweet with the daffodils she'd left on the windowsill earlier in the week.

The flat felt quiet, but not in the heavy way it had when she'd first arrived months ago. Now it felt lived-in, like her space.

She dropped her satchel by the chair, toed off her shoes, and stood in the centre of the room for a moment, letting the silence settle. Her body felt heavy from the day — not in a bad way, but enough to make her shoulders ache for release.

A shower first.

She padded into the small bathroom, peeled off her work clothes, and stepped under the spray. The water was lukewarm at first, then warmed enough to soothe the lingering tension in her muscles. She tilted her head back, letting it run through her curls, and closed her eyes.

For a moment, she let her thoughts drift blank.

But they didn't stay blank for long.

Roman's words returned to her, uninvited: "You should meet someone nice. Someone uncomplicated."

She clenched her jaw, rinsing the soap from her hands as though she could wash the sting of it away.

Why did it bother her so much? He was a man she barely knew, who had made it abundantly clear he wanted distance. And yet, the quiet lanes felt emptier without him.

When she stepped out, wrapping herself in the softest towel she owned, she caught her reflection in the steamed mirror. Her hair clung in damp ringlets to her shoulders, her skin flushed pink from the heat. She looked... like herself. But different.

She dressed simply — soft leggings, an oversized jumper — then drifted into the kitchen corner of the flat.

Coffee, she decided.

The kettle hissed as she spooned instant granules into her chipped white mug. The smell filled the little room, grounding her.

Her stomach growled, but when she opened the fridge, nothing appealed to her. Leftover pasta? Half a carton of soup? She closed the door without taking anything, leaning against the counter with her mug.

Eat now, or wait for the pub?

She'd never been much good at eating alone.

She carried the coffee to the armchair by the window and sat, pulling her knees up beneath her. Outside, the last of the sunset bled into the rooftops, a soft pink giving way to indigo.

The flat was quiet but comfortable. Safe.

And yet her mind kept straying — to the square, to the orchard, to a pair of green eyes she couldn't seem to forget.

Her phone buzzed on the side table.

Dad.

She smiled faintly and swiped to answer. "Hi, Dad."

"Emmy!" His voice was bright, though with that ever-present undercurrent of concern. "How's my girl? How's the big city?"

"It's a village, Dad," she said, laughing softly.

"Ah, well. Feels big when you're not here with us."

"It's good. Busy. The Spring Festival's this weekend — the whole place looks like something out of a postcard. Lanterns, bunting, all of it."

"That sounds lovely. You're going, I hope?"

"Yes," she said, swirling her coffee. "Actually… I'm going out tonight too. To the pub."

"The pub?"

She laughed at the surprise in his tone. "With a friend. June — she teaches at the school. She invited me."

"Well, good. You need friends out there. And to have fun."

"I am having fun," she said, softer now. "It's… nice. Being here. Feels like a fresh start."

There was a pause on the line. "You sound better," he said, his voice quieter. "I know it hasn't been easy, Em. But... I'm proud of you. You know that, right?"

Her throat tightened. "Thanks, Dad."

They chatted a little longer — her father updating her on neighbours back home, her reminding him to keep on top of his doctor's appointments — before she promised to call again soon and hung up.

The flat felt quiet when the call ended, but not in a lonely way.

She finished her coffee, set the mug in the sink, and crossed to the wardrobe.

What did one wear to the pub here?

She sifted through her clothes, settling on a dark green blouse and fitted jeans. Casual but not careless. She blow-dried her curls until they fell loose and soft around her shoulders, added a touch of eyeliner, and finished with lipstick that was just a shade bolder than her usual.

When she caught herself in the mirror, she almost didn't recognise the woman staring back.

\* \* \*

The Crown was already alive when she arrived.

It wasn't large — a low-ceilinged building with whitewashed walls and dark timber beams — but the warmth hit her the moment she stepped inside. Conversation hummed, glasses clinked, and the smell of cider and something savoury wafted from the kitchen.

"Emmy!"

June waved from a table near the fireplace, where two other teachers sat — Arun Bhatt and a woman Emmy hadn't met yet, who June quickly introduced as Rebecca, one of the teaching assistants.

"You made it!" June grinned as Emmy slid into the empty seat beside her. "I was half-worried you'd hermit yourself away with a book."

"I considered it," Emmy admitted, "but you're very persuasive."

"Damn right I am. Drink?"

Emmy glanced at the chalkboard menu behind the bar. "Cider, please."

"Good choice," June said approvingly, before flagging the barman.

They spent the first half-hour swapping school stories — Arun's ill-fated attempt at a Year Three recorder lesson, Rebecca's horror tale of supervising a messy art project, June's dramatic retelling of her morning battle with her cat.

"And he looked proud of himself," June said, gesturing animatedly with her glass. "Like, 'Look at me, Mum, providing for the family.' Meanwhile, I'm chasing him with a towel trying not to scream."

Emmy laughed, feeling some of the week's tension ease out of her shoulders.

At some point, the conversation drifted to the festival.

"Biggest event of the year," Rebecca said. "Dancing, music, food… it's magical. Especially in the evening when the lanterns are lit."

"You're going, aren't you, Emmy?" June asked, a glint of mischief in her eye.

"Yes," Emmy said, sipping her cider. "I was planning to."

"With anyone… particular?" June pressed, her voice teasing.

Emmy rolled her eyes. "You're relentless."

"Only because you're easy to fluster," June said with a grin. "Let me guess — you're hoping to run into the mysterious tall, dark and handsome."

Rebecca perked up. "Who is this?!"

June grinned like a cat who'd caught a mouse. "The man who lives out near the orchard. Broody, mysterious, tall — Emmy's been spotted walking with him."

"He's just a friend," Emmy said quickly, though the words tasted defensive even to her.

"Mm-hm," June said, unconvinced.

Rebecca leaned in, intrigued. "Is he single? Asking for... research purposes."

That earned another round of laughter, which Emmy joined in, though a small part of her twisted at the thought.

The evening stretched on with more drinks, more laughter, and the kind of lightness Emmy hadn't realised she'd been missing. For a little while, she didn't think about Roman at all.

But when she stepped back out into the cool night air, the stars bright above the quiet village, her thoughts drifted inevitably back to him.

She wondered if he'd be at the festival.

And, though she wouldn't admit it to anyone — even herself — she hoped he would.

The pub had grown louder as the evening stretched on, the hum of conversation blending with the clink of glasses and the occasional burst of laughter from a nearby table. Emmy leaned back in her chair, a little flushed from cider and the warmth of the fire.

"You know," she said, glancing between June and Rebecca, "I wasn't sure what to expect when I moved here, but... people are kinder than I imagined. It feels safe. Friendly."

Rebecca, mid-sip of her drink, lowered her glass with a smirk. "Oh, you'll be just fine here." She paused for dramatic effect, eyes glinting. "Especially with the Wandering Man keeping watch."

"The what?" Emmy asked, eyebrows knitting in confusion.

June groaned. "Oh no. Here we go."

Rebecca ignored her, leaning in as though about to share a secret. "It's an old village story. Been around for... well, no one really knows how long. Supposedly, there's this man — they call him the Wandering Man — who shows up when someone's in trouble. Pulls people out of ditches, helps them home in the dead of night, that sort of thing. Then he disappears before anyone can thank him. Like he was never there."

Emmy tilted her head, amused. "That's... oddly comforting? Like a guardian angel."

"Or a creepy woodsman," June said, sipping her cider.

Rebecca waved her off. "It's harmless. My gran used to tell me she believed in him. Swore her own gran had seen him once."

Emmy smiled faintly. "So what — he just wanders around saving people?"

"Pretty much. Hence the name."

From the next table, an older man who had been nursing a pint turned slightly toward them. "You talking about the Wandering Man?" His voice was rough with age, but curious.

Rebecca grinned. "See? Everyone knows him."

The man chuckled, shaking his head. "Aye. My grandparents used to tell me stories. Said their parents told them the same. Never saw him myself, mind, but the tale's been around longer than I have. Some say it's just folks looking out for each other, but…" He trailed off with a shrug. "Funny how many people claim to have seen someone when they needed help most."

Emmy let the words settle, her curiosity piqued.

A story, passed down through generations. A nameless figure who appeared only when needed.

She tried to laugh it off, but a small part of her couldn't help wondering.

"Sounds like I moved to the right place, then," she said lightly.

Rebecca raised her glass. "Exactly. You'll be just fine, Emmy. This place looks after its own."

They clinked their glasses together, the warmth of the pub wrapping around them like a blanket, though Emmy couldn't quite shake the strange little shiver that crept down her spine.

As the night wound down, the warmth of the pub seemed to sink into Emmy's bones. The clinking of glasses dulled to a steady hum, conversations turning softer, laughter looser.

Arun Bhatt reappeared from the bar, balancing a fresh pint and a packet of crisps. "Sorry," he said with a sheepish grin as he slid back into his chair. "Got cornered by Margaret from the parish council. She's very passionate about bunting placement."

"That's one way to put it," June teased.

"Don't let her fool you," Rebecca added. "He loves a gossip."

Arun raised his pint in mock defence. "If knowing the difference between violet and lilac bunting makes me a gossip, then so be it."

Emmy chuckled, the easy banter settling over her like a blanket. She hadn't realised how much she'd missed this — sitting in a circle of people, no pretence, no tiptoeing around the edges of conversation. Just being part of something.

By the time they were ready to leave, the crowd had thinned, leaving only the die-hards nursing their final pints near the bar. Emmy stepped out into the crisp night with June and Rebecca, the chill air biting her flushed skin. Arun lingered behind, chatting amiably with someone at the door.

"Glad you came out," June said, nudging her lightly. "You're not half bad at socialising."

"I'll try not to take that as a compliment," Emmy said with a smile.

June grinned. "Festival next, yeah? You're coming with me. Non-negotiable."

Emmy nodded, though her thoughts drifted elsewhere. The festival. Lanterns lighting the streets. Music in the air. Crowds mingling in the square.

And maybe, just maybe, a familiar face in the crowd.

When she finally made it back to her flat, Emmy paused at the window, looking out at the village below. The bunting fluttered faintly in the breeze, lanterns swaying gently in the square like promises of what was to come.

Friendly. Safe.

And yet, the pub story echoed in her mind — the Wandering Man, appearing when needed, vanishing before anyone could thank him.

She switched off the light and let the room fall into shadow, the faint hum of the village night settling around her.

The festival would be here soon.

And she couldn't shake the feeling that it would change everything.

# Chapter 13

The morning of the festival dawned bright and blustery, the kind of spring day that couldn't decide between sunshine and the occasional soft drizzle. Emmy woke to the distant hum of activity — car doors slamming, voices carrying through the narrow streets, and somewhere far off, the faint, cheerful sound of a fiddle tuning up.

She lingered in bed for a while, cocooned in the warmth of her duvet, staring at the ceiling as the morning light crept across her little flat. Today wasn't just another day — it felt as though the whole village had been waiting for this one.

By the time she'd showered and dressed, the streets outside had transformed. Emmy pulled on a soft cream blouse tucked into a pale-yellow skirt that skimmed her knees, then shrugged on a light denim jacket, the sleeves rolled at her wrists. She pinned back a section of her dark curls with a simple gold clip, the rest falling in soft ringlets to her shoulders. Her outfit felt bright, easy — something that matched the occasion.

When she stepped outside, the breeze was cool enough to bring colour to her cheeks, but the sun filtered through the clouds in golden bursts, warming the cobblestones beneath her feet.

The square was unrecognisable. Overnight, it had become a living, breathing patchwork of colour and movement.

Long strings of bunting stretched between the buildings, their triangular flags dancing in the wind. Lanterns hung from the eaves of the shops, swaying gently with every gust, catching the sunlight in their painted glass panes. Stalls lined the perimeter of the square, each one a small explosion of life — tables groaning under baskets of hand-stitched linens, trays of sugared buns still steaming in the cool air, and jars of homemade jams and pickles stacked neatly like tiny jewels.

The smells were intoxicating: roasting meat from a spit turning slowly near the fountain, sharp tangs of fresh herbs bundled together with twine, the sweetness of honeyed nuts spilling from little paper cones in the hands of children.

Musicians gathered at the far end of the square, the strains of a fiddle weaving through the steady beat of a drum. Two young boys kicked a football between the press of legs, their mothers calling after them good-naturedly, while an older woman in a broad-brimmed hat adjusted the display of her flower stall, coaxing a particularly stubborn tulip into standing taller.

Emmy paused at the edge of it all, breathing it in.

For a moment, she simply wandered, letting the sights and sounds wash over her. She stopped to watch a man carve delicate patterns into wooden spoons, his hands steady despite the breeze. At another stall, she ran her fingers lightly over handwoven scarves dyed in shades of blue and green that reminded her of the sea.

She bought a small bag of sugared almonds from a cheerful, red-faced vendor, thanking him before popping one into her mouth. The crunch of the sugar gave way to the soft bite of the nut, the sweetness lingering on her tongue as she continued to explore.

It felt like the whole village was here. Families strolled together, their children darting ahead to tug eagerly at the edges of stalls. Couples lingered at the cider tent, laughing as they shared steaming cups. Even the usual quiet corners of the square seemed alive, the festival breathing warmth into every stone and shadow.

Emmy felt lighter than she had in weeks. She didn't need to think about work, or about her past, or about anything beyond this — the present moment, wrapped in colour and sound.

She drifted toward the centre of the square, where a small crowd had gathered around a juggler balancing precariously on a wooden crate. His flaming torches flashed in the air as he tossed them higher and higher, the crowd gasping and clapping at each impossible catch.

"Emmy!"

She turned at the sound of her name to see June waving wildly from beside a cider tent, Rebecca at her side with two paper cups in hand. Arun was there too, laughing as he tried to juggle three enormous bags of something resembling homemade fudge.

"You made it!" June called, weaving through the crowd to pull her into a quick hug. "And you look like you belong in one of those fancy festival brochures."

"Please don't make me pose for one," Emmy said with a laugh.

"Nonsense," June said, thrusting a warm cup into her hands. "Mulled cider. Trust me, you won't survive this day without it."

Rebecca grinned. "She's not wrong. It's dangerously good."

Emmy smiled and accepted the cup, the heat seeping pleasantly through the paper and into her chilled fingers. "This is incredible. I've never seen the square like this."

"And this is only the morning," Rebecca said. "Wait until tonight. They'll light the lanterns and there's dancing in the courtyard behind The Crown."

"You're dancing," June added matter-of-factly.

"I didn't agree to that."

"You will after two more of those ciders," Arun said, nodding toward her drink.

They laughed together, the easy camaraderie wrapping around Emmy like a warm scarf as they drifted toward the stalls.

They wandered together through the stalls, sampling slices of tangy cheese, warm sugared pastries, and a questionable but surprisingly tasty pickled vegetable concoction offered by an elderly woman with more enthusiasm than salesmanship. Everywhere Emmy looked, there was something to take in — bright garlands of flowers, children with painted faces darting between the adults, the mouthwatering scent of roasting meats drifting from a grill.

At the edge of the square, Emmy paused at a stall displaying jars of golden honey and beeswax candles carved into intricate shapes. She reached for one shaped like a fox, admiring the detail.

"Ah! Miss Trevelyn!"

Emmy turned to see a familiar face — Mr. Peterson, the PE teacher, striding toward her with the same brisk energy he carried into the school gymnasium. His windbreaker was replaced with a tweed cap and scarf, though he still somehow looked like he was about to coach someone through a sprint.

"Enjoying yourself?" he asked, clasping her hand briefly.

"Very much," Emmy said, smiling. "This is incredible. I had no idea the festival was this big."

"Oh, this is nothing yet," he said. "Wait until the evening. You'll hear the music halfway across the village." He tipped his cap toward June and Rebecca in greeting before nodding at Arun, who gave a polite wave. "See you at the tug-of-war later?"

"Absolutely not," June said flatly.

Peterson laughed, unbothered, before striding off toward the cider tent.

As Emmy turned back toward the honey stall, a small hand tugged at her skirt.

"Miss Trevelyn!"

She looked down to see Ellis — one of her quieter Year Four students — grinning up at her, his face painted like a tiger, whiskers lopsided and nose smudged.

"Ellis! You look ferocious," Emmy said warmly. "Are you having fun?"

He nodded vigorously. "Mum let me have a candy apple and a hot dog!"

"Well," Emmy said, crouching slightly to meet his gaze, "that sounds like a very lucky day."

A woman approached, carrying two cups of tea. She looked like Ellis in the eyes, though her hair was streaked with early grey.

"Miss Trevelyn," she said, offering a smile. "Ellis talks about you all the time. We're so glad he's settling in."

Emmy felt a small bloom of warmth in her chest. "He's doing brilliantly," she said. "Always the first to help tidy up at the end of class."

Ellis grinned proudly at his mother.

"Well, we won't keep you," the woman said. "Enjoy the day."

"You too," Emmy replied, waving them off as they rejoined the crowd.

Rebecca elbowed her gently. "You're practically a celebrity."

"Hardly," Emmy said, though she couldn't help smiling.

As they moved on, Arun stopped to purchase an absurdly large paper cone of sugared nuts, offering some around as they passed a stall selling second-hand books. June had her eye on a string of handmade bracelets, while Rebecca bartered with a woman over a woven basket.

The juggler in the square was replaced by a trio of dancers, their feet tapping sharply against a makeshift stage as a fiddler and accordionist played a lively tune. Emmy stopped to watch for a moment, caught up in the rhythm of it, the laughter of the crowd spilling into the music.

This — all of it — felt alive in a way she hadn't realised she'd been missing.

They wandered away from the centre of the square, following a little side lane that had been transformed into a row of game stalls. Here, the atmosphere was different — less bustling than the main square, with smaller clusters of people laughing and cheering each other on.

"Right," June announced, coming to a stop. "We're doing this."

Emmy followed her gaze to a coconut shy, the coconuts lined neatly on their perches like smug little sentinels.

"Oh no," Emmy said, already laughing. "I am not embarrassing myself in front of half the village."

"Absolutely yes, you are." June was already handing over coins to the man running the stall — a barrel-chested fellow in a patched waistcoat, who grinned like he'd seen this conversation play out countless times.

Rebecca folded her arms, smirking. "This should be good."

June stepped up with dramatic flair, taking her first shot like she was about to make history. The ball thudded harmlessly against the wooden frame.

"Strong form," Arun said gravely, biting back a laugh.

"Oh, hush." June took another ball, this one at least wobbling a coconut before it resettled stubbornly in place.

"Third time's the charm," Emmy said sweetly.

"Third time is when I throw it at you instead," June replied, though her final throw wasn't much better.

Arun stepped up next and, with an easy toss, knocked one clean off its perch.

Rebecca whistled. "Show-off."

"Pure skill," Arun said, deadpan.

They moved on, still laughing, toward a ring toss stall, where the prizes ranged from little keychains to enormous stuffed animals that looked impossible to win. Emmy surprised herself by landing two rings in quick succession, earning a small plush rabbit that June immediately named Gerald.

"He's part of the group now," June said solemnly, tucking the toy under her arm. "We're taking him everywhere."

The smell of frying food lured them to a nearby stall, where a cheerful woman with flour-dusted hands served paper cones brimming with hot chips, doused liberally with salt and vinegar. The first bite was sharp and comforting, warming Emmy's fingers as much as her stomach. They ate leaning against a low wall, watching the world pass by.

"That," June declared between mouthfuls, "is the real reason anyone comes to this festival."

Rebecca pointed to a narrow, purple-draped tent tucked between two larger stalls. Madame Orielle — Palm Readings & Fortunes, the hand-painted sign declared.

"No," Emmy said immediately.

"Yes," June countered, already steering her toward it. "You can't go to a festival and not get your fortune told. It's the law."

Inside, the air was close with incense — heady sandalwood and something faintly floral. The tent was dim, lit by a single lantern on a round table draped in embroidered cloth.

A woman sat behind it, her fingers heavy with silver rings, her dark eyes sharp and assessing as they settled on Emmy.

"Please," Madame Orielle said softly, gesturing to the seat opposite her.

Emmy hesitated, but June nudged her forward.

She sat.

"Your hand," the fortune teller said, extending her own.

Emmy placed her palm in hers, feeling the cool press of metal and the warmth of skin. The woman traced the lines of her hand with one finger, silent for a long moment.

"You stand at a crossing," Madame Orielle murmured at last, her accent curling strangely around the words. "One path you walk already. One waits for you unseen."

Emmy frowned slightly. "And… what am I meant to do with that?"

The woman's lips curved in a small, knowing smile. "Not all roads are meant to be clear before you take them."

And just like that, she released Emmy's hand.

Outside, the sunlight felt brighter, the air cooler.

"Well?" June demanded, practically bouncing. "Was it good? Are you destined for glory? Or scandal?"

Emmy shook her head, smiling despite herself. "She said I'm standing at a crossing."

"Oh, that's suitably mysterious," Rebecca said, linking her arm through Emmy's. "Come on. We need another cider after that."

"Agreed," June said, already steering them back toward the tent they'd passed earlier.

The cider tent was even busier now, a knot of villagers gathered beneath its canvas roof, laughing and shouting over the cheerful din. The air was rich with the scent of spiced apples and mulled wine, and the occasional waft of roasted chestnuts from a nearby brazier. Emmy joined the short queue with June and Rebecca, her fingers already tingling in anticipation of the warmth of the drink.

Behind them, someone was telling an animated story about a near-win at the ring toss, their words punctuated by bursts of laughter. A little further off, a boy Emmy recognised from Year Four darted between legs with his face painted like a badger, his mother calling after him with exasperated fondness.

Emmy cradled her drink when it came, inhaling the fragrant steam as they stepped aside to make space for the next group.

"You know," June said, leaning against a wooden post, "I think you're becoming a proper local. Look at you — cider in hand, Gerald the Rabbit under your arm—"

Emmy rolled her eyes. "You're the one carrying Gerald."

"Details." June grinned, nudging her shoulder. "Next thing you know, you'll be judging the chutney competition."

Rebecca groaned. "Don't bring up the chutney competition. My aunt still hasn't forgiven the judges from last year."

Their easy chatter mingled with the festival noise — the clinking of mugs, the lively notes of a fiddle from the stage at the square's centre, the rise and fall of dozens of conversations at once.

Emmy let herself be swept up in it, the warmth of the cider and the company smoothing away the lingering tension she hadn't realised she'd been carrying.

She glanced past the crowd, toward the quieter edges of the square where the bustle thinned out into shaded walkways and bookstalls.

That's when she saw him.

Roman.

He stood by one of Aubrey's makeshift book tables, half in shadow beneath the awning, idly turning over a hardback in his hands. He looked almost as though he belonged to another scene entirely — his dark coat and calm stillness a stark contrast to the whirl of colour and movement around him.

Emmy froze before she could stop herself, the warmth in her chest shifting into something more complicated.

"Friend of yours?" Rebecca followed her gaze, raising an eyebrow.

Emmy blinked. "Sort of," she said, the word feeling inadequate.

Rebecca smirked. "Interesting 'sort of.'"

Before Emmy could reply, June reappeared from the pie stall with Arun behind her, arms full of crinkling paper bags. "Right," she declared. "Food, drink, and Gerald. We're unstoppable."

But Emmy barely heard her. Her attention was still caught on Roman, standing so quietly on the edge of it all.

He looked up as if sensing her gaze. For the briefest moment, their eyes met across the crowd — a flicker of recognition, of something unspoken — before a pair of villagers passed between them, cutting off her view.

By the time she looked back, he was gone.

Emmy stood still for a moment, the world of the festival carrying on around her — the laughter, the music, the calls of vendors — but none of it quite touching her. She scanned the edges of the square, searching for that dark coat, that easy stillness that seemed so at odds with the chaos of the day.

Nothing.

"Emmy?"

June's voice jolted her back. She turned to find her friend looking at her curiously, a paper bag of steaming pasties in one hand.

"Sorry," Emmy said quickly, tucking a loose curl behind her ear. "I thought I saw someone I knew."

June gave her a look that said she didn't entirely believe her, but she didn't press. "Come on," she said, nudging her. "We've got about ten minutes before Arun eats all of these."

Rebecca appeared at her other side, already unwrapping a pasty of her own. "If he does, we're staging an intervention."

They moved together back toward the main square, weaving through the press of people. Emmy let herself be swept along, the warmth of the cider and the comfort of her friends pulling her back into the present.

But every so often, she caught herself glancing toward the quieter corners of the festival.

For someone who didn't like crowds; Roman had a way of lingering in her mind.

The day rolled on in a blur of colour and sound — more food than Emmy thought she could possibly eat, another ill-fated attempt by June at the coconut shy, a lively group dance she refused to be dragged into but enjoyed watching from the sidelines.

As the sun began to dip, Emmy lingered at the edge of the square, cider cooling in her hands as the evening's hum settled into something different than the festival, she'd first walked into hours ago. The earlier chaos — children running wild, June's relentless dragging from one stall to another, Rebecca's exasperated bartering with a chutney vendor — had softened.

Lanterns now glowed overhead, strung in lazy arcs across the square, their golden light catching the colours of the bunting. Musicians had shifted to slower tunes, their fiddles and mandolins plucking out melodies that seemed to sway in time with the crowd. Couples danced in loose circles near the fountain, laughter softened by the night air. The cider tent had grown rowdier, though — a chorus of voices singing over each other, cheers and laughter rolling out from under its canvas roof.

"Come on," June said, reappearing at Emmy's elbow with Rebecca in tow, both holding pasties. "You've been standing there like you're posing for a painting."

Emmy blinked, shaking herself back to the present. "I'm just watching," she said, smiling faintly.

"You need another drink," Rebecca said decisively. "And probably one of these." She offered her pasty.

Emmy waved it off with a laugh. "If I eat anything else, I'll roll back to the flat."

Arun joined them, balancing two steaming cups of something that smelled suspiciously of mulled wine. "This place at night is the only thing keeping me from transferring to a different school," he said, passing one to June.

"Don't joke about that," June replied. "We'd miss you."

Arun smirked. "You'd miss my lesson plans. Not me."

Emmy let their chatter wash over her, watching as June gestured animatedly with her cup, nearly spilling its contents on an unsuspecting villager. She laughed, but her mind wasn't wholly there.

Her gaze drifted again — unbidden — to the edges of the square.

The spot where she'd seen him earlier.

Roman.

She hadn't imagined it. That brief, charged meeting of eyes had been real. Even now, her stomach tightened at the memory, though she couldn't explain why.

Her friends didn't notice her distraction, too caught up in Arun's retelling of some minor drama in the staffroom earlier that week. Emmy forced a polite laugh where it felt appropriate, but the longer she stood there, the more the press of the crowd seemed to weigh on her.

The air felt thick, the heat of so many bodies blurring with the tang of cider and the sweetness of roasting chestnuts.

She needed a moment. Just a breath.

"I'm going to get some air," she said, interrupting June mid-sentence.

June gave her a mock-suspicious look. "Don't vanish. I'm making you dance before the night's over."

"Threats," Emmy replied with a small smile. "I'll be back."

She weaved her way through the square, the music fading slightly as she slipped between stalls and clusters of chatting villagers. Away from the crush, the night felt cooler, the breeze teasing loose curls against her face.

Near the far edge of the square, a small line of tables had been set up — Aubrey's impromptu bookstall among them. Most of the books were half-hidden in shadow now, the shopkeeper himself nowhere to be seen, likely off enjoying the festival proper.

And there he was.

Roman.

He stood beside the stall, a half-finished drink in one hand — cider, by the look of it — as he thumbed idly through the spine of an old hardback. His coat was unbuttoned, his posture loose but deliberate, like someone quietly observing rather than participating. Even with the drink in his hand, there was something distant about him, as though the laughter and music all belonged to another world.

Emmy's steps slowed.

She considered turning back — retreating into the safety of the crowd and her friends — but Roman looked up, sensing her before she could slip away.

Their eyes met, and the faintest glimmer of a smile touched his lips.

"Miss Trevelyn," he said, his voice calm and steady despite the din behind them.

"Roman," she replied, her throat a little drier than she'd expected.

"I didn't expect to see you here."

He tilted his head, glancing toward the glowing square. "The festival has been held for centuries. It seemed wrong not to be here, at least for a while."

There it was again — that way of speaking. Not just the words, but the weight of them, as though he carried more history than one person should.

"Are you enjoying it?" she asked, stepping closer.

His green eyes flicked back to hers. "Enjoying?" He seemed to consider the word. "Perhaps not as others do. But I find it… grounding."

"Grounding?"

He gestured lightly with his drink. "Traditions like these survive because they connect people to something bigger than themselves. Even if they don't realise it."

Emmy found herself smiling faintly. "That's a very philosophical take on face painting and coconut shies."

The corner of his mouth curved, almost a laugh. "And yet, there is something enduring in it. These same paths have been walked by others long before us."

She tilted her head. "You sound like you've been coming to this festival longer than anyone else here."

"Perhaps I have."

It was said so casually, with such composure, that Emmy couldn't tell whether he was teasing or simply telling the truth.

"Have you really?" she pressed, curiosity winning over caution.

Roman's gaze lingered on hers for a moment, something flickering there before he looked away. "Long enough," he said quietly, noncommittal yet somehow more than an answer.

Emmy wanted to ask more — about what he meant, about him — but she hesitated. She didn't know why, only that pushing felt wrong.

Instead, she said, "I don't ever see you in the square".

"I prefer to keep to myself," he said simply. "But I walk these streets often enough."

She thought of the woods, of the manor beyond them. "It must be nice, living out there. Quiet."

"Peaceful," he agreed, though there was something in his tone — an undercurrent, like the word carried another meaning entirely.

For a moment, they fell silent. Emmy let her gaze wander to the square, the glow of lanterns catching on the glassy surface of the fountain, the music still winding softly through the night.

"I'm glad I came," she said eventually, almost to herself. "It feels… alive here. Like this village is more than just somewhere people live."

Roman looked at her then, fully, his expression softened by something she couldn't name. "And are you alive here?"

The question caught her off guard. "I think so," she said slowly. "I feel like I can finally start over here. Like I'm not defined by anything but myself."

He nodded slightly, as if her words held weight for him. "Starting over," he murmured, almost to himself. "It is no small thing."

She glanced at him. "You make it sound like you've done it before."

Roman's lips curved into the faintest ghost of a smile. "Once or twice."

It was such a non-answer that Emmy almost laughed. "Are you always this cryptic?"

"Only when I don't know someone well enough to be otherwise."

"Is that your way of saying I need to earn straightforward answers?"

"Perhaps."

This time she did laugh, shaking her head. "That's not exactly encouraging."

Roman tilted his head, considering her. "Would you prefer me easy to read?"

"I'd settle for mildly less mysterious," she said lightly.

"Mystery serves its purpose."

"And what purpose is that?"

"To keep people guessing."

Emmy gave him a look. "Well, you're succeeding."

His faint smile widened just slightly.

Emmy smiled, shaking her head. "You sound like someone who's very used to avoiding questions."

His gaze met hers briefly, then returned to the horizon. "Perhaps I am."

It wasn't defensive, just... honest. She found herself wanting to know why.

"I suppose that makes sense," she said after a moment. "If you keep to yourself out there. People must ask questions when they don't know you."

"They do," he said evenly. "It rarely ends in anything worthwhile."

Emmy tilted her head, studying him. "You don't like people knowing about you?"

"I prefer not to be the subject of idle curiosity," he replied. Then, softer, "You'd be surprised how often people mistake curiosity for care."

She didn't know what to say to that. It sounded like something born from experience, something lived, and it made her wonder again just how much more there was to him than he allowed people to see.

"Maybe," she said after a moment, "but curiosity can be care. At least a little."

He turned his head toward her, and for the first time that evening, his smile reached his eyes. "You believe that?"

"I wouldn't be talking to you if I didn't."

The smile lingered for a beat before he looked away. "Then perhaps you're an exception."

They stood in companionable silence, the music from the square drifting faintly through the cool air.

Emmy glanced down at the drink in his hand. "So you do join in a little," she said, nodding toward the cup.

Roman glanced at it as if he'd forgotten it was there. "Cider seemed appropriate."

"Appropriate," she echoed with a laugh. "Not enjoyable?"

He considered, then said simply, "It has its merits."

"That's a glowing review if I've ever heard one."

He allowed the faintest chuckle. "Perhaps I'm difficult to impress."

"Or just difficult, full stop."

That earned her another glance, sharper this time — but with an edge of humour. "Careful, Miss Trevelyn. That sounded like a challenge."

"Maybe it is."

He regarded her for a moment longer, and she wondered what exactly he saw when he looked at her like that — like he was weighing something far heavier than her words.

"Why do you stay out there?" she asked suddenly, gesturing vaguely toward the woods beyond the village. "On that big estate. You could live anywhere closer. You'd barely be noticed here in town."

Roman was quiet for a long time. When he finally spoke, his voice was measured. "It was my family's home. Long before I was here. And some places," he added softly, "you don't leave. Not really."

The way he said it made her chest tighten. It wasn't sentimentality. It was something deeper — like the house wasn't just bricks and mortar but a tether.

"You must have a lot of memories there," she said gently.

Roman's eyes lingered on the horizon. "More than I care to count."

She wanted to ask what kind of memories, but something in his posture — that quiet, almost imperceptible stillness — told her not to push.

Instead, she said, "You talk like someone who's seen a lot."

For a moment, she thought he might deflect. But then he said quietly, "I have."

And that was all. No elaboration. No invitation to dig deeper.

She swallowed the urge to fill the silence.

The music shifted, a slower tune now, distant laughter rising and falling from the square. A group passed by, heading back toward the dancing, their voices carrying easily on the breeze.

Roman glanced toward them, then back at her. "Do you dance?"

The question surprised her. "Not if I can help it," she said with a small laugh.

"Why not?"

"I'm terrible at it."

"That's not really an answer."

"It is if you've ever seen me try."

His mouth curved, a ghost of a smile. "Perhaps someday I'll see for myself."

"Not tonight."

"As you wish."

He didn't press, but there was a quiet amusement in his tone that made her wonder if he'd intended to.

For a while, they simply stood there, the world reduced to the glow of the lanterns, the faint chill of the night air, and the low hum of distant music.

Then Roman straightened slightly, as though settling on something he'd been debating.

"Miss Trevelyn," he said, his voice careful, deliberate.

She looked at him. "Yes?"

"Would you allow me to call on you sometime?"

Her breath caught, though she managed a steady, "Call on me?"

He inclined his head. "Properly."

"Properly," she echoed, her lips tugging into a small, bemused smile. "That's... very formal."

"Old habits," he said lightly. "I try not to forget them."

There was no irony in it. No apology. Just the quiet dignity of someone who meant what he said.

"I'd like that," Emmy replied, surprising herself with how easily the words came.

Roman's expression softened — just a fraction, but enough to make her chest tighten. "Then I shall speak to Aubrey about where to leave a note."

Of course he would, Emmy thought, suppressing a laugh. A note. Courting. So utterly Roman.

She didn't mind.

The music swelled faintly in the distance, laughter spilling across the night air, but here — in this quiet pocket of lantern glow and shadow — it felt like something else entirely.

For a moment, she wondered if this was how it felt to be seen. Truly seen.

And for once, she didn't want to run from it.

Something flickered across his face — not quite a smile, but something close — before his gaze shifted toward the far side of the square. "Are you hungry?"

Emmy gave a small laugh. "I was just thinking about food, actually".

The air between them eased, the earlier carefulness giving way to something more familiar. Roman gestured for her to follow, and they began to weave their way through the press of festival-goers. The glow of hanging lanterns caught in her hair, glinting off the gentle curls, while the shifting light traced the edges of his dark coat.

They passed the fiddler, the same one who'd been standing near the cider stall earlier. Now, his bow moved faster, pulling a tune lively enough to have children clapping and skipping in a rough circle while parents stood nearby, clapping along. Roman's gaze lingered a moment before they moved on.

The food stalls occupied the far edge of the square, each with its own halo of light and its own enticing scent. There were trays of sugared almonds, strings of sausages sizzling over charcoal, trays of fried dough dusted with powdered sugar. Voices carried from every direction — traders calling out their wares, people laughing at shared jokes, the scrape of ladles on metal pots.

Roman slowed near a smaller stall, one tucked slightly between two larger ones. It was run by an older couple, their hands moving with quiet efficiency as they ladled stew into paper bowls. The smell was rich and savoury — a broth darkened by hours of slow cooking, with hints of thyme, rosemary, and pepper.

"This," Roman said quietly, almost to himself, as if it were a certainty rather than a choice.

"You've had it before?" Emmy asked, her eyes drawn to the steam curling into the cool air.

He inclined his head. "Many times." Then, catching himself, he added more lightly, "Years ago. It's… a tradition here."

The woman behind the stall glanced between them with a knowing smile. "Two?" she asked, already ladling.

Roman looked to Emmy for confirmation. She nodded, and he said, "Two, please."

The couple moved with practiced hands — a ladle's sweep into each bowl, a wedge of bread tucked neatly at the side, a brief murmur of "Mind the heat."

Emmy cradled her bowl, letting the warmth seep into her chilled fingers. They stepped aside to a quieter stretch of wall, sheltered enough that they could see the whole square without being jostled. The music was softer here, the fiddler's tune drifting on the air like a thread of colour in the background.

She took her first spoonful, the broth rich on her tongue, and let out an involuntary hum of appreciation. "That's incredible. What's in it?"

Roman glanced down at his own bowl as though reading it. "Root vegetables. A little beef. A great deal of patience."

She laughed softly. "That's the poetic way of saying you won't tell me the recipe, isn't it?"

"I wouldn't dream of depriving you of the mystery," he said, his mouth curving faintly.

"You're not much of a sharer?"

191

"Not when it comes to recipes." He tore his bread in two anyway and offered her half.

She accepted, smiling as she dipped it into the broth. "Thank you. And here I thought you were going to make me beg for it."

"I cannot imagine you have had to beg for anything," he replied.

"Not yet," she said lightly, and took another bite.

For a few minutes they ate without speaking, the warmth of the stew working its way through the chill of the evening. From this spot, Emmy could see the lanterns swaying overhead, the soft shadows they cast dancing against the stone buildings. A child ran past with a streamer trailing behind her, giggling as her father gave chase. Somewhere, someone's dog barked once and then again.

"This is lovely," Emmy said at last.

"The festival?"

She nodded. "The whole thing. It feels... different here. Like time slows down a little."

His gaze lingered on her, something unreadable behind it. "Perhaps it does."

They finished their bowls slowly, the last of the bread used to catch every drop. When they returned them to the stall, the older woman behind the counter gave a warm smile and told them to come back before the night ended — "Best batch of the season," she said with quiet pride.

From there, they let the tide of people carry them further into the square. The music shifted — now a deeper, rolling rhythm of drum and fiddle that had people linking arms and stepping in time. The air was thick with the smell of frying batter, roasting chestnuts, and spiced cider. Every few steps brought a new sight — a child tugging at her mother's hand toward the bright colours of a ribbon stall, an elderly man in a flat cap showing off a carved wooden whistle, teenagers clustered around a game of ring toss.

Roman's stride was easy, unhurried, yet he somehow always managed to create a little space around them, guiding her subtly away from the most chaotic knots of the crowd. Emmy noticed the way people seemed to part for him without thought, a ripple of awareness that she couldn't quite explain.

They paused at a stall where a young man was turning skewers of meat over a bed of glowing coals, the juices hissing as they hit the heat. Roman bought one and handed it to her, the wooden stick warm in her fingers. She took a bite — tender, smoky, with a sharp edge of spice — and made a soft sound of approval.

"I see," Roman murmured, "you are not a difficult person to please."

"That's not true," she said with mock indignation. "I have very high standards. You just happen to be standing in the middle of my favourite kind of evening."

"And what kind is that?"

"One where the food is good, the air smells like sugar, and there's no paperwork to mark in the morning."

His mouth twitched at that, but he didn't argue.

They wandered toward the quieter end of the square where the games were set up — hoop toss, dart throws, and a stall where people tried to knock tin cans off a wooden shelf. The prizes were mostly cheap — stuffed animals, sweets in cellophane, keychains — but the laughter ringing out from the players was unguarded and genuine.

"Do you ever play these?" Emmy asked.

Roman gave a faint shake of his head. "Not in many years."

"Then tonight's the night," she declared, already fishing in her coat pocket for a coin.

The man running the hoop toss grinned when he saw her approach. "Three tries for a pound, miss."

Roman stepped forward before she could pay, placing the coin on the counter without a word. Emmy gave him a look, but he only gestured toward the three rings now set in front of her.

Her first throw landed wide, the ring bouncing harmlessly off the base of the stand. She winced. The second was closer, sliding over the post before wobbling off. The third landed neatly, and she let out a triumphant little laugh.

The stallholder offered her a choice of prizes, and she picked a small, soft toy in the shape of a fox. "For my bookshelf," she said as they walked away.

The night deepened, the glow from the lanterns seeming warmer against the cool air. A light breeze stirred the edges of Emmy's jacket, carrying with it the faintest scent of woodsmoke. She realised she had been smiling for much of the evening without meaning to.

"Thank you," she said suddenly.

He glanced at her. "For what?"

"For tonight. For... not rushing."

Roman's eyes softened, the shadows shifting in them like something long held and rarely shared. "Some things," he said quietly, "are not meant to be rushed."

They stood for a moment, the sounds of the festival swirling around them, neither quite moving to end the night.

They drifted toward the edge of the square, where the press of the crowd eased and the sounds of the festival became a muted hum behind them. Roman walked with his hands loosely clasped behind his back, his posture as steady and unhurried as the rest of him. A few stray voices floated on the cool evening air, laughter echoing from somewhere near the cider stall.

After a moment of quiet, he glanced at her.

"What else do you enjoy?"

She smiled faintly. "Aside from soup and fox-shaped prizes?"

"Yes," he said, with the smallest hint of amusement. "I have already gathered you prefer evenings that don't demand haste. But what fills your time when there is no festival?"

She thought about it for a moment. "Nature," she said finally. "Animals. Wildlife. I like places where I can just... listen to the world without too much interruption. The sound of wind in the trees, water moving over stones, birds calling in the morning."

Roman gave a slow nod, his eyes on her profile as though committing the words to memory. "That is not an answer I hear often. People tend to prefer noise. Distraction."

"I've had enough of both," she admitted, her gaze dropping briefly to the cobblestones. "I think that's why I came here. I needed somewhere that could breathe."

"And has it?"

"Yes." She glanced sideways at him. "And no. It's... different here. Slower, but in a way that makes you notice things. The colour of the leaves changing. The way the sky looks just before rain."

They reached a quieter lane that sloped gently away from the square, lanterns casting pools of amber light at regular intervals. A cat darted across their path, its tail high before vanishing into a garden. Emmy watched it go, smiling to herself.

Roman spoke again, his tone softer now. "Animals, you said. Do you keep any?"

"Not here. My parents have a dog — a big, soft thing who thinks he's still a puppy even though he's older than he realises. I used to take him on long walks through the woods near our house." She paused, tucking a strand of hair behind her ear. "I miss that. But I don't think a flat above a bookshop is quite right for a Labrador."

"No," Roman agreed, "perhaps not."

They walked on, their steps unhurried, until the faint scent of roasting chestnuts drifted toward them from another side street. Roman glanced in the direction of the smell, then back at her. "Shall we?"

Emmy nodded, and they followed it to a small cart tended by a man in a wool cap, the coals glowing red beneath the roasting pan. Roman bought a small paper bag and handed it to her, the heat radiating through the thin paper. She broke one open, steam curling into the cool night air.

"Perfect," she murmured, popping it into her mouth.

Roman watched her with a quiet expression she couldn't quite read.

They lingered there, the warmth of the chestnuts in their hands, before the man tipped his cap and turned back to tend his coals. The two of them retraced their steps toward the main square, though neither seemed in a hurry to return to the thickest part of the crowd.

As they rounded the corner, Emmy caught sight of a group of children she recognised from school, racing past with ribbons streaming from their hands. One of them spotted her and waved, calling, "Miss Trevelyn!" She waved back, her smile widening as they vanished into the crowd again.

Roman glanced at her. "You are well-liked."

She laughed softly. "They're good kids. A bit loud, but good."

"Loudness," he said, "is not always a flaw."

They walked a little further, pausing near the fountain where the water caught the lantern light in shifting patterns. Emmy found herself thinking that, for all the noise and movement of the festival, this was her favourite part — these small pauses, where the air seemed easier to breathe.

They lingered by the fountain, the sound of the water soft beneath the hum of the festival. Lantern light caught in the ripples, casting tiny reflections across Roman's coat. Emmy shifted the warm paper bag of chestnuts between her hands, glancing up at him.

"You've asked me a lot about what I enjoy," she said, "but you haven't said much about yourself."

Roman's gaze held hers for a moment before he looked toward the fountain again. "There is not much to tell."

"I doubt that," Emmy replied, her tone light but curious. "You strike me as someone who notices things. And people like that usually have a lot worth telling."

He gave the smallest of smiles. "I do enjoy nature. Perhaps for the same reasons you do. It is… unhurried. Honest. It does not pretend to be something it is not." He paused, as if weighing how much to share. "I am fortunate to have so much of it around me. The land near my home is quiet — woods, fields, the pond. I've watched generations of birds nest there, year after year. Some return without fail."

Her brow lifted slightly. "Generations?"

"A figure of speech," he said quickly, though there was something in his voice — a trace of distance — that made her wonder. "I did have horses once. A small stable. But I travel more than I used to. It became too difficult to care for them properly, so I found them good homes."

"That must have been hard."

"It was." His voice was low, almost a hum. "I still hear them sometimes, in memory. The sound of hooves on frost. The scent of the stables on a cold morning."

Emmy hesitated. "Do you keep any animals now?"

"A cat," he said, a faint thread of amusement in his tone. "If you can call him that. He comes and goes as he pleases, sometimes gone for weeks before appearing again as though he never left. He stays a few days, demands to be fed and admired, then vanishes."

"He sounds very self-assured."

"He is," he agreed. "He was not mine, at first. I think he simply chose the house, and by extension, me."

Emmy smiled at that. "I think that's how it works with cats."

They fell into a comfortable silence, the kind that didn't need to be filled. Somewhere behind them, a fiddler's bow struck up a slow tune, and the scent of spiced cider drifted on the air.

They began walking again, the path bending them back toward the wider square where the lanterns swayed gently against the night. A group of children rushed past, the tallest carrying a toy shield, their boots drumming against the cobblestones. Emmy instinctively stepped closer to Roman to avoid being jostled, her paper bag of chestnuts brushing against his coat.

Roman slowed his pace, letting the noise of the crowd fade just enough for their conversation to settle again. "It's a rare thing," he said quietly, "to live somewhere that hasn't been swallowed up by noise."

"You mean the village?"

He inclined his head. "Here, things move in their own time. The same families have lived in some of these houses for generations. The butcher's shop has been run by the same bloodline since before the railway came. And the bakery... the oven there has been in use for more than a century."

She glanced toward him, curiosity flickering in her eyes. "You seem to know a lot about the history here."

"I've had time to notice," he said simply, but there was a flicker in his expression — not quite a smile, not quite a frown.

They passed a stall strung with garlands of dried herbs, the air scented faintly with rosemary and sage. Roman's gaze lingered briefly on the bundles before turning back to her. "It's easy to forget how rare it is, this kind of continuity. In the city, buildings rise and fall in the span of a decade. Here... you can still walk the same paths someone took two hundred years ago and know they'd recognise the shape of them."

There was a weight in his words that made Emmy study him for a moment. "And you prefer it that way?"

"I do," he said after a pause. "There's a steadiness in it. A sense that life is allowed to be lived at its proper pace."

She smiled faintly. "That's probably why you seem so… patient. Like nothing could rush you."

Roman looked ahead, his expression unreadable. "Patience is easier when you're not waiting for something."

She didn't press him on it, sensing the shift in his tone. Instead, they walked on, the crowd thinning as they moved toward one of the quieter lanes. A pair of elderly men stood outside the pub doorway, arguing cheerfully over the outcome of a darts match, their laughter echoing in the cool air.

As they reached the turning that would take her back toward Aubrey's, the sound of laughter carried from the square ahead. A small cluster of villagers stood near the lantern-lit stalls, June among them, her cheeks flushed from drink.

Emmy slowed, turning back to Roman with a faint smile. "I should go before they start wondering where I've disappeared to."

Roman gave a small nod, his green eyes steady on her. "Of course. Thank you for keeping me company."

"I should be the one thanking you," she said softly. Her hand lingered on the strap of her bag as if she might say more. "It was… nice. Walking with you."

His mouth curved, subtle but warm. "Then perhaps we might do it again."

Her chest gave a flutter she couldn't quite disguise. "Perhaps," she echoed, before drawing in a breath and stepping back. "Goodnight, Roman."

"Goodnight, Emmy."

She slipped away toward the group, her steps reluctant, and as soon as she was in earshot June's voice rang out, mischievous and far too loud.

"Well, well! Look who's been sneaking off with tall, dark, and handsome!"

Emmy laughed, trying to wave her off as the others leaned in with curious grins. "It wasn't like that."

"Oh, don't you 'wasn't like that' me," June teased, eyes sparkling with mischief. "We all saw you—moonlight, lanterns, strolling like something out of a film. You'll have the whole village talking by morning."

Emmy shook her head, cheeks warming despite herself.

June nudged her with a knowing wink. "I'm playing. I think you have got good taste."

The others laughed, and Emmy could only join in, her heart still racing from the parting she wasn't ready to let go of.

# Chapter 14

The staffroom was already humming by the time Emmy stepped in, a steady drone of voices layered over the gurgle of the kettle and the occasional clink of teaspoons against mugs. Coats were draped over chair backs, folders were stacked haphazardly on the spare table, and the air smelled faintly of toast — someone had clearly beaten her to the communal toaster.

The school headmaster John Everly stood at the far end of the room, his clipboard tucked beneath one arm, glasses halfway down his nose. "Alright, everyone, settle in," he called over the chatter, a faint smile tugging at the corner of his mouth. "Just a few things before we send you all off to your classes."

Emmy slid into the empty chair beside June, who was busy scribbling something in the margin of her planner. June offered a warm glance of greeting without lifting her pen.

"First," Everly began, scanning his notes, "we've confirmed that next Friday we'll be hosting our local history event. The Historical Society has arranged for a guest speaker — chap by the name of Thomas Harding — to come in and talk to the children about the village's past. He'll be bringing along some artefacts for a sort of… well, show and tell. The idea is to get them hands-on with history."

A murmur of interest went around the room.

"Artefacts?" June raised an eyebrow. "What sort of artefacts? We're not letting Year Six loose with swords, are we?"

A ripple of laughter broke out. Everly's smile deepened. "Nothing quite so dangerous. We're talking old photographs, maps, a few tools, maybe some pieces of pottery. All safe, but still tangible. Something they can see and touch rather than read about in a book."

June leaned closer to Emmy and whispered, "I can already see the sticky fingerprints on a seventeenth-century candlestick."

Emmy suppressed a smile. "Let's hope he's bringing polish."

Everly continued, "I'll send around a rota so classes can take turns. It'll be set up in the hall all morning, smaller groups at a time so we don't overwhelm Mr Harding, the table, or each other. Please prep the children beforehand — we'd like them to have questions ready. Thoughtful ones." He lifted his brows over his glasses. "Not just 'How much is it worth?'"

"That rules out half my lot, then," Arun Bhatt said from the back, earning another round of chuckles.

"Risk assessment is printed and in your trays," Everly added. "We'll cordon off the display with those low museum ropes so no one topples a Tudor tankard with their backpack. Volunteers for the morning crowd control?" A smattering of reluctant hands rose. "Thank you, saints among us. Right, moving on. Playground duty rota — check your slots, please. Fire drill this Thursday, second period. Seating plans to be updated and left on your desks. And a gentle plea from Mrs. Keane: label your lunch in the fridge. Someone ate her yoghurt yesterday and there's a list of suspects."

Groans and theatrical gasps. "Justice for Keane," came a dry comment from Mr Peterson, the PE teacher, tipping his chin at Mrs Keane, who looked both put-upon and amused.

"And lastly," Everly said, "thank you for all your efforts with the Spring Festival displays. The village council was glowing about the children's work." His expression softened. "They were right to be."

Chairs scraped, conversations rose. June clicked her pen shut. "You've got break duty with me, haven't you?"

"Yes," Emmy said, closing her planner and standing. "We're by the field gate."

"Perfect," June said. "I'll bring my traffic-cone voice and we'll keep the peace."

They joined the flow into the corridor, the whiteboard outside the staffroom scrawled with reminders and doodles of smiley faces drawn by someone with chalky hands. The corridor smelled faintly of dry-erase pens and new books. Through the glass to the playground, the morning lay blue and bright, a fine sheet of cloud stretched high and thin, promising neither rain nor heat, only a steady kind of day.

Outside, the air had a bite, fresh enough that the children bounced against it, coats flapping like small capes. The playground unfurled: painted hopscotch grids in pastel squares; a climbing frame with its bark-chip moat; a low wall that all the Year Twos believed doubled as an Olympic beam. The noise rose at once — a joyful, ragged tapestry of calls, shrieks, laughter, the thud of footballs against shoe leather.

Emmy and June took their place near the gate to the field, where the grass sloped away to a boundary hedge studded with last year's blackberry thorns. From here they could see the full sweep: the chalked-out netball court with its lopsided post, the bench with flaking green paint, the corner where the quiet ones tended to drift in pairs.

"Cold," June said, tucking her hands into her coat pockets. "But not awful."

"Bracing," Emmy said, and meant it. She liked the feel of it, the way the air seemed to clarify the edges of things.

A pair of Year Three boys barrelled past, the football a meteor between them. "Boots away from knees, please," June called without looking, and they veered to the left by instinct alone. A whistle trilled from the far corner where Mr Peterson had stationed himself; somewhere a recorder honked a rogue note as if a child had smuggled it into break.

"Right," June said, scanning, "triage time. Spot the first drama."

"The girls by the rope," Emmy said. Three Year Fours were trying to coordinate a double-Dutch skipping sequence, the ropes slapping the tarmac, feet tangling. On the second attempt, one girl stumbled, then laughed, then tried again. Emmy felt her mouth curve without thinking. "They'll get it."

"They always do," June said. "Tenacity is just stubbornness with better PR."

A smaller figure detached herself from the quiet corner: Sophie, hands in the pockets of her coat, eyes observant, moving with the small, careful steps of someone who liked to keep her balance in sight. She stopped near Emmy but didn't speak — just hovered within orbit, as if proximity was its own kind of hello. Emmy dipped her head in greeting. "Morning, Sophie."

Sophie gave a quick smile and looked away again, watching two boys push a tyre that must have escaped from the PE shed. It bumped and wobbled across the yard, two more children joining the chase, squeals rising. June nudged Emmy, not unkindly. "You have the quiet ones trained to know where to find you."

"It's mutual," Emmy said softly. She lifted a hand when a small girl ran past trailing a scarf like a comet tail. "Scarves stay round necks, sweetie, not round ankles."

The scarf was obediently looped back up.

"So," June began again, voice light, eyes on the scuffle brewing near the bench, "you disappeared rather briskly on Saturday night."

"I got distracted," Emmy said, smiling. "I got caught up in the festivities."

"Mmm," June replied. "That sounds suspiciously like a cover for something delightfully interesting." She tossed Emmy a sidelong glance. "You've been... thoughtful since."

Emmy adjusted the lanyard at her neck. "Just— It was a big night. A lot of people. A lot to take in."

"And a certain someone?"

Emmy's breath made a small fog as she exhaled. She let her gaze sweep the yard: the pairs of friend's shoulder to shoulder; the cluster of Year Twos building a very determined castle out of sticks that didn't want to stay where sticks were told. "He was there," she said, keeping her tone even. "We talked. It was... nice." The word felt inadequate. "He's different, June. There's a way he... listens. And how he moves through a crowd without ever seeming to push. Old-fashioned is the easy word, but that's not all of it."

June's mouth tipped at one corner. "Go on."

"It's a feeling," Emmy said, surprised to hear it aloud. "As if he carries a kind of quiet that isn't empty. Like he's from somewhere that doesn't rush. I can't place it. It's— I don't know. A mystery."

June didn't tease. She tracked a child sprinting toward the fence and pre-empted a climb with a warning look that had the child think better of it. "You like a mystery," she said mildly. "And you deserve something that isn't noise."

Before Emmy could answer, the tyre-chase ended in a tangle and a thud. Emmy was already moving, the duty bag slung cross-body thumping lightly against her hip. "Alright, what happened?" she asked, kneeling to eye level with a boy clutching his shin and trying very hard not to cry. A smear of bark chip clung to his trouser leg, and a thin graze reddened his skin.

"It bumped me," he said, affronted by the betrayal of physics.

"Let's have a look." Emmy dabbed at the graze with a wipe from the kit, the sharp antiseptic smell briefly cutting through the cold air. "Not too bad. Brave face." She passed him a plaster printed with cartoon stars. He stared at the stars as if they were a medal and nodded, the wobble in his mouth steadying.

"Ball stays away from the climbing frame," June told the tyre brigade when they arrived, sheepish. "You know that."

"We forgot," one said.

"Try remembering," June said, but her tone was not unkind.

As the cluster dispersed, Emmy handed the wipe to June to tuck into the small rubbish pouch. "You were saying?" June prompted, almost as if they'd only paused a television show and were now hitting play again.

Emmy glanced toward the hedge where a blackbird hopped, head cocked, a small punctuation mark of life most adults would miss and most children would chase. "He asked to see me again," she said, not quite believing how simply that settled into the air.

June's eyebrows climbed, then softened. "And?"

"And I said yes." Emmy let it sit there. The word yes felt like a pebble dropped in a still pond, ripples spreading, not alarming, just… widening the edges of her day.

June's smile was genuine. "Good. You're allowed nice things."

Emmy laughed under her breath. "You say that like I ration them."

"Most of us do," June said. "Learned behaviour. We keep ourselves tidy and sensible and don't take up too much space. Then, once in a while, something good taps us on the shoulder and we look over it to see if it was meant for somebody else." She tipped her chin at the yard. "You spend all day telling small humans they're allowed joy. It's alright to keep some for yourself."

A shout cleaved the air, sharp enough to cut through their conversation. Two Year Fours, faces flushed, were in a tug-of-war over a skipping rope, each planted like a tree determined to grow in the exact same square foot of earth.

June's sigh held ten years of playground duty. "Your turn or mine?"

"I've got it," Emmy said, heading across the tarmac. She slowed before she reached them, letting the last three steps be unhurried. "We don't pull in ways that make wrists sore," she said, voice low and steady. "We share or we swap. Which do you prefer?"

"Share," one muttered.

"Swap," the other countered, then looked at his opponent and laughed despite himself.

"Two minutes each," Emmy said, holding out a hand for the rope. "I'll count them. Fair?"

They nodded. The knot of tension loosened, and within moments the rope thudded rhythmically against the ground and feet were finding the beat again.

By the time Emmy rejoined June, Mr Peterson had drifted past and executed a surprisingly nimble grab of a stray ball. "Five points to whoever stops hitting the fence," he called, lobbing it back with a spin that had the boys gape.

"You see," June murmured, "he keeps that up and they'll make him a demigod."

"They already have," Emmy said, smiling.

For a while, the yard showed its gentler face. The Year Twos abandoned their stick castle to gather round a ladybird discovered on the bench, solemn with reverence. Someone started a game of 'What's the time, Mr Wolf?' and the chorus of "Dinner time!" rolled over the tarmac like a tide. The quiet corner filled with the soft murmur of paired conversation; Sophie had found a friend to plait strands of grass and was humming under her breath, content.

June nudged her shoulder lightly. "Back to the topic of tapping-on-the-shoulder good things: what do you want next, with him?"

Emmy opened her mouth, then closed it again. Honesty asked to be simple. "I don't know. That's the point. I like not knowing in a way that isn't frightening."

"Then lean into that," June said. "Let it be slow. You like slow."

A small girl thrust a mitten at them like a presentation item. "Found this," she declared.

"Brilliant," June said, receiving the mitten with ceremonial care. "We'll do a lost-and-found fashion show at lunch."

The girl beamed and ran off.

"Do you ever have the feeling," Emmy said quietly, "that you're exactly where you're meant to be, and at the same time you're aware that something is about to change the shape of it?"

June's answering look was understanding without being probing. "You've only been here a little while. Of course it's changing shape. You're making a life. It's allowed to surprise you."

The bell at the wall flashed red and gave its single tone — not the loud, insistent drill bell, but the softer one that signalled the end of break. The children groaned, the way children always do, then collected themselves into lines that were more intention than geometry. Teachers appeared at doorways like magnets, drawing their classes in with calls of names and the universal promise that there might be stickers later.

Emmy and June held back, doing the sweep for stragglers: the boy who always insisted on one more kick; the girl who needed to tuck her scarf properly; the two friends finishing a whispered secret that clearly couldn't wait. When the yard finally exhaled into quiet, they shared the small, satisfied look of co-conspirators who'd steered a ship through busy waters.

"Coffee?" June said.

"Please," Emmy replied.

* * *

The day unrolled in the steady work of it. Literacy with her Year Fours: vivid verbs and a debate about whether "slurped" was more satisfying than "sipped" when writing about soup. (Consensus: yes, but only if you wanted to annoy someone in the next room.) Guided reading at a horseshoe table, three children bent over a page while Emmy gently coaxed a shy answer from Ellis, who had opinions but preferred to hold them the way a person holds a bird — gently and muffled. Spelling practice, where a child raised a hand to ask if "quiet" and "quite" were cousins who didn't like each other anymore. Maths on the late morning, blocks and bead strings and the small eruption of triumph when something that had been foggy came suddenly, deliciously clear.

At midday, the hall smelled of gravy and baked potatoes and something sweet that might become crumble. Emmy drifted through with her tray — a rectangle of school shepherd's pie, peas the exact green of peas everywhere — and sat with June at a table by the windows. The sunlight lay in generous rectangles across the scuffed floor, catching dust motes like lazy snow. The hum of voices was oddly soothing, children negotiating swaps (carrots for custard) with the gravity of diplomats.

"History event should be good," June said between sips of tea. "Harding did a talk here years ago. The kids loved the replica coins. He let them pretend to pay for things at a stall."

"That sounds brilliant," Emmy said. "We could set up a little market. Tie it to vocabulary. Barter. Trade. Worth."

June pointed her fork like a gavel. "And we can fashion ruffs out of paper doilies. Townsend will riot."

They grinned, and for a moment Emmy was aware of a quietness in herself that didn't feel like absence. It felt like space.

After lunch came a short assembly — Mr John Everly congratulating a group on their charity bake sale, a reminder to put lunch trays in the correct bins (an aspiration more than a reality). Back in the classroom, a spontaneous discussion about the difference between weather and climate broke out when a child asked why April felt like three different months at once. Emmy drew a quick diagram on the whiteboard — sun, cloud, a cartoon umbrella — and was rewarded with a chorus of "Ohhhhh" that made her quietly happy.

As the afternoon thinned toward its closing bell, Emmy tidied the edges: collected reading records, straightened the book corner, left a note on the board about tomorrow's PE kit. The clock nudged three. Coats were found under chairs, under tables, under other coats.

"Line up at the door please," she said, and the room arranged itself in that eager, wriggling line that always went a fraction crooked near the middle. "You were brilliant today. See you tomorrow."

The corridor exhaled again into the grounds. Outside, the light had shifted into the honeyed softness of late afternoon. The field's hedge wore its weak spring green like a promise. On the far side of the playground, the gate stood open to the narrow lane where parents gathered in familiar clusters, greeting one another in rhythms that had the comfort of liturgy.

This was a different kind of supervision — not the whistle-and-wipe triage of break, but the mellow, watchful unspooling of the day. Children peeled off into hugs; siblings quarrelled and were re-bonded by a biscuit; a pram squeaked over the tarmac and soothed to stillness by a rocking motion perfected over many miles.

Sophie's mother stood a little apart at first, scanning, then catching Emmy's eye with a small lift of her hand. She waited until her daughter had sprinted into her side and tucked herself neatly under her arm like a bird under a wing. Only then did she approach, smile gentle, green coat buttoned to the throat against the chill that always arrived early in the shade of the school wall.

"Miss Trevelyn," she said. Her voice held gratitude before the words had even formed. "I wanted to say thank you."

Emmy shook her head lightly. "You don't have to—"

"I want to," the woman said, softer. "Sophie's... she's happier. You see her. You don't rush her when she needs a minute, and she comes home talking about things I can tell mattered to her that day. Yesterday it was... pinecones, and the word 'whisper' and why it looks like it should have an 'h' sound everywhere." She laughed, then looked like she might cry. "It's small, but it's not small."

Emmy felt the words land where good words land — in the space inside that had room for them. "She's a thoughtful girl," she said. "She notices the details most people step over. That's a gift."

Sophie peered up, cheeks pink with the cold, the ghost of shyness retreating. "Mum, can I show Miss Trevelyn the picture I drew?"

"Of course," her mother said, finding the folded paper in the satchel and smoothing it against her palm. A pencil drawing of a feather, surprisingly delicate, lines layered with care. Emmy leaned in.

"It's beautiful," she said. "You caught the curve. And the little barbs — see how they're not all even? You noticed that."

Sophie's mouth made the smallest upward bow, pride almost — almost — allowed to be visible. "There was a feather by the hedge. I didn't take it. I just looked."

"That's the clever bit," Emmy said. "You looked properly."

They chatted a little longer — the history day next week ("We'll have artefacts in the hall. Ask Sophie to think of a question she'd like to ask."); the letter about library books due ("We'll find another she loves."). Then the stream at the gates thinned, and goodbyes were said. Sophie waved once, like a secret signal, and was gone, hand in her mother's, shoes scuffing the lane in a rhythm Emmy found she could have identified with her eyes closed.

The playground emptied in ripples. The last child was handed to a grandparent in a flat cap; the last buggy turned the corner; the last echo of laughter thinned into the ordinary village sound of a bus braking somewhere and a dog deciding to object to it.

Emmy stood by the gate a moment longer, the metal cool beneath her palm, and let the day settle. The sky had the palest wash of gold near the horizon, like light steeped through paper. Behind her, through the building's windows, a few classrooms still glowed: the late-markers, the after-school club, June's room with the paper planets that always seemed to be in a better orbit than anyone else's.

"Good shift?" June's voice floated from behind, accompanied by the squeak of the lost-and-found box being dragged back indoors.

"Quiet," Emmy said. "In the good way."

June hooked the box onto her hip and nudged the gate with her toe. "And you?" Emmy added. "Your soap opera?"

"Oh, the usual," June said. "A dramatic breakup between two best friends that lasted from 1:07 to 1:12. A rogue conker used as currency. A near mutiny over who gets the blue skipping rope tomorrow. Peace has been restored, treaties signed. For now."

They walked back toward the building together, their footsteps crisp on the tarmac. The corridor took them in with a warmer breath — the smell of paper and glue sticks and the faintest sweetness of the crumble that had perfumed lunchtime. They set the lost-and-found box by the office door, a colourful jumble of hats and a single glittery glove lying on top like a crown.

June touched Emmy's arm lightly. "I meant what I said, by the way. About good things that tap you on the shoulder. If he asks again… you're allowed to say yes again."

Emmy's smile was small but sure. "I know." She paused. "I did."

"I'm glad."

They parted at the fork in the corridor — June to chase a photocopier that never quite believed in settings, Emmy to her classroom to line up the pencils in jars and straighten the books in the corner, the small rituals that felt like putting a room to bed. On the whiteboard she wrote, in neat, looping script: Tomorrow: History Questions — bring one good one. She underlined good and smiled to herself, wondering how many would be about swords despite John's speech.

At the door she paused and looked back at the room: the chairs tucked in, the soft rug aligned, the stack of spelling books waiting for her later with a cup of tea. It seemed a simple thing, but it filled her — this order made for children to come into. She turned off the lights; the room exhaled into dusk.

Outside again, the last of the afternoon made a pale ribbon above the rooftops. Emmy locked the playground gate, checked it twice, and tucked the keys back into her coat pocket, her satchel finding its familiar place against her hip. She took the path along the low stone wall, where the hedge cut the wind and the small sounds of the village replaced the day's chorus: a bicycle bell far off; a shop door opening with its soft jangle; the murmured rise and fall of voices that had the same comfort as birds at evening.

She reached the street and paused, the scent of baking drifting from somewhere — cinnamon and something citrus. A cat lifted its head on a windowsill and blinked slowly, granting her the privilege of existing. Emmy smiled at it, the kind of smile one has for a stranger who has done nothing but be content in front of you.

Her phone buzzed in her pocket — a message from June: Forgot to say — your display on descriptive language got a gold star from Everly. He said "textbook" and then looked proud like he'd invented you. Pub Friday?

Emmy typed back: Yes to pub. And thank you. See you tomorrow!

She slid the phone away and set off toward the square, where the lamps would be flicking on by the time she reached Aubrey's. The day felt properly full — patched together by the small kindnesses and practicalities that made a life, and threaded through, quieter, by a sense of something unfurling she didn't need to name.

She let the not-naming be a comfort and walked on.

The lane from the school ran gently downhill, lined with plane trees just beginning to show their new green, the buds tight and glossy like thoughts not yet spoken. A light wind travelled along the terrace fronts, lifting the faint scent of laundry from somewhere — cotton and soap and the lemon tang of someone's cleaner. Cars ticked as they cooled, parents' voices drifted in soft exchanges about tea and homework, and a bike bell chimed twice in the distance as if clearing a path for the evening.

Emmy didn't hurry. The day still hummed quietly inside her — Sophie's careful feather; June's warm, teasing counsel; the contented order of a classroom put to bed. The village widened by degrees, terrace houses giving way to shopfronts; the pavement changed from smooth tarmac to the old, uneven flagstones that reminded you not to take your footing for granted. A pair of teenagers sat on the low wall outside the pharmacy sharing a paper bag of chips, steam rising into the cool; they nodded hello in that shy, adolescent way that's half greeting and half camouflage.

The square was softened by the hour — lamps not yet fully bright, but beginning to assert themselves against the thinning light. The bakery's front blinds were half down, the gold of the interior folded neatly away for morning. A cluster of daffodils in the planter by the noticeboard had survived another day of children's curious hands. The Crown's door stood open a few inches, letting out a ribbon of woodsmoke and the clink of glasses. And there, tucked a little back from the corner, Aubrey's window glowed with its dependable amber, the display as inviting as a hearth: spines turned out like confidences, a small chalkboard reading New Arrivals & Old Favourites in a hand steady enough to suggest practice.

She hesitated only a moment before crossing to the door. The bell above it gave its familiar tink — and, overlapping that small note, a deeper sound moved through the shop like breath: a measured tick... tock, firm as a heartbeat.

Emmy paused on the threshold, surprise blooming. "Is that...?"

Aubrey looked up from behind the counter. He was rearranging a stack of paperbacks in that way only bookshop owners can, half attention on the covers' faces, half on how the tower would keep its dignity if one impatient hand tugged from the middle. "Evening, Miss Trevelyn," he said, his smile creasing the soft lines around his eyes. "And yes. You're not imagining it."

She stepped in fully, letting the door hush closed behind her. The sound filled the space in an old, generous way, sitting beneath the room like the keel of a boat. She turned toward the back corner where the grandfather clock had stood for as long as she'd been coming to the shop — tall, dark wood, its face a little clouded, its brass hands elegant if forgotten. It had always been a gentle, silent presence, like an elderly relative asleep by the fire. Now its pendulum swung with purpose, and the seconds counted themselves aloud, composed and unhurried.

"It's working," she said, unable to keep the brightness out of her voice. "I've never heard it."

"Nor has anyone under forty," Aubrey said dryly, coming round the counter as if to greet the clock too. "It hasn't ticked properly in… well. Longer than I've had the lease. It was my father's before me and quiet even then. Decoration, mostly. Authority without function." He put a hand on the clock's flank, fond. "Until today."

"What happened?"

Aubrey's mouth twitched, the kind of smile that wasn't quite sure of itself yet. "Roman Vandrelle happened."

The name landed gently, like a coin on felt. Emmy looked from Aubrey to the clock and back again. "He fixed it?"

"He did," Aubrey said, and even in those two words there was baffled admiration. "Came in this morning to return a book — or perhaps to return silence to something that shouldn't have been silent, I'm not sure now — and asked if I minded him having a look. I minded very much, of course," he added, with a gesture that tried to be stern and failed. "It's an antique and there are people one pays handsomely to fiddle with such things. But he had a… I don't know… the manner of someone who has asked permission in shops like this before and been trusted. He had a little leather case." Aubrey made a shape in the air: narrow, old, the sort of object that suggests competence because it has been carried for years. "Said he wouldn't touch what he shouldn't."

"What did he do?"

"Talked to it," Aubrey said, surprising himself with the answer. "Not literally, I don't suppose. But he stood with it as if it had a temperament. Took the hood off, gentle as a hat. Looked at the plates and the anchor. Said something about the verge being worn and the bushings having had a hard life." He shook his head, still half enchanted. "Moved as if he knew exactly where long fingers had been before. As if he'd seen its kind younger."

Emmy felt her mouth curve. "And you let him?"

"I hovered," Aubrey admitted, spreading his hands. "Like a mother hen with a degree in catastrophising. But the way he handled it — as if time were not a thing to be hurried — you trust a person like that. He took the works out onto a cloth like a surgeon. Cleaned, adjusted. I fetched him tea because I had to do something with my hands." He glanced at the clock, pride and relief sharing space in his expression. "By one o'clock it was ticking. By two it was keeping time better than the till. At three it struck the hour and two ladies in the travel section jumped and then clapped."

As if to affirm the tale, the pendulum swung on, scything the seconds with patient grace. The shop's air seemed clearer for it — as if the sound pulled the dust motes into a more dignified drift.

Emmy stepped closer to the case. The face wasn't grand — no gilded moon, no painted arch — but it was honest and handsome, its numerals a little worn where fingers had set them right after power cuts in years past. The brass had the glow of something that had never been allowed to forget its worth.

"He didn't want paying," Aubrey said, as if he needed a witness to this part. "Wouldn't hear of it. Took his note back and said a thing that has been worrying and reassuring me in equal measure ever since."

"What did he say?"

"'It's better if it keeps time, isn't it?'" Aubrey mimicked lightly, though not unkindly. "As if clocks that don't tick are a moral failing. Then he packed his tools away and nodded once, like we'd both agreed time needed minding, and left."

Emmy let out a small breath of laughter. "That sounds like him."

"You know him, then?" Aubrey asked, tilting his head with the nosiness that is really just care wearing an apron.

"Only a little," she said carefully, not trusting the word "know" to hold without spilling. "We've talked."

"Hmm." Aubrey's eyes softened. "He's an odd one. Kind, in that old way that makes you behave better yourself. When he was peering in there," he nodded at the works behind the face, "he said something about the wheel-cut looking hand-finished and the plate pins being 'as they were when they left the bench.' I nearly asked him whose bench and when, but he

227

said it like a person says 'morning' — a fact rather than a story."

Emmy felt that sentence fix itself in her mind like a thumb-mark in soft wax. She didn't poke at it. "It's beautiful," she said, and meant the sound as much as the object.

Aubrey gave the case a quiet pat, as if you could pat time and have it purr. "I'll have to get used to the chime again. The quiet had become part of the shop without me noticing. But this… it feels like setting the bones."

"When will it strike?"

"In six minutes, if we're counting properly," he said, with a glance at his watch. "I know because I've checked three times. Come — I'll show you the new editions while we wait."

They moved through the aisles together, the shop a soft maze of paper and cloth and ink, the sort of scent that reminds you reading is as physical as it is imagined. Aubrey plucked a slim hardback from a shelf. "Local walks," he said, handing it to her. "A new print. Proper maps, not the sort that assume you're a crow. You strike me as someone who likes to know where the stile actually is."

"Very much," Emmy said, flipping it open. The pages lay obedient and clear; paths traced through hedged lanes, small ponds marked with ovals so neat you could hear the frogs already. "This is perfect."

He led her to another display. "And these — essays about British weather through the centuries. Surprisingly charming. Makes you feel less cross at drizzle if you can imagine a seventeenth-century vicar being cross about it first."

She laughed. "You're very good at selling books."

"I'm very good at knowing what people like and pretending the books chose them," Aubrey said. "It's a shop trick. And a kindness, when it works."

The clock cleared its throat — that's what it felt like — and then struck six, the first bell round and sure, filling the room's corners and then the street beyond with a sound that was at once home and theatre. The second chime followed with the same clean authority. Aubrey closed his eyes briefly, as if matching his own pulse to the measure.

"I'd forgotten," he said, opening them again with a small astonishment. "It makes everything else go about its business more sensibly."

Emmy listened until the final note settled. "I think you're right."

He wrapped her chosen book in brown paper with an ease that suggested he'd been doing it since before he could shave, tucked a small paper slip under the twine with the shop's name on it, and rang the till. "And if you see Mr Vandrelle," he added, as casually as a man can who rehearsed not sounding too impressed, "tell him I've ordered him not to fix anything else unless he lets me thank him with something other than tea."

"I'll tell him," Emmy said, aware that she probably wouldn't — not because she wanted to keep the moment for herself, but because some sentences felt better left in the air like pollen, free to land where they might. "Thank you, Aubrey."

"Always," he said, with theatre and sincerity in equal measure. "Take care in the cold. It pretends to be finished with us and then misbehaves at night."

She stepped out into early evening again, the bell chiming behind her, the deep tick… tock slipping out into the square like a low tide. The lamps had found their footing now, clarity gathering beneath them in circles; across the way, a man emerged from the barbers with his hair clipped close and his neck goose-prickled in the air, and a dog on a lead made a determined inspection of the base of the noticeboard as if the day's events had been posted there in scents.

Emmy tucked the wrapped book into her satchel, the paper's rasp a small pleasure. She found herself glancing toward the end of the street that led, eventually, to the long line of trees and something beyond them she would not name right now. It wasn't longing, exactly; more the feeling you get when a melody you recognise passes by a window. She turned the other way and headed for her stairs.

The stairwell to the flat above the shop collected the day's smells the way a pocket collects small coins: the sweetness of paper and ink from below, the faint damp of old plaster, someone's faint floral perfume lingering like a polite guest. Inside, she set the satchel on the chair by the window and put the kettle on with a clack that had, even now, the power to settle her. She loosened her hair from its pin, shook out the long black curls, and opened the window a fraction to let the evening in — cool, laced with the distant promise of rain that might not arrive.

While the water heated, she stood at the glass. People moved below with that particular end-of-day gait that isn't exactly hurry and isn't exactly leisure. In a first-floor window opposite, a woman drew her curtains and then opened them again, reconsidering the line of dusk. A pair of students in scarves walked past arguing cordially about whether a tomato was fruit or vegetable and what that meant ethically for pizza. Emmy smiled to herself.

The kettle clicked. She made tea in her favourite mug — the one with the chipped rim that turned out to be exactly where her lip wanted to go — and carried it to the window. For a moment she let her eyes defocus so the street became only shape and colour, the way a painter might test a composition. It had the right balance: light, movement, a quiet centre.

Her phone lay on the side table where she'd left it, screen nudging with a message from her father that was just a photograph of the dog in a ridiculous new bandana (Mum's doing. Help.). Emmy laughed and typed back a heart and he looks proud, admit it. She hesitated, then tapped the green call button next to Mum. The ring thrummed in her ear — once, twice — and then the familiar click.

"Darling!" Her mother's voice warmed the line like sunlight. "I was just saying we haven't heard your voice in a couple of days, only your father's daft photos."

"You love his daft photos," Emmy said, curling her feet under her on the chair.

"I do," her mum admitted cheerfully. "He thinks the dog is a poet and must be documented at all times. How are you, my love? How's the village?"

"Good," Emmy said, and found she meant it in the round, full way. "Busy in the best way. We had staff meeting this morning — we're having a history day next Friday. A man is bringing artefacts for the children."

"Ooh," her mother said, the ooh of someone who enjoys vicarious school days. "Will there be costumes? You know I live for a costume."

They talked about small things, which is to say they talked about everything that matters when you are far apart. Emmy's mother described the new woman at the supermarket who packed tomatoes with reverence and potatoes like she'd rather not. She reported that Mrs Kavanagh from the end house had fallen in love with a dance class on Tuesday evenings and now tried to recruit from the bus stop with all the zeal of a friendly cult. She said the neighbour's apple tree had finally been pruned and now looked "like a figure skater in a sensible cardigan."

"Made any friends yet I should be jealous of?" her mother added, playing it light.

"June," Emmy said promptly. "You'd like her. She left a life that didn't fit to make room for one that did. She's… brave in a way that looks ordinary from the outside."

"Ah," her mother said, with that note that says a person is seen.

They moved around the edges of the topic without naming it — as families do — until her mum, buoyed by warmth and mischief, dipped a toe in. "And are you… seeing anyone? Or thinking about seeing anyone? I must draft my nosiness for proper use."

Emmy's laugh was soft. "Mum."

"I know, I know," her mother said quickly. "I'm not pushing. You take your time. You take all the time. I'm only here to cheer from the sidelines and send biscuits."

"There… might be someone," Emmy said, and heard her own surprise in the way the sentence landed. "We've spoken. He's— different."

"Oh?" The single syllable did a lot of hopeful work.

"Old-fashioned," Emmy tried, aware of how little that said. "Careful. Kind in a way that feels like a steady place to stand. I don't know anything important about him yet. That's… odd to say out loud."

"You don't have to know important things fast," her mother said, firm and gentle at once. "You only have to feel whether you can breathe near them."

"I can," Emmy said, and it was a relief to admit it.

"Then that's enough for now," her mum said. "And if it becomes not enough, you'll know, and I'll arrive with a holdall and a very sharp opinion. Until then — I am happy for you, my love."

They drifted to other subjects — a recipe her mother was intent on perfecting ("The secret is patience and too much butter"), a half-made scarf that insisted on frogging itself at night, a television show Emmy pretended not to watch and her mother pretended not to enjoy. The call lengthened comfortably, then thinned in the agreeable way of calls that can end without anyone feeling short-changed.

"Sleep well," her mother said.

"I will," Emmy said. "Love you."

"Love you more," her mother returned, as ritual demanded, and the line clicked into the kind of silence that is not empty but stored.

Emmy sat for a moment after, phone warm in her palm, the tea tilting lukewarm toward cold. The room had gathered the blue of evening; outside, lamps had fully taken up their post. She stood, drew the curtains most of the way but left them a hand's width open — a habit she'd never been able to justify, only obey — and set her mug in the sink with a small, satisfied chime.

# Chapter 15

The following week had settled into the kind of rhythm that sneaks up on you and then, once noticed, makes you oddly proud. Monday had been a neat row of small wins — Ellis finally offering an answer in guided reading without being coaxed, the class deciding en masse that "whisper" did in fact deserve its silent h, and June managing to charm the photocopier into behaving for a full ten minutes. Tuesday brought rain so fine it felt like walking through breath; the children came in flushed and exuberant from PE, the hall smelling of rubber soles and damp hair, and Emmy showed them how commas could make a sentence breathe. On Wednesday she took her class to the hall to practise questions for History Day, and a boy who usually asked only about biscuits raised his hand to inquire, with great seriousness, whether old spoons "remembered the mouths they'd met." (Emmy had told him she suspected they remembered the hands more, and he'd nodded as if this satisfied a private theory.)

June had been her cheerful, slightly chaotic orbit through all of it — appearing in doorways with a handful of lost and found hats, calmly defusing a lunchtime standoff over whose turn it was to sit on the blue beanbag, slipping Emmy a note during staff briefing that read, Paper doilies acquired. Prepare your ruff. Aubrey had leaned out of his doorway on Wednesday to inform Emmy that the clock had kept perfect time for two days and he felt personally improved by it. Even Mr Everly had been unflappably pleased: "Your descriptive writing display is excellent, Miss Trevelyn. Quite textbook." (June had mouthed 'told you' from behind him.)

By the last bell on Thursday, the sky had settled into that pale, steady light that comes when the weather can't quite commit to cloud or sun. Emmy saw her class off at the gate — a chorus of bye Miss! that always made her feel a thin ribbon of tenderness pull from chest to fingertips — and gathered the room back into itself: straightening the books in the corner, lining up pencils with their points facing the same way, erasing the day's date from the whiteboard and writing tomorrow's with the neat loops she'd learned from her mother. She liked leaving a room ready for the next set of footsteps; it felt like an invitation to tomorrow.

She considered going straight home, briefly. The thought of her flat — the quiet, the kettle, the square through the window — was attractive in a soft, padded way. But the air outside the classroom door had the kind of brightness that asks to be walked in, and there was an itch in her legs that school corridors couldn't soothe. She sent June a message — Going for a small wander. Need to un-crinkle my brain. Pub tomorrow? — locked her classroom, signed herself off in the office, and stepped into the cool.

The route to the river was already becoming a habit: out of the school gates, past the small run of cottages where someone always seemed to be pruning roses regardless of season; along the lane that narrowed between two old brick walls furred with moss; across the little triangle of green with its tilted bench and varnished noticeboard. A blackbird hopped ahead of her for a while, as if escorting her to the edge of its jurisdiction, then shot into the hedge with a reprimanding chack at something only it could see.

A family crossed ahead of her — two parents, a toddler in a pushchair brandishing a stuffed rabbit by the ear — and Emmy caught the mother's eye, exchanged that small, tired, happy smile that means we're almost at tea-time, keep going. She liked these anonymous recognitions, the brief rhythms that made a place feel held.

The river path began after the pub car park, where a flat stretch of tarmac gave way to a narrow trod that ran along the top of the bank, hedged on one side and edged on the other with long grass that would, by high summer, be the colour of old gold. Today it was a greener promise, blades fat with moisture, beaded lightly from a passing shower. The river itself

238

wore its usual expression of mild surprise, as if still impressed it had been given room to move. Not grand — no cliffs, no thundering rush — just steady water slipping around reeds and past the flat stones where children came to launch leaf boats when they should have been on their way home.

Emmy's shoulders dropped half an inch with the first sight of it. It happened every time, this physical easing — as if the lines on the day's page were being loosened. The path, kept to the right of the water by a scatter of hawthorn and a few sentinel willows, was pleasantly uneven. Her shoes found their grip easily. A pair of ducks idled near the bank, industriously uninterested in anything but their own route, and the air held that particular river smell — leaf-rot and stone, a sweetness that wasn't sugar but something older.

She took her time. She passed the old stile with its smoothed top rail (so many hands, so many crossings), the sawn stump that gave away the tree that had once leaned just so over the bend, the little outcrop where the council had put a bench years ago and forgotten to varnish it since. A child's chalk drawing still faintly haunted the stone: a sun with exuberant rays, a stick figure holding a balloon, Mum written in a tidy, careful hand.

Two dog walkers approached from the far side, leads looped over their wrists. They nodded the way walkers do, a civility that needs no words. Emmy stepped aside on the grassy

239

verge to let a small pack of terriers pass, their little legs a determined blur. One paused to consider her shoe with sceptical interest, then thought better of it and trotted on, as if deciding she was not the sort to go around smelling of interesting things.

The river's slow bend opened into a small, shallow pool where the water widened and took a breath. On the near bank the grass was flattened in two or three places where people had sat, alone or in pairs, to watch or think or eat something wrapped in paper. Emmy had eaten an apple at lunchtime and half a sandwich — she'd been distracted marking spelling and then Sophie had wanted to show her something — and now she could feel the other half, wrapped in waxed paper in her satchel, a small promise she hadn't realised she'd kept.

She found her preferred spot on the bank, where the slope was gentle enough you didn't feel you'd tip in if you leaned the wrong way. She perched, satchel tucked between her ankles, and looked. Sometimes she looked without thinking anything, letting her eyes drift across the water as if it were music. Today, the week moved through her again in quiet images — the classroom light at mid-morning, June's scarf whipped sideways by the playground wind, Aubrey's pleased face at the chime. She took the sandwich out — cheese and tomato — and unwrapped it, the paper sighing. She bit and chewed and let the simple salt and sweetness clean her mouth of school coffee.

A hiss of movement, a drift of white on the bend, caught her eye. Then another. And then, in that way they have of materialising all at once like a spell spoken under breath, the family of swans appeared from the far curve and slid into the broad place in the river, regal without effort. Two adults — necks a long question mark smoothed into certainty — and three cygnets, still grey and fluffy around the edges, their down catching the light so they looked like smudges of cloud coming loose.

Emmy's breath did a small, involuntary thing, somewhere between delight and respect. Even from where she sat, she could see the adult pair's watchfulness — the slight angling of their bodies so the cygnets were always between them and the bank, the minimal, purposeful adjustments of webbed feet under the surface. The river carried them as if consulted.

She broke off the corner of her sandwich and crumbled it between her fingers, scattering a few pieces onto the water with a kind of childish hope she hadn't remembered having in a while. The current took them and the nearest adult swan turned its head, one bright eye — so dark it read as black — holding, calculating. It glided closer in three measured strokes, the wake folding the river into neat pleats. Up close, their grandeur was less theatrical and more engineering: the heft of the body under the sleek, the articulate hinge of the neck, the untroubled slide of it through cold water.

241

"Hello," Emmy said, too softly for anything but herself and perhaps the swan to hear. "I'm sorry I scared you before."

She tossed another small piece, then another; the cygnets, bolder than she expected, peeped forward and took them with quick, earnest nibbles, their bills still a softer colour, their movements a shade clumsier — practice for grace. The adults allowed it, watching her with that steady appraisal that swans have made their signature for centuries, as if to say we have survived because we do not hurry our judgements.

Emmy laughed, quietly. "Glad I am forgiven," she murmured.

A small crunch on the path behind and to the left made her turn. Footsteps approached — slow, a little uneven, a careful, companionable pace. Emmy looked up to see a woman in a pale blue coat and a knitted hat walked gently along the trod with a carer at her elbow. The woman's hair, where it escaped beneath the hat, was the soft white of magnolia petals; her face was that beautiful kind of lined that looks like a map of kindness. The carer, younger, wore a navy fleece with a logo Emmy recognised from the local nursing home, and good walking shoes. Their hands were not clasped, exactly, but they moved in the geometry of people who knew how to walk together without tugging.

"Mind if we pause here a moment?" the carer asked, her voice pitched politely, the way you speak to another walker who has claimed a view for a while.

"Of course," Emmy said, shifting a little to make the implicit space explicit. "They've picked the best spot to show off."

"They always do," the older woman said, her voice warm, vowels long and English in that very old way. She looked at the swans with an attention that felt like conversation. "There were two last year," she added, almost to herself. "One of the little ones disappeared in the flood and the other made it through. We worried, didn't we, Hazel?"

The carer — Hazel — nodded. "We did. And here they are again."

The older woman's eyes left the swans and found Emmy's with a courtesy that made Emmy straighten a little. "You're the teacher," she said, not as a question but as a pleasant deduction. "You live above the bookshop."

Emmy smiled. "Guilty on both counts."

"Ada," the woman said, touching her chest lightly. "Though I have been other names to other people." She extended a hand that was thin but steady, the web of veins on the back like an exquisite etching. "And this is Hazel. She keeps me honest."

Hazel dipped her head. "And dry, when possible. Ada is very good at finding the mud."

"I am," Ada agreed. "It's magnetic." Her gaze returned to the water. "I used to come down here with my brother when we were little. He'd try to convince the swans to be horses. They declined." She looked sideways at Emmy, conspiratorial. "We were not from horse money."

Emmy laughed. "No one is, until they are."

Ada's eyes sparkled. "Quite. We fed them crusts and were told off by Mrs Wilkes for encouraging bad behaviour. She said they'd follow us home and live in the washtub."

"I'd read that book," Hazel said, deadpan.

"So would I," Emmy said, breaking another corner from her sandwich and holding it out. "Would you like—?"

Ada took the piece between careful fingers and crumbled it to dust with the deliberation of someone who has learned the exact pressure of bread and age. "Thank you." She scattered it with a sweep, and a cygnet peeped, delighted, before realising boldness requires practice and hanging back until the adult approved.

"Don't fall in," Hazel murmured, a warning wrapped in affection.

"I'm not allowed to fall in on Thursdays," Ada said. "Fridays, perhaps. We'll see." She breathed in, a small, appreciative sound. "It smells the same, you know. The river. People change their soaps, but the river keeps its perfume."

That last word made Emmy think of her mother, of the way she would stand by the back door and identify seasons by the way they handled the air. "It does," she agreed. "It's nice to meet you properly, Ada. I think I've seen you in the square."

"Oh, I collect the square," Ada said. "I put it in my pocket and take it back to my chair." Her tone shifted just a fraction, not darker, but threaded with something older. "We had a power cut last winter. Do you remember? All candles and neighbours knocking on the door with flasks. They moved us from the home because they were worried and some... some gentleman came down and made sure the lane was clear. I thought he was a dream until Hazel confirmed him."

Hazel's mouth tilted. "He was real enough. Very useful in a crisis. Kept people calm. Tall fellow."

Ada looked at Emmy as if testing kindness with a spoon. "You have kind eyes," she said. "You won't laugh if I say something odd, will you?"

"No," Emmy said, softly. "Never."

Ada nodded, satisfied. "I thought he looked like a story I was told when I was a girl. About someone who walked the lanes and the river and... well." She glanced at the swans again, as if the water could hold back what it didn't need right now. "He had a way of being that made people breathe properly."

She smiled, quick, bright. "Perhaps I am sentimental. The swans disapprove."

"The swans disapprove of everything," Hazel said. "That's their job." She touched Ada's sleeve lightly. "Shall we head back before it chills?"

"In a minute," Ada said, and looked at Emmy again. Ada reached out as if to pat Emmy's hand, then thought better of leaning and settled for the air version, which somehow was as good. "It's nice to see new people who look like they intend to stay."

Emmy felt that land somewhere she hadn't known was ready to receive it. "I think I do," she said, and was surprised by how certain it sounded.

"Good," Ada said, and then, after another appreciative look at the swans — who had decided they were bored of bread and were ready to be bored of people — she allowed Hazel to guide her gently back onto the path. "Lovely to meet you, dear. Hazel, mind that root. It tripped me last time and we had words."

They moved on at their companionable pace, Ada talking about something to do with a neighbour's plum tree and Hazel listening the way good listeners do — with the whole face, not just the ears. Emmy watched them for a while, then looked back at the river, which had gone on doing what rivers do: carry, reflect, not hurry.

Her sandwich was nearly finished. She saved the last bite for herself and ate it on a long, slow chew, tasting the cool of the tomato and the way the cheese softened at the edges. The cygnets had drifted farther out, practising being distant, and the adult pair were content to let them pretend independence while staying close enough to remind it where home was. A breeze pulled a few strands of her hair loose; she tucked them behind her ear and closed her eyes, just for a breath, and let the sound of water file her thoughts back into their proper drawers.

When she stood, the bank held the faint print of her sitting weight like a polite memory. She brushed a crumb from her coat, folded the wax paper neatly into the satchel, and felt the pleasant heaviness in her legs that meant she'd walk a bit more before turning back. The path west would take her over the small wooden footbridge and along the field edge where the hedgerow thickened with elder; east would keep her close to the village, dipping back into familiar streets before the light went. She chose west, not out of rebellion, but because the day's long lines felt like they wanted the company of longer ones.

She took three steps, then paused and looked back. The swans had re-ordered themselves into a procession, the cygnets properly in the centre now, and for some reason this efficiency pleased her. She raised a hand in an instinctive wordless goodbye — to them, to Ada, to the first stretch of river — and then followed the path into the curve of evening.

# Chapter 16

Emmy left her flat earlier than usual, the village not quite awake but already promising itself it would be. The square held a pale, silvery light; shop blinds were half-raised like eyelids at half mast, and a milk crate sat by the café door with a note tucked under the topmost bottle. She liked the village in this first hour, when it felt like a secret she'd arrived early enough to hear.

She took the longer way to school, looping past the bakery on the corner. The window glass had fogged in soft ovals where heat met morning air, and the smell—warm bread, sugar, a trace of cinnamon—met her on the pavement like a greeting. She pushed inside.

"Morning, Miss Trevelyn," called Mrs Harcourt, cheeks pink from the ovens. "You're out with the larks. What can I tempt you with?"

"A small sourdough, please," Emmy said, unbuttoning her coat. "And… two buttered baps to take away." The day was History Day, and buttered baps at ten-thirty felt like sensible foresight.

"Excellent choices," Mrs Harcourt approved, already reaching for paper bags.

Two men in flat caps sat by the window with mugs of tea and the brisk intimacy of people who have shared the same morning table for twenty years. Their voices drifted under the clink of cups and the soft hiss from the kitchen.

"...told you they'd fence it off forever," one said. "Council loves a fence."

"Aye, and then some chap turns up and sorts it. Quiet as you like," the other replied. "Had the boards up and new ones down before I'd finished me tea. Rails too—solid work, not the decorative rubbish."

Emmy kept her gaze on the tray of iced buns, heat rising faintly onto her face from the glass. The first man snorted.

"Who was he, then?"

"Dunno," came the answer, a shrug audible in the word. "Tall. Dark hair. Didn't give a name. But he knew what he was doing. You can feel it under your boots again. Proper bridge, that."

Mrs Harcourt slid the sourdough into a bag and leaned in conspiratorially as she set it on the counter. "They mean the old footbridge by the mill stream," she said in a lower voice, smiling. "I went over it yesterday. Not a wobble in it. Whoever did it saved us a lot of form filling."

"Whoever did it," the nearer man added, raising his mug in a miniature toast to the air, "did it right."

Emmy paid and tucked the warm bags into her satchel. She didn't comment; the detail slotted itself into a quiet drawer in her mind, ready to be taken out later and turned over in better light. Outside, the morning had brightened by a shade. She crossed the square with the small, deliberate satisfaction of a person carrying still-warm bread.

* * *

The school gates were already propped open. A bunting of laminated history facts—Henry VIII's wives in smiling cartoon, a bay-windowed coaching inn from 1721—fluttered along the fence. In the office, Avril the office manager was half-buried in clipboards.

"Good morning, Emmy! Mr Harding from the county museum phoned; he's on his way with a van full of treasures. The hall is ours all morning." She lowered her voice. "And the caretaker has found extra crowd-control rope."

"Bliss," Emmy said. "I brought bribery." She lifted the paper bag of baps.

"You're a saint."

In the staffroom, June had spread a sheet of brown paper across the table and was drawing a sign with a black marker: PLEASE TOUCH WITH YOUR EYES.

"That'll work," Emmy said, setting the bread down.

"It'll work for exactly three minutes," June replied. "Then we'll pivot to 'Gentle hands or communal shame.'" She capped the pen and looked Emmy over with mock severity. "You look suspiciously content for this hour."

"Bread," Emmy said.

"Ah." June inhaled theatrically. "Holy sacrament."

Teachers drifted in, layering the room with steam and chatter. Mr Peterson balanced a stack of gym mats for the hall ("Children fall more when they're excited about pottery"), Miss Townsend attached name cards to lanyards, and Arun arrived last with a Tupperware of flapjacks and the air of a man who had negotiated with a toddler about socks.

At half eight, the van pulled up, and with it, Mr Thomas Harding of the county museum: late fifties, quick-eyed, wearing the sort of tweed that had seen honest rain. He shook hands as if he enjoyed the business of meeting people, then supervised the unload with the gentle command of a person who could coax a cat from a tree and have it thank him for the instruction.

The hall transformed. Long tables, draped with calico, became islands of another time. A case of coins glinted softly under a plexiglass cover—Edward VI to George V, a lineage of faces and mottoes. Hand-thrown pots sat in a shallow cradle of foam, their lips chipped where other hands had used them and put them down too hard. There were iron nails hand-forged and slightly crooked, a pewter spoon with its bowl reshaped by centuries of stirring, a clasp knife whose hinge creaked like an old door. A child-sized smock and a coarse linen cap hung from pegs, prop ghosts waiting for volunteers.

"Teachers first," Mr Harding insisted when the last table was set. "You must be armoured with answers you haven't had to invent."

They went round like a small, eager tour group. He encouraged them to touch—carefully, clean-handed—and to describe before naming.

"What do you notice?" he asked at each table, eyes dancing.

"That the spoon's thinner on one side," Emmy said, turning it gently in her fingers. "As if a right-hander always stirred the same way."

"Exactly," he said, delighted. "Our bodies leave history before our names do."

At ten, the first class arrived, wide-eyed and simultaneously reverent and wiggly. Emmy's Year Fours were third in the rota—enough time for her to settle jittery ones and coach questions, not so late their energy fell off a cliff. She knelt to eye level with Sophie.

"What will you ask?" she said quietly.

Sophie's brow furrowed in thought. "If the smock belonged to someone small, does the smallness stay in it?"

Emmy's mouth tugged into a smile. "That's a beautiful question."

The hall filled and emptied in tides. Children rotated through in tighter groups while the others sketched, wrote, or tried caps and smocks and the art of fastening a cloak without strangling oneself. The sound was a happy buzz layered over the occasional metallic clink. At the coin table, a boy declared he could smell the past ("It smells like pennies and old rain"), and Mr Harding looked as gratified as if he'd written a book and found it read.

Between classes, Emmy slipped to the door for a breath of corridor cool. Parents had begun to congregate at the gates for the mid-morning deliveries of forgotten lunchboxes and PE kits, their chatter rolling along the fence. She caught a fragment as two women passed the office, voices amused.

"…walked over the mill stream yesterday. I swear it's new under my feet."

"It is. Well—new old. Someone's fixed it. Annie says he did it in two days."

"He who?"

"No idea. A man, apparently. Tall. Quiet. You know how people are—no one knows and everyone knows."

They moved on, and Emmy stood there a beat too long, the corridor air cool on her face. Then she went back inside and helped a child decide whether his question about Tudor toilets should be expressed to a visiting professional or saved for fiction.

At break, the staffroom turned into a small encampment of satisfied adults. The baps disappeared. June divided the last one with judicial fairness and made a show of selecting the larger half for Emmy. Arun passed flapjacks and confided that his own class had tried to trade a modern fifty-pence piece for a Charles II farthing "to see if Mr Harding was paying attention." He was.

"How are you liking him?" June asked Emmy through a mouthful of buttered bread, chin tilted toward the hall.

"He's wonderful," Emmy said. "He listens like he's collecting each sentence to put in a drawer."

June nodded, satisfied. "Good for the children to see that adults can love things without owning them."

When Emmy's class finally took their turn in the hall, she felt that little swell of private pride that teaching sometimes lit in her; the kind you didn't show on your face, because it would make you insufferable, but kept in your chest so you could take it out on bad days and remember. Her pupils moved carefully, even the exuberant ones. Sophie hovered near the clothing rail and then, after a small inhale, reached to touch the linen with two fingers, the way one touches water to test its truth.

Mr Harding caught Emmy's eye across the coins and mouthed, Good class. Emmy felt herself grin like a child.

"Miss Trevelyn," said a voice at her elbow. It was John Everly, appearing with his clipboard at the precise moment his presence seemed most official and least intrusive. "Splendid work. Your questions wall is a triumph. Also—please remind your lot that the replica wax seals are not edible."

"Consider them un-edified," Emmy said. "We'll stick to flapjacks."

By noon the tables looked handsomely used and the children's sketch pages had filled with odd, beautiful details— nicks, dents, grain, wear. Emmy shepherded her class back to their room, hung up caps and cloaks, and worked with them to write two-sentence captions that required noticing and not guessing.

This spoon is thin on one side because someone always stirred the same way.

The smock smells like air when it has been outside.

She stood back and looked at the results and thought: yes. This is education.

At lunchtime, the hall did its other job, smelling now of gravy and mash. Mr Harding ate at the end of the long table with the staff, and the conversation slid easily from dates and dynasties to the ethics of handling objects to whether custard should be poured or dolloped. He told a short story about a farmer who had used a Roman roof tile as a doorstep for forty years because "it was the perfect shape," and June responded that most perfect things had likely been discovered by people who weren't looking for perfection at the time.

After, while the last plates were cleared and a classroom assistant chased a rogue carrot across the floor with a damp towel, Emmy walked back through the corridor toward the staffroom for ten minutes of quiet. She passed the main doors and saw, through glass, the square in its noon brightness. A couple with a pushchair crossed toward the post office; Aubrey stood in his doorway talking animatedly to Mr Lyle, hands making little arcs in the air; someone had pinned a new notice to the board.

For a beat, she pictured the bridge—old stones, the curve of its small arch, water pressing at its ankles—and the imagined sound of footsteps over it that didn't creak anymore. The thought of it pleased her far beyond utility. A small thing done well, without a name attached. The village would carry on across it as if it had always been so.

In the staffroom, June had abducted the last of the tea and was peering into the tin as if willing leaves to multiply. "We are rationing," she announced when Emmy came in. "Only those who can answer a history question may drink."

Emmy dropped into the chair opposite. "Ask me about spoons."

June laughed and slid the mug across anyway. "How's your heart?"

"Full," Emmy admitted. "Yours?"

"Same," June said, then softer, a smile playing at one corner of her mouth. "Also—I overheard something funny at the gates earlier. The old footbridge's been fixed."

Emmy lifted her mug but didn't drink at once. "So I heard."

June watched her, knowing when not to press. "This place is good at looking after itself," she said finally, as if that were all that needed saying.

Emmy nodded. Outside, the clock in the square struck one, each note a measured reassurance. The afternoon would be full again—tidy, purposeful—and then she would walk home past the bakery and the bookshop, and perhaps, without deciding to, she might take the lane that led toward the mill stream and the repaired bridge. Not to make a mystery of it. Only to walk the new-old sound of boards underfoot and see how good work sits in the body when you don't rush it.

She finished her tea, stood, and picked up her pile of exercise books. "Back to it," she said.

"Back to it," June echoed, and they parted with the ease of people who would find each other again in a corridor soon enough, carrying different mugs and the same good work.

The afternoon slid into its steady rhythm, the energy of the morning history sessions mellowing into the quiet hum of handwriting and end-of-day tidying. Emmy's pupils were bent over their final sketches and captions, their faces creased in concentration as they filled the last white spaces. A few tried to draw the smock in the exact proportions they remembered; others focused on close-ups of coins or the strange little clasp knife. Sophie sat with her tongue caught in the corner of her mouth, shading the spoon until its bowl looked worn thin enough to break.

When the bell for home time approached, Emmy had them stack their chairs and line up by the coat pegs. There was a cheerful flurry of voices and the muffled thud of lunchboxes being stuffed into bags. She shepherded them out, past the display of history-day work they'd hung in the corridor.

At the school gates, the parents were waiting in the soft gold of late afternoon light, the square just beyond busy with the everyday exchange of news and errands. A mother with a toddler waved; another crouched to zip her son into his jacket before he dashed toward the park. Emmy handed over Sophie to her dad, who thanked her and asked whether the "smock thing" had survived the onslaught.

"It did," Emmy said with a smile. "Still the same size, too."

A familiar voice called her name. Aubrey was walking by with a paper bag from the greengrocer's, pausing to chat as if the gates were the natural place to do so.

"Afternoon, Miss Trevelyn. How's the day been? All full of Kings and Queens?"

"Something like that," she said, shifting her satchel. "I heard the old footbridge is repaired."

Aubrey's brows lifted. "Aye. Went over it this morning. Solid as you like." He lowered his voice, leaning in slightly. "You'll laugh — the council didn't fix it. Some man did. Quiet sort. Just turned up and got on with it."

"Do you know who?" Emmy asked lightly.

"No idea. Didn't give a name. Just… worked. Mind you, it's been done properly. None of your quick-patch business." Aubrey looked faintly impressed, which for him was almost effusive. "Anyway, I'll let you get on — see you in the shop sometime."

She smiled and let the conversation end there, though the remark joined the others she'd overheard that day, each small detail about an unnamed man building its own shape in her thoughts.

The children's numbers thinned as the last few parents arrived, until only the playground supervisors remained, locking the gates behind them. Emmy waved to June across the yard and began the short walk toward the square.

Later, over a simple supper, she thought again of the bridge, and the voices in the bakery, and the way the village seemed to absorb these quiet acts without fuss. She didn't put a name to it — not yet — but the thought stayed with her all the same.

Emmy rinsed her plate in the small kitchen sink, the warm water steaming faintly in the cooler air. Outside, the lane was quiet now — only the occasional car passing, or the faint sound of footsteps heading toward the pub. She left the plate to dry on the rack and wandered into the living room, switching on the lamp by the sofa. Its soft amber light pooled across the arm of the chair and caught in the framed photograph on the side table — her parents at the coast, standing in front of the old lighthouse they loved to visit.

The picture made her smile without thinking, and before the smile could fade, she reached for her phone. It was later than she usually called, but she knew her mum would still be awake. The line rang twice before a familiar voice answered, warm and unmistakably hers.

"Emmeline Trevelyn — twice in one week, what have I done to deserve this?"

Emmy laughed and curled herself into the corner of the sofa. "I thought I'd better check in before you start thinking I've forgotten you."

"I wouldn't dare," her mum said. "How's my village girl?"

The question brought a small swell of warmth to Emmy's chest. "Good. Busy. We had a history day at school, so there's been… costumes, artefacts, curious questions from six-year-olds."

Her mum chuckled. "Sounds like your sort of chaos. Did you dress up?"

"Absolutely not. I left that to the experts," Emmy said, smiling at the memory of Sophie in the too-big smock. "Though I did have to mediate a tug-of-war over an old spoon."

They talked for a while about work, Emmy listening to her mum's updates on neighbours back home, a new café that had opened on the high street, the weather ("Wet, as always").

By the time they said goodnight, the warmth of the conversation lingered. Emmy set the phone down on the arm of the sofa and rubbed her thumb over the corner of the cushion absentmindedly. She had half a mind to stay in for the evening, curl up with a book, and let the day sink into her quietly — but she'd promised June she'd come out for a drink tonight, and she knew cancelling now would be more than just rude; it would be disappointing.

Pushing herself up, she padded into the bedroom and flicked on the light. The faint scent of her rose hand cream from earlier still hung in the air. She pulled open the wardrobe doors, scanning the hangers for something casual enough for the pub but still a little more than her work attire. Her fingers landed on a soft cream blouse with lace detailing at the cuffs and the navy skirt she liked — the one that fell just below her knees and moved easily when she walked.

She dressed quickly, then moved into the small bathroom. The mirror reflected her slightly flushed cheeks from the warmth of the flat. She touched up her makeup — a sweep of powder, a fresh coat of mascara, and the soft rose lipstick she kept for evenings. Her hair, still carrying a faint wave from the morning, she left loose, letting the curls frame her face naturally.

Back in the living room, she reached for her jacket from the peg by the door, pausing to glance out of the window. The street was hushed but for a couple of voices drifting up from further down the lane. She slipped her phone into her bag, checked she had her keys, and gave the flat one last glance — the lamplight still pooling in the corner, the framed photo of her parents steady on the side table.

She stepped out into the cool evening air, pulling the door shut behind her. The night smelled faintly of woodsmoke and damp stone, and the faint glow from the pub's sign two streets over promised warmth and company. Emmy set off toward it, her steps light and unhurried, ready to see June.

# Chapter 17

The morning sunlight was softer than it had been in months, spilling over the rooftops in a pale golden wash that caught the edges of every slate and chimney pot. The air still carried the faint bite of the night just passed, but beneath it there was something new — a green freshness that hinted at the weeks ahead.

Emmy lingered at her kitchen window, mug in hand, letting the breeze drift in. Her long black curls, with a mind of their own, were gathered loosely over one shoulder, catching the light like threads of silk.

She'd once been someone who welcomed mornings like this — who would lace up her trainers before breakfast and head out without overthinking it. Running had been her way of clearing the cobwebs, of reminding herself she had a place in the world. Since moving here, though, the habit had slipped. There was always a reason to wait — a busy school day, a late night, a reluctance to be spotted pounding down a lane like an intruder in someone else's life.

Today, though, felt different.

She set her empty mug down, padded into her bedroom, and pulled on running leggings and a light top. She tied her hair back into a ponytail, tucking away the strands she knew would still escape, and zipped up a thin jacket. She caught her reflection in the wardrobe mirror — cheeks a little fuller from a winter of comfort food, eyes alert despite the early hour.

Her trainers were waiting by the door, still faintly dusted with the city grit from months ago. She bent to tie them, the familiar pressure against her arches sparking a little memory of what it used to feel like to run before the world settled heavily on her shoulders.

When she opened the front door, the scent of damp grass, faint woodsmoke, and something floral drifting from a neighbour's garden met her all at once. She was just stepping over the threshold when she saw the letterbox flap sitting slightly open.

A sliver of thick cream envelope was poking through, its edges catching the light.

Curious, she pulled it free. The paper was soft beneath her fingers, her name — Emmeline Trevelyn — written in a steady, deliberate hand that belonged to someone who never dashed off anything.

She glanced up and down the lane.

Carefully, she broke the seal. Inside was a single folded card.

If you are free this afternoon, I would be honoured if you might join me. The orchard is particularly beautiful in the spring light. I believe you might enjoy it. — R

Her lips curved before she could stop them. There was something about the way he phrased things, the formality wrapped around an invitation, that made her chest feel warmer than the sunshine. She turned the card over — blank on the back — before slipping it back into the envelope.

She tucked it onto the little hall table and pulled her door shut. The run would still happen — she needed the movement — but now there was a hum in the background of her mind, a low and pleasant anticipation.

The lane was waking slowly as she jogged toward the green. Curtains twitched. Somewhere nearby, a kettle clicked off. The bakery's scent curled down the street — warm dough, sugar, something fruity — making her stomach protest her light breakfast.

She passed Mrs. Simmonds from the post office, who raised a hand in greeting, and a paper boy on his bicycle weaving lazily in the middle of the road. He looked up, startled, as Emmy passed; he called out a polite "Morning, Miss!" before wobbling off into the safety of the verge.

The village shrank behind her as the road dipped toward the fields. Hedgerows ran thick with new growth, white with blossom in some places, tangled with bramble and ivy in others. Emmy slowed near the stile at the river bend, breathing in the sight — water catching the sunlight in shards, the distant shape of a heron lifting into the air.

She found her rhythm again along the towpath, the steady slap of her trainers against packed earth and the faint rasp of her own breath filling her ears. A fisherman sat hunched at the bank, rod angled over the water, his eyes on the float. He didn't turn as she passed.

The run became less about exercise and more about noticing: the way a cluster of daffodils leaned toward the sun; the flash of a moorhen disappearing into reeds; the low hum of bees already at work in the wildflowers edging the path.

By the time she looped back toward the village, her pulse was steady, her hair clinging damply to her temples. She slowed to a walk near the green, letting herself cool down before stepping back into the neater edges of her street.

At home, she toed off her trainers at the door, hung her jacket on its hook, and leaned against the wall for a moment, catching sight again of the cream envelope on the hall table.

The card's words seemed to wait there, quietly patient.

This afternoon, she thought, and smiled.

She showered while the flat steamed, letting hot water beat the run out of her calves until they loosened. When she came out, she wrapped her hair in a towel and padded barefoot to the kitchen, the tiles cool under her feet. The cream envelope sat where she'd left it on the hall table, angled like it had been placed with ceremony. She picked it up again without meaning to and read the note once more. The words did nothing new and still managed to rearrange her insides.

She propped it against the little bowl where she kept keys and loose change and made coffee. The smell stitched the morning together—fresh, sure, familiar. She ate toast standing up by the sink and then, remembering herself, sat at the small table to finish it properly. Between sips she wrote a few lines in her notebook, not because she needed to but because it kept her hands steady:

Market—apples, thyme. Don't overthink clothes. It's only a walk. (It is not only a walk.)

She closed the cover and laughed quietly at herself.

The square was gathering pace by the time she went out. A delivery van idled near the grocer, and two teenagers wrestled a lopsided A-board into obedience outside the café. In Aubrey's window, a fresh display had appeared: a pyramid of paperbacks with green spines and a chalkboard that read Rivers, Lanes & Ways: Walks for People Who Like To Look.

Aubrey himself was on a step stool inside, adjusting the angle of a cover by a degree as if that were the difference between someone buying the book and leaving it behind. He spotted her and hopped down with surprising agility, opening the door before she even touched the handle.

"You look like someone who has already walked today," he said, approving, and the bell chimed behind her.

"I did," Emmy admitted. "Haven't in a while. It felt... right."

"Walking usually is," he said. "It's the closest thing to thinking with your feet." He waved vaguely toward the display. "I suspected you'd come in to argue with me about maps."

"I don't argue," she said. "I make observations."

"Which is arguing's polite cousin." He slid the new, smaller edition from under the counter without being asked. "Here. No squinting required."

She turned the pages. The paths she already knew were there, but tidier somehow, like someone had ironed them. "Perfect," she said. "Put it on my tab?"

"Your tab is a myth," Aubrey said, twinkling. "But yes." He wrapped the book in brown paper with practised ease, tucked a little slip with the shop name under the string, then leaned a hip against the counter. "Big plans today?"

Emmy hesitated, aware of how quickly news travelled in a place where everyone pretended it didn't. "A walk," she said, keeping her tone even. "This afternoon."

"Excellent." He nodded as if she'd said something sensible about pensions. "Take the left turn after the willow if

270

you're going toward the orchard. It's less muddy. And watch the stile; the top rail bites."

She almost asked him how he knew where she was headed, then decided everyone here knew where everyone was headed; it was part of the charm and half the danger. "Thanks," she said.

"Of course," he replied, then lowered his voice a touch. "And Emmy—if you are walking with someone who listens as well as he speaks, say the things you mean. It's terribly efficient."

She coloured, more at the kindness than the implication. "I'll… try."

Back outside, she cut across to the grocer for thyme and apples and, on impulse, a small jar of honey. Mr Lyle approved of all three items as if they were civic choices and sent her on her way with a paper bag and a reminder to rotate her apples so they wouldn't sulk. She passed the noticeboard—SPRING MARKET VOLUNTEERS tacked up at a fresh angle—and a woman in a moss-green coat who was coaxing a reluctant spaniel past the post office with promises the dog clearly did not believe.

By late morning, a bright, slanting light had taken the edges off the cool. Emmy cleaned her flat because it was the kind of nervous energy that could be disguised as productivity: she wiped the kitchen counters until they were certain of themselves, shook out the rug by the door where the river had dried into fine dust on her soles, and wrestled her hair into obedience with a little oil and a lot of persuasion. She tried on two blouses and rejected both. A third—a soft white with a small row of covered buttons and sleeves that skimmed her wrists—felt like a decision made by someone with sense. With her navy skirt and the boots that could handle a path without complaining, she looked like herself without looking like she'd tried to look like herself.

She checked the time more often than she needed to. Twelve-thirty. Twelve thirty-six. She told herself she wasn't counting; she was preparing. At one she ate a small lunch she could barely taste—tomato and mozzarella, bread torn into patient hunks—and then she washed the plate because leaving it felt like bad luck.

At half one, June texted. Pub later? I have news of an outrageous cat and a perfectly reasonable person he lives with.

Emmy typed: Maybe not tonight—walk this afternoon. Rain check?

A bubble, then: Walk in good company?

I think so, she sent, and the three dots appeared, disappeared, reappeared. Finally: Be yourself x.

She put the phone down and stood very still for a moment, letting the encouragement settle where it wanted to. Then she went to the mirror and re-checked nothing at all.

Because time will always move whether you watch it or not, the hands nudged round until the question of whether to leave became the fact of leaving. Emmy slipped the cream envelope into her satchel as if carrying the note with her would prevent some misunderstanding of place or purpose, then took her jacket from the peg and locked the door behind her.

The light outside had deepened into afternoon. The square wore its friendly face. A bicycle bell chimed; someone coaxed a pram up the curb with theatrical struggle and then laughed at themselves. Emmy crossed the street, the soles of her boots tapping a quiet pattern on the paving.

She took the route Aubrey had suggested without letting herself admit it: past the willow whose branches had outlived winter and were now an indecisive green, along a narrow trod that skirted the edge of a meadow, and through the hedgerow break where a stile did indeed threaten to bite if you placed your palm in the wrong place. She remembered at the last second and slid her hand along the smoother spot worn by generations of other hands. This pleased her more than it should have.

Out here the village thinned into fields and fences and the industry of small creatures. A pheasant startled from the verge with an affronted clatter. Further on, a wren worked earnestly at the low thorn, disappearing and reappearing like a stitch. Emmy slowed her pace to something between hurry and dawdle and then, unable to stand herself, laughed and let her feet choose something closer to steady.

She thought about conversation topics and immediately discarded them because nothing kills conversation like planning it. She thought about what the orchard would look like—blossom just on the turn, perhaps, white and pink froth against dark boughs—and whether he'd meant this very afternoon when he wrote this afternoon or a more elastic idea of it. She thought about how his handwriting made her want to find an ink pen and a quiet table and write letters to no one.

At the bend where the path met a copse, she stopped to listen. The light changed under the trees, dappled, moving; a blackbird ran an extravagant scale and then decided that was enough of that for now. Emmy leaned into a gate and watched the dust motes lift in a shaft of sun and tried not to look like a person rehearsing how to greet someone.

She reached the outer edge of Roman's land earlier than she meant to. The long, tree-lined drive held its own weather— half shadow, half whispers of last year's leaves—drawing the eye like a corridor. The orchard gate sat off to the right, modest, ironwork curled at the top where someone had decided simple things should also be lovely. She could see the orchard beyond in pieces: a branch hung with buds; a square of grass scattered with petal-fall; the suggestion of an old stone wall.

Emmy checked the time and discovered she was ten minutes early, which is to say, exactly herself. She stood just outside the gate and let her eyes move over what could be seen without peering. The hens were somewhere nearby—the faint impression of their commentary carried on the air—but she couldn't see them yet. A breeze lifted and the orchard answered it; leaves made that soft conversation they have when the weather is not threatening but wants to be included.

Bootsteps sounded on packed earth—measured, unhurried—and she turned before she could pretend she hadn't heard.

Roman came along the orchard path as if the path belonged to him and he belonged to it—a man precisely in his place. He wore a dark jacket open over an off-white shirt, the sleeves rolled once at the wrist like he'd been doing something practical and decent and stopped in the middle of doing it. His hair—black, with that slight wave at the ends that never quite behaved—caught the light and made it look like he'd borrowed a fraction of the afternoon. His eyes were the green she kept telling herself she might have exaggerated—until she saw them and knew she hadn't.

He paused a polite distance from the gate and inclined his head the way he always did, as if greeting were an art worth doing properly. "Miss Trevelyn," he said, then corrected himself with a small, apologetic smile. "Emmy."

She hoped the fact that her heart had chosen that moment to show off wasn't visible from the outside. "Roman," she said, and was glad her voice behaved.

"I'm grateful you could come," he said, and there was nothing in the sentence that tried to be more important than it was. "The orchard is... generous today."

She glanced past him at the sweep of trees. "It looks beautiful from here."

"It will allow us closer," he said, as if asking a favour of an old friend. He opened the gate and stood aside. "If you'll trust me not to let you trip over the world."

"I'll risk it," she said lightly, and stepped through. The iron was cool under her palm; the grass on the other side cushioned her footfall and made her step quieter than she expected. Roman closed the gate behind them with a click that sounded like punctuation rather than warning.

For a moment neither of them moved. A pair of hens materialised from the left, looking harried and highly opinionated, and stalked off with the important business of being hens. Somewhere toward the centre of the orchard, a bee climbed into a blossom and made a sound that was not quite a hum and not quite a purr but satisfied both definitions.

Roman gestured toward the trees, then tucked his hands loosely behind his back because he never seemed to know what to do with them when he wasn't picking something up or setting something down. "May I?" he asked, and when she nodded he started walking, slow enough that it counted as company rather than a tour.

They moved under boughs just beginning to commit to blossom, the white and faintest pink like breath caught on wood. The air smelled softly of green and a sweetness that hadn't decided what fruit it would become. Emmy felt her shoulders drop the half inch they always did in places that belonged to weather and time more than people.

"Do you remember the names?" she asked, tilting her head at the nearest tree, its trunk rough, its branches generous.

"I do." The answer held affection without fuss. He touched the bark with his fingertips the way a person touches a friend's sleeve. "This one is Blenheim Orange. That, Egremont Russet. And there—" he pointed, not lifting his hand too high—"Worcester Pearmain. Names that sound as if they were decided by people who liked walking home slowly."

Emmy smiled. "How do you keep them all in your head?"

"I look at them rather than past them," he said simply. "And they're very obliging if you pay attention."

They walked on. A low stone wall made a boundary most things respected but didn't fear. Beyond, she could see the line of the pond in the distance, flat as polished slate from here, waiting for any breeze with opinions. The hens commentary continued, punctuated by a self-important cluck like punctuation.

"When did you plant these?" she asked.

He considered. "Some of them were here before me," he said, and she knew it was one of his careful sentences. "Others… I added as the house asked for company. That pear there"—he slowed so they could look—"was a gift from a friend with very strong feelings about puddings."

She glanced up at him. "You collect friends by their desserts?"

"It works as well as any system," he said gravely, then: "What would yours be?"

She pretended to think. "Treacle tart. Or anything with lemon."

"I had a feeling about lemon." The smallest smile as if he'd earned a point no one else knew they were keeping score for. "I remember you noticing the tree by the walled garden the first time you were here."

She felt, absurdly, like she was being seen in a way that had nothing to do with scrutiny. "It's hard not to," she said. "It looks like a quiet sun."

"It does," he agreed, pleased with the description. "Would you like to see it again before the day pretends it isn't spring?"

"Yes."

They angled toward the walled garden, conversation finding its own pace between steps. Emmy asked about the hens; he described them as colleagues with mixed reliability and a tendency to unionise. She asked if he drew out here; he admitted he did, sometimes, when light and patience coincided. He asked about her class and listened like the right answer wasn't the tidy one but the true one. The gate to the walled garden gave with the gentle complaint of old hinges, and the lemon tree stood a few feet in, held against the wall where warmth collects.

It had put out new leaves that were glossy as if freshly varnished. A few tight buds showed white at the tips where they were testing how much of themselves the air would tolerate.

Emmy stood with her hands lightly clasped in front of her so she wouldn't put them where they didn't belong. "Your mother planted it," she said, not a question—he'd said as much before—but an offering of knowledge back to its source.

"She did," he said, looking at the tree as if it were both present and not. "She liked the idea of fruit that smelled like brightness."

"That's exactly how it smells," Emmy said, and leaned in until the waxy leaves brushed her cheek. The scent was sharp and clean and hopeful. "Thank you for inviting me," she added, turning slightly so she could say it to him without making it sound like a comment to the tree.

He met her gaze for half a beat longer than politeness demanded. "Thank you for coming," he said. The words had no decoration and didn't need any.

A breeze lifted and the garden answered with a busy rustle. Somewhere near the wall a robin considered them and decided they were harmless. Roman glanced toward the far side of the garden, thoughtful. "Would you like to sit a while?" he asked. "There's a little bench in the sun that pretends to be warmer than the day."

"I would," Emmy said. It came out soft, certain.

They walked together toward the light falling in a square against the brick, their shadows running ahead and overlapping before they reached the bench. He let her sit first and then took the far end, leaving enough space to be respectful and not so much that the space became the subject. For a time neither of them spoke. The silence wasn't empty. It held the hum of an early bee, the distant water, the occasional comment from a hen who had found—or lost—something of significance.

When he finally spoke, he did it as if he were putting a small, valuable thing on the table between them. "I'm not very practised at this," he said. "The… inviting. The being invited. I've discovered I'm better at fixing things than starting them."

Emmy found her own hands had folded in her lap, thumb circling the base of her ring finger. "I'm not very practised either," she said, honest enough that the words made the air feel clearer. "But I like walking. And I like sitting. And I like the bit where you don't have to fill every corner with talk."

He looked relieved and, for a second, younger. "So do I."

She let the quiet settle again, this time with the knowledge that it was a shared choice rather than an accident, and looked past him at the lemon leaves trembling minutely in a breeze that didn't make it to the bench. The afternoon was properly here now. The light had shifted into something rounder, more forgiving. The house, beyond the wall, kept its watch without interfering.

Emmy thought of the note in her satchel and of the sure, careful way the letters had made her name into something you addressed rather than used. She thought of the orchard gate and how he'd waited a few paces inside it instead of looming like a cliché on the other side. She thought—because sometimes you have to think the thing plainly so it doesn't haunt you—that this, right now, was exactly what she wanted: not declaration, not revelation, not a scene where everyone in a square turns to look; only the slow, unembarrassed building of something that might hold.

She turned back to him. "Show me the rest?" she asked.

His answering nod was small, pleased. "With pleasure," he said, standing, and offered his hand in that old-fashioned way of his—not to pull her up, exactly, but in acknowledgment that rising together is easier.

She took it. His palm was warm, steady; he let go once she'd found her footing, as if the moment were the thing and not the holding. They stepped back into the orchard light, leaving the bench to keep their place, and walked on.

Roman led her along a narrow flagstone path that stitched the orchard to the house, their steps soft on the moss that had crept up between the stones. As they turned the corner past a lilac bush just beginning to think about flowering, the kitchen door stood open to a short terrace of old brick. A small table waited there in a trapezoid of sun, set with an ease that suggested habit rather than performance: a linen cloth the colour of cream, two plain plates, forks and knives with narrow handles, a small vase holding a sprig of something green, and—most insistently—a loaf of bread cooling on a wooden board, steam lifting in pale threads from its slashed top.

The smell hit her first: warm, clean, and a little sweet, like a promise made tangible. Roman set his hand lightly to the back of a chair, an invitation rather than an instruction.

"Please," he said. "Sit. It won't offend me if you tear into the bread like a heathen. In truth, I'd be flattered."

Emmy laughed and slid into the chair. Up close, the loaf looked almost alive—crust crackled like tree bark, the score bloomed wide to show a tender crumb. Beside it, he had arranged other things with the same unshowy care: a shallow dish of pale butter with a white-handled knife resting across it; a wedge of a firm, nutty cheese; a little bowl of green olives; a plate of pears and apples that must have come from winter stores; a jar of honey the colour of late afternoon. In a jug, water caught the light and sent it back in wavering strokes across the linen.

He took the other chair with the kind of upright comfort that made you want to sit straighter yourself. "I hope you don't mind simple," he said. "I've learned that simple done properly covers a multitude of sins."

"It looks perfect," Emmy said, unable to keep her eyes from drifting back to the loaf. "Did you…?"

"Bake it?" His mouth tipped. "This morning. Before the orchard decided to be hospitable."

He picked up the bread knife and held it like a violinist might hold a bow—familiar, precise—and drew it through the crust in slow, even strokes. The blade whispered; the crust gave way; the crumb parted to show a pale, aerated interior that sighed very slightly as if relieved to be seen.

He slid the first slice onto her plate and the second onto his own, then rested the knife and pushed the butter nearer to the reach of both of them.

"Go on," he said, with the conspirator's softness of a man inviting a friend into mischief.

Emmy didn't need telling twice. She took a slice still warm enough to sting the fingers, spread butter that melted as it touched, and bit. The taste unfurled—nutty, tender, with that little sweetness that only comes from bread that has taken its time. She closed her eyes without meaning to and made a small sound that was not conversation but was certainly communication.

Roman looked pleased in a way that had nothing of pride and everything of relief. "Good," he said, a verdict that included her as judge and jury.

"Good is too small a word," she said when she could. "This is… You've ruined me for supermarket bread forever."

"That is a consequence I can live with," he replied, buttering his own slice with absentminded care. "I like the doing of it. The hands are occupied, and the house smells as if it has intentions."

They ate for a while with that contented quiet broken only by the sounds food likes to make: crust giving way, butter spreading, a knife tapping a plate. Bees worked in the border nearby with the steady industry of beings who have known their job so long they no longer need to boast. From the orchard, a hen offered an opinion and another answered, their conversation moving like an old couple's E-flat and B-flat through the trees.

Emmy drizzled honey onto her second slice and watched the thread of it catch sunlight on its way down. "This is indecent," she murmured, mouth curved.

"What's life for, otherwise?" Roman said, but something in the line of his mouth softened, as if it always surprised him to see pleasure arrive and sit down politely.

She reached for the apples next, choosing a small one that felt dense in the hand. "From here?" she asked.

"From a tree that does not like to be hurried," he said. "Stored in the cold room where it can keep its dignity." He watched her bite as if waiting for the apple to introduce itself properly. When it did—crisp, sweet, a little floral at the end— he nodded, satisfied on the apple's behalf.

They moved on to the cheese, to olives tasting of brine and sun, to pear slices arranged with the unconscious neatness of someone who cannot help but line edges up. Conversation ambled with them. She asked about the bread and he talked yeast and time, the way warmth helps but impatience never does. He mentioned proving in a bowl he favoured and she asked why that one, and he answered, "It's the right size for hope to rise without getting ahead of itself," as if that were obvious.

"And you?" he asked, after she'd described a school morning wherein a child had managed to combine a question about Roman numerals with a question about Roman soldiers "just to be efficient." "What is the difference between a good day and a merely survivable one?"

"Good days have room in them," she said, thinking as she spoke. "Space between things. Moments when the children surprise me with what they notice, or when one of them who never puts a hand up… puts a hand up. A merely survivable day is packed too full of the wrong kind of noise."

He considered that with the seriousness he gave to fruit trees and weather. "Noise is a tax we levy on ourselves," he said finally. "I have become an expert at avoiding penalties."

It was a neat line, but the way his gaze shifted just beyond her shoulder told her there was a longer paragraph behind it he had no intention of reading out. She did not press. The afternoon light had widened, finding its way onto the table so the water glass threw moving, watery prisms onto the linen and her wrist.

Roman rose with a small apology of a movement. "If you'll excuse me a moment," he said. "I promised you something sweet."

"I thought this was the something sweet," she teased, lifting her honeyed bread.

"This is the overture," he said, and vanished into the kitchen.

She watched the door as if the act of looking would keep the moment in its proper shape. Through the open gap she saw the cool interior—flagged floor, a wide old table with the scuffs of generations, a dresser lined with plain white crockery and, here and there, pieces with a thinner, older glaze that caught the light differently. The scent of lemon reached her first—clean, bright, warm in a way that wasn't heat but memory—and then he returned, carrying a shallow tray with both hands.

On it stood two delicate glasses, wide-bowled and footed, each filled with a pale, whipped cloud that held its shape like a well-made promise. The surface of each had been dusted with the finest curl of lemon zest so faint it was more suggestion than garnish.

He set one before her and one before himself and sat again, a small, almost private satisfaction in the set of his shoulders. "Syllabub," he said, the word soft in his mouth. "Properly made, not tamed. Lemon, a little sugar, cream, and something that makes it lift." A pause, the very slightest shadow of mischief. "The lemons are from the tree."

Her smile arrived before her reply. "Your mother's tree."

He inclined his head, not dismissing the sentiment that sat behind the phrase. "It has been generous this week." He lifted his own spoon, then waited for her to taste first, a courtesy that felt as old as the glassware.

Emmy dipped her spoon and felt the resistance give delicately. The first mouthful bloomed—cool cream carrying the brightness of lemon without harshness, a tiny bite underneath that made the whole thing less innocent and more alive. She blinked, surprised into stillness, then went back again just to make sure she hadn't imagined the rightness of it.

"I've never had anything like this," she said at last, speaking around a laugh. "It's… light and sharp and…" She searched for a word that wouldn't sound performative. "Happy."

Roman relaxed as if a muscle he'd forgotten tensing had let go. "Then it has done its work."

"How do you know this?" she asked, spoon lifted, glass sending a thin beam of light across her knuckles. "It feels like… an old recipe made by someone who knows what it's meant to be."

He toyed with the stem of his glass. "My mother made it," he said, and the sentence held so much in so few words that Emmy was careful with her silence. "And before her, someone else. Recipes are the only family trees some people keep. I have collected a few."

"I'd like to learn it," she said, then softened it because the wanting sounded like more than dessert. "Someday. If you'd show me."

"Gladly," he said, and something eased between them—a line tied with a little knot that could be held without tightening.

They ate slowly. Syllabub is not a dessert that wants to be hurried; it collapses if you insult it with haste. They gave it its dignity. When she set her spoon down finally, a faint ring of lemon scent still hovered in the air like a benediction. She looked at the glass, the last smear of cream marking the curve, and thought that if contentment had a texture, it might be this one.

Roman collected the plates and the little glasses with a discreet competence that never made her feel she should have jumped up to help. When he returned, he brought a pot of something steaming and two cups.

"Herbs," he said, pouring. "Lemon balm and mint. To persuade the afternoon to last."

They sat with the cups warming their hands. The tea tasted green and clean, like the idea of a garden rendered drinkable. A breeze came and went, making the linen breathe under her fingers. Beyond the gate, a duck arrowed across the far end of the pond and left a wavering V that the light filled obediently.

"Do you draw here?" she asked, remembering his earlier mention.

"When the light is polite," he said. "And when I can bear to be patient without fiddling." He hesitated. "I can show you, if you like."

"I would," she said, something quick sparking in her chest that she told herself was about paper and charcoal and not about being invited further in.

He led her along the terrace, down two shallow steps into the cool of the kitchen, and through into a room that had the workman's calm of a place made to be used: pine table marked with a constellation of tiny cuts and stains, a shelf of jars holding things that could be spoons or seeds or nails, a basket of folded linen, another of onions. On one wall, a row of sketches was tacked up without ceremony. Charcoal studies, mostly—leaves, a particular twist of branch, the curve of a hen's back as she settled, the lemon tree in three different winters and one summer, the pond, a gate latch.

Emmy stood in the doorway as if stepping further might obligate the drawings to explain themselves. "They're... careful," she said. "Not fussy. Like you've kept the bits that matter most and let the rest be implied."

He smiled a little, a dimple appearing in one cheek like a secret he sometimes forgot to tuck away. "That's the game I play with myself," he said. "What belongs. What is noise."

Her eyes fell on one page set a little apart: a study of a hand holding a coin—not posed but mid-turn, the thumb across the face, the wrist relaxed. The hand looked ordinary and kind. The coin, older than anything else in the room, wore the softened features of a monarch whose name Emmy could not have placed in that moment if asked. She didn't ask. She felt certain that some questions were bridges you only crossed when there was a reason to go to the other side.

Roman watched her looking without fidgeting or apology. "These are for me," he said. "I don't show them often. Not because they're precious, but because the world is very good at speaking over quiet things."

"I like quiet things," she said, and felt the truth of it all the way down.

He inclined his head as if they had agreed a principle that might be useful later. "Shall we walk again? The afternoon is being generous and I'd rather not offend it."

They went back out the kitchen door, leaving behind the cups breathing mint and lemon balm and the tray with its two little glasses empty but perfumed. The terrace warmed her ankles as they stepped into light. In the orchard the shadows had grown longer, pooling at the feet of trees like contented dogs. He took her a different way this time, skirting the edge of the pond where reeds stood like a well-behaved crowd and a single swan made mild adjustments as though in quiet conversation with the idea of its own reflection.

Roman kept to the pace she set without making a ceremony of it. Where a root humped the path, he said, "Mind that," in the tone of someone pointing out a step to a friend rather than shepherding. Where the path narrowed between a hawthorn and the low wall, he fell in behind her so the leaves wouldn't brush her face.

They looped past the walled garden again, the lemon tree catching the sun so that the new growth looked east-African bright against English brick. She reached out without thinking and brushed a fingertip along a leaf, then brought her hand to her face and smiled when the scent lifted just enough to be more than suggestion.

"I've never had dessert like that," she said, the thought arriving late and still important. "It was... It tasted like... beginnings."

Roman's answering smile was small and unguarded, the kind he might have offered a much younger version of himself for managing a difficult task. "Then I made it properly," he said. "It's meant for Tuesdays that try to be Mondays and for afternoons that choose not to be evenings. It forgives."

Emmy laughed. "Dessert that forgives. The world could use more of that."

They walked on with the kind of ease that felt earned rather than lucky. A robin dipped from a branch to the path in front of them and cocked its head in the brusque, businesslike way of robins who know their importance. From the stable block, the soft, dusty smell of old straw drifted out, joined by a faint metallic tang of oiled hinges. Somewhere a door clicked and then went quiet, the house exhaling again into its habitual secrecy.

They came to the little pier at the pond's edge. The rowing boat was tied up there, paint worn at the gunwale where hands had rubbed over time. Roman touched the rope as one might touch the shoulder of a good companion.

"Another day," he said. "When the air's kinder. She's a summer friend, not a spring one."

"I'd like that," Emmy said, and meant the whole sentence—the boat, the day, the suggestion of more days layered gently on top of this one.

They stood watching the slow ripple when a wind fingerprint crossed the pond. In the pattern it left, she saw the lemon syllabub's surface again, that faint tremble that spoke of delicacy held by confidence. The thought made her foolishly happy.

As the sun shifted, the orchard stepped very slightly toward evening. The air cooled by a degree. Somewhere at the margin of the grounds a gate clanged faintly, not urgent, only real. Roman looked toward the sound and then back to her, as if measuring whether to let the day continue its work or argue with it.

"I should walk you back to the gate," he said. It wasn't a dismissal; it was a continuation with good manners.

"I'll allow it," she said, smiling, and he matched it with one of his own.

On the way, they fell into talk that did not need to be clever to count: the stubbornness of nettles, the talent of swallows when they returned, whether rain remembered where it had already been. At the orchard gate he paused with his hand on the latch and turned to her with a seriousness that was not heavy.

"Thank you," he said. "For trusting me with your afternoon."

"You trusted me with your bread," she returned. "I think that makes us even."

"Hardly," he said, and there was a playful injury in it that made her want to stay longer and find out what would make them even by his measure. Instead, she only nodded, because some things were better left as thread pulled a little and not yet woven.

He opened the gate. On the village side the path looked wider than it had on the way in, as if it had been stretching quietly in anticipation of being used again. Emmy stepped through and turned back because it felt wrong not to.

"Thank you."

"You're very welcome," he said. The sunlight found his eyes and made them the green of hawthorn just before it explodes into leaf.

He did not lean to kiss her. He did not hover as if to a point. He only stood there, exactly himself, and let the quiet carry what it could. Emmy smiled—the kind that takes the place of touch when touch would be too loud—and then set her feet on the path home, the taste of lemon and cream lingering like a small, forgiving benediction at the back of her throat.

As she walked, she looked down at her hands as if they had been busy with something complicated and had managed it. Somewhere behind her, a hen offered a last remark on the day's proceedings, firm and satisfied. Ahead, the village waited in its afternoon manners. And under her ribs, something steady and unashamed took one small step forward and then— because it had finally learned how—held its ground.

# Chapter 18

By mid-morning, the village was restless with wind. The sky was a pale, unsettled blue, clouds moving faster than they should, and every so often a gust came in from the bay sharp enough to rattle loose shutters. The air wasn't cold exactly, but it had a certain edge to it, as though the day were in the middle of deciding what it meant to be.

Emmy had finished her marking earlier than expected. The thought of sitting in the quiet house with nothing but the hum of the fridge for company didn't appeal, so she'd pulled on her coat and scarf and set out with no plan other than to be out among the sounds of other people's days.

The wind tugged at her skirt and lifted strands of hair against her cheek. On the main street, the bakery's chairs clinked faintly against their tables, left out despite the weather. A few tourists braved the breeze, their jackets zipped high, while locals passed with their heads lowered in that practical, wind-defying way.

Instead of following the route she usually took toward the quay, Emmy let herself drift into one of the side streets — narrower, quieter, the kind where the upper floors of the houses leaned toward each other as though to share a word.

That was where she saw it.

The shop front wasn't flashy; it simply sat there, its paintwork fresh but unassuming, as though it had always been part of the street. The sign above the door read Morrow & Mend in gold paint that caught the shifting light, and beneath, in smaller lettering: Repairs & Curiosities.

She slowed, curiosity drawing her toward the front window. The glass had that faint ripple of age, making the display inside shimmer gently when she moved her head. A small table stood just behind the glass, arranged with a careful sort of disorder: a pair of porcelain candlesticks, a carved wooden box with a missing clasp, several framed botanical sketches browned at the edges.

At the centre, propped at a slight angle as if to best catch the light, was a walnut writing box. Its brass corners glowed warmly despite the dullness of age, and a fine vine inlay curled across its lid, so delicate it seemed almost like a shadow. Through the slight gap of its open lid, she could see pale velvet and the cloudy gleam of glass inkwells.

A sudden gust pressed at her back, making the glass rattle faintly in its frame. Without thinking too much about it, Emmy reached for the door. The bell above gave a soft, uncertain chime as she stepped inside.

The air was different here — cooler, still, scented with beeswax polish and lavender, with a faint underlying tang of old metal. The light fell in softened pools through lace curtains, touching the edges of shelves and the corners of framed prints.

Behind the counter stood a man in a neat wool waistcoat, spectacles low on his nose. He looked up from a ledger as she entered. His expression was polite but reserved, as though weighing whether she might be here for business or just to pass the time.

"Afternoon," he said, his voice low but clear.

"Hello," Emmy returned, lowering her own voice without meaning to. "I'm just looking."

"That's how most people begin," he replied mildly, closing the ledger.

She moved toward the central table, letting her fingers rest lightly on its polished edge. Up close, the writing set was even finer than it had looked from outside. The brass corners showed faint, soft scratches; the velvet inside had worn to a paler shade in the places most used.

The shopkeeper stepped around the counter, hands loose at his sides. "Georgian," he said, stopping just short of her. "Early, I'd say, judging by the shellac. Came in this morning."

He unlatched the lid and opened it with the unhurried care of someone who enjoyed the act. Inside, the two square inkwells sat neatly in their places, their shoulders clouded with age. A narrow compartment held a bone-handled penknife with a blade that had clearly been sharpened many times. In one corner rested a small, plain seal, a narrow carved band circling its middle.

"It's beautiful," Emmy murmured, leaning slightly closer.

"It is," he agreed. "And rare to find one so well kept. No ink rot in the wells, no corrosion in the fittings. Whoever owned it took real care."

She almost reached out, but stopped herself. "Is it for sale?"

"It was," he said with a small, regretful smile. "Sold an hour after it came in. A gentleman took it without haggling. Paid in full."

"Quick," she said.

"Some things find their next home faster than others." He closed the lid again, the hinges silent, and latched it with the same deliberate precision. "Still, I like to keep them out until they leave. Let them be seen a little before they vanish."

Emmy gave it one last look before moving on to the shelves. She took her time, letting her eyes pass over glass paperweights, old postcards written in a neat looping hand, and an assortment of pocket watches whose faces seemed to hold their own miniature moons. Nothing else caught her quite the way the writing set had.

When she finally stepped outside again, the wind was waiting for her — stronger now, pulling at her scarf and carrying with it the briny tang of the bay. The sunlight had thinned behind the faster-moving clouds, giving the air a restless brightness.

And there he was.

Roman stood a short distance from the shop, one shoulder to the ivy-covered wall, a brown-paper parcel tucked neatly under his arm. The wind teased at the edges of his coat, but he didn't move to stop it. His eyes found hers almost as soon as she saw him.

"You looked as though you'd been deciding whether to come back out at all," he said, a glint of humour at the edge of his voice.

"It's warmer in there," she answered, pulling her scarf tighter as another gust ran the length of the street.

"I imagine so." His gaze flicked briefly toward the shop window, then back to her. "Find anything?"

"There was a writing set," she said. "Walnut, brass corners, vine inlay. Georgian, apparently."

He nodded once, as though the description required no further clarification. "Did you buy it?"

"It was already sold. This morning—someone took it without hesitating."

"Some things don't wait around," he said, not looking at her when he said it.

They began to walk without needing to agree on a direction, heading downhill toward the quay. The smell of salt and tarred rope thickened with each step; gulls wheeled and cried above the moorings, and the masts made their small metallic music whenever a gust caught a halyard. The harbour wall wore its gloss of old spray; along the slipway a pair of oilskins flapped on hooks like wind-bothered flags.

"Do you go into that shop often?" she asked.

"Occasionally," he said. "It's a place where patience is rewarded. You never know what you'll find."

"That's what he said," she murmured, thinking of the careful way the shopkeeper had closed the lid. "He kept it out even though it was sold. 'Let it be seen a little before it vanishes.'"

"A decent philosophy," Roman said. "For objects. For days."

They paused where the quay broadened into a small apron of stone. Water shouldered the wall in slow breaths; a coil of hemp lay like a sleeping animal on the bollard. The wind arrived in tidy squalls, strong enough to lift the ends of her scarf and make her laugh under her breath at the suddenness of it.

"What about you?" she asked, nodding at the parcel under his arm. "Errand, or rescue?"

"A small sale," he said. "Freeing a corner of a room. That's a kind of rescue, I suppose."

"And do you feel lighter?"

"Lighter," he said. "And curious about the next life of a thing."

They let the silence settle, not the awkward kind but the sort that lets you hear what the place is saying — the slap of a wave against the steps, the pip of a sandpiper stitching along the waterline, the high, wire-like croon of wind at the mastheads. Above the harbour the clouds were knitting themselves into longer seams, sliding faster than the rest of the sky.

"Walk the harbour wall?" Roman asked, angling his head toward the short run that led out and then back, the view of the bay widening with each step.

She nodded. "If it doesn't blow us into the water."

"It won't. It only pretends at drama," he said, and they set off, keeping to the inside where the stone kept a hand on their shoulders.

As they walked, the village revealed itself in pieces: the slate roofs stacked like cards, the café awning snapping, a fisherman's dog watching the tide with professional suspicion. Roman adjusted his pace to hers without telegraphing it. Emmy noticed the small, inkish shadow at the tip of one of his fingers when the wind flicked the paper at his elbow; she told herself it could be any pen's fault and nothing more.

"You mentioned patience," she said. "With objects. Do you have it?"

"When it's asked for honestly," he said. "Less so when it's used as an excuse."

They reached the end of the wall and turned back, the wind now on their faces, cooler and carrying more salt. Out beyond the bay, a darker band of cloud had formed, low and slow-moving.

"Come up by the old mill?" he suggested. "The lane's a touch more sheltered. You can laugh at fewer things trying to take your hat."

"I'll allow my hat to remain unmocked," she said, smiling.

They left the harbour behind, turning into the narrower lane that wound between stone walls tufted with grass. The wind still reached them here, but in softened bursts. Ahead, the silhouette of the mill rose against the sky, its sails long gone but the stonework still steady. Somewhere beyond it lay the copse and the ponds he had mentioned once before — and, further still, the orchard where the wind moved differently through the leaves.

The day was still deciding what it wanted to be, but Emmy had the feeling it was leaning toward something.

They carried on along the narrowing lane, the harbour's bustle falling away behind them until only the wind and the soft scrape of their steps remained. Here, the air felt cleaner, the salt tang faint now, replaced by the cooler scent of moss and damp leaves. The wind, blustery by the water, came in quieter bursts, nudging her scarf and stirring loose strands of hair against her cheek. The lane climbed gently, never quite revealing what came next, turning just enough to keep the view in pieces.

Stone walls flanked them on either side, their tops furred with cushions of moss and little crowns of grass. In places the stones bulged outward after years of settling; in others, they tucked inward, a long, slow exhale made rock. Ferns had found the gaps and declared them permanent. Emmy let her fingers trail once along the lichen-silvered edge of a stone and felt the cool damp bite into her fingertips before she tucked her hand back into her coat sleeve.

A rook flapped up from somewhere ahead, scolding nothing in particular. The great body of the mill came into view around the next bend: sails long gone, but the tower still broad-shouldered and steady, as if the hill had grown it on purpose. The wooden door was shut, iron fittings browned and pitted; beside it, the shallow pond fretted under the breeze. Rings of ripples moved outward and met each other in brief, polite collisions; the reed heads whispered as if passing on gossip they didn't want to own. A dragonfly looped low over the surface and vanished into the rushes, its brief flash of brightness swallowed by the wind.

"It's always so still here," she said, slowing a little as her eyes took the place in.

Roman didn't stop, but his gaze lingered. "Still isn't the same as empty," he said. "Places remember the work that's been done. The walls keep it, even when the hands are gone."

It wasn't sentiment exactly. More a quiet acknowledgement, like the way you nod to someone who taught you something and then let you go. She thought of his house and of the rooms she hadn't yet seen, and wondered what those walls kept of him.

The lane tipped upward a little and the air changed again—less brine, more green. The orchard announced itself subtly at first, a low-fence scent of cold grass and a sweetness from apples past their best. Through a break in the right-hand wall she could see the first ranks of trees, their trunks rough and dark, the last leaves clinging like coins saved from spending.

Roman slowed and nodded toward the gap. "Step through there. Best view of the village, if you ask me."

She ducked through. The grass gave underfoot, damp but not unfriendly. The orchard rolled down the slope in rows not quite straight enough to be proud of themselves. From here, the village looked as if it had been arranged by a careful hand: rooftops overlapping, chimneys set at companionable angles, the harbour a pale crescent cupping darker water. Beyond it, the sky was busy with itself—clouds knitting long seams, sliding faster than the land could follow.

The wind here was a breath rather than a shove. It moved the branches lightly, made a soft sound in the hedges. Somewhere a gate clicked open and then back again, as if it had thought better of going out. The faint thread of woodsmoke found her and held for a moment before the wind decided it belonged elsewhere.

"You were right," she said, turning back toward the lane.

"I usually am," he replied. The corner of his mouth acknowledged the joke and then declined to linger on it.

She returned to the track, brushing a little moss from her sleeve. They walked without talking for a time, the kind of silence that didn't test the air for weakness. Emmy counted three strides and then stopped counting, letting the sounds of the place do the remembering for her: a twig snapping somewhere under a hedge, the dull thud of something wooden settled down in a yard, a gull's voice carried inland thin as wire.

"Do you miss the noise?" she asked after a while. "The harbour. People."

"I like it at the edges," he said. "Close enough to hear when the day is in a good mood. Far enough that it doesn't have to perform."

"That's how I feel about crowds," she said. "I like passing through them. I don't like being assigned to them."

He considered that, and she felt him consider it. "You like to stand where you can see the door," he said. "And where you can leave without anyone minding."

"You make that sound unfriendly."

"It's not," he said. "It's a preference for doorways."

"Do you collect those too?" she asked lightly. "Preferences."

"I keep a short list," he said. "It fits in a pocket."

"What's on it?"

He thought, and the thought made him a fraction softer, as if his attention warmed the thing it touched. "Good bread. Candles that don't smoke. A chair you don't have to explain. A window that shows you the weather honestly." He glanced at her. "And food that knows where it came from."

"That's cheating," she said. "You put three cooking-related things on a five-item list."

"Bread and candles are not strictly culinary."

"They go with meals," she said. "And windows go with eating if you care about weather."

"Then I've betrayed myself."

"Only a little."

They came to another break in the wall where a branch had dropped across the gap and stayed. Roman lifted it aside, and she noticed the inkish shadow at the tip of his index finger again, as if a fountain pen had argued and won. It could have

307

been anything—ink, oil, a bruised edge of something—but she filed it away because her mind collected such things when it cared.

"Do you write?" she asked, surprising herself with the question.

"I do," he said, not deflecting. "Lists. Letters when they're needed. Notes to future selves that I often ignore."

"On paper."

"Usually." He glanced down at his hand as if he were quietly amused by the evidence. "You?"

"Lesson plans. Which feel like writing until I look at them the next morning." She smiled. "And things for no one. Lists with more thoughts than errands. Sentences that don't go anywhere yet."

"That's respectable," he said. "Not everything has to arrive."

"Mr. Morrow said something like that," she offered. "Let a thing be seen before it vanishes."

"Mr. Morrow has patience," he said. "And a good eye for when to do nothing."

"I envy that," she said.

"Doing nothing is harder when you are kind," he said. "You mistake silence for neglect."

"And what do you mistake it for?"

"A tool," he said, as if the answer had been paid for already. "Sometimes the only one left."

They walked on until the orchard's rows thinned and the lane widened just enough to let two people pass without one of them becoming wall. The wind returned in a cleaner push; a cloud moved across the light and made the damp grass a darker green.

"Tomorrow evening, I'll be in the orangery," he said, as if the thought had been rehearsing and had chosen its cue.

She turned her head, and the wind took the moment to lift a curl across her cheek. "Doing what?"

"Cooking," he said simply. "Something from the garden that ought to be eaten fresh. And something sweet—the last of the lemons from my mother's tree."

"The last," she repeated. "That sounds ceremonial."

"It's practical," he said. "And a little ceremonial. You like lemons."

"I told you that once."

"Once is enough," he said. "I notice the things people like. It makes cooking for them easier."

"And the orangery?" she asked, though the image had already started to paint itself.

"It's warmer when the wind's up," he said. "And the light in the glass at dusk is worth seeing. We'll need candles—the wiring isn't to be trusted. I prefer it that way. Candles make people linger."

"And you want me to linger?" She let the tease sit at the edge of the question.

"I wouldn't invite you if I didn't."

The picture arrived fully: the orangery darkening, panes going from windows to mirrors, little flames steadying themselves after the first draft, a table that didn't ask to be admired, only used. The smell of soil worked but not exhausted. The clean brightness of a lemon lifted and then set down with care.

"What are you making?" she asked.

"Broad beans, if the pods hold until tomorrow. Olive oil, garlic. Bread, of course." He allowed the smallest pause. "And lemon tart—the kind that asks you to sit with it."

"That sounds dangerously close to romantic."

"Not dangerous," he said. "Just honest."

She looked at him closely then; he didn't look away, and he didn't look too long. It felt like being measured for a coat by someone who wanted it to fit and didn't especially care whether you admired the cut.

"I could bring something," she said. "Wine? Or a story, if you're collecting those as well."

"A story, if you like," he said. "Wine if it's not a burden. But neither is necessary. Just yourself."

She let that settle. The wind hushed long enough to make the quiet feel like a decision. "I'll come."

"I know," he said, and the certainty didn't push—it held.

They walked on, the lane levelling out for a stretch before dipping gently toward the village again. Through a gap in the hedge she caught the bay, darker now under the clouds sinking lower into themselves. A gull wrote a briefly illegible line across the sky and then left it to the wind to interpret. The orchard's smell thinned into a general green, then into the chalk and old salt of stone.

They rounded a bend where the wall sat lower and a bench had been made from a plank and two crates whose previous jobs had not involved hospitality. Roman glanced at it, then at her. "A minute?"

She sat, and he stayed standing a foot or two away rather than crowd the rest of the bench. From here, the orchard tilted away in soft terraces, the trees working their quiet language with the wind. The sky had shaved its blue thinner still; the band of brightness on the water had narrowed to a modest stripe.

"Tell me the start of the story," he said, not as a test but as a kindness, the way you ask a child what they've found so they can enjoy telling you.

She thought. "The start is that I moved here to be less tired," she said. "That worked for about a week. Then I learned that being tired is sometimes a habit pretending to be a place."

"And the middle?"

"The middle," she said, "is that I am learning where to stand so that the wind helps and doesn't merely rearrange my hair."

"And the end?"

"I don't know yet," she said. "But tomorrow there's lemon tart."

"That's a respectable end," he said. "Or a middle that behaves like one."

A woodpigeon sounded certain and was ignored by everything that knew better. Emmy stood, and the bench, relieved of duty, creaked less. Roman stepped back to let her take the path first. The wind changed its mind and pushed from a slightly new direction, curious rather than stern.

They walked until the lane widened again and the walls gave way to hedge. The first rooftops came up to meet them; the gulls were closer, the sound of a door being shut more human and less weather. The hour felt like a sleeve you could slip into if you didn't hurry.

"Will you pass Morrow & Mend again?" he asked, as if it didn't matter and might.

"Probably. I want to see what he puts in the empty space. Some people are brave about leaving a hole. Others can't bear it."

"He'll leave it," Roman said. "He's stubborn where patience is concerned."

"You say that like you know."

"I often sell through him," he said, not making a point of it. "He respects absences. Lets them do their work."

"What do you sell?" she asked, and then checked herself. "Sorry. That's nosy."

"It is," he said, pleased by the accuracy rather than offended by the question. "A print this time. A small thing that took a larger corner than it had earned. We'll see if it breathes better in another room."

They reached the place where the lane met the little street that tilted down to the quay. The wind funnelled through it and came at them briskly, lifting the ends of her scarf and making the sign over a door clack against its hook. Down the way, the shop's window blinked in the light as someone moved past; for a moment she could see the pale rectangle where the writing set had sat, the ghost of it more visible than glass.

They came to the small choice-point where she would angle left toward home and he would carry on along the upper path. He slowed as if the lane itself had asked for a moment of formality.

"Tomorrow evening?" he asked.

"Tomorrow evening," she echoed.

"Come to the side gate," he added, quieter, as if it were one of those small practicalities that keep larger things honest. "The front catches the wind."

"I'll find it," she said. "I have a map in my head already."

"Good," he said, which did not say, I hoped you would.

They paused there, and everything around them decided to be moderately noisy so that the quiet between them could feel deliberate: a van bumped a gear and changed its mind, a gull revised its opinion and told everyone, a door let itself be shut twice. The wind pressed and then took its hand away.

"Thank you for the walk," she said. "It felt longer than it was."

"That's how I count a good one," he said. He shifted the parcel under his arm as if it should have remembered to be lighter by now. "Tomorrow."

She let the smile begin where it wanted, in her eyes, and said, "Tomorrow."

He stepped back the small half-foot that turns space into permission, and she took the left-hand turn. The bell over Morrow & Mend chimed as someone else went in. Through the glass the blank shape of absence waited to be either honoured or disguised.

# Chapter 19

By the following evening, the wind had picked up where it left off the day before—still blustery, but with a sharper, more insistent edge, as though it were rehearsing for something larger. All day it had rattled gutters and bent the heads of the last flowers, slipping into classrooms through the smallest cracks and stirring papers just enough to be distracting.

Emmy had thought about Roman's invitation more than she meant to, the way a single sentence can take root and quietly grow while the rest of the day goes about its business. Between lessons—between the chatter and squeak of shoes and the bright, necessary noise of children—she found herself picturing the orangery he'd described: glass turning dusk into mirrors, candles standing like small certainties, the faint warmth of soil and citrus in the air.

Now, with the village settling into its evening, she fastened her coat, smoothed her scarf, and stepped out. Lamps flicked on behind curtains. A door caught the wind and shut twice. The harbour was hidden by the fall of the lane, but she could hear water in conversation with stone.

She took the side path he'd told her—between laurel and an old outbuilding whose wall had learned to lean without falling. Ivy brushed her sleeve as though to take attendance. The side gate appeared, old wood and honest latch, and when she lifted it the hinge offered a low, approving creak, the sound of something opened for the right reason.

Beyond, the orangery waited—light pooled against glass, flickering gently as though it had a heartbeat. Inside, the shapes of plants leaned toward the warmth, their leaves casting soft, moving shadows against the walls. She knocked once, and when the wind carried the sound away she knocked again.

The door tugged against a draft and then yielded. Roman stood with a dish towel over one shoulder, sleeves rolled, the lantern-warmth behind him waking the green in his eyes.

"You found it," he said, stepping back.

"It wanted to be found," she replied.

The air changed as soon as she stepped in. The glass hummed faintly under the wind's broad hand, but the room kept its own weather. The scent was layered—fresh earth, rosemary, the faint brightness of lemon drifting from the far corner where the familiar tree stood, its leaves shifting faintly in the draft.

Candles burned everywhere she looked: lined along brick shelves, gathered in brass holders on the long table, set into the niches of old plant stands. Their light caught on the panes, doubled itself in reflections, and softened the edges of everything it touched.

"It's beautiful in here," she said, turning slowly. The glass ceiling disappeared into shadow above, its framework crisscrossing like the lines of an old sketch. Terra-cotta pots filled with green shapes sat on every available surface, some kept in tidy rows, others allowed to spill wherever they pleased.

Roman set her coat over the back of a chair near the door. "I light more candles than is strictly necessary," he said, glancing toward the shelves, "but the wiring doesn't always behave, and I've learned not to argue with it."

"I'm glad it misbehaves," she said. "It suits the place."

"Rooms change with the light," he replied. "Some of them are at their best when the day's done."

She glanced toward him. "And this one?"

"This one prefers evenings," he said, a faint curve at the corner of his mouth.

He gestured toward the table but didn't sit yet, bringing over two glasses of wine instead. The glass was cool in her hand, the candlelight swimming faintly in the surface.

"You're not from here," he said, watching her over the rim of his own glass.

"No," she admitted. "I needed a fresh start."

His gaze held hers. "From what?"

She let her eyes rest on the nearest candle for a moment. "Something bad. Something that took longer than it should to get past. I thought I was fine for a while, but I wasn't—not really. When I was ready, I decided the best thing was to start again. Somewhere new. Somewhere that didn't know me or what I'd been through."

He didn't rush to respond. "A place without history," he said at last. "Those are harder to find than people think."

"This one came close enough," she said, her smile small but sure.

"And now?"

"Now it's mine. Not perfect, but mine. I like that I can walk down the street and not be tripping over ghosts."

Roman nodded, something unreadable in his expression. "I understand that more than you might think. It's why I move around so much."

"You've done this before?"

"Many times," he said. "I never expect to stay long. I keep my life light enough to carry."

"That sounds freeing," she said, though there was a thread of doubt in her tone.

"It can be," he replied. "It also means you never truly belong anywhere."

"And here? You've been here longer than you planned."

"Yes." His gaze drifted briefly toward the glass, where the wind pressed and the candles shivered in their reflections. "This land, this estate, it has been in my family for generations. I keep it on; it's still standing when I return. It lets me be here without asking for anything I can't give."

She tilted her head. "Do you think you'll leave?"

"I've learned never to promise I won't," he said. "But right now..." His eyes came back to hers. "Right now, I'm still here."

"Well," she said softly, "it would be a shame if you suddenly vanished. I'm getting used to your company."

That drew a warmer smile from him than she'd seen before—quick, but unguarded. "Getting used to my company? Dangerous territory."

"I'll risk it," she said, and the words settled between them with a tidy confidence that made the orangery seem to lean in and listen.

Roman's smile held for the length of a heartbeat. "Then I'll try not to make you regret it," he said, and crossed to the counter where a shallow pan was already warming in the candlelit penumbra.

Oil answered with a soft sizzle. He scattered in thin coins of garlic that shivered and turned pale around the edges, then added broad beans with an easy shake of the wrist. The scent lifted—green, clean, edged with warmth. Emmy let her eyes drift across the room—the leaves that shone along their ribs, the old brick low-wall running the length of the glass, the candles kept in their good behaviour by a steadying hand in the air. Outside, the wind considered the panes, pressed once, and withdrew without comment.

Roman brought a board of bread, the crust still whispering from the knife. "Best with the oil first," he said, nodding at a shallow dish where pepper bloomed dark in the middle like a small storm inside a calm sea.

She tore a piece, dipped, tasted. "You've gone straight for advantage."

"That would be cheating," he said, amused. "This is only hospitality."

"And you don't entertain much," she said, more statement than question.

"Almost never." He divided the beans between two plates and set one in front of her before sitting at the near corner—close enough for conversation, far enough for ease. "Most nights it's me, a book, and a lot of candles."

"Because the wiring 'doesn't behave.'" She lifted a brow.

His gaze flicked to her and back to the plate. "It gives people softer edges." After a beat: "You look good in it."

A pleasant, totally inconvenient warmth rose to her cheeks. "The candles will be insufferable now that they've been complimented."

"They already were," he said, smiling.

They began as meals ought: bread first—an agreement; beans next with some broiled salmon he had prepared earlier— the peppered oil as punctuation. Roman topped up her glass and then his own, turning the bottle with an absent care that made even that small act feel like part of the conversation.

"Why me?" she asked after a moment. "If you almost never ask anyone in."

"Because you notice things," he said, plainly, "you are different – intriguing".

They ate. The room warmed in the specific way places do when talk has been given space to take its coat off. The bottle, meanwhile, cooperated. When their glasses dipped below the halfway mark, Roman poured until each was honestly matched.

"Tell me something you don't usually tell others," Emmy paused, "Plainly."

He considered, tracing the rim of his glass with a thumb. "All right. I don't sleep well the first night in new rooms. I check the latch twice. I like knowing where the first-aid tin is, and I keep one lemon in the kitchen even when I'm down to ends. I move more than I should because leaving a place before I'm needed has always felt safer than being asked to stay."

She listened, glass loose in her hand. "That was very plain."

"You asked."

"And here?" she asked. "Do you still check the latch twice?"

"Tonight," he said, glancing toward the door with a wry tilt of his mouth, "probably three times."

"Because of the wind?"

"Because you're here."

The line landed without flourish and stayed. She didn't move to catch it; she didn't need to. "What about you?" he asked. "Something you don't usually say."

"I'm trying to be brave," she said. "Not in grand ways. Just... answering the door when it knocks. Saying yes to dinners that come with candles. Trusting that a new place can be mine, not just where I'm keeping my things." She tapped her glass lightly, almost self-mockery. "Finishing what's in front of me."

"That last one I can help with," he said, and nudged some more salmon closer.

They cleared the plate between them without haste. When there was only pepper-salted oil left, he slid the dish aside and brought the tart from the low shelf. No garnish. No apology. He cut two neat slices as if line and angle were small respects paid to what they were about to claim.

"Moment of truth," he said.

She took a forkful and closed her eyes because the lemon asked politely for the same attention she'd given to the beans. When she opened them, he wasn't staring, only waiting with that steadiness that felt like rescue from the worst kind of fuss.

"It's exactly itself," she said. "In a good way."

His breath let go as if a small task had been meant and completed. "Empty plate for applause?"

"Empty plate for applause," she agreed, and set about proving it.

They lingered—forks slow, conversation easy. The bottle surrendered the last of itself; she split it evenly, then gave him an extra finger for the work done, and he pushed a mouthful back into hers by moving his glass the smallest inch until equity returned.

"Do you ever miss more noise?" she asked, gesturing toward the quiet that had chosen them. "Crowded tables? Too many chairs? People talking over each other?"

"Sometimes," he said. "For an hour. Then I remember I like hearing a whole sentence as it was meant."

"You like sentences," she said. "You handle them carefully."

"I learned to after breaking a few."

She tipped her head. "On purpose?"

"By habit," he admitted. "Leaving can do that. You start finishing conversations in advance, as if you're helping. You're not."

"What about tonight?" she asked, voice steadier than she felt. "Are we finishing any conversations early?"

"No," he said, firm and soft at once. "Not this one."

He rose to gather plates, and she rose too on instinct. "Sit," he said, but without insistence.

"I'm better at standing next to people while tasks get done," she said, following him. "Besides, I can dry."

"Then dry," he conceded, and handed her a towel. They worked without choreography, and somehow every hand found the right thing: her catching a glass as he set it down, him sliding the board toward her before she asked. Their fingers touched once over a fork—nothing dramatic, only the particular kind of contact that lives a few beats longer than physics requires. Neither of them commented; both of them noticed.

He set the last plate into the rack and turned the tap. Steam lifted and wrote a brief private sentence against the pane. When it cleared, their reflections resolved in the glass— candle-soft, companioned.

"How's your brave going?" he asked lightly, passing her a square of linen she didn't need.

She smiled. "Better than average."

"On a scale?"

"On a scale. Today started at seven. You've brought it up to an eight-and-a-half."

"I'll aim for nine next time," he said.

"'Next time' sounds like optimism," she said, folding the towel.

"It's a plan," he said. "I like plans that can be eaten."

"That's a narrow category."

"It's the best one."

They returned to the table without quite deciding to. The candles had been doing their mathematics; their scale had tipped toward the hour that invites honest talk and makes bravado look slightly overdressed. The wind came in long bands now, pressing and letting go, pressing and letting go, like an animal deciding whether to sit. Roman reached for the bottle, confirmed it was empty, and considered the evidence.

"We appear to have told the right amount of truth," he said.

"How can you tell?"

"The wine agreed to run out exactly here," he said, and that was absurd and felt true.

Emmy traced a fingertip around a circle of wax on the table, then looked up. "Can I ask something nosy?"

"You've earned one."

"Earlier you said you invite almost no one in. If I'd said no tonight—if I'd decided I wasn't ready—would you have asked again?"

"I would have waited," he said, simple as the knife beside the board. "Then I'd have asked once more. After that I'd have let you ask, if you wanted to."

She weighed the shape of that. "Thank you."

"For what?"

"For telling me the part where you stop," she said. "It matters to know the edge of a person's insistence."

"I have fewer edges than rules," he said. "But the ones I keep, I keep clean."

Her smile said she'd catalogued that for later. "And your rules?"

"Feed people. Don't talk over them. Let the room look its best. Step wide at the broken paving even if you've mended it three times already."

"Practical poetry," she teased.

"You asked for fewer riddles," he reminded her.

She leaned an elbow on the table, chin briefly propped in her hand. "Do you like me?" The words came out lighter than they had felt in the turn, like a coin tapped on a counter to prove it's real.

"Yes," he said, with an ease that made her breath change. "I like talking with you. I like the way you look around a place before you sit in it. I like that you tell the truth without turning it into a performance. And I like—" he paused, not for drama, only to be accurate—"that it feels easy to make food for you."

The air between them did a small, serious thing that neither of them tried to name. She didn't look away. "I like you too," she said. "You don't make me feel watched. You make me feel... seen." She laughed softly at herself. "Which is a sentence that would make me roll my eyes if I weren't the one saying it."

"It's a good sentence," he said. "You should keep it."

They sat in the gentle absurdity of having said something simple and survived it. Outside, the wind ran its hand along the glass as if testing for loose screws. The orangery held. A candle near the door guttered once; Roman leaned to turn it slightly, and the flame steadied—small, obedient, bright.

She stood first, partly because the room had begun to fold into that shape it takes when people should be walked to the door, partly because standing allowed her to breathe without counting. He took her coat from the chair and held it without comment; she slid into it and smoothed the cuff, suddenly mindful of sleeves and hems as if the evening had tuned every ordinary thing.

At the door, the glass returned them in double—their candle versions and their wind-outline versions, both true.

Roman braced the panel against the push of weather and looked past her briefly to where the path turned.

"Step wide by the laurel," he said. "It lies."

"I remember," she said, and then, quieter, "Thank you for tonight."

"Thank you for coming," he said. "And for staying long enough for the bottle to be honest."

He opened the door. Cold air introduced itself and got over the pleasantries quickly. They walked together to the side gate. The hinge gave its low, approving note, as if keeping its own guestbook.

"Before you go," he said, stopping there, "one more plain thing."

She met his eyes.

"I don't entertain much because I don't want the house to learn the wrong people," he said. "It's not a grand principle— just a way of keeping it kind to be here. You make it kinder."

She couldn't think of anything clever, so she didn't try. "I'm glad," she said. "And for what it's worth, you've made this place feel kinder to me, too."

He nodded, a small motion that looked like agreement with something much larger. "Again," he said—no question in it, only the right-sized promise.

"Again," she returned, and the word fit.

# Chapter 20

By morning the wind had moved from rehearsal to performance. It came off the bay in long, muscular bands that found every loose slate and muttered at every hinge, scraping at the edges of the day as though trying them on for size. The sky had the look of something layered wrong—grey on grey, with a pale seam where the light kept trying to get a word in.

Emmy woke twice before her alarm intervened, the old building speaking in its weather-voice—the chime of the shop sign below, a faint knock from somewhere under the eaves, the steady hiss of air along the sash windows. She lay still for a moment, letting last night arrange itself in her mind: the quiet luxury of the orangery, the lemon-scented air, the easy, gentle warmth of conversation, and the word again settling somewhere she could reach it.

From her window she could see the lane rearranging itself: a stray flyer tumbling end over end; a man fastening down a stack of crates with a tarpaulin, the straps flapping like impatient ribbons; a neighbour pressing on a bin lid with a tap that said stay put. The harbour was hidden beyond the drop of the street, but she could hear it anyway—water shouldering stone, the rope-voices of halyards talking to their masts. For no particular reason, she pictured Roman checking the latch on his side gate twice, as if the second time were a matter of courtesy.

At school, the wind intruded everywhere—through the old frames, under the fire door, along the spine of the corridor where it could make its presence felt. The children tilted toward the windows at each sudden gust, then back again as if they'd been trained in some quiet art of weather manners. Emmy kept the morning practical and steady: fractions that refused to misbehave, a map exercise that kept hands busy, a story that could be paused wherever the wind demanded.

By midday, the headmaster appeared in the doorway with his coat still buttoned and his tone already decided. "We'll close early," he announced. "The forecast's worsening— parents will want to collect while the lanes are passable."

The afternoon dissolved into small, sensible departures— boots clattering on the steps, coats tugged close, children leaning into the wind on their way to waiting cars. Emmy tidied the classroom into a version of itself that could be left overnight: pens corralled, paper weighted, windows latched and then latched again. She left a small chalk note for the morning on the corner of the board (Page 43. Bring patience.) before switching off the lights.

The streets were already bracing for what was coming. Two men carried a length of timber between them without needing to speak. The café had drawn its sign inside. A gull crouched on the lamppost as if reconsidering its career.

By the time she climbed the narrow outside stairs to her flat above the bookshop, the wind was funnelling hard along the side of the building. The shop sign swung in short, aggravated arcs. She pushed inside, set her bag down, and had just started filling the kettle when a knock came—firm and deliberate, with a rhythm that said this is not the wind pretending to be a guest.

Roman stood there, collar turned up, hair unsettled by the gusts. In one hand he held a cloth-wrapped loaf, in the other a bottle of milk.

"I thought you might be short on supplies," he said, stepping back a little so she could take them without fighting the wind. "Bread's mine—made this morning. Milk's from the shop before they decided they'd had enough of the weather."

The bread was still warm through the cloth. She glanced at the loaf before meeting his eyes. "Thank you."

"There's a weather warning in place," he told her. "It'll get worse before it gets better. I'll check on you later, if that's all right."

"It's more than all right," she said, meaning it.

For a moment his gaze stayed with hers, as if to be sure the arrangement was understood, then he gave a short nod. "Keep your windows stubborn," he said.

"And you keep your latches honest," she replied.

The wind took him down the steps and along the lane before she could think of anything else to say. She shut the door, set the bread and milk on the counter, and stood there a moment listening to the flat find its own weather again.

The storm had been building all day, carrying itself along the rooftops like an uninvited guest. By nightfall it had claimed the street entirely, the wind sweeping rain in fierce, diagonal sheets. The streetlamp outside Emmy's flat above the bookshop swayed faintly, casting its pale-yellow light over cobbles slick with running water. Roof tiles clattered somewhere out of sight, followed by the sharp snap of a branch giving way.

Emmy sat with a book open in her lap, though her eyes hadn't settled on the page in some time. Candlelight softened the small, mismatched furnishings of the flat, the scent of the bread Roman had given her earlier still lingering in the warm air. She glanced at it once — still wrapped neatly on the counter — but left it untouched.

The sudden knock at her front door startled her enough to make her sit up straighter. She rose and crossed the room, the sound of rain intensifying as she unlatched the door.

June stood there, rain dripping from her hood, cheeks pink from the cold. "Emmy, sorry to drop in like this, but the nursing home's in trouble. A branch has smashed through one of the lounge windows. They've moved most of the residents, but they're short-staffed — some can't make it through in this weather. Can you come help?"

"Of course," Emmy said without hesitation, stepping back. "Come in a moment — you're soaked."

June ducked inside, lowering her hood and brushing rain from her sleeves. "It's getting worse out there. They need all hands."

Emmy was already pulling her charcoal wool coat from the hook, fastening it tight at the collar. From the back of the door, she took her satin headscarf, shook it out, and tied it snugly under her chin to protect her curls from the rain. Gloves on, scarf tucked in, she grabbed her torch from the windowsill.

"All right," she said. "Let's go."

They stepped into the storm together. The wind pressed hard against them, carrying bursts of icy rain that stung Emmy's cheeks. The cobbles were slick beneath their boots, water streaming in narrow, urgent rivers toward the drains. A branch in the churchyard overhead thrashed violently, spraying them with cold droplets; another limb had already split and lay sprawled across the road, its bark slick under the swaying streetlamp. Further along, shards of slate from a nearby roof glittered wetly where they'd fallen.

By the time they reached the nursing home, both women's coats were damp at the seams and the air was thick with the smell of wet stone and salt from the sea. The automatic doors opened into a wave of warmth, tea, and disinfectant.

Inside, the place was alive with movement. Staff hurried through the halls, carrying blankets and armfuls of towels. A few residents had been brought into the main corridor, bundled in layers, their eyes following every passerby. The lighting had that slightly dimmed quality of a building running on a backup system — steady enough, but with a faint buzz and hum behind it.

A brisk voice called from halfway down the corridor. "June — over here!"

Annie, the nursing home's deputy manager, strode toward them, her short silver-streaked hair flattened by the damp, a clipboard under one arm. She was in her fifties, with quick, assessing eyes that seemed to take in every detail at once. Even in the storm's chaos, her tone was calm but edged with urgency, the voice of someone who'd worked through enough emergencies to know that panic never helped.

334

After quick introductions, Annie explained that the East lounge window has been destroyed and gestured towards the side corridor. "We've got a tarpaulin over it, but the wind's still pushing through. I need you," she nodded to June, "in the back lounge with the residents from that wing. Emmy, you're with me for now."

The dining room had been turned into a temporary refuge for residents from the damaged lounge. Candles flickered in jars along the tables in case the power failed, their light trembling over worried faces. Emmy began helping to adjust blankets and pour tea, speaking softly to those unsettled by the noise of the storm.

From the corner of her eye, she saw movement in the side lounge through an open doorway — a jagged gap in the glass where the branch had broken through, rain still needling its way in. Two figures worked at securing a heavy tarpaulin over the frame. It took her a moment to recognise one of them as Roman, his hair damp, sleeves rolled to the elbow. He moved with precise, unhurried confidence, holding the tarp in place as another man tied it off. The candlelight caught on the damp curve of his jaw as he glanced outside to judge the wind.

A loud crack startled the room — not thunder, but something nearer. Emmy turned to see a window latch in the dining room give way under the strain of the wind, letting in a sudden spatter of rain. She grabbed a towel from a nearby chair and pressed it against the gap until Annie appeared at her shoulder with a strip of strong tape.

"Good — hold it there," Annie said, her fingers quick and sure as she sealed the latch. "That should keep it till morning."

Minutes later, another gust made the tarpaulin in the side lounge snap like a sail. Emmy glimpsed Roman leaning his weight against it, securing the corner while a younger staff member retied the rope with clumsy urgency.

The building seemed to react in waves — as soon as one problem was managed, another appeared. Annie directed them to the east corridor, where rainwater was creeping steadily in under the garden door. Towels had been propped against the threshold, but the wind kept pushing the water further. Emmy and two carers moved residents slowly, wrapping them tightly in extra blankets as they wheeled chairs toward the back lounge.

Halfway through the move, a loud bang echoed down the hall — one of the fire doors had blown open. Emmy felt the cold rush of air whip through the corridor. Roman was there almost instantly, bracing the door and pulling it shut against the wind before helping the nearest resident to safety.

As they passed the side lounge again, Emmy caught sight of him speaking to a silver-haired woman in the corner. He crouched slightly to meet her gaze, his voice low, and she looked at him with an expression so intent it seemed to hold the space between them still. Whatever they were saying was lost in the background noise, but Emmy felt a flicker of something she couldn't name before she moved on.

Over the next hour, the storm showed no signs of letting up. Water began dripping steadily from a join in the ceiling of the small reading room, and a pair of staff hurried to set a bucket beneath it. The tarpaulin needed checking twice more when the wind threatened to lift it. Emmy fetched more blankets from the laundry, helped calm a resident convinced the noise outside was "the roof coming down," and coaxed another into accepting a hot drink when she insisted she wasn't cold despite shivering.

Once, the lights flickered sharply and the emergency lamps hummed on for a few seconds before the main supply steadied again. Annie worked the room like a conductor, dispatching help where it was needed, her sharp eye catching things before they became problems — a loose curtain cord, a chair too close to the draft of a door.

Through it all, Roman moved between tasks — checking a door, steadying a chair leg, helping a carer lift a stubborn window back into place against the wind. He was quiet but never idle, stepping in exactly where needed.

By the time the worst began to pass, the rain had eased to a steady curtain and the wind had lost its sharpest edge. Residents dozed in chairs, the back lounge warm with the scent of tea and old wool. Staff began moving more slowly, voices quieter. Annie finally allowed herself a breath, leaning briefly against the wall before pushing away again to make one last round.

When Emmy and June finally stepped outside, the lane shone dark and wet under the swaying lamps. The air smelled of rain-washed stone and salt, the storm now only muttering at the edges of the night. Emmy tightened her scarf and fell into step beside June, the image of Roman in the lounge — and that unreadable exchange with the silver-haired woman — still lodged in her thoughts.

# Chapter 21

The wind had finally stopped arguing with the rooftops. In its place lay a thin, washed light, the sort that made every slate and puddle look newly-invented. Emmy woke before her alarm, not to noise but to the absence of it, and for a long, honest minute she did nothing but listen: the tick of the radiator cooling, the small clack of the bookshop sign below as it settled from a night of clattering, the slow breath of the lane finding its morning again.

When she pushed back the curtain a fraction, the street presented itself like a picture after a storm scene was painted and wiped away again. Leaves had migrated to places leaves did not belong. A single roof tile lay neat as a plate by the kerb. The old plane tree at the bend had shed a limb, cleanly, and the broken end showed a pale, shocked interior. The gutter along the opposite eaves glinted with too much water, then spilled a quiet silver over the downpipe. The world smelt of wet stone and the faint iron of disturbed earth.

She stood there with her palm on the cold glass, and the night came back to her-the draught elbowing its way around the sash, the rain rattling like impatient applause, the way the wind had gathered itself and pushed in one long, confident shove that made the whole building square its shoulders. Somewhere in the dark, a sign had gone from clack to clang to a drawn-out rattle so constant it turned into silence by persistence alone. And beneath it all, the steady thread of purpose that had pulled her through the night: a knock at the door, June's voice rushed and practical, the choice to step into the weather and make herself useful at the nursing home while the sky rehearsed what ruin looked like.

Now the rehearsal was over. The set stood untidy. Someone would have to sweep up, right the chairs, write the report.

Emmy wrapped her robe tighter and went to put the kettle on. The flat felt like a small boat beached after a rough sea-safe, yes, but with the memory of toss and tilt still in its boards. She found the satin headscarf she'd tied last night against the wind and shook it out, the fabric catching the weak light in a soft sheen. She draped it over the radiator by habit, though it was nearly dry, and set a mug on the counter with the deliberate care of someone who had not slept enough to trust herself with speed.

When the tea was ready, she took it to the window and leaned on the sill. The lane was already busy in the very particular way small places are busy after weather: not with traffic, but with people carrying things. A man with a hammer and two lengths of batten. A woman with a broom whose bristles had a permanent splay.

Aubrey appeared on the street from his shop below; sleepless-looking but tidy as ever, propped the bookshop door with his elbow while he checked the pavement for broken glass. He tilted his head up, caught her watching, and gave a small salute Emmy returned it with the mug and mouthed, *You okay?* He nodded in a way that said: I will be once I've tidied this up.

* * *

Emmy dressed in layers-soft blouse; the warm jumper she liked because the colour forgave tiredness; skirt; tights; boots; the practical coat that had already learned the village. She tied the satin scarf over her hair again, not to keep it dry now but to catch the wind's habit of tossing. At the door, she paused, hand on the knob, unreasonably struck by the thought that once she stepped into the morning, she would keep finding last night in it.

On the street the air was cooler than it looked. The puddles had turned into mirrors bright enough to make her blink. Above, a patch of honest blue sky opened and closed like a trick. She crossed toward the square, boots making small sounds that the day did not mind, and turned by instinct down the route that led to the nursing home. She had meant to go later, after a second mug and perhaps toast, but she felt the desire to check on how things looked in the daylight.

The village showed its wounds with humility. Roofs here and there were missing slates that lay in orderly fragments below like broken scales. The bakery had lost one of the letters from it's sign. The iron gate by the church leaned, its hinge protesting when a man with helpful shoulders tried the latch and then propped it with a stone. At the corner near the post office, the public noticeboard had lost three sheets and gained a thicket of tacks; the card for guitar lessons hung on by a final brave perforation. A gull strutted in the centre of the road as if promoted by the absence of wind to a supervisory role. The harbour, visible in slivers, looked scoured clean and slightly offended about it.

She met Mrs. Lyle from the greengrocer's sweeping the threshold in brisk, penitent strokes. "Morning, love," the woman puffed, "you were out in it last night, weren't you?"

"I was," Emmy said. "The home needed hands."

"Aye, well, bless you for it," Mrs. Lyle said, as if Emmy had signed up to more than one night's usefulness. "Annie's a marvel, but there aren't enough arms for all the lifting." She nodded at Emmy's scarf. "That's sensible. Mind, there's talk there's another burst due this afternoon, smaller than last night but meaner. You take care."

"I will," Emmy said. Mrs. Lyle resumed sweeping as if safety were something you could brush into a neat pile and lift away.

At the edge of the square stood a tree that had decided on one short-lived rebellion against the wind; a bough as thick as Emmy's thigh had been torn and left in a tidy, vegetative collapse across the pavement. Two men were sawing it into sections with a rhythm that made a sort of music, the saws' complaint softened by the damp. Emmy stepped around the trunk and continued.

At the florist's, an open cardboard box sat on the step with a hand-lettered sign: *Wind-bruised blooms - help yourself.* Without quite meaning to, Emmy plucked two anemones by their soft stems and tucked them into her coat pocket. There was no one to see her do it-Mrs. Penwell had gone inside to argue with vases-and the flowers' existence in the pocket felt like a small gladness smuggled through customs.

She had thought the route to the nursing home would be empty. It was not. Villages distribute people to tasks the way tides distribute weed, and ahead of her she saw evidence of that tide: Mr. Hadley, whose limp was a barometer, carried a roll of plastic sheeting; the caretaker from the school moved with purpose and a staple gun; a teenager walked a dog much larger than herself and looked to be reconsidering the terms of their friendship. Each person nodded when their eyes met hers with the coherent civility of a place that had survived a thing and was now embarrassed about the mess.

She kept expecting-reflex more than hope-to see Roman somewhere among them: the particular geometry of his posture against the wind, the way he made weather look like an option rather than a decree. She did not. That absence did not mean anything, she told herself. People had their own corners to tend. And yet she found herself checking doorways and side lanes the way one looks for a word that ought to sit at the tip of the tongue.

The nursing home came into view around a bend, its Victorian frontage handsome even in exhaustion. The bay windows wore rain-streaks like tear tracks. One pane on the east side had been replaced in the night with a sheet of plywood already spotted with damp. Sandbags made a modest wall along the lower step where the wind had bullied water in. The signboard that usually announced *TEA THURSDAYS OPEN TO ALL* had been laid flat to prevent it from sailing to France.

A man in a high-visibility vest stood at the gate, ticking names and intentions from a clipboard. He recognised Emmy and waved her through without asking for either. Inside the small lobby the smell of disinfectant did battle with the sweeter smell of stewed fruit-someone had been kind to the morning with sugar-and won only on the edges. The light in here had the greenish cast of old glass. The noticeboard bore weathered reminders about hearing-aid batteries and hairdresser days; a sheet hastily tacked over it read *ALL WELL - PLEASE RING AND WAIT* in letters written with the sort of pen found only in desk drawers.

Annie came from the direction of the office as if conjured by the thought of her. She had the same plait as last night, but today it looked as though it had negotiated terms rather than been dragged into service. Her cheeks were flushed, and her sleeves were rolled in a way that suggested sleeves had learned not to argue with her. A pencil sat behind one ear like a permanent idea.

"Oh, thank goodness," she said, and if the words were formula, the warmth was not. "Emmy-are you all right? You were a marvel yesterday."

"I'm fine," Emmy said, and found that she almost meant it. "Is everyone-?"

"Shaken and stirred," Annie said dryly. "But we've done the rounds. No injuries beyond a bruise or two and one stubborn splintered sash that will not be spoken politely to. We had to close off the east lounge after the window went. Temporary boarding's up. The glazier says he'll try for this afternoon if the wind doesn't fancy his ladder." She took a half-step closer, the way practical people do when the subject leans from lists toward humans. "Would you stay a bit? We've the morning staff, but we're short on the sort of hands that can carry a tray and a conversation at once."

"I can do that," Emmy said, and almost laughed at the relief she felt at being given something so simple to do. "Where would you like me?"

"Tea rounds first," Annie said, thrusting a clipboard into her hands. "I've marked the rooms where people didn't fancy the bustle. After that, if you're up for it, sit with anyone who looks like they're waiting for a storm that's already passed. That's most of us." She paused, eyes softening. "You were steady last night. Thank you."

"I wasn't steady," Emmy said honestly. "I just... had something to do."

"That'll do it," Annie said, as if she had been waiting all morning for someone to say something precise. "Kitchen's through there. Mind the cord-they're drying towels."

The kitchen felt like the first normal room she'd stepped into since the storm: square, warm, tiled in a pattern that forgave feet. A volunteer with an expression of industrious mercy poured tea from two enormous brown pots that could have been enlisted in any century. "One sugar for Ms. Vickers," he said without looking up, "three for Mr. Kemble, none for Mrs. Roe unless you want her to tell you about her heart-she will tell you anyway." He slid a plate of custard creams toward her with the sort of flourish one reserves for medicine.

Emmy loaded a tray, the muscle memory of carrying cups finding her wrists. As she moved along the corridor the morning arranged itself into small scenes. A television in the lounge muttered the news with its voice turned down to politeness. The smell of stewed apples grew stronger near the dining room. Somewhere a radio thought about being cheerful and decided on something middle-of-the-road instead.

Mr. Kemble-ex-postman, always in a cardigan that believed in buttons-opened for her before she knocked, as if he had been expecting tea like a post. "Morning, Miss Emmy," he said. "Well done on the weather last night. Could have been worse, mind. Nineteen seventy-nine blew the shed clean off the allotments. Chickens wandering about like they'd changed their minds about staying."

"I'll keep that in mind when I do my report," Emmy said solemnly, and put three sugars in his mug while he pretended to look scandalised. They spoke for a few minutes about roofs and pigeons, and when she left he blessed her in a way that made her feel momentarily like a vicar.

Mrs. Roe-bright-eyed, bones like birds-took her tea without sugar and then told Emmy about her heart anyway, but with such vim that it felt less like a complaint than a diary entry that had been waiting for a fresh page. "We were lucky," she concluded, lifting her chin toward the boarded lounge. "Could have been right through us. Did you see that gentleman helping with the window last night? Quick hands."

"I did," Emmy said, because there was no way to answer that without answering it. "A lot of people turned up."

"They do," Mrs. Roe said. "That's the thing about this place. People turn up. Then they go home the next day and complain about the damp." She laughed at herself and waved Emmy out with the back of her hand in the affectionate way of people who have earned the right to be imperious in slippers.

In the corridor Mr. Fleming, who had spent forty years under cars and now trusted nothing with fewer than four wheels, was arguing amiably with a young man from maintenance about the correct angle for a temporary brace. "Your brace will hold," Mr. Fleming conceded as Emmy passed, "but that's not the point. The point is that mine will hold while also looking right." The young man looked delighted to be corrected, which was perhaps the point after all.

Emmy followed Annie's pencil marks to a room at the end of the hall. The door stood ajar, balanced on the sort of hinge that still remembered the old craftsman who'd fitted it. The room itself was neat in the way small rooms learn to be: a bed made crisply, a chair with a shawl over its arm, a table that knew how to hold only what it must. In the chair sat the silver-haired woman from last night.

In the storm's churn and urgency, Emmy had only absorbed the outline of her. Now, in this increased gentleness, she saw detail: hair like new frost pulled back in a modest coil, skin that had the thinned transparency of parchment, a mouth that had learned not to say things until they were worth the effort. The woman's eyes, though-those were very much awake. They were the grey-green of evening water. When Emmy stepped in with the tray, those eyes lifted and held her in a look that recognised more than politeness would have required.

"Good morning," Emmy said. "Tea?"

"If we must observe such conventions," the woman replied, the dryness of the words softened by the quickness of a smile. "Milk, no sugar. And if you can, set it where the saucer won't wobble. I don't trust saucers since nineteen sixty-two."

Emmy obliged and asked, because curiosity felt like the kindest form of attention, "What did a saucer do to you in sixty-two?"

"Leapt," the woman said crisply. "Off a tray. Into my lap. In church, no less. I was wearing a dress that would never forgive me, and the vicar thought I had given my soul to the

Lord on the spot." She sipped, eyes not leaving Emmy's face. "You were here last night."

"I was," Emmy said, setting the plate of biscuits where they could be accepted without becoming an admission. "You were very calm."

"Calm is just shock with good breeding," the woman said. "Sit down a moment. You'll make me anxious hovering like that. I'm not a convalescent, only a resident."

Emmy obeyed, perching on the spare chair. From this angle she could see where a picture had been taken down from the wall to prevent it falling; a rectangle of brighter paint marked the place where a landscape had once been allowed to make the room look larger. On the bedside table lay a folded handkerchief, worn thin at the edges but ironed with fidelity. The woman's hands, resting on the blanket, had the slender architecture of age-blue map-lines visible beneath the skin, knuckles like small hillocks. One finger wore a simple gold band that had been polished, not because anyone else would see it, but because she knew when something had earned polish.

"What should I call you?" Emmy asked, and if the question was procedural, her voice made it feel like an invitation.

"Esther, for everyone except the people who call me Mrs. Bell," the woman said. "And you are the bookshop flat, though I assume you also have a name."

"Emmy," she said. "I brought biscuits I'm not supposed to offer before ten."

"Rules bend better when biscuits are involved," Esther said, and took one with the neat decisiveness of a person who had not wasted biscuits on indecision in seventy-odd years. "You live above the bookshop? I lived above a shop once. The things one hears from above-confidences of tills, secrets of the broom. Are you settled?"

"I think so," Emmy said. "Enough to know which floorboard not to step on when I want my neighbours to believe I'm a ghost."

"Good," Esther said. "The world has enough people who wait to live until the weather improves." She glanced toward the curtained window and the faint, relentless bright behind it. "It will not, so you must."

They spoke for a few minutes of the sort of things talk knows to use while it is learning whether it can be trusted. Emmy asked if Esther wanted the shawl moved; Esther said no, the draught from the window liked to tease her ankles and the shawl would only encourage it. Emmy asked if the tea was too strong; Esther said tea is only too strong if it prevents you seeing your reflection in it; otherwise it is simply a fact of the

351

day. When silence came, it was brief and ordinary, and Emmy thought to use it to move on to the next room.

"Wait," Esther said, not urgently but with the gravity of a person who had learned to spend their breath carefully. "Would you come back when you have done your rounds?"

"Of course," Emmy said, though the question opened in her a pocket of alarm she could not name. "Do you need anything?"

"Yes," Esther said. "A listener." She lifted the biscuit as though it were a glass. "And perhaps one of these without your pretending I'm convalescing."

"I'll smuggle it," Emmy said. "That way it won't count."

Esther's mouth did the small, pleased thing again that did not quite reach smile but improved the air. "Good. Go along with you. There are people down the corridor who take to tea like faith."

When Emmy stepped back into the hallway, she found Annie had materialised again, this time with a roll of tape and an expression that suggested she had coaxed a dishwasher into performing beyond its station and would do so again if necessary. "How is she?" Annie asked, following Emmy's glance toward Esther's room.

"Sharp," Emmy said, which covered a good deal. "She asked me to come back."

Annie's mouth softened. "She will have a story for you. She's one of the ones who keeps them like seed in a tin-only taken down when there's good ground."

"Is she all right after last night?" Emmy asked carefully. "She looked-"

"As if she were watching a thing she'd seen before," Annie supplied. "She was steady. Many weren't. I was not." She blew a strand of hair from her forehead. "We had help. You saw. It is one thing to train for emergencies and another to become one."

Emmy did not ask the question that tried to climb into her mouth-*Who helped?*-because the question would have announced itself as loaded and she had not yet paid for ammunition. Instead she said, "Is there anything that needs lifting?"

"Everything," Annie said cheerfully. "But not until after tea."


By the time Emmy finished the round, the rhythm of the place had swung a little closer to what she imagined normal sounded like. Dishes clinked, the washing machine in the small laundry thumped with a quarrelsome dignity, and someone in the lounge had found a station that insisted on flutes. In the corridor a volunteer with a toolbox replaced the hinge pin on a door that had taken to squeaking as a protest; he tapped the pin in with the handle of a screwdriver and then, unasked, gave the hinge a drop of oil the colour of amber. The squeak vanished and the door, surprised at its own silence, closed politely thereafter.

In one room a woman named Olive showed Emmy a photograph of herself taken in nineteen fifty-eight in a bathing costume she claimed had caused traffic to stop on the promenade; Emmy, who believed this completely, told her so, and Olive spent the next ten minutes radiant with a sort of borrowed youth that felt like the only useful invention time had given anyone that morning.

In another, Mr. Avery held Emmy hostage with a story about a football match in nineteen seventy-three that could be proven because a lad from three streets over had broken his wrist on the same day, and therefore whenever the wrist ached it would rain. Emmy nodded solemnly and promised to pass this meteorological marvel to Annie, who, he assured her, would understand the science of it immediately.

Between rooms she saw small kindnesses pass between staff and residents like notes folded and left under mugs: a hand taken without comment when a step was high; a chair drawn just-so without making it into a performance; two seconds of conspiratorial eye contact over a joke too old to be told out loud anymore. She did not see Roman. There was no reason for him to be here now. And yet the fact of his absence began to feel like a texture as much as the presence of anyone else-a lack that shaped the surface of the morning, the way missing tiles shaped the roofline.

When the tea things were done and the trolley pushed back to the kitchen with the final, grateful rattle of work well sent away, Emmy found the corridor outside Esther's room empty. She paused, set her hand briefly against the cool wall to steady the odd tilt in her thoughts, and knocked.

"Come," Esther called, as though she had been fully expecting an appointment. "If you have contraband, close the door."

"I do," Emmy said, stepping in and setting two biscuits on the saucer as though she were guilty of a small, happy crime. "And I brought more tea."

"You are a woman of discernment," Esther said. She gestured to the chair. "Please. I should like to use your quiet."

"My-?"

"Your quiet," Esther said, as if the word were perfectly ordinary. "You carry it well. People who have been through hard weather sometimes rattle afterward. You don't rattle. You ring true. It is useful, if you can stand it."

Emmy sat. "I can stand it," she said, half-wondering if that were true and deciding it could be for the length of a conversation.

Esther looked at the curtained window for a long, measured beat, and Emmy felt the moment turn in the air like a key in a lock. "Last night," Esther said, "I saw a face I knew."

She said it with the composure of someone reporting the time, and yet something in the words lifted the hairs on Emmy's arms. "Someone from the village?" Emmy asked. She kept her voice low, a shade of colour softer than usual, as if she were speaking in a church where she did not know the rules yet.

"Someone from the world," Esther said, which was not an answer in the useful sense but told Emmy a great deal about the size of the story now taking its breath. "He was here, as he has been before."

Emmy felt the conversation incline toward an edge and made herself a surface sturdy enough to hold it. "Would you like to tell me?" she asked, the way she would have asked a child in her class if they wanted to show her where it hurt without making a fuss of the hurting.

"Yes," Esther said, and folded one hand over the other as though the gesture kept something precise from slipping away. "But you must allow me to start in the wrong place. Stories are not doors. They are fields. One enters where the hedges permit."

"All right," Emmy said, and meant it. She was aware, at the far edge of her attention, of the hallway's faint sound and the building's-tired breathing.

Esther took a breath like the settling of a quilt. "When I was six," she said, "the river took hold of me and changed its mind."

She stopped there, not for drama but for breath, and Emmy's hands went still in her lap as if the air had asked for that quiet. "I'm listening," she said, and in that sentence, she gave away more of herself than she had planned to.

"Good," Esther said, almost to herself. "Because it is a ridiculous thing to say, and yet it is true, and I have been trying to repay the truth of it with good telling for eighty years." She took a sip of tea, grimaced at its temperature, and smiled because the grimace amused her. "But before I tell you the river, I need to tell you the lane. There was a lane then that is not a lane now-no, do not look like that; they hide lanes the way they hide old bones under pavements. It ran behind the mill and came out where the allotments are, and there was a man who walked it. We called him the wandering man. Not because he was without home exactly, but because he belonged wherever his feet were, which is a different sort of ownership."

Emmy sat very still. The word *wandering* sounded like a stone dropped into a well and bouncing off smooth sides on the way down. She had the sudden, backward thought that she

357

knew the sound his boots would make on gravel, which was absurd. She kept her face even and her eyes on Esther's, and willed her pulse to choose a pace that would not embarrass them both.

"I will tell you the rest," Esther said, and the words were gentle and absolute, "when you have warmed that tea again. It is an old story and it asks for heat." She lifted the cup slightly. "And I would prefer not to waste a good listener on a lukewarm truth."

Emmy stood, not too quickly, the sense of the room gathering itself like skirts to step over a threshold. "I'll fetch us fresh," she said, hearing that her voice had gone careful without going thin. "I won't be long."

"Take your time," Esther said, eyes on her in that measuring way that had nothing to do with suspicion and everything to do with deciding whether a person could be trusted to carry a thing. "I have already waited decades."

In the corridor the light seemed both brighter and farther away. Emmy carried the empty cups to the kitchen on a tray that felt heavier than logic allowed and set about the practicalities that had made sense all morning: kettle on; fresh pot; milk in a small jug with a blue ring around its belly; two spoons; two new biscuits, though she told herself this was not contraband but hospitality. While the water heated she leaned back against the counter and watched the steam begin to pearl and then billow. The noise and business of the place-voices, footsteps, the occasional cheerful clatter-moved around her like a river around a steady rock.

Roman's absence was in that movement like a negative shape. You could fill a mould with water and learn what the mould had been by the shape that set; you could fill a morning with cups and chatter and still feel the space where a person was not. She had seen him last night-outside, in the crosswind, a dark line against the white tilt of the boarded window-and later, in the sudden quiet, he had stood with the silver-haired woman and spoken with the serious courtesy of someone who was telling the truth to time. She had not heard a word. She had only seen the line of his mouth and the way the woman's face had changed as if choosing, in a single moment, to remember or to forget.

"Don't stare at the kettle," the volunteer with the merciful expression said kindly, passing through with a crate of clean mugs. "She'll only take her spite out on the tea."

"I'm not staring," Emmy said, not quite truthfully. "I'm convincing."

"That's different," he said, and left her to it.

When the tea had brewed the correct, consoling colour, Emmy carried the tray back along the corridor. Her hands had stopped shaking sometime between the boiling and the pouring; her breath had found a quiet that did not feel like holding, only like keeping. At Esther's door she paused, made a quick, private agreement with herself not to argue with the story as it came, and knocked again.

"Enter," Esther said, with the good-tempered imperiousness of a person who had spent a lifetime deciding when to be imperious and had never abused the privilege. "Ah," she added when she saw the tray. "You've brought proof that the world can be persuaded to behave better the second time of asking."

"I have hopes," Emmy said, and set the cups down carefully. "You said you would tell me the rest."

"And I will," Esther said, leaning forward a little as though the act of telling itself would generate warmth. "But allow me one more wrong beginning." She glanced past Emmy's shoulder toward the corridor as if to ascertain the time and the weather. "Since last night, the village has been moving around like a person who knows they have forgotten something but cannot yet remember where they put it. You know that feeling?"

"I do," Emmy said softly, and thought of an antiques shop with its door half-open and a bell tied so it would not complain.

"Good," Esther said, as if Emmy had passed an examination she had not known she was taking. "Then you will understand the shape of this. I will make it plain. Last night I saw the wandering man. He is exactly as he was when he pulled me out of the water as a child. Exactly." She lifted her chin, not daring Emmy to doubt her but offering her certainty as a thing worth considering. "He has green eyes that have not learned to age."

The rest of the words did not come. Not yet. Esther sat back, as though her story had reached the edge of a page and refused to be squeezed into the margin. She set her fingers lightly against the gold band on her hand, turned it a quarter the way one might turn a coin for luck, and looked at the window. "We'll begin properly when the tea has the right courage," she said. "I have found that some truths ask to be poured hotter than others."

Emmy nodded and wrapped her hands around her cup as if her palms could lend heat to the drink. Her mind, a disciplined thing when it had to be, tried to put the pieces in an order that would make them harmless. A storm. A frightened night. An old woman's memory backed by adrenaline and gratitude. A face glimpsed and mistaken. Green eyes are not uncommon. And yet the tidy explanations kept slipping their moorings and drifting into water that did not admit to being charted. She kept her face arranged in the listening shape and reminded herself that being a good listener did not commit one to believing anything except the person who was speaking.

On the wall above the bed, the rectangle where the painting had been seemed to grow brighter, as though the paint remembered the light it had been denied and wanted to keep it. The building groaned softly-the ordinary complaint of timbers after weather. In the hall, a trolley rolled and then paused with a forgiving squeal. Annie's voice, farther away, gave an instruction that made the room feel looked after. The tea steamed.

"Very well," Esther said finally. "Let us try the door now instead of the field." She folded her hands and fixed Emmy with a look so frank that it erased years. "When I was six," she said again, "the river took hold of me and changed its mind. The man who changed its mind is the same man who stood in this corridor last night. He has not altered one minute since that day. And if that is impossible, then we are agreed about the size of the truth."

She smiled then, not with triumph but with a certain relief, as if she had paid a bill in full. "Drink," she said kindly. "Then I'll tell you why I am certain."

Emmy obeyed because the act of lifting the cup and sipping gave her body an instruction that was easier to follow than any her mind might attempt. The tea was, as promised, hotter, and carried with it the sober comfort of afternoons in winter when windows needed help to look friendly. She set the cup down. "I'm ready," she said. And she realised, with a complicated astonishment, that she was.

"Good," Esther said. "Because the next part is where sensible listeners usually stop me to apply logic. I do not mind logic. I admire it. But you must allow me to lay out all the pieces before you begin deciding which belong to which puzzle." She tapped the rim of her cup with the spoon, one light note that rang absolute. "After that, if you wish to insist the river and I conspired with memory to trick each other, you may. I will not be offended. I have had seventy years to practice not being offended."

Across the hall someone laughed, the sound lifting and then bending like a weathercock finding a wind. The morning had reached the ordinary noise that meant the day had made peace with its obligations. Emmy, who could usually find exactly where to place herself in a room, felt keenly that she was now sitting at the point where several rooms met. She did not know yet which door she would walk through when the story was finished. For the first time since moving here, she liked not knowing.

Esther drew a breath to continue.

The window gave a small rattle as if to clear its throat, and then the building settled again. Emmy set the fresh cups down and took her chair without fuss. Esther—because that was the name that suited her in this light—rested one thin hand on the saucer and, for a few seconds, simply listened to the quiet as though checking that the room would hold what she was about to put into it.

"When I was six," she said, as if resuming a sentence paused only for breath, "the river took hold of me and changed its mind."

Emmy kept her gaze soft and steady. The smell of damp plaster drifted faintly in from the corridor beyond the door; somewhere a hammer tapped, paused, tapped again.

"It was summer," Esther went on. "Hot enough that the cows stood in the pool above the weir and pretended to be stones. I was sent to fetch my brother—he had gone down to the water when he said he wouldn't—and I slipped on the bank by the alder where the ground gives way. You'll know the one, if you've learned the river like people here do." She tipped a look at Emmy and then away, granting her the ignorance of newcomers without malice. "I fell badly. Not in the way of stories—no noble arc, no splash like applause. I went in wrong, sideways, and the water had me by the waist before I could remember which way was air."

Her fingers made a small, unconscious shape on the arm of the chair, as if counting stones. "It was brown that day. Fast as a quarrel. I would have gone under. I did, I suppose. But then there were hands under my arms, and a voice in my ear that did not bother with comfort. 'Hold,' he said, and I did."

The smallest laugh lifted, surprised at itself. "You do, when someone says it properly."

Emmy heard the simple word as if it hung in the air, still carrying a little river in it.

"He took me to the bank as if the water had planned it that way, sat me down, put my head between my knees until the world allowed me back into it. I looked up, and he looked... calm. Not young or old, not then. Thirty, perhaps. Calm like a clock before clocks were cheap. Green eyes. You remember what frightened you and what saved you. Sometimes they're the same." She glanced toward the window as if the light there would agree with her. "He left as quietly as he came. Others pulled me upright; my brother swore he'd been there all along; I was smacked for running off—gently, as one smacks love when it does a foolish thing—and when we told the story later they called him the wandering man because a name is a way to put a fence around a thing you cannot keep."

Emmy swallowed a mouthful of tea to steady the thought forming and unforming behind her ribs. "People talk about him still?" she asked, keeping it light, as if discussing weather.

"They always have," Esther said. "Not every day. Not with the relish gossip likes. But he passes through a place and leaves the air different. There are mothers who say to children, 'Don't wander; the man will see you,' and children who grow and carry the nonsense in their pockets like a lucky coin. There are men who tell each other there's a fellow goes about doing good, which is always said with suspicion; and there are women who have once, and only once, met a kindness that arrived like a well-made door closing with a clean click. He does not stay. That is part of it. He cannot. Or won't."

She took a biscuit, broke it with care, and considered its halves. "Last night he was in the corridor outside the east lounge when the window went. I knew the shape of him in the way you know your own handwriting at a glance. He moved toward the harm as if harm had asked him to keep it company. He spoke to the lad from maintenance as if they had worked together a long time. He steadied me with the same hand—right hand; the left hovered, ready, as it did when I was a child—and when the worst noise stopped, he looked at me and there was the smallest... I will not say smile. Recognition, perhaps. There are people who make recognition feel like a safe place." She set the biscuit half down untouched. "He has not aged. Not one day."

"Memory plays tricks," Emmy said, in the same tone she had used in classrooms to ease fear that was learning its own size. "Especially after a night like that. The light—noise—adrenaline. It's easy to connect faces across years."

Esther accepted the point without the least sting. "It is. I have allowed memory to lay its little traps for me before. But this is not that. He is himself, exactly as he was. There are things you can argue with and things you must store as a question and leave alone. I am not trying to persuade you, child. I am telling you what is true for me."

Emmy nodded, grateful for the absence of demand in the woman's voice. She let her eyes slide, briefly, to the doorway, where the corridor's draught lifted the edge of the curtain. In the space left by that small movement her mind laid out sensible explanations like neat tools: the wandering man was a village myth children had grown into; there had been a helpful stranger last night; green eyes belonged to half the world. The sensible explanations sat there obediently and, unhelpfully, felt thin.

"You called him the wandering man," she said. "Did you ever learn his name?"

"No," Esther said. "Once, I thought I had. Decades ago. I asked a woman who had seen him in another town, and she said a name that did not suit him—too modern; it rattled on him like a borrowed belt—and then she laughed and said, no, she had decided it for herself because she could not bear the thought of a nameless kindness. You see how we are." Her fingers, still elegant, traced an absent-minded circle on the saucer. "He came once more for me, after the river. Long after. A winter storm. The sort that drops snow in a clean sheet over the hill and then lays ice like glass where the lane pretends to be a path. I fell. He was there, like a sentence you wish you'd said but somehow find written for you anyway. He did not speak his name. He never does."

Emmy felt a small stab of annoyance at herself for the way her heart paid attention. She set her cup down, balanced its sound carefully on the saucer's edge, and said, lightly, "I'm glad you felt looked after, last night and then. That's what matters."

Esther's mouth tilted, not unkindly. "Is it?" She let the thought go in the same breath, merciful. "Well. The biscuits are correct. Whoever is in charge of them should be promoted."

"I'll pass that up the chain," Emmy said, and they both smiled, the river and the night set aside as if in a drawer for later.

A small clatter came from the corridor—toolbox meeting floor. Annie's voice, calm as a spirit level, followed: "No harm done." A moment later she tapped on the door and leaned in, eyes going first, as always, to the person in the chair. "How are we in here?"

"Enlightened and fed," Esther said. "Your girl listens properly. Don't give her the floors to scrub when there are minds about in need of polishing."

"Noted," Annie said with an obedient solemnity that made Emmy laugh. "Glazier's here now," she added to Emmy, voice dropping into the practical. "He's brought his tallest ladders and his shortest patience. If you're able, can you sit with Mr. Kemble while we've the bang-and-crash going on? He pretends he's deaf to it, but he starts narrating football scores from the seventies and the nurses begin to lose the will to breathe."

"I can," Emmy said, rising. "Mrs. Bell—Esther, I'll come back before I go, if you like."

"I do like," Esther said. As Emmy reached the door, Esther's voice followed her, softer. "Child—don't be too quick to file a thing where it cannot be reached. The mind is too tidy for its own good."

"I'll… keep the drawer unlocked," Emmy said, and felt the odd relief of having admitted she had considered the drawer in the first place.

The corridor had filled with a different kind of noise now—boards lifting, a ladder testing its feet, the workmen's shorthand that makes a language of instruction and assurance. Emmy sat with Mr. Kemble and his cardigan and dutifully admired the way his sugar dissolved with three stirs and not a revolution more. He did not narrate football. He told her instead about the way letters gained weight in winter and the small triumph of a correctly stuck stamp. "A whole world can go wrong for want of a corner pressed," he said, and Emmy agreed, feeling companionably foolish for having never thought of stamps as moral objects.

When a particularly assertive clunk shivered the floorboards, Mrs. Roe announced to the room at large that the building must have its sighs like any living thing and the best way to help was to drink tea with conviction. Emmy handed out conviction in cups and discussed, with Olive of the famous bathing costume, whether hyacinths preferred south light or praise (they settled on both).

The glazier—narrow, weathered, all tendon and competence—came and went in the periphery, his ladder an extra spine for the house. The wind probed once, was refused, and drooped into sulks. Somewhere a kettle protested, was soothed, was replaced. She did not see him. She caught herself noticing that she did not see him, and put the noticing away without driving a nail through it.

Near noon the building changed key. People began to hunger; staff moved with that briskness which can be mistaken for urgency until you see the hands lowering plates with care; the radio discovered a song too cheerful for the day and then thought better of it. Annie appeared with a clipboard and a gentleness the clipboard did not diminish.

"You've done a morning and then some," she said to Emmy. "Will you stay for a bowl of soup? We make a credible soup."

"I will, if I can be of use another hour," Emmy said, because something in her did not want to loosen its hold on the work yet.

"You can always be of use," Annie said, with the quiet conviction of a woman who had divided usefulness into more kinds than most. "After you eat, I'll have you walk Mrs. Bell down to the conservatory—the light's better there and she likes to feel she's supervising."

Mrs. Bell, then. Emmy held the name the way one holds a newly-learned street—turn it in your mind until it sits where it will be found again.

The soup was exactly what soup should be when a house has suffered—simple, hot, not clever. She ate with the others at the end of the corridor on a small table that could be folded if the day wanted it. A volunteer put a slice of bread on her plate without asking and said, "Don't argue," and she didn't.

When she went back to Esther's room, the woman had already pulled her shawl up as if to consent to movement. "Shall we take on the conservatory?" she asked. "I like the glass when it has remembered its place."

"I'll wheel you if you prefer," Emmy offered, glancing at the sturdy chair by the wall.

"Walked in, will walk out," Esther said, and Emmy, who understood the sometimes-stubborn arithmetic of dignity, simply offered her arm.

They went slowly along the corridor, around the workman's ladder, past the newly-glazed pane that wore its clarity with a modest pride. In the conservatory the light did its best with a sky that had not decided which story to tell. The plants on the sill looked a little apologetic for the state of their leaves. Esther chose a chair where she could see the garden and the door.

"You will think me fanciful," she said once they had settled, "but I have always liked doors. A door says, 'Choose.' Walls say 'End.' I prefer a choice, even a small one. Sit, child. Don't hover like a helpful cloud."

Emmy sat. The conservatory smelled of damp soil and lemon antibacterial. A single fly traced the window as if it had left a note there and could not remember where. A breeze worried the gap at the bottom of the outer door and then gave up for lack of an argument.

"I shall not trouble you with more of last night's fairy-tale," Esther said after a while, tone almost jaunty, as if they had both agreed to store the improbable in a cool cupboard. "Only—if this place one day needs hands again, and you knock and a stranger open, trust that he has been practicing the task longer than you have been alive."

"I will remember," Emmy said, meaning only that she would remember that sentence belonged to this woman, on this day, in this light.

# Chapter 22

By the next morning, the village had resumed that purposeful murmur it wears after trouble, the kind that says nothing is entirely fixed and everything is being seen to. Emmy woke with the odd, clean feeling that follows a hard day well spent—the nursing home corridors still in her ears, Esther's voice folded like a pressed leaf between the pages of her thoughts. She lay for a minute and listened: gulls testing their vowels, the shop sign below deciding on a dignified creak, a van door thudding shut as if putting an argument to bed.

She made tea and stood at the window with the mug tucked under her chin, watching light sift down the lane. The storm's fingerprints were still everywhere, but fainter now: a roof patched with a square of new slate that didn't match, a stack of sawn branches waiting beside the church wall, the florist's awning tied into obedience with better knots than yesterday. The air had a rinsed, metallic brightness. Puddles held small skies in their bowls.

When she stepped out, her scarf caught the faint breeze and the world smelled of damp wood and warmed stone.

"Emmy!" June's voice sailed across the square like a flag that knew exactly where it meant to fly. She emerged from the school lane with a bundle of files under one arm and her hair pinned with the briskness of someone who had negotiated with both weather and bureaucracy and won the second if not the first.

"You're out early," Emmy said, meeting her halfway. "How's the school roof?"

"Sulking," June said cheerfully. "We've got two classrooms with decorative water features and a corridor that thinks it's a canal. The council have been—" she searched for the right word and decided on accuracy— "present. Which is to say, a man with a clipboard pointed meaningfully at the ceiling and said 'hmm' in three different tones."

Emmy laughed despite herself. "Does 'hmm' cover repairs?"

"Apparently it covers the idea of repairs," June said. "But we've jumped the sensible hurdles. The upshot is: school's closed for the week." She lifted her eyebrows with theatrical gravity. "Emergency works, safeguarding, that sort of thing. Parents are already walking the streets looking betrayed. Expect to be asked to teach long division on your doorstep by lunchtime."

"A whole week?" Emmy said, part sympathy, part private relief at the unexpected pocket of time. "Are you all right?"

"I'm fine," June said, and looked it—wind-pinched, bright-eyed, shoulders squared to the work of ferrying messages and calming small catastrophes. "We'll get the tarpaulins up today, proper roofers in tomorrow, and if the gods are kind and the paperwork is dull, we'll be back to chaos-as-usual by Monday. In the meantime, try not to spend all your sudden holiday mooning about in windows. Go and buy a scandalous pastry. Or," she added, eyes gleaming with mischief, "make excellent use of your free time with your mysterious friend..."

"June," Emmy said, rolling her eyes.

"What?" June said, entirely innocent. "Text me if you fancy a walk later, unless you're otherwise employed rescuing hearts. Now go, before I conscript you to supervise a queue of parents who've just found out phonics is not a personality."

They parted with a squeeze of hands, June striding off toward the school and Emmy drifting into the square's slow orbit. The bakery had its door propped, warmth exhaling in fragrant waves. Two men carried a pane of glass between them with the cautious grace of waiters balancing a great, invisible dessert. The ironmongers had a hand-written sign that read Storm stock at the back, as if the weather were something one could rummage for in a bin.

On the edge of the square, near the antiques shop, a woman stood frowning at a shop sign that had worked itself loose at the hinge. She held a screwdriver as though it might be venomous. A gust shouldered through the gap between buildings; the sign flapped once and threatened to twist free altogether.

Before Emmy could cross to help, a man was already there—coat buttoned, sleeves unbothered by the work. He steadied the sign with one hand and, with the other, took the screwdriver the way someone accepts a note of music they already know how to play. He loosened the remaining screw, set the sign flat on the pavement, and then flipped the hinge-pin out with a small, neat tap of something from his pocket— brass, familiar—slid the pin back through the aligned holes, tightened both screws to the exact hush of wood well-pleased, and lifted the sign back into place. It swung once, experimentally, and then settled as if it had always been pinned to that precise degree of obedience.

"Thank you," the woman said, relief running through the two words like warm water.

"It wanted to be fixed," he said, that old-world mildness in his voice, and handed back the screwdriver as if returning a pen. He half-turned, and Emmy saw his profile first—the calm line of it, the quiet alertness—and then the unmistakable green of his eyes when he looked up and across.

Roman.

The world did not tilt. It only admitted that it had been leaning toward this moment and could now stand easier. He gave the woman a small, courteous nod and stepped back from the doorway. The woman, emboldened by the sort of gratitude that makes people chatty, started telling him about her cousin's greenhouse and the way storms always pick on weak screws. He listened as if screws were the beginning of an interesting essay.

Emmy felt, absurdly, like someone who had been told a secret and then immediately asked not to repeat it to herself. Esther's voice rose in her mind for the briefest second—the wandering man, exactly as he was—but she closed the thought like a drawer without checking what was inside. Storms pull stories out of people; faces get mixed up in fear and gratitude; green eyes belong to more heads than one. She was not going to be the sort of woman who stitched a myth to the nearest coat.

He looked up again, and this time the look found her. A flicker—recognition, a quiet yes—moved through his expression, and then that fractional softening at the corner of his mouth that counted as a smile when he didn't spend it lavishly. He excused himself from the conversation with the exact right sentence—"If it drops again, leave it; I'll pass later"—and crossed the space between them at an unhurried, practical pace, as if the morning were a room they both happened to be in.

"Good morning," he said. His voice had it's usual lantern-warmth, but today there was something else in it too—a gentler check-in, a measure taken without fuss. "How are you after the storm?"

"Better for it being today," Emmy said. "And you?"

He considered the sky as though answering it first. "Dry," he said, almost amused at his own plainness, and then: "Tired in the useful way." Up close, he looked exactly himself and a little more so: a smudge of dust at the cuff, a faint line of sleeplessness that didn't ask for sympathy, the precise way he stood, as if he always made space for other people even when there was not quite enough pavement.

"June's declared school a canal and advised it is closed it for the week," Emmy said. "I'm officially redundant until the roof decides to behave."

"Then the village will test your resistance to being borrowed," he said. "It's very persuasive when it wants hands."

"I've noticed," she said, and found she liked that he assumed she would be useful before she offered it.

He glanced past her to the square where the glass-bearers negotiated a corner. "Careful," he said, not to her but to the air, and the air obliged. When he looked back, a thought had settled in his eyes, like a bird deciding a branch suited it.

"Have you breakfasted?" he asked, mild as a weather question.

"Badly," she said. "Tea and the heel of yesterday's bread."

"An honest meal," he said. "But not a cheerful one."

"I can be bribed," she said before she thought better of it, and a small, quiet satisfaction crossed his face at the proof that she would meet him where conversation wanted to go.

"Then let me be bribery," he said, and inclined his head toward the bakery. "Walk?"

They crossed the short distance together, falling into step without deciding to. It wasn't the sort of walk that needed noise; there was plenty of that in the street—the saw's two-note song as someone trimmed a limb into sense, a child's triumphant whoop at the discovery of a stick that would, briefly, be a sword. Inside the bakery, warmth lifted to meet them and the air spoke cinnamon as if making a case for joy. He bought two pastries and a small paper bag that made the sound of sugared things, and when they were outside again he handed her one of the chocolate croissants without ceremony.

"Diplomacy," he said, as if that explained chocolate at ten in the morning, and she laughed because it did.

They ate leaning against the low iron railing that pretended to separate the square from the lane. The croissant gave way with a clean tear, steam and chocolate, and Emmy decided that some kinds of gratitude ought to be said out loud. "Thank you," she said. "I'll try not to form an attachment to this exact moment and expect it to repeat."

"That's where disappointment lives," he said. "In the identical. Better to like the rhyme."

"The rhyme," she repeated, amused. "You make even breakfast sound literary."

"Occupational hazard," he said. "Some things insist on being called by their better names."

She felt the smile before she knew she was wearing it. "Like storms insisting they're rehearsals."

"Or doors insisting they're choices," he returned, quick as the matching line in a poem. For a second their eyes held in the warm cold of the morning, and the square went on around them, busy enough to keep them private.

A boy pedalled past, feet a blur, and yelled to no one in particular, "They've fixed the window!" as if this were news of national importance. Roman watched him go with the same calm attention he gave everything that moved under its own power. "Good," he said, and the word was the exact size of the boy's triumph.

He brushed his hands, as if setting away flour that wasn't there, and looked back at her. "I've repairs at home," he said— practical, unadorned—and only then, a half-breath later, let the more particular rhythm of him in. "The outbuildings took exception to the wind. They've stood for longer than most neighbours' memories, but last night reminded them they're not invincible." He said it simply, as if remarking on tide lines. "I'll see what I can persuade back into sense."

She pictured, uninvited, the long, low roofs she'd glimpsed once beyond his wall, and the soft, green-dark smell of timber and old hinges. "You're handy," she said. "I saw you saving a sign from disgrace."

"A hinge is only a hinge," he said, with enough self-mockery to make the sentence a smile. "And a day like this is mostly hinges. Things wanting to swing the right way again."

There was a space then, not empty, between the next words and the last. He looked at her the way people look at weather before deciding whether to take a coat. "Perhaps," he said, and the word was as gentle as a hand turning a page, "you might come by tomorrow—if you can spare a little time from your sudden holiday. I could use a second opinion on the damage." A beat, the faintest curve at his mouth. "And I suspect yours would be more honest than mine."

Emmy blinked at him, surprised not so much by the invitation itself, but by how lightly he had placed it between them, as if it were no heavier than the steam curling from the roll in her hands. "You'd trust me to give an honest opinion on a roof?" she asked, half-teasing.

"On honesty—yes," Roman said, steady as stone. "On roofs—well, we'll let the timber argue back if you're wrong."

She laughed, softer than she meant to. "Tomorrow then," she said, pretending to think it over, though the answer had already settled in her chest. "If you don't mind me intruding."

"If I minded," he replied, "I wouldn't ask."

The wind nudged between them, tugging at her scarf, carrying the brine-smell from the harbour up the lane. For a moment they both turned their heads toward it, as though listening to the same low music. When her gaze came back, his had not moved.

"You're certain you want company while you're mending?" she asked. "Most people prefer solitude when hammering nails."

"I've had solitude," he said quietly. "It doesn't offer much conversation."

There was something in his tone—gentle but weighted— that made her pulse catch, though he gave her no more than that. He turned his roll in his hand, a tiny deliberate pause, and then shifted the subject as if allowing her to breathe.

"And what will you do with an empty school week?"

"Sleep," she said instantly, then grinned at his raised brow. "Or at least that was my first thought. But knowing me, I'll end up fussing with lessons or catching up on things I've put off. I'm terrible at real idleness."

"Most people are," Roman said. "We like to believe rest is simple, but it takes more discipline than work."

"You sound like you've thought about it," she said.

"I've had practice," he murmured, then, catching himself, added with a half-smile, "Too much time alone does make one philosophical."

For a while they stood in companionable silence, watching the square unspool itself: a cart rattling over uneven cobbles, a pair of children trailing sticks along the iron railing, a man opening shutters with the grumble of hinges that had suffered too much rain. The day had the strange peace that follows a storm, fragile but generous.

At last, Roman dusted his hands against each other and said, "I should leave you to your morning. But—" He hesitated, a rare crack in his usual certainty. "Tomorrow, then. Come when the day feels willing."

She smiled, not hiding the warmth that rose in her at his awkwardness. "I'll come by after breakfast. That should give you time to scold your roofs without me watching."

His mouth curved. "They behave better without an audience... Tomorrow," he echoed, as though the word had a shape he was memorising. Then, with a small incline of his head, he stepped back, the space between them widening like the parting of two lines in a sketch, each unfinished but already suggesting the picture.

Emmy carried the warmth of that exchange with her as she walked back through the square. The day had tilted subtly, the light a little brighter, the air sharper against her cheeks. She noticed things she might have missed—how the mason had propped his tools carefully under a tarpaulin, how the florist's window gleamed from a hasty polish, how even the puddles seemed to catch more sky than they should have held.

When she reached her flat, she set the remains of the sugared pastry on a plate, poured fresh tea, and tried to busy herself with small tasks—straightening the books she'd borrowed from the shop below, folding the blanket at the foot of her bed, writing out a rough plan for lessons she might never use if the roofers worked quickly. But her thoughts kept returning to tomorrow.

The truth was, she wanted to see his world again—the orangery, the quiet gravity of his house, the sense that time bent differently on his grounds. It wasn't just curiosity anymore. It was the way he looked at her, as though her presence steadied something in him.

She caught herself smiling at nothing and, with a shake of her head, went to put the kettle on again.

# Chapter 23

The next morning; Emmy smiled as she crossed the square, choosing the side path that would take her toward Roman's house.

The further she went, the more the storm's mark showed. Branches lay scattered, ivy torn from old walls, the grass flattened in wide, uneven swathes. Yet the air carried that rare sharpness storms sometimes leave behind, as though the world had been rinsed clean.

When she reached the iron gates, she paused. They were open—she had only ever seen them closed. Today they stood wide, almost beckoning. After a moment, she stepped through. The track wound gently toward the outbuildings first, stone structures huddled in a row. Their roofs bore the storm's temper—slates slipped, moss scattered—but they stood firm.

From the nearest shed came the scrape and thud of someone at work. Roman emerged a moment later, a coil of rope in one hand, his sleeves rolled. His hair had dried only partway, swept back to reveal the sharp lines of his brow.

When he saw her, his expression softened—as though he'd half expected her.

"You braved the wreckage," he said.

"I did," she answered, taking in the sight of him, the open shed, the rope. "Though I'm not sure if I came to check on you or to see if you needed rescuing."

A flicker of amusement crossed his face. "From a falling beam? That would be a sight."

"Don't tempt me," she said, stepping closer. Inside, the shed smelled of damp wood and iron. Timber leaned against the wall, and a cart sat on its side with a broken wheel.

"The storm loosened a beam," Roman explained. "I thought I'd put it back before it decides to fall."

"With rope?"

"And nails, eventually," he replied. "Rope is persuasion. Nails are permanence."

She glanced past him at the rafters, where a pigeon shifted near its nest. "You've been at this since dawn, haven't you?"

He shrugged lightly. "There's order in mending what storms leave behind." Then, more softly, "Though I didn't think you'd really come."

"I wanted to," she said simply.

For a moment the air between them was filled with the calls of gulls and the drip of water from the gutters. Roman's expression changed—something quiet, almost unguarded.

"Well," he said at last, "since you're here, perhaps you might stay a while. I can offer less charm than the orangery, but there's bread cooling in the kitchen. And coffee, if you don't mind it plain."

She smiled. "I think I can manage plain."

His mouth curved faintly. "Then come inside. Let the roof beams wait their turn."

He stepped aside, gesturing her toward the house beyond.

The kitchen greeted her with warmth and the faint smell of woodsmoke. Its stone floor still carried damp prints from Roman's boots, but the long table had been cleared, a loaf resting on a board with its crust cracked just enough to release steam.

Roman set down the rope and wiped his hands. "Eggs too, if you'll allow me to play host."

"You've been mending roofs since dawn and you're still offering to cook?" Emmy teased, slipping her scarf from her neck.

He glanced over his shoulder with the ghost of a smile. "I've been feeding myself for quite a while. You'll forgive me if the presentation lacks ceremony."

"I'll survive," she said, settling at the table.

He moved with a kind of unhurried efficiency, taking down a pan from its hook and cracking the eggs with steady

388

taps against the rim. The yolks slipped into the pan, hissing faintly when they touched the butter already melting there. The smell was immediate—rich, warm, comforting.

Emmy leaned her chin against her hand, watching him. His sleeves were still rolled, the lines of his forearms catching the glow of the window's light. There was nothing rehearsed about him here, no distance, no polite guard. Just a man at his stove, turning eggs, slicing bread, pouring coffee into two cups that didn't quite match.

He set her plate in front of her, the eggs bright against the fresh bread, and sat opposite with his own. "Plain fare," he said, "but it will keep you from fainting in the wind."

"It's perfect," Emmy said honestly. She hadn't realised until that moment how hungry she was.

They ate in a silence that wasn't strained but companionable, the kind that let the sound of cutlery and the occasional settling creak of the beams fill the space. When he finally looked up, there was a faint amusement in his expression.

"What?" she asked, smiling despite herself.

"You're easier to feed than I expected."

"That's not much of a compliment."

"It is," he said, sipping his coffee. "I was half afraid you'd be too polite to eat."

"Trust me, I don't pass up food." She paused, then added more softly, "Especially not when it's this good."

That earned her the smallest bow of his head before he leaned back in his chair. His gaze flicked toward the window, then back to her. "Speaking of unexpected visitors—one turned up this morning."

"Oh?"

"The stray cat," he said, as though it were an ordinary remark. "I'd not seen it for weeks. Thought perhaps it had moved on. But when I opened one of the sheds earlier…" He let the rest trail, a note of surprise still woven into his tone. "Not a tom at all, as I assumed. She's very much female. And—" He paused, half-smiling. "Heavily pregnant. She's made herself a nest in a corner, as if she owns the place."

Emmy sat forward slightly, her fork forgotten. "Really?"

He nodded, finishing his coffee before standing. "Come. You should see her. She seems determined to be admired."

They stepped back into the crisp air. The sun, though weak, struck bright against the wet grass, and gulls wheeled overhead. Roman led her past the first shed to a smaller one tucked close against a low wall. Its door leaned, protesting faintly when he pushed it open.

The smell inside was of straw and old wood, mixed with something faintly musky. In the corner, on a heap of straw and folded sacking, lay the cat. Her fur was patchy but thick, her green eyes wide and watchful. She shifted slightly when they entered, but didn't move, her sides rising and falling in a steady rhythm.

"She found this on her own," Roman said quietly, his voice gentler now. "I don't recall leaving that sacking there, but perhaps she dragged it herself."

Emmy crouched a little, her scarf slipping forward as she peered at the animal. And then she blinked. Something about the shape of her face, the white blaze across her nose—familiar.

"I've seen her before," she murmured.

Roman glanced down at her. "You have?"

"Yes. In the square." Emmy's lips curved. "Same markings."

The cat gave a small, throaty sound, as though confirming the claim.

Roman leaned one hand against the doorframe, studying the animal with a faint frown of thought. "So she's made a circuit of the village. And chosen here, of all places, to see her kittens into the world."

Emmy looked up at him, the corners of her eyes warming. "Because she knows you'll look after her."

He gave a soft, rueful sound. "Or because my shed is dry."

"She knew what she was doing," Emmy countered gently.

Their eyes held for a moment, the damp smell of straw and the quiet sound of the cat's breathing filling the air between them.

The cat shifted again, curling her paws under her chin, content enough to accept their quiet presence. A gust pressed against the shed's walls, rattling the wood, but inside it felt oddly peaceful—like the storm had spent itself and left only a hush behind.

Roman crouched down beside Emmy, careful not to crowd her. "She'll need food. Milk, certainly. Something more substantial if she's to feed a litter."

"You sound like you've done this before," Emmy said, glancing at him.

He tilted his head. "Not in recent years. But animals tend to find their way to me. I suppose it's a habit learned long ago."

Emmy smiled faintly. "I should have guessed. You're the type who doesn't send strays away."

"Not if they knock at the right door," he said lightly.

Her breath caught a little at that, though he hadn't looked at her when he said it. She touched her scarf as if adjusting it, letting the moment pass before speaking again. "Do you think she'll be all right here?"

"Yes," Roman replied, watching the cat settle deeper into her straw bed. "This is one place the wind can't reach. She's chosen wisely."

Emmy traced a small circle in the dust with her boot tip. "I don't suppose you'll name her."

He gave her a sidelong look. "Do you think she'd tolerate one?"

"Cats tolerate nothing," Emmy said, grinning. "But I think you should. She deserves at least that much."

Roman's mouth curved. "Then I'll leave it to you."

"Me?"

"You will have more creativity for such things," he said, as if that settled the matter.

Emmy looked back at the cat, who blinked once, unbothered. "I'll have to think on it," she said softly. "Something that suits her... and her kittens."

They rose together, and Roman closed the door gently behind them, leaving the cat in her borrowed sanctuary. The air outside smelled of damp earth and faint smoke from a chimney further off. The grass was still wet enough to cling to the hems of Emmy's skirt, but she hardly noticed.

Roman walked a pace slower than usual, letting her match him as they crossed back toward the main path. His shoulders looked less guarded, less solitary somehow, as though the simple act of showing her the cat had made him easier to read.

"You take everything seriously, don't you?" Emmy said after a moment, her tone light.

He arched a brow. "Do I?"

"Yes. Even a cat showing up in your shed becomes an omen worth noting."

"Perhaps it is," he replied evenly.

She laughed. "You don't give much away, do you?"

He looked at her then, properly, the green of his eyes sharpened by the light. "I give what I can."

It wasn't the sort of answer she'd expected. The words lingered in her mind as they reached the main house again, where the kitchen still smelled faintly of coffee and warm bread. She set her scarf on the back of the chair, letting her curls breathe free.

Roman leaned against the doorframe, watching her with that same measured steadiness. "You're quieter today," he said at last.

Emmy smoothed her sleeve, half-smiling. "I suppose I'm still hearing the storm in my head. And… it's not often I have breakfast cooked for me by someone who isn't family."

His expression softened. "Then I'm glad to have made the exception."

There was no artifice in the way he said it, no charm layered in for effect. It was simple, and somehow that made it land more deeply than any rehearsed compliment might have.

Emmy felt a warmth creep into her cheeks. She busied herself gathering her scarf again, though she wasn't quite ready to leave.

Roman seemed to notice. He straightened, brushing a fleck of straw from his sleeve. "Stay a while longer, if you'd like. There's no rush to the day."

She hesitated only a moment before sitting again at the table. "If you're sure I'm not keeping you from your repairs."

"The roof can wait," he said quietly.

Their talk stretched then, meandering from the storm's aftermath to the old stories of the village—the kind Emmy had begun to collect almost without meaning to. Roman listened more than he spoke, but when he did, his observations carried weight, like stones placed carefully in a stream. And every so often, when she said something that surprised him, he smiled—not the fleeting curve she'd grown used to, but something warmer, truer.

By the time she finally rose to leave, the sun had pushed through enough clouds to strike gold across the wet fields. Roman walked her to the gate, his hand resting lightly against the wood as he opened it for her.

"Thank you," Emmy said softly.

"For what?"

"For breakfast. For… letting me see your shed."

His mouth quirked at that. "My pleasure."

She stepped through, pausing with her scarf in hand. The wind caught at her curls, lifting them. "I'll think on a name," she said.

"I'll hold you to it," he replied.

For a moment they stood there, the air holding something almost unspoken. Then Emmy smiled, and Roman inclined his head in that old-fashioned way of his, as if closing a chapter without ending it.

She turned down the lane, the damp cobbles gleaming beneath her boots. Behind her, she thought she heard the shed door creak again, as if the cat had shifted in her nest—settling, waiting, exactly where she meant to be.

# Chapter 24

Emmy balanced her mug of tea on the arm of the sofa, phone tucked to her ear as she leaned back against the cushions. The flat smelled faintly of rain, the windows still damp from the night before, though the sun had finally broken through. She heard the familiar crackle of her mother's voice before the line steadied.

"Emmeline? Can you hear me?"

"Loud and clear," Emmy said, smiling into the receiver.

Her mother exhaled a sound that was almost a laugh. "Every time there's a storm I picture you being blown half across the country. You'd better tell me you've still got a roof over your head."

"I do," Emmy said, glancing upward as if to make sure. The ceiling looked as tired as it always did, but intact. "I survived, don't worry. The whole village rattled, though. They've closed the school for a week while they check the building over."

"That's sensible." A pause, then, gently: "And you, love? You sound… lighter. Better."

Emmy let the silence hover before answering. "I am. It's taken a while, but I think I'm finally where I'm meant to be. Starting again was the right thing. Hard, but right."

Her father's voice rumbled in from the background: "We're proud of you, Emmeline. You've done what most people would never dare."

The words warmed her, though they also pricked something fragile. "It didn't feel brave at the time. It felt like running."

Her mother made a soft, disapproving sound. "No. It was choosing. There's a difference."

Emmy swallowed, tracing the rim of her mug with one finger. "You know it wasn't easy, what happened before. For a long time, I felt like I didn't exist anymore. Like I was just... surviving someone else's anger. I thought maybe that was all life was going to be. But here, it's quieter. I can breathe. I feel like myself again."

The line was quiet, but Emmy could picture her mother's expression — the way she pressed her lips together when she was holding back words, or tears.

"You're stronger than you realise," her mother said at last. "It's good to hear you sounding like you again. Properly you."

Her father coughed, then added, with gruff affection, "And don't forget, if that wind blows the roof off, you're always welcome back here."

Emmy laughed softly. "I'll keep that in mind."

They lingered on small things after that — her father's allotment, her mother's book club, the neighbour's new puppy — ordinary details that wrapped around Emmy like a blanket. By the time the call ended, she felt steadier than she had in days.

She placed the phone on the table and sat for a moment, listening to the creaks of the old flat as though it were settling with her. The storm had passed, at least for now. Outside, she could hear the street sweeping itself back together — someone hammering at a loose shutter, the whine of a drill, gulls crying above the harbour.

She pulled on her running shoes and stood, stretching until her muscles protested. It was time. She'd told herself she'd start running again weeks ago, but today, with the sun back and her parents' voices still in her ear, she finally felt ready.

The morning air still carried the storm's edge. Emmy felt it the moment she stepped out of her flat, pulling her scarf tighter beneath her chin. A freshness lingered, sharp and damp, like the village had been scrubbed clean overnight but hadn't quite dried. The gulls wheeled low, their cries sharper than usual, carried on a wind that hadn't yet decided if it was finished with its mischief.

She started at a jog, feet slapping lightly on the slick cobbles. Her satin headscarf, knotted securely, kept the dampness from her curls, though every now and then a gust tugged at it playfully. She headed down toward the harbour, past shuttered shopfronts where chalkboards leaned blank against doorways. Someone had propped a ladder against the baker's roof, tiles stacked neatly at its base, ready to replace those the storm had claimed. The whole village seemed to be tidying itself, piece by piece, as though embarrassed at having been caught in disarray.

Her route took her along the narrow street that ran parallel to the sea wall. The air tasted faintly of salt, and somewhere a door creaked in the wind. She passed Mrs. Calloway, broom in hand, who gave her a bemused smile.

"Morning, Miss Trevelyn. You'll catch your death running in this weather."

Emmy laughed, breath already quickening. "It's warmer when you're moving."

The harbour came into view, the water restless but no longer angry. Boats strained against their moorings, one with its mast still lashed, splintered from the night before. Men moved carefully along the decks, checking lines, hammering at damaged planks. It looked almost choreographed — the whole community quietly, stubbornly putting itself back together.

Emmy slowed as she passed, watching their bent heads, their steady rhythm, and felt something like admiration.

She pushed herself harder as the lane rose steeply past the harbour. Her legs burned, lungs tight, but she welcomed it. Once, runs like this had been about escape — pounding footsteps covering the noise of arguments in her old flat, the sick heaviness in her chest chasing her into the dark. But now the rhythm felt different. It wasn't flight, it was presence. Her body's insistence that she was here, alive, moving forward on her own terms.

She slowed at the edge of the fields, where the lane gave way to hedgerows dripping with rain. A kestrel hovered in the wind, wings quivering, before diving toward the rough grass. Emmy stopped just long enough to watch, breathing hard, and felt a strange kinship with the bird — suspended, but purposeful.

By the time she turned back toward the village, her limbs ached with pleasant fatigue. The rooftops reappeared, damp slates shining in a patch of sunlight that broke briefly through the clouds. The bell tower stood firm, as though it had withstood far worse storms in its time.

She walked the last stretch to cool down, breath clouding in the crisp air. The sound of boots scuffing gravel reached her ears. Looking up, she saw Roman coming from the grocers, a sack slung over one shoulder. It was bulkier than she'd have managed with such ease, but he bore it without strain, his stride steady.

As he drew closer, she caught the bold black letters stamped across the sack: CAT FOOD.

"That's a fair haul," she said, grinning despite her breathlessness. "Planning to open a cattery?"

His eyes lit faintly. "Not quite. Just making sure I'm ready. It won't be long now."

Emmy's grin softened. She didn't need him to explain— the stray had made herself comfortable in his outbuilding days ago, and the swell of her belly left little doubt as to what was coming.

"Smart," Emmy said. "I've heard they eat like wolves when there are mouths to feed."

Roman gave a small, almost amused shake of his head. "She already does. I can only imagine what's ahead." There was a softness in his tone—reluctant, maybe, but fond. It warmed Emmy's chest in a way she hadn't expected.

"Still," she teased lightly, "better than her turning up in your kitchen."

The corner of his mouth ticked. "I'd sooner she didn't. But she's earned her place, I suppose."

The air between them lingered, quiet but companionable. Emmy tugged at her laces to loosen them, more to steady herself than out of real need. "And you? Storm repairs?"

Roman inclined his head slightly. "The courtyard took the worst of it. Pots shattered, soil scattered, one of the trees leaning where it shouldn't. It needs putting right."

She imagined him there, sleeves rolled, hands in earth and stone. The picture suited him too well.

He adjusted the sack on his shoulder, then added—deliberately, almost carefully: "I thought perhaps you might join me. For a meal. Today. Say, at one?"

The directness of it stopped her for a beat. "Sorry?"

"Today," he clarified. His voice wasn't careless—if anything, it was deliberately plain, as though he wanted to leave no room for misreading. "I'd like to cook for you. A quiet meal, nothing grand. One o'clock?"

The world seemed to tilt, just slightly. Emmy blinked, the words catching somewhere between surprise and anticipation.

"One o'clock," she repeated, more to steady herself than anything else.

"If you're free," he added.

Her lips curved almost before she could stop them. "And if I'm not?"

The faintest, rarest flicker of play touched his mouth. "Then I'll resign myself to a lonely meal and far too much food."

They held each other's gaze a fraction too long, the air charged with something unspoken. Emmy cleared her throat lightly. "Well… to spare you the tragedy of excessive food, I suppose I'd better come."

Roman's smile deepened—not broad, not careless, but real. "Then it's settled."

"One o'clock," she echoed.

He inclined his head, almost a bow, before shifting the sack again. "Until then."

And with that, he moved down the lane, the sack balanced effortlessly against his shoulder. Emmy watched him until the bend swallowed him from sight.

When she finally turned toward her own door, she realised she was smiling—helplessly, stupidly smiling, her pulse quick in her throat. She pressed her back to the wood once she slipped inside, the ordinary smell of her flat wrapping around her, layered now with something else: anticipation.

One o'clock. Hours away, but already the day had changed its shape around it.

\* \* \*

By midday the clouds had broken just enough to let light through, a pale, shifting wash across the village rooftops. Emmy checked the clock for what must have been the fifth time, then gave herself a quiet shake. She had showered, dressed, tidied the same stack of books on her table twice. Her reflection in the small mirror by the door had already suffered her inspection more than once—curly hair pinned and coaxed, makeup light but present, skirt smoothed so many times it could have flattened stone.

She wasn't sure what she was nervous about. It wasn't as though she hadn't sat with Roman before. But this was different. He had invited her—not as a polite convenience, not as an accident of place, but deliberately.

At ten minutes to one, she tugged her scarf against the wind and set out. The estate gates stood just beyond the lane, their ironwork catching the weak light like ink strokes on paper. Beyond, the house rose with its familiar silhouette, though she swore it looked larger with the anticipation wound in her chest.

Roman met her at the door, his shirtsleeves rolled despite the chill, a faint dusting of flour at the edge of his cuff. The sight of it tugged something unexpectedly soft at her heart.

"You're prompt," he said, a curve at his mouth.

"You invited me," she replied. "I wasn't about to be late."

He stepped aside, letting her in. The hall was broad but not grandiose; its age spoke more than any ornament, wood polished by hands and years. He didn't lead her toward the dining room, though, or the orangery she remembered. Instead, he guided her down a quieter passage, one lined with tall doors whose hinges murmured as they passed.

Then he stopped at a wide set of glass-paned doors and pushed them open.

The world shifted.

The courtyard opened like another country within the house—a square of sky framed by stone walls, its heart claimed by a tree that stretched upward, branches feathering into leaves just brushing the air above. Light slipped through and dappled the flagstones, catching on petals and glass alike.

A fountain, simple but graceful, stood at the centre: water spilling from a stone basin into a shallow pool, the sound steady and low, as though it had no need to hurry. Moss softened its edges, bright against pale stone, and lily leaves floated in the water's calm surface.

Around the edges, flowers grew in bursts of colour—old roses climbing the walls, their stems woven with ivy; pots of lavender releasing a faint sweetness each time the breeze shifted; herbs spilling from terracotta planters, rosemary and thyme brushing her sleeve as she passed.

Stone benches sat in the shade, worn smooth at their edges. A wrought-iron table stood off to one side, already laid for two with simple white plates, wineglasses catching the light, and candles ready to be lit when dusk came.

Emmy's breath caught. It was like stepping into the heart of a secret—half garden, half room, utterly private.

She turned slowly, taking it in. "Roman… it's beautiful."

He watched her, not the courtyard. "It's survived a great many storms," he said softly. "Though I had to put some of it right again this week."

Her eyes found the edges where soil still bore the signs of being swept, pots shifted back into place, a few broken shards gathered neatly against the wall. Yet even in its imperfection it held a kind of timelessness, as though it had been waiting for centuries to be admired again.

"I had no idea this was here," she murmured.

"You wouldn't," he said simply. "It isn't for most."

Her gaze met his, something unspoken passing in the space between them. She looked back at the fountain, at the way the water traced its endless path. "It feels… like it doesn't belong to the world outside. Like you could forget time here."

Roman's mouth shifted, just slightly. "Perhaps that's why I keep it."

She turned back to him, her pulse lifting in her throat. "You did all this yourself?"

"In parts," he admitted. "Stone doesn't lay itself, and plants don't tend themselves. But it's less a matter of making than of listening. The place tells you what it wants to be."

Emmy let her fingers brush the rosemary at her side. "And you listen."

"I try," he said.

The quiet between them was not empty but full, brimming with the sound of the fountain and the light shifting across leaves. Emmy felt the strangeness of standing in the heart of his home—where the world narrowed to four walls and a sky—and realised how much he had trusted her by opening it.

"Shall we?" he asked, gesturing toward the table.

She nodded, and as she moved toward it she glanced once more at the fountain, the tree, the flowers climbing toward air. She thought of her own flat, with its small window and its books stacked where they could fit, and felt an ache she couldn't quite name—something between awe and longing.

Roman pulled out a chair for her. His gestures were always careful, deliberate, as though each one carried weight. As she sat, she caught the faint scent of baking and herbs that seemed to come not only from the courtyard but from the kitchen beyond.

Whatever he had prepared, she thought, it would taste of history and care, just as this place did.

And as he poured the wine, steady and unhurried, Emmy felt her nerves soften—not vanish, but ease—into the rhythm of water and light and the quiet of stone.

Emmy leaned back in her chair, letting her gaze sweep across the fountain, the walls softened by vines, the tree that seemed to reach as if it had always belonged here.

"It really is beautiful out here," she said, her voice hushed without meaning it to be. "Like a dream. Like somewhere a person would come to... to remember how to breathe."

Roman's eyes followed hers, though the weight of his attention was never really on the walls or the flowers. "That was always its purpose," he said quietly. "The estate was built with this place in mind."

She looked back at him, brow lifting. "Really? You mean... from the start?"

"Yes." He rested his forearms lightly on the table, hands folded loosely. "My father began the build. He wanted a home that opened inward as much as it faced outward—a place that kept its heart safe. After he passed, it fell to me to see it finished." His eyes flicked briefly toward the tree at the centre, its branches shifting faintly in the wind above. "My mother loved this courtyard most of all. When she was... unwell, she spent her days here. It became her sanctuary."

Emmy's throat tightened at the simplicity with which he said it, the weight that seemed folded into each word. She followed his gaze to the stone benches, imagining someone seated there, pale in the shade, drawing strength from the fountain's steady music.

"It feels like it," she said softly. "Like the whole house is holding its breath around this space."

He gave the faintest of nods. "Perhaps it is."

For a while the water filled the pause between them, the sound unhurried, timeless. Emmy traced her fingers along the rim of her glass, her thoughts catching on something he had said.

"I'm surprised," she admitted, turning back to him. "I thought this house must be… much older. Hundreds of years, at least." Her lips curved as she added, "And you hardly look old enough to have had a hand in building it yourself."

Roman's mouth tilted at one corner—half smile, half shadow. "Appearances are often deceiving."

She blinked at him, half amused, half puzzled, the flicker of his words lodging somewhere in the quiet of her thoughts. "You mean I'd be surprised?"

"Very," he said, and though the warmth in his eyes gentled the words, something in his tone suggested a truth larger than she could yet see.

The fountain trickled on, as if it had overheard secrets before and would again.

Roman rose with an unhurried grace, setting aside his wine glass. "The food will lose its patience if I don't bring it out," he said, the faint humour in his tone breaking the weight of the moment.

Emmy smiled, watching him disappear through the arched doorway to the kitchen. The courtyard breathed around her: the fountain's steady murmur, the soft scuff of leaves shifting above, sunlight dappled into moving coins across the flagstones and the cloth. The air held rosemary and thyme and the clean mineral coolness of stone after rain.

When he returned, he carried a wide earthenware dish that looked older than either of them by centuries. Steam curled from the lid; the fragrance came first—herb-bright, citrus-lifted, the warm, savoury depth of roasted meat.

He set it down with quiet assurance. "Chicken in mustard and wine," he said. "A recipe my mother favoured. I've added a few touches—lemon for brightness, rosemary from the garden. It keeps the dish alive."

Emmy laughed softly, surprised despite herself. "You make it sound like a family heirloom."

"In some ways, it is." He lifted the lid; the scent deepened, generous and comforting. Beside it, he set a dark-crusted loaf, still warm, and a small bowl of early greens glossed with oil that caught the afternoon sun in thin, golden threads.

"You made all this?" she asked, leaning forward despite herself.

"Cooking isn't so different from anything else," he said, carving with the neat economy of long practice. "Patience. Attention. A respect for what came before."

"You make patience sound like an art."

"It is." He set a plate before her, then one for himself. "An art most people rush past."

The first bite stopped her talking: tender chicken, mustard's heat softened into something round by the wine, lemon glowing at the edges, rosemary breathing through. It tasted like care. Like a memory made present.

"Roman," she said, setting her fork down for a moment, "this is… it's better than any restaurant. I'm not exaggerating."

A line eased at the corner of his mouth—almost a smile. "Then I've succeeded."

For a while they ate, the fountain speaking its low, continuous sentence, a small wind tilting the sunlight on the table. When conversation returned, it did so naturally, as if the courtyard itself had made room for it.

"You said once you came here for a fresh start," he said, resting his knife lightly against the plate.

Emmy's gaze fell to her hands. She drew a breath. "I did." Another breath, steadier. "When my last relationship ended, I went home first. To my parents. It was the only place I could think to go. I told myself I'd stay a week. I stayed longer." She glanced up, offered a quick, apologetic smile. "They made it easy to stop, to rest. To be small for a bit. But I realised I couldn't live there and pretend I hadn't broken something open. I was safe…but I was becoming a guest in my own life."

He didn't interrupt. The afternoon light shifted a fraction across his knuckles; the water went on speaking in the middle ground.

412

"So I started looking." Her voice was quiet but sure now. "For a place that didn't know me, or what I'd been through. Somewhere I could be new without explaining why. The village felt... honest. A little scuffed, a little stubborn. It made sense."

He inclined his head once, as if acknowledging a compass point found.

"My last relationship wasn't dramatic at the start," she went on. "Just words. Corrections. The kind that makes you smaller without quite noticing. Then came the arguments, the blame, doors slammed harder each time. And when it crossed into..." She paused, the word like a stone she chose to set down. "Bruises. That was the line. I knew if I didn't leave, I'd lose the part of me that could."

The courtyard seemed to listen. A leaf let go somewhere above and landed without sound.

"You left," Roman said, not as a question but a marker.

"I did." Her eyes shone but held. "It took me too long, but I did."

Something shifted in his face—no pity, no anger, only a quiet recognition, as if her story illuminated a map he already knew by heart. His hands, relaxed a moment earlier, had curled; he made them open gently on the table.

"You were stronger than you think," he said. "Strength doesn't wait until it feels ready. It shows itself when it has to."

She let out a breath that almost became a laugh. "You always talk like that. Like you've lived it already."

For once he didn't retreat into a silence that closed the subject. He held her gaze, steady, a softness there she hadn't seen before. "Maybe I have," he said.

The words settled between them like a small, bright weight. She didn't press. The light moved again; a bird quickened through the branches; the wine in their glasses caught a pale flare and then went still.

After a time, she smiled, the heaviness lifting just enough to let warmth back in. "Well. If you keep feeding me like this, I might forgive you for being so mysterious."

That drew a quiet, genuine sound from him—near to a laugh. "Then I'll consider myself warned."

They ate a little more, not to fill silence but because the food deserved it. When he tore the bread and passed her a piece, their fingers brushed—a simple contact, ordinary in any other place. Here, it felt like a promise that didn't need words: you're here; you're seen; you're safe.

Emmy leaned back in her chair, her plate mostly finished, fingers curled lightly around the stem of her glass. The sunlight had softened now, no longer direct, broken into shifting patterns by the branches overhead. It seemed to wrap them in a gentler quiet.

She studied him for a moment—the way his profile held stillness, the lines at the corner of his eyes when he glanced down. She hesitated, then spoke with the courage that came from wine and the comfort of the courtyard.

"Can I ask you something a little personal?"

Roman's eyes flicked to hers. He didn't smile this time, but neither did he close the door. "You can ask. Whether I answer is another matter."

She laughed softly. "Fair enough." She traced the rim of her glass once with her fingertip before continuing. "Have you ever been in love?"

For the first time all afternoon, his composure seemed to waver. Not collapse, but tilt, like a shadow shifting where you didn't expect it. He didn't answer immediately, and Emmy felt almost tempted to take the question back.

At last, he nodded once, as if acknowledging something long buried. "Yes."

The quiet was different now—not awkward, but charged, like a page that had just been turned. Emmy leaned in a little, waiting. "And?"

Roman set his glass down. He looked at the fountain as if its voice might lend him words. "It was a long time ago. Longer than I sometimes care to admit. She was…" His mouth curved, faint and private. "Brave. She had a way of walking into a room as though she belonged there, whether anyone agreed or not. And she laughed often. It was… contagious."

Emmy smiled, picturing the ghost of someone she'd never know. "It sounds like you loved her very much."

"I did," he said simply. The words landed with more weight than any flourish could have given them.

"So… what happened?" she asked gently.

His gaze lingered on the courtyard's tree, its branches swaying faintly as though stirred by some memory. For a long while, he said nothing, and Emmy wondered if he'd simply let the silence answer for him. But then he spoke, low and careful.

"Some things… don't last. Not because the love is less, but because the world around it won't allow it. She wanted things I couldn't give. A life that moved forward in ways mine… didn't. I tried to hold it together, for her. But love, if it's to mean anything, shouldn't be a cage."

The phrasing struck Emmy—beautiful, yet tinged with something deeper than regret. She tilted her head, searching his expression. "So you ended it?"

He breathed out slowly, a sound half like a sigh. "Yes. It was the only mercy I could offer."

Emmy's chest tightened, imagining the pain of such a choice. She set her glass aside, her voice softer still. "That must have been hard."

Roman finally looked at her. His eyes caught the fractured sunlight, green deepened by shadow, and for the first time she saw not just mystery but something raw, something he wasn't used to showing. "Some things never stop being hard."

Her throat worked as she swallowed. The air between them had shifted again—less playful now, more fragile, as though they were both standing at the edge of something neither could quite name. She wanted to reach across the table, to close the space his words had opened, but she wasn't sure if it would be welcome.

Instead, she said quietly, "I'm sorry."

He gave the faintest shake of his head. "Don't be. It taught me what love costs. And what it gives, if only for a time."

The fountain kept speaking; a bird crossed overhead, scattering brief shadows across the stone. Emmy let the moment rest, her heart steady but full.

After a while, she smiled, small but genuine. "For what it's worth, I'm glad you told me."

Roman's gaze softened, his voice almost a murmur. "For what it's worth… so am I."

The words seemed to linger long after they were spoken, hanging between them like the golden flecks of light shifting over the courtyard. Emmy lowered her gaze to her hands, clasped together on the table, before daring a glance back at him.

Roman's posture was still composed, but there was a tension in him—like a man used to holding himself at a distance, suddenly aware that he'd let something slip free.

Emmy took a breath. "It doesn't sound like you regret loving her. Even if it ended."

His mouth curved faintly, but not in amusement. "No. To regret love would be to regret being human. And I wouldn't trade that."

Something about the way he said it—like a confession wrapped in poetry—made her chest tighten. She hesitated, then reached for her glass again, if only to steady herself. Her fingers brushed the stem clumsily, and before she could catch it, the glass tipped sideways.

Wine spread across the table in a thin crimson stream.

"Oh, I'm so sorry," she said quickly, reaching for the napkin at her side.

But Roman was faster. He caught the glass upright in one swift movement, and his hand covered hers before she could blot at the spill. The contact was brief—her skin warmed instantly under his touch—but he didn't pull away right away.

Their eyes met across the small, simple point of connection.

Emmy's breath faltered. His hand was cool, steady, as though it belonged exactly where it was.

Roman seemed to realise the same thing in the same heartbeat. He released her gently, as though careful not to startle her. He took the napkin himself, dabbing at the wine with deliberate precision. "No harm done," he said, his voice softer than before.

But his gaze lifted again, and this time he didn't look away.

Emmy found herself smiling—nervous, but unable to stop. "You're very quick."

"Years of practice," he murmured, though something in the weight of his tone suggested the words carried more than clumsy wine glasses.

The silence that followed wasn't heavy now—it was charged in a different way, like the brief pause before rain. Emmy rested her chin lightly in her hand, studying him.

"You talk like someone who's lived twice as much as he lets on," she said, teasing lightly, though her voice wavered with a sincerity she hadn't meant to reveal.

Roman's lips curved into that faint, knowing smile again—the one that always seemed to mean more than it said. "And you talk like someone who notices more than she should."

She laughed, a low, quiet sound. "Maybe I do."

For a long moment, they simply looked at one another, the air thick with something unnamed but unmistakable.

Roman's hand rested still on the table now, close enough that if she stretched her fingers, she could touch it again.

And though neither of them moved, it felt like something had shifted—a thread drawn between them, fine but unbreakable.

A light breeze moved through the courtyard, setting the lavender heads nodding. Roman reached toward the nearest stem, pinched a sprig free, and turned it once between his fingers as if measuring its colour against the afternoon.

"May I?" he asked.

Emmy felt the question land in more than one place. She nodded.

He stepped closer—not hurried, never hurried—and tucked the lavender behind her ear with a care that felt older than habit. His fingertips brushed her temple, a touch so slight it might have been accidental if not for the way his gaze held hers while he did it.

"There," he said. "It suits you."

She laughed under her breath, the sound small but unguarded. "I'll smell like your garden."

"You already do," he said, and the faintest warmth loosened his voice.

They let the quiet settle again, newly shaped. A gull called somewhere beyond the glass; water kept its steady run in the basin. Roman's hand fell back to the table, but he didn't step away.

"I wasn't planning to rush off," she said, half-teasing, half-confessing.

"Good," he replied, as if that settled something in him. "I hoped you wouldn't."

He lifted the platter to clear space, the easy domestic motion at odds with the formality she sometimes felt from him. "There's something for after," he added, a ghost of mischief passing over his mouth. "If you'll humour me."

"What have you made?"

"Lemon posset," he said. "Old recipe. New patience."

"That sounds like you," she said, smiling.

"It does." He nodded toward her chair. "Stay. I'll bring it out."

He disappeared through the arch; the courtyard reshaped itself around his absence. Emmy lifted a hand to the sprig tucked at her ear, unsure why the small thing undid her more than any grand gesture could have. When he returned, he carried two small glasses set on a narrow wooden board, their surfaces faintly clouded, sunshine caught in their pale depth. He set them down and slid one toward her, along with two thin spoons.

She tasted first: cool, silken, lemon bright without sharpness. It seemed to carry the afternoon in it, the filtered light, the hum of the fountain.

"Oh," she said, surprised into honesty. "Roman—this is… perfect."

"Then that's two successes in one day," he said, lightly pleased.

They ate in companionable quiet. A petal let go somewhere above and drifted down, spinning, to rest near her saucer. Emmy watched it land and then glanced at him, the question that had hovered between them since lunch finding its shape again, gentler now.

"Thank you for telling me about her," she said. "You didn't have to."

"I know," he replied. "I wanted to give you something true."

She let that sit. The lavender's scent rose when she turned, a small reminder against her cheek.

"What happens next?" she asked, not quite meaning the afternoon.

Roman weighed his answer, as if he were checking the balance of it in his hand. "We go slowly," he said at last. "We learn the shape of things as they are, not as we imagine them. And we are kind to whatever we find."

She looked down, smiling despite the sudden pressure in her chest. "I can do slow."

"I thought you might."

They finished the posset, swapping the last spoonfuls with quiet jokes about fairness and portion sizes. When the dishes were cleared to the side, Roman stood and offered his hand—not ceremony, simply invitation.

"Walk with me," he said.

They moved the long way round the courtyard, not to see anything new but to see the same things more closely. He showed her the faint chisel mark on the corner stone—his father's hand, he said, without adornment—and the line along the paving where a crack had been mended so precisely you'd miss it unless someone loved the place enough to point. At a low wall he paused, eyes turned toward the house, listening the way one listens for weather.

"I'll check on her later," he said, meaning the cat without needing to name her. "It feels close."

Emmy nodded. The thought didn't scare her; it steadied her. "I'll help," she said.

"I was hoping you'd say that."

They returned to the table as the sun thinned a fraction, light sliding to a softer angle across the stone. Roman poured water; Emmy tucked her feet under her chair, lavender still anchored at her ear, an ordinary grace note that made everything else ring.

"Tell me what you're reading," he said, and she did—two novels and a slim book of poems she'd found shelved crooked in the shop downstairs. He listened with that still attention of his, not interrupting, only asking a question when it added to what she wanted to say. When he spoke in turn, it was to offer one quiet memory of a line that had saved him once on a winter afternoon, the words themselves unimportant, the saving plain.

Time went on without urgency. The glass above ticked faintly as it adjusted to the cooling air; somewhere a door in the house thudded softly shut, the old timbers answering with a small, approving groan. Roman refilled her glass. The lavender shifted when she laughed. Nothing demanded an ending.

"Stay awhile longer," he said, though she was already staying.

"I will."


The hours folded in quietly, the sort of afternoon where time didn't announce itself but slid by in soft increments—like the sun slowly shifting across the courtyard stone. They walked together along the long corridor that flanked the orangery, their steps echoing against flagstones worn down by centuries.

Roman showed her the library briefly—shelves lined in uneven rows of books, their spines faded in different shades of brown, inked titles almost rubbed away with age. Emmy's fingertips hovered over them, curious, though she resisted the temptation to pry.

Later, they returned to the courtyard where the soft trickle of water fell from the fountain's stone lip, the air gently fragrant with herbs and trailing roses. They talked without urgency, about small things and larger ones, laughter finding its way into their pauses. Emmy told him about the chaos of teaching her youngest pupils to write in cursive and how the "g"s always came out like miniature disasters. Roman smiled at that—his laugh quieter, contained, but unmistakably genuine.

It surprised her how easy it became. The silences no longer felt like cliffs she needed to fill, but steady ground. Sometimes they simply sat, side by side on the cold stone bench by the fountain, Emmy with her skirts gathered close to keep the damp at bay, Roman with his long legs stretched forward, a hand idly tracing a pattern on the moss-slick stone at his side. When the wind rose and shivered the branches above, he glanced at her as if to check she wasn't chilled, and she felt the warmth of that look more keenly than the shawl at her shoulders.

By the time shadows began lengthening and the light softened toward evening, Emmy almost forgot the outside world existed at all. She might have been in another century, kept in this walled garden of stone and quiet green.

Roman stirred at last, as though recalling something. "I should look in on her," he said, his voice lowering with thought.

"On who?" Emmy asked, turning to him.

"The cat," he replied. "It won't be long before her litter comes. If you don't mind—would you like to see her?"

There was no hesitation in Emmy's answer. "Of course."

They left the sheltered courtyard, passing through a side corridor where cool drafts whispered against the glassless windows. The path to the outbuildings wound across a stretch of uneven cobbles, the stones damp from earlier rain, their hollows catching little mirrors of water. The sky above had begun to deepen into muted blues and silvers, the evening breeze carrying the scent of wet leaves and earth.

The outbuilding itself stood slightly apart, weathered but sturdy, its timber beams darkened with age. Roman lifted the latch carefully, letting Emmy step through first. Inside, the air smelled of hay and woodsmoke long since absorbed into the walls. Shafts of dimming daylight pressed through gaps in the roof boards, lighting the dust in suspended motes.

In one corner, on a bed of straw Roman must have arranged earlier, the stray cat lay curled. Her body shifted with uneasy ripples, paws kneading against the straw, ears flicking back at their approach.

"Oh," Emmy whispered, her heart tugging. "She's started."

Roman crouched down, movements unhurried, and the cat stilled slightly, blinking at him with wide, liquid eyes. He reached out a steadying hand but didn't touch, simply keeping his presence close enough to calm her. "She's been restless all morning," he murmured. "I thought it might be today."

Emmy knelt beside him, her skirts brushing the straw. She felt a strange mix of awe and worry, the rawness of new life pressing close. "What should we do?"

"Mostly nothing," Roman said gently. "Nature knows the way better than we do. But sometimes—" he glanced at her, a wry flicker of a smile "—a little encouragement helps."

The first contraction rippled visibly through the cat's body, and she let out a low, plaintive sound. Emmy's instinctive hand hovered, and Roman placed his lightly beneath hers, guiding her fingers nearer. "There," he said. "She'll take comfort in your nearness."

Their hands almost brushed, and Emmy felt her breath catch at the warmth of his skin, the steadiness in it. She focused on the cat, though, stroking lightly along the air just above her flank.

Minutes stretched, punctuated by small gasps and rustles. Then, with a sudden shift of motion, the first tiny kitten came—slick, fragile, trembling against the straw. The mother turned immediately, instinct ruling, and Emmy pressed a hand to her chest, moved beyond words.

Roman, calm as though he'd seen it many times before, reached for a clean scrap of cloth folded neatly on the ledge beside him. "She'll do most of the work herself," he explained softly, "but sometimes the little ones need a hand." He dabbed gently, careful not to interfere with the mother, and laid the cloth aside.

Another contraction came, then another kitten, this one letting out a startlingly loud mewl as it found the air. Emmy laughed softly through the lump in her throat, her eyes bright. "They're so small," she whispered. "So impossibly small."

Roman's lips curved in a rare, unguarded smile. "Small things endure. You'd be surprised how fierce they are."

The cat continued, the rhythm of birth unfolding until at last four kittens nestled against her, each no bigger than Emmy's palm, their tiny bodies pressing close for warmth. The mother's sides rose and fell, exhausted but content, her purr faint but steady.

Emmy's gaze lingered on the new family, her chest swelling with a tender ache she hadn't expected. "I've never seen anything like it," she said softly.

Roman's reply was quiet, reflective. "It never loses its wonder. New life—against all odds."

They remained kneeling side by side, the straw prickling beneath their knees, their shoulders brushing without either shifting away. The kittens rooted blindly for milk, their small cries threading through the hush of the outbuilding.

Emmy tilted her head, glancing at him. Candlelight would have suited the moment, but instead the fading daylight caught his profile, all sharp lines softened by shadow. Something unreadable stirred in his expression as he watched the kittens—something both wistful and deeply protective.

"You've done this before," she said gently. It wasn't a question.

His eyes flicked toward hers, thoughtful. "Yes." A pause, then: "Enough times to know how fragile beginnings are."

Emmy studied him in the quiet that followed, aware of how near they were, of the rare warmth in his voice. She didn't press further, though curiosity itched at her. Instead, she looked back to the kittens, letting the moment stand as it was: tender, whole, unspoken.

The air in the outbuilding grew cooler as the light slipped further away. Roman eventually rose, offering her his hand to help her up from the straw. She took it without thinking, the clasp firm, steadying her far more than it needed to.

"Come," he said softly. "They'll be all right now. Let's leave her to rest."

Outside, the sky had deepened into indigo, and the first stars pricked through where the clouds had begun to break. Emmy lingered at the threshold, her pulse still quickened by the closeness of it all—the birth, the kittens, Roman's steady presence beside her.

As they walked back toward the courtyard, she felt the lavender sprig still tucked in her hair, its faint fragrance rising whenever the breeze caught. She wondered if he'd notice it again, or if it was meant only for that one small, perfect moment hours ago.

Either way, the day had taken root in her. And she sensed—though she didn't yet know how to name it—that something between them had, too.

# Chapter 25

A few days had passed since the kittens were born, and the rhythm of Emmy's week had folded itself back into the ordinary. She had spent most of her time upstairs in her flat, catching up on the pile of children's books waiting to be marked, lesson plans half-finished, and the quiet but endless rotation of housekeeping. The kind of things that never seemed urgent until they built into little towers of guilt on her desk.

It had been strangely comforting, though — to ground herself in the familiar after the intensity of that day with Roman, crouched beside the straw, both of them hushed as if the world itself held its breath for the stray's new family. Since then, she had not seen him, though the image of him gently lifting one of the newborn kittens to settle it closer to its mother had kept replaying, stubborn and vivid.

Saturday arrived with a clean, bright light that made the village look freshly painted. Emmy had opened her window to let in the morning, hair pinned loosely back, when she heard the low, steady hum of an engine. Looking down, she blinked in surprise. Roman's dark-green Land Rover was idling outside the shopfront, boxy and solid, as if it had always belonged to him and the village both.

When she stepped out, he leaned across to push open the stubborn passenger door, the gesture almost habitual.

"I didn't know you drove," Emmy said, smiling as she climbed in.

"I prefer to walk," Roman replied, glancing over as he settled the gearstick into place. "It slows the world. You notice more that way — the air, the soil, the sound of birds' wings. You feel the ground carry you." His mouth quirked, almost apologetic. "But Gibside isn't on the doorstep. Driving is essential this time."

"Gibside?"

"Have you been?"

She shook her head.

"Then today's your introduction," he said simply, starting the engine properly. "It's a National Trust estate now — woodland, old ruins, a chapel, an avenue so long you'll forget you ever came to the end of it. If you don't fall in love with it, I'll eat my coat."

The ride out of the village followed lanes hemmed in by hawthorn and stone walls, the hedgerows swollen with green. Emmy watched the fields rolling past, sunlight flickering through gaps, and found herself strangely soothed by the quietness between them. No radio, no chatter for the sake of it. Just the steady patience of the old Land Rover and the occasional low call of wood pigeons.

By the time they reached the entrance gates of Gibside, the sky had opened up wider, pale blue streaked with slow clouds. They pulled in beneath tall brick piers topped with carved stone, and beyond stretched a long, straight avenue lined with towering trees, their branches arching overhead like a cathedral nave.

Emmy caught her breath. "Oh—"

Roman smiled, as though he'd been waiting for that. "The Grand Walk. Nearly three hundred years of people coming here just to stand where you're standing. The National Trust look after it now — they've cleared the storm damage, but the bones of it remain. You'll see."

They set out on foot. Gravel crunched beneath their shoes, the long avenue pulling them forward as if it had its own gravity. The air smelled sharp with pine and damp earth, washed clean by the storm earlier in the week. Children's voices carried faintly ahead, and a dog barked with uncomplicated joy.

As they walked, Emmy tilted her head back to take it in — the way the trunks seemed impossibly tall, the canopy layering the sky into patches of green and light. "It feels... staged," she said softly. "Like a painting, or a set."

433

Roman's voice was low, carrying an old resonance. "That was the intention. Designed for spectacle, for declaration. People used to promenade here in their best coats, showing themselves off beneath trees that would outlive them all." He glanced at her. "The guidebooks will tell you the dates and names. But walking here — that's the truth of it."

They passed a clearing where the Derwent river curved below, catching the light like spilled silver. Further on, the great column came into view, rising against the sky with Liberty poised at its peak, torch raised high.

"She looks smaller than I imagined," Emmy said.

Roman's eyes lifted. "They call her Liberty, though her features are more English than Roman. Originally, the torch was gilded — it caught the light for miles. Now the leaflets don't mention that. Or that it was meant as a kind of challenge, visible to rivals across the valley. A reminder that wealth could reach higher than principle."

Emmy looked at him. "You know all that from the Trust boards?"

His mouth curved, but he didn't answer directly. "Something like that."

They carried on, toward the Palladian chapel that gleamed pale against the blue. Its symmetry struck Emmy first — elegant, balanced, proud. Inside, the air was cool and carried the faintest scent of old stone. Sunlight broke in coloured pools through tall windows, painting the pews with soft gold.

Roman stood near a column, his hand briefly brushing the stone as if in greeting. "They say James Paine designed it," he murmured, "and they're not wrong. But a local mason did more than his share — you can see it in the marks high on the cornice. His initials are still there, though few notice."

Emmy tilted her head, hearing something in his tone. He spoke less like a man recalling facts, more like one remembering a conversation. "You and your thin places," she teased, though gently.

Roman only smiled faintly, but his eyes lingered on the high windows, green catching the sunlight until they seemed almost bright.

They wandered on through woodland paths, where pine needles softened each step and shafts of sun angled down through storm-broken gaps. Birds darted between branches, restless with the season. Emmy breathed deeply, the air resinous and clean. The sound of the river reached them again — a steady rush that invited silence rather than speech.

When the path dipped toward the bank, Roman held out a hand without fuss. Emmy took it because she wanted to, and because it felt natural, and for a few steps longer than necessary she didn't let go.

By the time they returned to the estate's heart, the sun was past its highest point, and they followed a sign down toward a small tea room tucked in what had once been a stable block.

The smell of warm scones drifted out as they stepped inside. Roman ordered without hesitation — two scones with strawberry jam and clotted cream, and a pot of strong tea.

Emmy laughed as they carried the tray out. "Strawberry? I thought you'd be the lemon-curd sort."

"Lemon has its place," he said with a flicker of amusement. "But tradition deserves its turn."

They sat side by side, the stone bench cool beneath them, the taste of strawberry sharp and sweet, the cream thick and soft. Emmy found herself laughing when a smear caught at the corner of her mouth, and Roman, after the briefest pause, reached across with his thumb to brush it away. The touch was light, gone in a heartbeat, but it left her warmer than the sun.

Later, they walked again, slower this time. The path curved back toward the river where a great willow swept down to touch the water. Its branches swayed, curtain-like, stirring with the breeze.

They stopped beneath it, half-hidden from the rest of the world. Emmy tilted her face up, the play of leaves scattering sunlight over her hair.

Roman reached without seeming to think, plucking a stray leaf caught there. For a moment he hesitated, then tucked it gently behind her ear, his fingers brushing her temple.

The sound of the river filled the quiet that followed. Emmy felt it all — the space between them narrowing, the weight of things unspoken.

But neither moved further.

The moment held, suspended like the willow's branches, then softened into something quieter. A kind of peace.

They stood there until the light shifted, before turning back along the path together.


The path they followed sloped gently, gravel crunching underfoot, guiding them toward another stretch of trees where the canopy broke and sunlight pooled. A weathered wooden sign pointed them toward the walled garden. Emmy's curiosity brightened instantly—she had always loved enclosed gardens, the promise of something hidden within stone and brick, its own little world sealed away.

Roman glanced sideways at her expression and smiled faintly. "You'll like this," he said, almost as if reading her thoughts.

"I already do," she admitted. "I love the idea of a garden behind walls—it feels secret, even if it's open to everyone."

When they reached the entrance, Emmy stopped in her tracks. The tall brick walls rose like sentinels, streaked with age and softened by ivy. The wide iron gate stood open, as though inviting them in. Beyond, a tapestry of flowers and greenery spilled across neat paths, framed by espaliered fruit trees climbing the very walls themselves.

Emmy drew in her breath. "It's like walking into a painting."

Roman's eyes followed her gaze. "They first laid this garden out in the mid-eighteenth century. Functional at first—fruit, vegetables, herbs. Then it grew into something more ornamental. A way of showing prosperity as much as providing for the house."

"You sound like one of the National Trust guides," Emmy teased.

"I've read more than a few pamphlets," he answered easily, though the faint curve of his mouth suggested otherwise.

As they walked the gravel paths, Emmy let her hand drift out, brushing the lavender, the neat borders of roses and foxglove. Butterflies scattered in their wake. A gardener knelt at one of the beds further down, humming under her breath, but otherwise the garden was quiet, carrying only the sound of bees at work and the faint rustle of leaves overhead.

Roman paused near a tree where tiny green fruit swelled among the branches. "Apple," he said. "They still train them along the walls like they did in the old days. Warmer here, sheltered—the fruit thrives better."

Emmy tilted her head at him. "I'm starting to suspect you know more than the pamphlets."

He gave a small laugh, but didn't elaborate. Instead, he bent down and pinched a sprig of rosemary from a pot near the path, rolling it lightly between his fingers until the scent rose. He offered it to her, and Emmy took it without hesitation, pressing it to her nose.

"It's lovely," she said softly. "Simple, but—comforting."

"Some things don't need to change," he replied. "Rosemary then, rosemary now. Always the same."

They wandered on, stopping now and then to admire the symmetry of beds and the playful bursts of colour where tulips had broken through. Emmy found herself slowing, not because she was tired, but because she wanted to savour every step, every angle, each new view the paths offered.

They came at last to a circular bench around the base of a young lime tree, its pale leaves trembling faintly in the breeze. Emmy sat, smoothing her skirt beneath her, while Roman leaned a shoulder against the trunk, arms loosely folded.

"This place feels…safe," she murmured. "Like the world outside could disappear for a while, and you wouldn't know."

"That was the point," Roman said. "A place for quiet. For retreat." His eyes drifted upward to where the walls met the sky. "I suppose we all need that sometimes."

She studied him for a moment, the way the dappled sunlight softened the lines of his face. There was a stillness about him here, as if the garden had given him a rare permission to rest.

"You sound like you know it personally," she said carefully.

Roman didn't answer right away. When he did, it was with a small, almost rueful smile. "Perhaps I've known a few gardens like this."

They lingered until the breeze shifted, carrying with it the distant toll of the chapel bell somewhere across the estate. Emmy stood, brushing a streak of dust from her palm. "Shall we keep exploring?"

Roman offered a nod, and together they left the walled garden, stepping back into the broader sweep of Gibside.

\* \* \*

The rest of the afternoon unfolded in layers—paths that led them to shaded woodland walks, Roman pointing out details Emmy would never have noticed alone: the faint outline of an old icehouse half-buried by moss, the foundations of a forgotten building marked only by stones sinking into earth.

At the ruined banqueting house, Emmy tilted her head back, tracing the empty windows with her gaze. Roman explained how it once overlooked grand processions and gatherings, though now it stood hollow, its only guests the crows. Emmy tried to imagine the place alive, music drifting through its arched doorways, gowns sweeping across its floors.

"You have a gift for making it feel real," she told him as they stood together in the doorway.

"History never disappears," he said quietly. "It only waits for someone to notice it again."

The words stayed with her as they looped back toward the chapel, its tall spire cutting clean against the sky. Roman walked a little closer now, his stride unhurried, his voice low when he spoke. Emmy matched her steps to his, realizing with a soft certainty that the space between them had been shrinking all day, not with intention, but as though it were the most natural thing in the world.

By the time they returned to the entrance, the light had shifted, carrying the first signs of evening in its weight. Emmy glanced at Roman, her cheeks still warm from the hours spent in his company.

"Thank you," she said, her voice gentle but full. "For bringing me here. It was…more than I expected."

Roman met her eyes, and in his expression, she caught a flicker of something unguarded. "Then I'm glad."

The car park was quieting, most visitors already gone. A hush had settled over the estate, broken only by the sound of gravel beneath their shoes as they crossed back to Roman's car. The evening light stretched low and gold across the treetops, the chapel spire cutting sharp against the sky. Emmy lingered, reluctant to let the day fold away so quickly.

Roman opened the passenger door for her. The old-fashioned courtesy might have seemed unusual in someone else, but from him it felt natural, a gesture without performance. Inside, the air held the faint scent of leather and cedar. He moved unhurriedly, the kind of patience that never seemed to notice time pressing.

They pulled out along the winding road, hedgerows darkening as dusk thickened. Emmy sat back, watching the rhythm of his hands on the wheel. He drove as he walked—measured, attentive, unbothered by haste. No sharp jerks, no impatience. Every movement belonged to its moment.

"You drive like you're listening to something," she said after a while.

Roman's mouth lifted faintly. "Perhaps I am."

"What do you mean?"

He kept his gaze on the road. "Engines have their own language. So do roads. Most people ignore them—force their

442

way along. But if you pay attention, they guide you. Tell you when to ease, when to wait. It's not so different from walking a path in the woods."

Emmy smiled, turning to the darkening window. "Trust you to make driving poetic."

"Only truthful," he said simply.

The road bent through a copse, shadows knitting together overhead. For a moment the car seemed suspended in half-light, and she felt again that odd hush that always accompanied him—the sense that when he spoke, everything else leaned out of the way to listen.

"You seemed very at home at Gibside," she said softly.

Roman's expression shifted, not guarded exactly, but thoughtful. "Some places… they hold their peace better than others. You step inside and feel it immediately. That kind of quiet is rare."

"It was beautiful," Emmy murmured. "The gardens, the chapel… I don't think I'll forget today."

"Nor will I," he said, almost too quietly for her to catch.

The silence that followed wasn't empty—it felt thick, alive, carrying something unspoken between them. Emmy let her cheek rest against the cool glass of the window, her heart steady but fuller than usual, her thoughts looping back through the day: the walled garden, the stories he'd told, the sense of time folding strangely around him.

\* \* \*

By the time they reached the village, lamps glowed warm behind curtains. Roman slowed into the narrower lane, pulling up outside the bookshop with its upstairs flat. The familiar sight seemed softened somehow by the day she had spent.

He switched off the engine but didn't move at once. The car held its own hush, the tick of cooling metal mingling with the distant hush of wind against rooftops. Emmy turned toward him, a curl falling loose at her temple.

"I had a really lovely day," she said, the words simple but weighted.

Roman's green eyes found hers in the half-light. "So did I."

There was no rush in him, no leaning forward, just that steady presence, as though he would allow the moment to belong to her if she needed it to.

"Thank you," she said, softer still. "For showing me something I'd never have found alone."

His mouth curved faintly. "You notice more than most. That's why it's easy to share."

The way he said it—quiet, assured—settled into her chest like warmth. Emmy stepped out of the car, pausing with her hand still on the door. Roman leaned slightly across the wheel, his profile cut by the glow of the streetlight.

"Goodnight, Emmy," he said, his voice lower, carrying a note she hadn't heard before.

She smiled, her cheeks warm despite the cool air. "Goodnight, Roman."

She climbed the stair to her flat, pausing at the window once inside. Below, his car pulled gently away, the tail-lights curving out of sight. Emmy pressed her fingertips to the glass, breath slipping slowly from her chest. The day had not ended; it had only deepened something she wasn't ready to name.

\* \* \*

*Roman's Reflection*

The lane narrowed as Roman steered his car out toward the main road, the familiar rattle of gravel under the tyres giving way to smoother tarmac. The wind had begun to ease, leaving the air damp with the memory of rain. He opened the window slightly, letting the cool air cut through the warmth that still clung to him—not from the drive, but from the afternoon.

Her laughter lingered. It had echoed under the canopy of trees, in the hollow of the old chapel, even across the stones of the walled garden. A sound that seemed to loosen something in him, as though the weight he had carried for centuries might briefly be set down. He should have known better than to let it settle so easily.

He gripped the wheel a little tighter. Time and again he had learned the same lesson: every closeness was temporary. He could not keep what the years would always steal from him. To offer his heart was to guarantee loss—not hers, but his.

And yet...

He saw again the way she had looked at the wildflowers pressed against the chapel wall, as though the smallest bloom deserved reverence. The way she had listened, not only to his words but to the silences between them. He had not spoken of anyone like that—not in decades, not in lifetimes.

His gaze flicked to the passenger seat, empty now, and for a moment he almost imagined she was still there, hands folded loosely in her lap, eyes alive with questions she didn't dare yet ask.

Roman exhaled, long and controlled. He knew he should draw back—make space, retreat into the safety of distance. But as the road stretched out ahead, he found no resolve in the thought, only a quiet admission: he wanted to see her again.

He wanted, against all caution, to keep her company a little longer.

The wheel turned beneath his hands, carrying him back toward the manor, and the candles that would burn there tonight without her.

# Chapter 26

The days that followed the trip to Gibside blurred into a softer rhythm, like pages turning without the need for a clock. Emmy found herself slipping back into school routine, though with a new sense of lightness in her step.

The children, who had been restless and excitable after a week away from the classroom, returned like a sudden flock, their chatter louder than usual, their energy spilling over in every direction. She spent the first morning fielding their stories about storm-damaged roofs, toppled trees, and the thrill of being off school when they weren't supposed to be. It took nearly half the day to coax them back into lessons, but by the afternoon, they were bent over their books again, pencils scratching in bursts of enthusiasm.

Emmy loved that about teaching—the way children could be resilient without knowing the word for it. Even after the storm had rattled their little village and sent tiles flying, they were still arguing over crayons and practicing sums as if the world had never so much as shivered.

In the staffroom, mugs of tea steamed on mismatched saucers, and the teachers fell into their familiar chorus of sighs and laughter. June was still laughing about the chaos of her form class when she announced, with a flourish, that one of the younger staff had just got engaged.

"Oh, you should've seen the ring," June said, setting her cup down with a clink. "Like something out of a fairy tale. He did it on the moors, can you imagine? Wind in her hair, wildflowers underfoot, and then down on one knee—though I'd have been terrified he'd drop it in the heather."

Laughter bubbled around the table, and Emmy found herself smiling, though there was a little tug inside her too. Not envy, exactly—more a wistful curiosity about what that kind of moment might feel like.

By the time she returned home that evening, the flat seemed quieter than usual, the stillness pressing in after the noise of children and colleagues. She caught herself listening for the soft padding of paws or the faint rustle of leaves, and then laughed at herself. She had been spending more time at Roman's estate than she had ever expected to—checking on the kittens, which had grown stronger and more wriggly by the day, and somehow finding excuses to linger for tea or a slow walk back down the drive.

Roman was careful with his invitations, never insistent, always leaving her the space to choose. Yet somehow, when she looked back, Emmy realised she had chosen "yes" almost every time.

The following Saturday arrived with a brightness that seemed to make promises of its own. Emmy woke early, the faint calls of gulls breaking through her half-dreams. She laced her trainers with the quick, practiced motions of habit regained—her runs had become regular again since the storm, each one a reminder that she was settling back into herself.

The village was quiet at first, her feet carrying her past the harbour where boats tugged at their moorings, the air sharp with salt. But as she rounded the high street, the smell of coffee drifted into her path, and she slowed. June was seated outside the little café, hair tied up messily, a mug steaming between her hands.

"Look who's finally keeping her promise," June teased, waving her free hand. "Back to the running track."

Emmy laughed, pushing a curl from her damp forehead. "I said I would, didn't I?"

"You did," June said. "I didn't believe you, but you did." She leaned back in her chair, eyeing Emmy fondly. "You look happier lately. Settled. Maybe it's this place working its magic on you."

Emmy hesitated, catching her breath. "Maybe it is."

June tilted her head. "School feels back to normal too, doesn't it? The kids are finally caught up. You can almost forget the week we lost."

"Almost," Emmy agreed. She stretched her arms lightly, keeping her legs warm. "It feels good to be back into routine though."

"You'll have to join me for a coffee one morning after your run," June said. "If you're not too busy."

"I'd like that," Emmy said honestly.

June's smile held a flicker of curiosity, but she let it pass. "Go on then, before you seize up. Don't let me keep you."

Emmy jogged on, warmth lingering from the brief exchange. When she turned back down toward her flat, sweat cooling on her temples, she felt not just exercised but steadied—ready for whatever the day might bring.

After a quick shower and breakfast, her thoughts drifted—as they so often did now—to Roman's estate. She told herself it was natural; she'd been helping with the kittens, after all. They were growing stronger, their tiny paws pushing them clumsily through the nest.

When she arrived, Roman was outside one of the outbuildings, sleeves rolled again, a sack of cat food resting against his leg.

"Morning," he called, his voice carrying easily.

Emmy smiled, slowing her steps. "You've been busy already."

"Someone has to keep them fed," he said, tipping his head toward the outbuilding. "They're loud enough to remind me." His hand rested briefly on the sack before he straightened. "You're here at a good time—they're awake."

Inside, the kittens were indeed stirring, their tiny bodies shifting in the straw. Emmy crouched, unable to help the soft sound that escaped her. "They're getting stronger."

"They are," Roman agreed, standing nearby with that calm watchfulness she'd come to recognise. "It never stops being a miracle, does it? Something so small, so fragile, and yet... determined to live."

Emmy glanced up at him, her cheeks warmed by the quiet sincerity in his voice. She hadn't thought of Roman as someone who might speak that way about anything, let alone a litter of kittens. And yet, here he was—kneeling on the straw, eyes soft with an almost reverent calm.

"Have you thought of names yet?" she asked, watching one of the tiny creatures shift closer to its mother. Its minuscule paws stretched as though it had conquered half the world already.

Roman's brow lifted slightly, as though the question had caught him off guard. "Names?"

"Yes," Emmy said, a little laugh escaping her. "You can't have kittens without names. It feels wrong. Even if they change later when they find homes."

He considered this, gaze returning to the cluster of small bodies pressed against their mother. "I suppose I haven't. They only just arrived. It feels… premature."

"Well, I've already named their mother," Emmy admitted, tucking her knees closer under her chin. She hesitated a moment, suddenly shy. "I call her Marigold."

"Marigold," Roman repeated, and the way he said it gave the word more gravity than she expected. "Why that?"

Emmy smiled faintly, eyes drifting to the cat. "She's tough. She survived storms and winters on her own, but she's still gentle. Marigolds are hardy like that—they grow in the most unlikely places. Bright, too. She deserves a name that says she's more than just some stray that wanders in and out of people's lives."

Roman's lips curved, but slowly, as though it were something he hadn't meant to let slip. "It suits her."

"Thank you." Emmy rested her chin in her hands, studying the tiny creatures with their blind fumbling and urgent little squeaks. "So, no ideas for the kittens?"

He shook his head lightly. "I'm not sure I trust myself with names. I tend to… keep things simple."

"Simple can be good," Emmy said. "Sometimes simple is what makes something stick."

Roman's gaze flicked to her, quick but steady. "And what would you name them?"

Emmy thought for a moment, scanning the bundle of fur. "Well… that one—" she gestured to the boldest, already crawling over its siblings as though the world was a hill it intended to climb, "—I'd call it Clover. For luck. Because it's clearly determined to make its own."

Roman tilted his head. "Clover," he repeated softly.

"And that tiny one," Emmy said, pointing to a kitten half-hidden beneath its mother, its paws feeble but persistent, "—maybe Fern. Because ferns always find a way to grow in the cracks where no one expects them."

His eyes lingered on her as she spoke, not just the words but the thought behind them. "You see more than most," he said quietly.

Emmy felt her throat tighten a little, not knowing how to respond. She gave a small shrug. "Maybe I just spend too much time in books."

Roman didn't argue. He turned back to the kittens, crouching low, his broad hand resting against the straw near them though he didn't touch. "Clover and Fern," he murmured, almost testing the names on his tongue. "Not bad."

"And the others?" Emmy nudged, watching his profile in the lamplight hush of the outbuilding.

Roman paused for a long moment. "Perhaps I'll need your help with the rest," he said finally. "You seem to have the knack."

Emmy smiled, pleased more than she expected to be. "Deal. But you have to choose at least one. No excuses."

He glanced at her, green eyes catching the faintest shimmer from the light. "Very well," he said, and then looked back at the smallest of the kittens—one curled stubbornly in a ball despite the chaos of its siblings around it. His mouth shifted, almost imperceptibly. "That one... Rose. Because even fragile things can carry thorns."

Emmy blinked at him, surprised. "That's... actually perfect."

"I told you," Roman said with a faint smile, "I keep things simple."

She leaned forward, watching the last unnamed kitten—a soft-grey one that seemed unusually alert, its tiny head lifting as if it could already sense the world outside the straw nest. Emmy smiled. "And this one... maybe Ash. Because it's small now, but there's a strength in it. Ash trees bend in storms but don't break."

Roman's gaze followed hers. "Ash," he echoed, voice low. He looked between the four of them—Clover, Fern, Rose, and

Ash—and for a fleeting moment, his expression softened into something almost unguarded. "Then they're named."

Emmy nodded, strangely satisfied by the finality of it. "They'll grow into them."

Roman's mouth curved in that small, rare way again. "I suspect you're right."

They lapsed into quiet for a moment, the only sounds the faint scrabble of paws against straw and the soft rasp of Marigold's breathing. Emmy rested her cheek on her knee, watching the small family with a warmth she hadn't realised she'd been missing.

"I used to want a cat," she said softly. "When I was younger. My parents said no—we travelled too much back then. Then later, I suppose… life got in the way. Maybe I forgot about it."

Roman glanced at her. "And now?"

She considered. "Now… I think I'd like the company. They make things feel alive."

His gaze lingered on her a moment longer before he turned back to the kittens. "Maybe Marigold knew that. Maybe that's why she came here."

Emmy smiled faintly, though her heart gave a small, inexplicable pull at his words. She looked down quickly at the straw, her hair slipping forward over her face.

They lingered a while longer in the straw-scented hush of the outbuilding, Emmy reluctant to leave the fragile new lives she'd just watched stumble their first clumsy steps. But when Marigold curled herself protectively around the kittens, her green eyes slipping half-shut in contentment, Roman rose and offered a hand to Emmy.

"Come," he said gently. "They'll sleep now. We should leave them their peace."

His hand was warm when she took it, steadying her as she stood. Emmy brushed straw from her skirt, tucking a curl behind her ear as she followed him back towards the main house. The storm had left its faint mark on the grounds still—fallen branches stacked neatly against a wall, dampness lingering in the air—but the courtyard glowed with a kind of quiet resilience.

When Roman opened the orangery doors, Emmy drew in a small breath. Afternoon light spilled across the mosaic tiles, softened by the high glass panes that caught glimmers of the outside sky. The scents of rosemary and jasmine hung in the air, curling faintly through the warmth.

On the table near the fountain sat a simple tray: two tall glasses filled with chilled water steeped with mint and slices of fruit, catching the light in delicate colours. A small plate of bread with butter and jam had been set out beside it.

"You've thought of everything," Emmy said, lowering herself into the chair he pulled out for her. Her eyes softened as she noticed the care in the details.

Roman set a glass before her, then one before himself, his movements unhurried. "I thought you might be hungry after the morning," he said quietly. "It takes more out of you than you realise, watching and waiting like that."

Emmy smiled as she lifted the glass, the coolness refreshing against her fingers. "You're right," she admitted with a laugh. "It's strange, isn't it? Watching them—it makes you forget time."

Roman's gaze held hers across the table, green eyes steady. "Some things are worth losing time to."

The words lingered between them, unhurried. Emmy took a sip to steady herself, the mint leaving a light coolness on her lips. She wanted to look away, but his eyes had that way of pulling her in, of making her feel as though he saw her even when she said nothing at all.

To break the spell, she glanced at the little plate. "This is lovely," she said softly. "You really didn't have to go to the trouble."

Roman leaned back slightly in his chair, one hand resting against the stem of his glass. "I wanted to," he said simply. His voice wasn't heavy with implication, yet the words carried weight all the same.

Emmy felt her chest tighten in a way she hadn't expected. "Well," she said gently, brushing a curl back from her face, "I'm glad you did. It would be a real shame if you suddenly decided to disappear. I think I'm getting used to having you around."

A flicker passed through his expression—subtle, but she caught it. "Then I suppose," he murmured, "I had better not disappoint you."

The heat that rose in her cheeks startled her. She reached for a piece of bread, spreading a little jam with the knife, though her hand felt less steady than usual. She broke off a corner, more to give herself something to do than from hunger.

As the quiet settled, Roman reached across the table and plucked a sprig of lavender from a small vase. With careful fingers, he leaned forward and tucked it lightly behind her ear. His touch was no more than a brush against her hair, yet Emmy's breath caught all the same.

"There," he said softly, almost amused. "Now you match the season."

Her laugh came lighter than she meant, betraying the warmth in her face. "That's terribly old-fashioned of you," she teased.

Roman only smiled, the expression rare but sincere. "Perhaps I am," he replied.

Emmy sat still for a moment, the lavender sprig holding its place in her curls, its fragrance mingling with the fresh green air of the orangery. She felt the warmth of Roman's hand linger at her temple even after he'd drawn it back, as though the gesture had pressed itself into her rather than just her hair.

"That suits you," he said, almost matter-of-factly, though his voice had softened.

Her lips curved faintly. "I'll take that as a compliment."

"You should," he replied, folding himself into the chair opposite. His posture was relaxed now, an ease that was rare to see in him. "You make simple things look... right. A sprig of lavender, sunlight through glass—it becomes something finer when you're in the middle of it."

Her cheeks warmed at that, though she tried to hide it by breaking off a small piece of bread. "You're in danger of sounding like a poet."

"Or perhaps a gardener," he said, glancing toward the rows of plants, "unable to resist pointing out what thrives in front of him."

They shared a quiet laugh, and for a little while they let the room itself speak—the bees flickering against the glass panes, the faint drip of water in a clay pot, the air carrying rosemary and soil.

Emmy leaned her elbows lightly against the table, turning her glass between her hands. "You know, I've lived above the bookshop for weeks now, and yet I feel I've barely seen this village properly. Between school and… well, life. It's too easy to fall into routines."

Roman tilted his head, studying her. "Routines can be safe. But they can also make the world smaller than it is."

"And you don't like small worlds?" she teased.

"I prefer ones that keep expanding," he answered. "New places, new… people." His eyes flicked toward her with deliberate subtlety.

She looked down quickly, though her smile betrayed her. "Well, I can't say I mind this part of my world expanding."

They let the words sit there a moment, not filling the silence too quickly. Then Roman reached for the small jar of jam between them, spreading it carefully across a slice of bread before setting it on the plate nearer her. "Try that," he said simply.

Emmy lifted it, taking a bite. Sweetness bloomed instantly across her tongue. "Strawberry?"

He nodded. "From the summer past. I keep a few jars. They remind me of the sun when the days are short."

Her smile widened. "So you do have a practical streak."

"Occasionally," he said, watching her with something deeper than amusement.

Minutes stretched and softened. They talked of lighter things—her students and their stubborn mispronunciations, the antics of the baker's dog, the stubborn ivy climbing one of his outer walls. Roman listened closely, adding his own dry observations now and then, his green eyes never drifting far from her face.

At some point the sun shifted, slanting low enough that it sent a streak of amber through the highest panes. Emmy brushed a curl from her face and said, "This really does feel like a dream sometimes. Sitting here. It's... different from everything else."

Roman didn't answer immediately. He reached out instead, steady, deliberate, until his hand rested just over hers where it lay on the table. His touch was cool at first, then warmed as their skin learned each other.

"Some dreams," he said at last, "you don't want to wake from."

Her breath caught at the quiet weight of it. She didn't pull away. Instead she turned her hand, lacing her fingers lightly with his. The movement was small, but it shifted everything— turned the moment from suggestion into something that belonged to them both.

The candles guttered faintly in their brass cups as a breeze pressed the glass. Outside, the storm's wreckage still lay across the village—branches, broken tiles, the faint smell of rain— but here inside, with his hand closing around hers, it felt as though the world had steadied.

They spoke less after that, content to let the day fold itself into longer silences, where every glance seemed to hold its own conversation.

The courtyard had grown hushed, the perfume of orange blossom and damp earth clinging to the cooling air. Roman rose, his hand still curved lightly around Emmy's, and to her quiet astonishment he didn't let go.

"Come," he said gently, his voice low and steady.

She let him guide her, the brush of his palm against hers sending warmth through her despite the evening's creeping chill. His stride was unhurried, his presence steady, as though he'd thought of this path before she had even agreed to follow. Emmy half-expected him to release her once they left the orangery, but his hand remained, grounding her as they walked.

The corridor they entered was quieter than any she had seen. Here the walls seemed older, lined with faded runners and the kind of oil paintings that carried centuries in their brushstrokes. The air smelled faintly of beeswax polish and stone, of a house that had known long silences.

At the far end, he paused before a tall gallery door and pushed it open. The space they entered seemed to stretch endlessly. Sunlight, softened to amber with the fading of the day, poured through arched windows, casting long stripes across the floorboards.

Emmy's steps slowed, her gaze caught by the paintings that lined the walls. Not landscapes this time, but portraits— faces in gilded frames, gazes that followed her with uncanny stillness. Her eyes came to rest on a large canvas near the centre: a woman seated beside a harpsichord, her gown a sweep of pale silk, her expression calm yet tinged with something distant.

"She's beautiful," Emmy whispered before she could stop herself.

Roman's gaze followed hers. His expression softened in a way she hadn't seen before, shadows shifting into something almost tender. "She was my mother," he said quietly.

Emmy blinked, startled. "Your—your mother? Did you commission this?"

Roman's lips curved faintly, though his eyes stayed on the painting. "No. I drew it."

Emmy turned sharply to him. "You?"

He inclined his head, almost reluctant, as if the admission cost him something. "I did. Many years ago."

For a moment she didn't know what to say. She studied the delicate shading, the way the folds of the gown caught light, the softness in the woman's features. "It looks like it belongs in a museum. It's... extraordinary."

He gave a quiet, almost humourless smile. "She sat for me often. She had patience." His voice grew gentler still. "When she fell ill, she preferred to rest here, in the light. This portrait... it was my way of keeping her close."

Emmy's throat tightened. She glanced at him, curiosity tugging despite herself. "How long has it been since she... since she passed?"

Roman's eyes remained fixed on the portrait. His silence stretched just long enough for Emmy to sense the weight of it. When he finally spoke, his voice was guarded. "A very long time. Longer than I sometimes care to measure."

She frowned faintly at the answer, puzzled, but the sorrow in his tone stopped her from pressing further. She simply nodded, letting it rest between them like something fragile.

Roman guided her on, their joined hands swinging ever so slightly as he led her to a stairwell at the far end of the gallery. The stone steps spiralled upward, the air cooler the higher they climbed. Emmy glanced around as they reached the landing, then followed him through another door.

The terrace opened around them. When Emmy stepped out, she stopped short, caught by the view. From here the valley unfurled in patchwork fields, the river winding silver through the trees, the faint outline of the harbour glinting where sea met sky.

"This house is huge," she said with a half-laugh, her voice edged with awe. "You always talk about liking solitude, but—

" she gestured broadly "—this isn't solitude, Roman. This is an entire world. You could lose people in here."

Roman's hand rested lightly on the balustrade, his gaze following the sweep of land below. His voice was quiet, thoughtful. "It wasn't always so empty. It was meant to hold family. And once, it did."

Emmy glanced at him, surprised by the flicker of something behind his calm expression. "So it was built with that in mind?"

"Yes." His eyes softened, distant. "My father planned it for our family. I finished much of it after he was gone, for my mother. She spent her last years in these walls. The house has been… quieter since."

Something in the way he said it—measured, but heavy with a history she couldn't place—made Emmy's chest tighten. She turned her gaze outward again, letting the silence stretch between them.

"I think I understand that," she murmured. "Houses can hold people, even after they're gone. Not just in portraits or things they left behind, but in the air somehow."

Roman's head inclined slightly, and though he said nothing, the flicker of recognition in his eyes told her he understood more than she had meant to reveal.

Her breath left her in a slow sigh. "It's why I came here, you know. To start over."

His attention returned to her, steady and patient.

"I don't think I've really told you," she continued, her fingers tracing the cold line of stone at the railing. "I was with someone, for years. Too long. It started small, like shadows at the edge of the day. And then, before I realised, the shadows were everything. I kept telling myself it was normal—everyone has arguments, bad days. But bad days turned into bruises. Into silence. Into hiding."

The words stuck in her throat. She hadn't expected them to come so easily here, with the sky stretched wide above and Roman's quiet presence beside her.

Roman moved without hesitation, slipping an arm lightly around her shoulders. The gesture startled her; she stiffened for a heartbeat, unused to such instinctive protection. But there was no demand in the hold, no pressure—only a steady warmth, offered without expectation.

Slowly, she leaned, letting her temple rest against his shoulder.

"I should have left sooner," she said quietly. "But it took time. In the end, I went back to my parents for a while, until I could breathe again. When I felt ready, I came here. Somewhere no one knew me as... that woman who stayed."

Roman's gaze fixed on the horizon, his voice low but firm. "You left. That choice is more than many ever find the strength to make. You chose yourself. That isn't weakness, Emmy. It's the bravest thing."

Her throat tightened at the certainty in his tone. She closed her eyes, letting his words root deep. And though the terrace opened wide to the valley, her world in that moment felt smaller, steadier, defined only by the quiet strength of the man beside her.

# Chapter 27

By Monday morning, the school playground was lively with the laughter and shrieks of children not quite ready to end the newfound freedom they experienced the previous week. Emmy stood near the railings with June, both clutching takeaway coffees against the chill of early spring. Their breath misted faintly in the cool air as they kept half an eye on the children darting around the yard, jackets unzipped and scarves trailing despite reminders.

"Sometimes I think we're glorified shepherds," June muttered with a small smile, watching one boy chase another in increasingly dangerous circles.

Emmy chuckled softly. "At least sheep don't argue back."

"True." June sipped her coffee, then nudged Emmy lightly with her elbow. "So. Are you going to tell me what has got you smiling at nothing?"

Emmy raised a brow, defensive. "Smiling?"

"Mm-hm," June said knowingly. "It's not nothing. I've known you long enough for that. You've got this… glow about you. And don't tell me it's the marking pile making you that happy."

Emmy hesitated, then sighed, her eyes scanning the playground. "It's Roman."

"I thought so," June said, pleased. "Go on then."

Emmy twisted the cardboard coffee sleeve between her fingers. "He's… different. Kind, thoughtful. He doesn't treat me like I'm fragile, but at the same time, I've never felt so safe with anyone."

June tilted her head, listening without teasing now. "That's something you desire?"

"It is." Emmy's voice softened. "It feels… surprising. Like I wasn't expecting it. He's not easy to read, but when he looks at me, it's like—" She broke off, blushing. "See, I'm doing it again. Sounding ridiculous."

"You don't sound ridiculous," June said firmly. "You sound like someone remembering what it's like to be happy. And honestly? You deserve that more than anyone."

Before Emmy could reply; a lorry shouldered into view with the careful swagger of something large in a small space. A pair of men in Hi-Viz jackets hopped down and began the practised ballet of unloading: scaffold poles laid in bright, ringing stacks; boards thumped into tidy piles; a bucket hoist clanking idly until it had purpose. Another van slid in behind, its side door whisked open to give up bundles of slate tied with wire. A smell travelled on the cool air—wet wood, old tar, rain-bothered stone warmed slightly by effort.

Emmy and June made their way inside and headed for the staff room; the headmaster John Everly was already there; sleeves rolled, mug in hand that had World's Okayest Head printed on it. He tapped a knuckle against the table and let the room settle.

"Right," he began, genial as always, "news of the roof, my favourite new hobby. The last of the slate goes on today, flashing replaced, ridge capped, and then—if we all clap loudly enough—scaffolding down by Friday. Hooray for modern miracles and Mr. Archer's elbow grease." He nodded toward the caretaker, who lifted his eyebrows modestly and saluted with a tea bag.

Laughter loosened the room.

The headmaster continued. "So, timetable adjustments: there will be noise, as you might have deduced from the small industrial estate in the playground. Year Two will have PE in the hall rather than outside this morning; sorry in advance to whoever follows them." A collective groan. "Please keep your classes away from the fenced areas and the coned walkway by the main doors. If you need to move between buildings, do it with the elegance of a cat and not the enthusiasm of a Labrador."

"Can confirm I am Labrador-coded," Mr. Ellis from Year Five said mournfully, patting his stomach. More laughter.

"First tranche of men up by nine," the head went on, "weather looks stable until late afternoon—touch wood, not the rafters. If you see anything worrying—more worrying than men standing on planks four storeys up—tell the office, and they'll tell me, and I'll tell someone who actually knows what a purlin is."

"What's a purlin?" June called.

"A thing I pretend to understand in front of governors," he said promptly, and the room gave him a round of appreciative claps.

There were the usual small notices: lost cardigan, please return if a Size Of A Tent turns up; choir after school moved to the library; Ms. Kemp's class to avoid the east corridor because it would be half a building site by lunch. Through all of it ran that gentle, joking current that made trouble into work and work into something close to pleasure.

As they filed out, June bumped Emmy with her shoulder. "I'll give you a fiver if you can keep them from plastering themselves to that window all morning."

"Make it ten," Emmy said. "We're doing fractions. The scaffolding will be the most compelling object any of them have ever seen."

"Set them to counting bolts," June suggested. "Learning through... rivets?"

"Close enough."

Emmy took the long way back to her room, past the hall where the caretaker was taping down cables with the solemnity of a surgeon, past the library where someone had propped open a box of new picture books like treasure. The building wore its scars with a kind of pride. The storm had rattled it, yes—lifted tiles, driven rain under the flashing, taught the gutters what they were for—but the bones had held, and now the flesh of it was nearly mended.

By five to nine her classroom had filled with the small weather of children. Coats flung, then retrieved and hung with varying accuracy. Lunch boxes displayed and judged, zipped again. A round of guess what my dog did, cut off by the register. Through it all, the faint outside racket grew—a clatter, a mutter, the high metallic ding of a coupler tightened to satisfaction. Emmy opened her mouth to begin the day and four hands went up, eyes slewing toward the window.

"Yes, Noah?"

"Miss, is that man going to fall off?"

"No," she said, serenely. "He is attached to that very nice belt, and the belt is attached to that very nice rope, and the rope is attached to that very nice scaffold, which is attached to the earth and the earth is attached to... well, itself."

Giggles. The tension released a notch.

"Can we watch?" Priya asked, the plea already plaited into her voice.

"You can watch in fractions," Emmy said, enjoying her own foolishness. "One quarter of the class at a time, for one minute. Meanwhile, we have quarter pizzas to draw." Groans softened into grins. She held up the laminated pizza circles they'd cut last term. "If you can prove to me that you can share this pretend pizza fairly, you may go and supervise the roofers, who will be devastated if you get the maths wrong."

The first group hovered at the window, solemn as magistrates. "He's carrying five slates," Toby reported. "No, six. Are they heavy?"

"Very," Emmy said. "He is very strong and very sensible and very tired of small people staring at him, so wave nicely and then come back to your chairs." The roofer in question, catching twenty-eight earnest eyes, grinned and gave a little salute. The class squeaked as softly as pride would allow.

The morning found its rhythm. Fractions smoothed themselves beneath patient fingers; the whiteboard flashed and yielded answers with saintly acceptance; pencils rolled and were rescued. Outside, the work went on—a saw whining then obedient; someone calling "Mind!" in the measured tone of someone who has called it a lot and always means it. When a slate skimmed, skittered, and was caught against a toe board with a quick clatter, the collective inhale in her room was audible. Emmy didn't turn her head.

"That," she said mildly, "was a very good demonstration of why we leave roofing to roofers and fractions to experts like us."

"Like you," Noah said, with the affectionate ruthlessness of children.

"Like us," she corrected, and moved among them with a hand on a shoulder here, a murmured "good" there, the quiet machinery of encouragement.

At break the yard was claimed by the business of small bodies who had been told not to run and therefore did so only in bursts that pretended not to be. The scaffolding had been threaded by then tight to the eaves—silver uprights, boards running level with the guttering, a tarpaulin folded ready like a tongue against sudden weather. One of the foremen—broad, cheerful, a pencil behind his ear—was showing a younger man how to seat a bracket, the teaching both brisk and kind. Emmy stood with June near the hopscotch and watched the children invent a game involving an imaginary dragon that had taken up residence in the skip.

"Look," June said, lifting her chin slightly. Across the street, where the railings that edged the green cast a sensible shadow on the pavement, a familiar figure walked with his hands clasped behind his back, head turned as if listening to the trees rather than looking at them. Roman's pace was unhurried, his coat open to the mild air, his gaze travelling along the line of the school—not lingering, not shying, simply acknowledging its fact in the village.

Emmy's heart did that small, disobedient thing it had learned. She kept her voice even. "He's early for ghosts," she said, because June understood the need for humour even when it wasn't very good.

June's smile was surface and sympathy. "Maybe he likes the sound of children not falling over."

"Optimistic," Emmy murmured. Roman reached the corner, paused briefly as if to read the community noticeboard that had probably not changed since last Thursday, and moved on. He didn't look toward the playground. Emmy, who had not intended to watch him, watched him until the hedges took him.

When the bell shepherded them back inside, the building breathed them in. The second lesson slid into the third with satisfying inevitability. Outside the window, a man's boots paced and paused along the boards; above, there was the occasional hollow chuck of a slate finding its place. The children, bribed by the promise of window minutes and the threat of losing them, worked beautifully, tongues peeking out at the corners of mouths, rulers lifted and replaced with reverence.

Just before lunch, a gust pushed from nowhere, made, perhaps, by the village funnelling itself the wrong way for a moment. It caught at a loose sheet of tarpaulin and snapped it like a flag; grit rattled down the window in a small, stinging scatter. Half the class jumped. Emmy lifted a hand without looking up.

"Outdoor weather report," she said, light. "Conclusion?"

"Wind," Priya said, already smiling.

"Solution?"

"Stay inside and eat," chorused three boys with perfect logic.

"An unanswerable argument," Emmy said, letting their laughter teach their shoulders to drop. She crossed to the window and, because the body is a barometer, put her palm to the glass. Cool. Gritty with the dust the storm had taught the old roof to shed. On the scaffold, two roofers bent their heads together over a line of flashing, gloved fingers precise. One of them reached to tighten a tie and gave the upright a practised shove to feel its truth. The whole grid replied with a small, reassuring: I'm here.

She pulled the blinds down to the first notch for lunch so the worst of the glare was gentled. In the staffroom, everyone ate as if someone else might steal it, as teachers always do. June had brought leftover couscous and was treating it with suspicious respect. Mr. Ellis had surrendered and gone to the bakery and was brandishing a cheese and onion pasty that made the room briefly religious. The headmaster came in with rain on his shoulders no one else had found and announced that the foreman had promised they were "on the home straight".

"Is that a roofing term?" June asked.

"It's a sports metaphor that hopes to distract governors from the invoice," he said. "But yes. Nearly there."

"Children?" someone asked through a mouthful of crisps.

"Deaf to the charms of fractions in the face of men with belts," Emmy said. "But otherwise generally obedient."

"Add that to the school motto," the headmaster said, amiably. He knocked on the door frame as he left, because he was the sort of man who knocked on things other people didn't notice and the building seemed to like him for it.

The afternoon began with handwriting, which lent the room a peaceful hum like bees in a field. Emmy moved between tables, tipping pages to catch the light, letting the slow curve of the children's letters tug her own breath into steadiness. Outside, a man whistled a tune she couldn't name, and the tinny radio tried to find the chorus and mostly failed. A gull clattered inelegantly along the ridge and was sent off by a roofer's flapping glove, the exchange so practised that Emmy smiled without looking.

When the last set of joined-up S's had been admired, she called them to the carpet for a story, the bribery she didn't bother to pretend wasn't bribery. They folded themselves down with the sleepy grace of small animals. She chose a book with pictures big enough to out-compete a scaffold and began in the voice that told them without telling them that all the edges were soft in here.

Halfway through the second page, there was a sound from above. Not the neat tap of a slate set home, not the cheerful argument of men about whether toast or bacon was the better breakfast, but a stuttering scrape as if something had not meant to move and then did. It travelled the length of the roof with a decisiveness that raised the small hairs at the nape of her neck. Emmy paused. Twenty-eight faces tipped up to hers, trusting her to tell them how to think about it.

"It's the roof having a little stretch," she said, the corner of her mouth acknowledging the silliness as what made it work. "Same as you when you've sat too long." She tapped the page. "Where were we? Ah yes—the fox had found a door."

The scrape subsided, replaced by the brisk clink of work resumed. The children let their breath out as one creature and leaned back into the story.

When the final bell let them go, the children went, all elastic and edges again, out into an afternoon that had finally found some blue. Emmy dismissed them to parents at the gate with the squidgy joy of a day done well, exchanged the litany of thanks and news ("We found his hat, it had fled under the radiator," "She says she needs to bring something for the class bear and we have no idea what that means") and stood for a moment once the flow had thinned, letting quiet come back. The scaffold, battened now nearly to the apex, looked like a ladder someone had thrown at the sky and had stick. A roofer straightened and rolled his shoulders. Another nudged a slate with the toe of his boot until it sat flush.

She turned to go back inside, the last of the children's voices skipping down the lane, and paused, her palm against the push plate of the door. It was nothing—only a tiny tremor through the metal, a vibration that might have been someone setting down a bundle of slates with a little too much enthusiasm. Still, it travelled along her bones like a note. She let the door swing back, took one last glance up along the bright ribs of the scaffold, and then stepped into the cool of the corridor, calling over her shoulder to the office, "Back in Year Three if anyone needs me!"

The corridor answered with its small, hollow echo. Somewhere, the radio on the scaffold finally found the chorus. Outside, a foreman lifted his chin and said to no one in particular, "Hold that tie a second," in the same voice you would use to ask for the salt at tea.

Inside her classroom, Emmy reached for the pile of books she hadn't finished marking at lunch, set them on the table by the window where the light was kindest, and sat with her pen uncapped, ready to pin small stars to small efforts. A gust bumped the blind against the frame and the slat clicked like a polite throat being cleared. She smiled, shook out her hand, and wrote in green ink, Good thinking. Explain your answer.

The scaffolding outside gave a faint groan, like old wood stretching. Emmy frowned but kept writing. She knew enough to recognise when her nerves were trying to make shadows into spectres.

A sharp rap at her door pulled her head up.

"Marking marathon?" Mr. Havers, the Year 5 teacher, leaned in with his habitual grin, a stack of worksheets balanced in one hand. His tie had slipped halfway down his shirt as though it had long since given up. "I swear, if this building doesn't bury us under paperwork first, it'll be under slate."

Emmy laughed lightly, shaking her head. "Don't say that while the scaffolding's still rattling."

He rolled his eyes, good-natured. "Whole circus out there. Can't believe we've been teaching under it. Anyway, tea's gone cold in the staffroom, don't bother." With a wave of his free hand, he vanished back down the corridor, his footsteps fading into the stairwell.

Emmy let the smile linger before returning to the open book. She bent over the neat but wobbly handwriting of one of her pupils, underlined a clever phrase, and noted, Excellent detail.

The last book slid back onto the pile, Emmy's green pen capped and set aside. She stacked the papers neatly, smoothing her palm over the top as though tidying her thoughts along with them. The room had that end-of-day stillness now, the kind that made her shoulders ease.

She slung her bag over her shoulder and gave the window one last wary glance. The scaffolding stood in its rigid skeleton outside, shadowing the side of the school. It looked harmless enough, but she couldn't shake the unease it stirred. With a small shake of her head, she flicked off the light and pulled her classroom door closed.

The corridor smelled faintly of polish and pencil shavings. Emmy passed a pair of teachers in quiet conversation near the staffroom.

"Goodnight, Emmy," one called.

"See you tomorrow," she answered with a smile, pushing through the heavy front doors and stepping into the cooling air.

Outside, the evening held the quiet weight of a week nearly done. The playground was empty, the faint marks of football games and skipping ropes still etched in the asphalt. Emmy adjusted her bag strap and started down the steps.

A groan of metal drifted through the air. She paused, frowning. It was low at first, almost dismissible—like a lorry's brakes somewhere down the road.

Then it came again. Louder. Sharper.

Her heart picked up. She turned her head just in time to see the scaffolding shudder, tilt forward, and with a shriek of splitting metal, give way.

The sound was monstrous—bolts snapping, planks cascading. Emmy froze, breath caught, as the structure pitched down towards her side of the yard. A spray of dust burst into the air, and the clatter of collapsing metal swallowed the world.

Instinct kicked in too late; she threw her hands up, half a scream forming—

—and then everything blurred.

Arms closed around her, firm and unyielding, pulling her back against a wall of strength. She barely had time to gasp before the world roared again: the scaffolding slammed into the ground with a force that made the pavement tremble. Metal struck stone, wood splintered, a storm of dust and grit filled the air.

Her head hit the ground hard and something sharp grazed past her ear. Emmy squeezed her eyes shut, clutching instinctively at the fabric across her chest—the sleeve of whoever had her.

When the racket subsided enough for her to hear her own ragged breath, she opened her eyes.

Roman.

He was crouched over her, one arm wrapped across her shoulders, the other braced against the ground as if he alone held back the chaos. His body was a shield, his face set with a stillness that did not belong in disaster. Dust had settled in his dark hair, his green eyes sharp in the haze.

Her relief shattered as her gaze dropped lower.

A jagged length of scaffolding had punched clean through the wooden boards when it fell—and through him. The metal rod jutted out from his side, the torn edges of his shirt darkening with blood.

"Roman!" Emmy's voice broke, high and panicked. She reached for him, not knowing what she could possibly do.

But he didn't flinch. Didn't groan. His jaw tightened, yes, but his eyes stayed locked on hers. Calm. Steady. As though her terror mattered more than the steel piercing his flesh.

"Emmy," he said quietly, his voice a low current beneath the ringing in her ears. "You're safe. That's what matters."

Safe? The word didn't make sense. She could feel the tremor in her hands, the heat of his blood dampening the sleeve under her grip. He should be collapsing, crying out, something—anything human. But instead, he shifted, rising carefully to his knees, the rod grotesquely still lodged in him.

Her breath caught. "You—you're hurt. Roman, you can't—"

But the look he gave her silenced the rest. Something unreadable, ancient, flickered in his gaze before he looked away, scanning the wreckage as if deciding what to do next.

Emmy's stomach lurched. The disbelief rattled inside her skull, clashing with the undeniable fact in front of her: Roman Vandrelle had been run through with steel, and he was still on his feet.

Still holding her steady.

Still impossibly alive.

Emmy froze. The weight of Roman's arm still shielded her, though the worst of the crash had already passed. All around them, the sound of scaffolding settling echoed in metallic groans, shards of slate skittered across the pavement, and dust drifted in the air.

Her eyes dropped to his side.

A steel rod had pierced straight through the fold of his coat, into him. She couldn't breathe. He should be dead.

"Roman—" Her voice broke, a dry gasp more than a word.

Still bent protectively over her, he met her gaze. Calm. His green eyes locked onto hers with a quiet steadiness that didn't belong in this moment of chaos.

"Stay still, Emmy," he said, his tone low, almost gentle, as if he were the one soothing her fear rather than the other way round.

She shook her head violently. "No—no, you're—" Her hands moved instinctively to press against his side, to stop the bleeding that had to be there, only to find her fingers coming away... not soaked in blood, but barely damp. Just a thin smear of red, nothing like the wound she expected.

He caught her wrists carefully, lowering her hands. "Don't," he whispered.

Then, before she could react, he straightened to his full height, bracing one hand on the scaffolding rod that speared him. With a controlled, almost effortless motion, he drew it out of his body. The sound was soft, sickening, metal against flesh—and then it was gone.

The rod clattered onto the stone.

Emmy's breath hitched sharply, her eyes fixed on him in terror and disbelief. "That's—" Her words tangled into silence.

Roman staggered only slightly, as though it were nothing more than pulling out a splinter. Already the wound was closing, the torn fabric of his coat stained but not spreading darker. His chest rose with one deep breath, steady again in seconds.

"It's fine," he said, quieter now, almost pleading. "I'm fine."

"No!" Emmy stepped back from him, her pulse racing so hard she felt dizzy. "That went through you. I saw it. You—"

Her throat constricted. Tears of shock pricked her eyes. Around them, a couple of passers-by shouted toward the site, checking if anyone was hurt, but no one seemed to notice Roman specifically. Dust still settled in the air, covering everything in a thin pale veil, like the world itself was holding its breath.

Roman looked at her with something raw in his face—regret, fear, an ache he couldn't hide. "Emmy…"

Her mind was a storm. No blood. No pain. Alive. Impossible.

"Tell me," she whispered, voice trembling. "How is that possible?!"

He didn't answer. Instead, he reached out as if to touch her cheek, then stopped, fingers curling back. His jaw tightened. His silence was louder than the chaos around them.

For the first time since she'd met him, Emmy felt a coldness slip between them, not from distance but from the truth he carried and couldn't yet speak.

Roman's hand fell back to his side, and before Emmy could press him again, the voices of the workmen drew nearer — heavy boots pounding, shouts of "Is everyone alright?" cutting through the dust and ringing in her ears.

Roman's head snapped toward the sound. His whole frame went taut, like a creature cornered. Without another word, he eased his arm from around her, the warmth gone in an instant.

"Roman—"

But he was already stepping back, his eyes dark with something she couldn't name. In the haze of dust, he turned sharply, slipping behind the fallen tangle of scaffold as if the chaos itself had swallowed him whole.

"Miss Trevelyn!" a voice called — one of the caretakers, jogging toward her with two workmen close behind. She tore her eyes from the space where Roman had stood only heartbeats ago.

"I— I'm fine," Emmy said, her voice uneven as she steadied herself. Her knees still felt untrustworthy, her pulse hammering. The men swarmed around, checking the heap of scaffolding, muttering about a faulty brace, lucky it hadn't gone worse.

Emmy nodded along, but her thoughts weren't with them. They were with the man who had taken the full force of the collapse, who should have been bleeding, broken — and who had walked away without a mark.

She pressed a trembling hand to her chest. No blood. No pain. Alive. Impossible.

And gone.

# Chapter 28

The world after the crash was a blur of urgency and half-heard voices. Emmy barely felt her legs carry her inside the school hall before she was pressed into a chair. Hands fluttered over her, checking for cuts, bruises, concussion. June crouched before her, one hand still clasping Emmy's wrist, as though afraid she might float away if she let go.

"Emmy—look at me. Are you hurt? Tell me honestly—"

"I'm fine," Emmy said, though the words rasped out dry. Fine. The least convincing word in the English language.

The paramedics arrived quickly, their green uniforms sharp against the grey stone walls. They asked her questions— What's your name? What day is it? Where does it hurt?—and though she answered every one, their expressions didn't soften. She was pale, they said. Her pulse was fast. Her pupils too wide.

"Shock," one decided, tugging gently at her elbow. "You've had a fright. Best you come with us to get you checked over properly."

She didn't argue. Her mind was still behind her, outside, fixed on the impossible sight of Roman standing with steel through him, impossibly whole.

* * *

At the hospital, light and sound seemed harsher. Strip bulbs glared down. The air smelled sharply of antiseptic, mixed with coffee long burned. A nurse clipped an oximeter to her finger, wrapped a cuff around her arm, slid a thermometer across her temple. Normal. All normal.

The doctor, a middle-aged man with kind eyes and a too-short tie, studied her vitals, then crouched slightly to meet her gaze.

"You've had a very lucky escape," he said, voice steady but not unfeeling. "That scaffolding could have fallen just a few feet closer and…" He didn't finish the sentence. He didn't need to. "You may not feel injured, but shock can mask things. I'd like to keep you in overnight for observation, make sure nothing develops. Concussions, bruising, even internal injuries sometimes take hours to appear."

June, who had insisted on riding in the ambulance with her, nodded fiercely as if Emmy might otherwise refuse. "She'll stay," she declared, speaking for her. "Of course she'll stay."

Emmy gave a dazed nod. She was compliant because she couldn't muster the energy not to be.

* * *

They settled her in a curtained cubicle, pale blankets pulled over her legs, a jug of water within reach. The steady beep of machines in the next bay, the occasional rolling squeak of a trolley, the intercom calling for a registrar—all of it wove around her, strangely unreal.

June sat with her until visiting hours ended, filling the silence with little bursts of chatter: how the staff had been brilliant at getting the children safely out, how parents were already on social media demanding answers from the contractors, how Emmy should let herself rest. Emmy nodded in the right places, murmured "yes" and "mm," but her thoughts were elsewhere. Always elsewhere.

She could still see it: Roman turning his head, eyes meeting hers, metal jutting clean through where flesh and bone should have failed. And then... nothing. No wound, no blood. Just Roman, alive, walking away.

* * *

After June left—squeezing her hand and promising to check in first thing—Emmy lay in the hospital bed, staring at the curtain that separated her from the next patient. The clock ticked in heavy, indifferent beats.

Sleep would not come.

Every time she closed her eyes, she saw him. Not the scaffolding. Not the fall. Him.

By two in the morning, she had sat up, restless, hands twisting in the thin blanket. By three, she was perched on the edge of the bed, head in her hands. By four, she was standing barefoot on the cold linoleum floor, heart hammering with a decision she couldn't ignore.

She couldn't stay here another minute, wrapped in white sheets and unanswered questions. She needed him. Needed the truth from his own lips.

When the nurse came to check her vitals again at half past four, Emmy asked—politely, firmly—if she could be discharged. She was alert, walking steadily, vital signs strong. The nurse looked uncertain, but after consulting with the doctor on duty, they agreed. "If anything changes, come straight back," the nurse said, helping her sign the paperwork.

"Of course," Emmy replied, though she had no intention of anything but one course of action.

\* \* \*

The sky was paling when Emmy stepped outside, a soft blue-grey hinting at dawn. The car park smelled faintly of wet tarmac and early-morning chill. She pulled her cardigan close and walked—past the bus stop, past the sleepy bakery van unloading flour, through the hushed square toward the hidden path that wound up to the manor.

Her body was exhausted. Her mind was a storm. But every step forward felt inevitable.

Roman could no longer run from her questions.

And she would no longer let him.

* * *

Emmy's shoes tapped quietly against the pavement. Each step was both too fast and not fast enough. The hospital wristband still clung to her arm, the plastic stiff against her skin, a reminder of where she should have been. But her feet carried her forward, up the hill, toward the manor that seemed to loom larger with each turn of the path.

She tried, uselessly, to order her thoughts.

What had she seen? Not a trick of light. Not an illusion born of panic. Steel had pierced him—she had seen it—and yet he'd stood there, whole, alive, as though the laws of the world had bent for him alone.

Her chest tightened. Her mind darted between terror and awe, between the memory of him shielding her and the unbearable silence in his eyes.

The gates to Roman's estate were open. Not flung wide, not inviting, but ajar—as though left that way by absent-mindedness, or perhaps intention. Emmy paused at the threshold, breath misting in the cool air, her hand brushing the iron as if it might bite.

For a heartbeat, she wondered if she should turn back. Go home. Pretend none of this had ever happened. Pretend she hadn't seen him defy death itself.

No, she couldn't – the thought withered almost instantly. She couldn't unknow. She couldn't forget. And she couldn't live with silence gnawing her insides raw.

She pushed through the gates.

The gravel crunched underfoot as she crossed the long, sweeping drive. The manor rose ahead, its windows catching the paling light, tall and watchful. The house looked ancient in the dawn, not just old but enduring, as though it had stood longer than time itself cared to measure.

Her stomach turned as she reached the steps. She'd been here before, walked through these doors, but never with such a storm of questions inside her. Never with her heart this loud in her ears.

The great door loomed before her. She lifted her hand, hesitated, then knocked. Once. Twice. The sound echoed into the hollow quiet.

No answer.

Her knuckles pressed again, firmer this time, before the weight of the door creaked open on its own. Not a dramatic swing, just a reluctant inching, as though the house itself had sighed.

Emmy stepped inside.

Inside, the air was cool, touched with the faintest hint of woodsmoke and something older—paper, stone, memory. Shadows stretched long in the hallway, the pale light of morning edging through the high windows and pooling against the tiled floor.

"Roman?"

Her voice trembled despite her resolve. The name felt fragile in the vastness of the house.

She stepped forward, her hand trailing against the carved banister, listening for the sound of footsteps, of life. Only the faint creak of wood answered her.

Then—soft, deliberate—the sound of steps on the stairs above.

Her breath caught.

A figure emerged slowly from the shadowed landing, descending with unhurried grace. Roman. His hand brushed the carved banister as he came down, his expression unreadable in the muted light, green eyes catching hers only once before sliding away.

When he reached the last step, the silence pressed thick between them.

"You're here," she said, though it sounded foolish on her lips.

"I am." His voice was quieter than usual, edged with something she couldn't place. He studied her for a long moment, his gaze sweeping over her face, her shoulders, as though searching for what she wasn't saying. Then, softer still: "How are you?"

The question seemed to settle everything else—the storm of unanswered doubts, the strangeness of what she'd seen. For a heartbeat, it was just kindness in his voice.

"I'm... fine," Emmy said, though the word didn't feel steady. "They said I was lucky. Just bruising, nothing broken. They wanted to keep me in longer, but I couldn't—" She broke off, pressing her lips together. She hadn't been able to stay when the only image in her mind was him, impossibly alive, vanishing before her eyes.

Roman inclined his head, relief flickering in his expression. "I was afraid," he admitted. His hand tightened slightly on the banister before he let it go. "Afraid you might not come."

"I wasn't going to stay away," she whispered. "I didn't get a chance to say thank you."

Something passed across his face then—an unreadable shadow, quickly smoothed. He gave the faintest nod toward a set of double doors opening off the hallway. "Come."

He moved ahead of her, pushing the heavy doors open.

The room beyond was vast, unlike any she had yet seen in the house. Panelled walls rose high into a shadowed ceiling, their carvings deep with age. A long rug stretched from door to hearth, patterned in faded threads that hinted at brighter days. And there, dominating the far wall, was a fireplace unlike any Emmy had known—its arch framed in pale stone, broad enough that three people might have stood inside it. Logs had already been set aflame, the fire leaping with a restless, consuming hunger.

Roman stood before it, half turned toward her, the light striking across his features so one side was etched in warmth, the other lost to shadow. His hands rested against the mantle, as though the stone itself steadied him.

"You look cold," he said at last, eyes flicking over her pale hands.

"I'm fine," she replied quickly, though she realised only then she had been shivering since she left the hospital.

"Still." He turned slightly, lifting the iron poker to shift a log deeper into the blaze. Sparks rushed upward, gilding the air in fleeting stars. The fire roared louder, filling the great lounge with a heat that wrapped around her at last. "Come closer."

She obeyed almost without thought, her steps soft against the rug.

Roman set the poker back in its stand and looked at her properly then, his expression carved sharp in firelight. "You should not have seen what you did. That truth was never meant for you."

The words struck her, a sting beneath the warmth. "You saved me. If it weren't for you, I—"

"You saw," he interrupted gently, though his tone carried weight. "You saw what no one should."

And the images came rushing back: the crash of scaffolding, his body shielding hers, the impossible sight of iron piercing him yet leaving no blood, no ruin, no death. Alive. Whole.

Her mouth dried. "I don't understand."

"You will," he murmured, gaze flicking briefly to the fire before finding hers again. "But once I speak it, there is no going back."

The logs cracked, spilling sparks that faded before they touched the rug. Emmy felt her pulse hammering as if it might split her chest. Still, she didn't look away.

"Then tell me."

Roman held her gaze for a long, silent moment. His shoulders rose with a deep breath, his jaw tightening as though he weighed the centuries against the fragile present. Then he exhaled slowly, almost like surrender.

"Sit," he said, gesturing to the high-backed chair angled toward the hearth. "This will not be easily told."

The fire cracked and spat, a cascade of sparks leaping up the chimney. Emmy felt the heat lick at her cheeks, but her hand in Roman's steadied her more than the flames. His palm was broad, cool against her warmth, as though even his blood carried the weight of centuries.

Roman didn't speak at once. He studied her, searching her expression for hesitation, fear — the reflex most people would have in the face of his truth. When he found none, only the stubborn determination in her wide eyes, something in him softened.

"You shouldn't want to hear this," he murmured, almost to himself. "Every time I've let someone close… it has ended the same. With distance. With grief. With their questions left unanswered."

"And yet," Emmy said gently, "I'm still here."

He gave a slow nod, the faintest smile tugging at his mouth — though it vanished quickly, replaced with gravity.

"When I was a boy," he began, voice low, "I thought death was a far-off thing. My father was strong, broad-shouldered, the kind of man who filled a room without trying. He worked the land, rode hard, hunted, laughed loud. To me, he was indestructible."

Roman's gaze dropped to the flames. "But death came anyway. Sudden. Cruel. I learned early that the world takes without warning."

Emmy's throat tightened. She remembered him telling her in passing that the house had been built by his father, finished by him for his mother. That old grief was written into every stone of this place.

"My mother..." He exhaled, the sound long and heavy. "She was softer, quieter. The house was hers after he was gone. I finished what he had begun so she could have peace here. But she too... slipped away." His jaw worked, green eyes glinting. "And yet I stayed."

The way he said it made Emmy's skin prickle. Not lived on, not survived. Stayed.

"It should have been me, Emmy," he said after a pause, his voice roughened. "My life should have ended when theirs did. But it didn't. It never does."

Emmy's fingers tightened around his hand. She wanted to pull him closer, to shoulder even a piece of the weight that bent him.

"Do you know how many generations I've watched come and go in this valley?" he asked suddenly, his voice turning sharp with memory. "How many faces I've seen born, grow, laugh, weep, die? Their children mourning them, then the children's children after that. Whole lineages pass like a season. And still, I remain."

His gaze snapped to hers, the firelight cutting his features into stark relief. "Do you know what that does to a man?"

Emmy swallowed, her words careful. "It must be... unbearable. But it doesn't make you less human."

A low, incredulous laugh escaped him, though it carried no humour. "Doesn't it? I have lived longer than any man should. I have buried every person I dared love. I have lived through witch trials, plagues, wars, famines... and still I wake each morning. I've become a ghost who happens to walk in daylight."

Emmy shook her head firmly. "No. You're not a ghost. You're sitting right here."

Roman searched her face, some internal war flickering in his eyes. Slowly, he eased back, their linked hands still resting between them.

"I have thought about telling someone," he admitted, voice quieter now. "About stepping forward, seeking answers. But I know what mankind does to what it cannot understand. I learned that lesson long ago."

Her brows knit. "The witch trials," she said softly, recalling his earlier words.

His jaw tensed. "I was dragged before a crowd once. Accused of things they couldn't name. Surviving what should have killed me... it frightened them. They chained me, questioned me, prepared the pyre. If not for fortune — and a kind soul who risked everything to help me escape — I would have burned that day. Do you wonder, then, why I keep to shadows?"

Emmy's stomach twisted. The thought of him, green eyes alight with flames that weren't firelight but execution, made her shiver. "Roman..."

He looked away, rising from the chair as if distance could cage what he had unleashed. "This is too much for you. I shouldn't have said any of it."

Emmy rose too, crossing the space quickly, her hand finding his again before he could step back. He looked down, startled, as her fingers wrapped tight around his.

"You don't get to decide what's too much for me," she said, her voice trembling but firm. "I asked you to tell me. And I meant it. I'm not going anywhere."

For a long moment, silence stretched between them, filled only by the hiss and crack of the fire. Then, at last, Roman's shoulders eased — not free of his burden, but no longer carrying it alone.

Roman's hand was still in hers, but he looked at it as though it were something he didn't quite recognise. His lips parted as if to argue, to push her away again for her own sake — but the words never came. Instead, he gave the smallest of nods, as though conceding to a battle he had no strength left to fight.

"You don't know what you're saying, Emmy," he said at last, his voice low, thickened with something she couldn't quite name. "You think you want the truth — but the truth cuts deeper than any blade."

"Then let it cut," she whispered.

He closed his eyes briefly, drawing in a slow breath, as though steadying himself against a tide that had been pressing at him for centuries. When he opened them again, the green in his gaze seemed almost too bright against the firelight.

"There was someone once," he began, and Emmy felt the air shift — heavy, fragile. "Her name was Elise."

The name alone carried a weight that made Emmy's heart tighten.

"She was… unlike anyone I'd met," Roman continued, his words halting at first, then flowing with reluctant rhythm.

"Sharp-minded, tender-hearted. She had a way of making the world less cruel simply by standing in it. For a time, I thought perhaps… perhaps I could remain. That I could ignore the curse, deny it, and live as if I were any other man."

Emmy's grip tightened on his hand. "What happened?"

Roman's eyes flicked to the fire, the shadows dancing across his face. "Time happened. She grew older. I did not."

The silence that followed was deafening. Emmy's breath caught.

"I tried, for as long as I could, to hide it. But years betray themselves in small ways. People notice when a man doesn't change. Whispers began. Suspicions. It put her in danger simply to love me. And when I realised that… I let her go." His voice broke slightly on the last word, like glass splintering beneath pressure.

Emmy felt her chest ache. She thought of this man, centuries of strength etched into his bearing, standing powerless before the one thing he could never outrun: time.

"You loved her," she said softly.

His jaw worked. He didn't deny it. "More than I should have. More than was wise. And when she passed…" His voice faltered, a flicker of pain crossing his features. "I buried her with my own hands. And then I walked on, while she remained beneath the earth."

Emmy swallowed hard, her eyes stinging. Without thinking, she raised her free hand and touched his arm, as though grounding him in the present. "That must have been unbearable."

Roman let out a strained laugh — not cruel, but hollow, carrying the weight of centuries. "It is the price of what I am. To love is to suffer. And yet..." His gaze met hers then, burning and unflinching. "Here you are. And I... I cannot help but care."

Emmy's breath caught. The honesty in his voice was raw, terrifying, beautiful.

"You don't have to carry it all alone anymore," she whispered.

For a moment, Roman looked at her as though she were something impossible — not fragile, not fleeting, but steady in the storm he had lived within for so long. Slowly, as though pulled by something greater than choice, he lifted his hand and brushed a loose curl from her cheek, letting his fingers linger just a breath too long.

The fire roared softly behind them. Outside, the wind rattled faintly against the high windows. But within the lounge, the world had narrowed to just the two of them — one immortal, one fleeting, yet both caught in a moment that felt suspended in time.

Roman's hand lingered against her cheek, warm despite the coolness that had seeped into Emmy's bones since the accident. His thumb brushed lightly against her skin, almost reverent, as though he feared she might vanish if he touched her too firmly.

Emmy's heart was beating so loudly she was sure he could hear it. She didn't move away. She couldn't. His closeness was both grounding and dizzying, the firelight painting shadows across his sharp cheekbones, glinting in the green of his eyes.

"Roman..." she breathed, her voice unsteady, more a confession than a name.

His expression softened, but sorrow remained etched into its edges. "You don't understand what you're asking," he said, though the words lacked conviction. They sounded like a man trying to convince himself, not her.

"I'm not asking for anything," she whispered back. "Just... don't pull away."

A muscle in his jaw twitched. His breath faltered. For a man who had lived centuries, he looked utterly undone by the simplicity of her words.

He leaned closer, so slowly it was as though he were moving through water. His hand still rested at her cheek, his other sliding over hers where it still held his, enclosing it in warmth. The space between them tightened, a fragile thread stretched taut.

Emmy's gaze dipped to his lips, unbidden. She caught herself, startled, and dragged her eyes back up to his — only to find him already watching her, caught in the same suspended pull.

The fire crackled behind them, throwing sparks that snapped in the silence.

He stopped, just shy of her, their foreheads nearly touching. His breath brushed her skin.

"If I cross this line," he said hoarsely, "there is no going back. Not for me."

Her chest rose and fell quickly, every nerve alive. "Maybe I don't want you to go back," she replied, the words trembling but true.

For the briefest second, Roman looked as though he might yield — centuries of restraint trembling under the weight of the present. His lips parted, his eyes closing ever so slightly, his hand tightening over hers.

But then he drew in a sharp breath, pulling himself back as though burned. He broke away just enough that the air cooled between them again, though not enough to erase the closeness.

Emmy's heart clenched. The space felt unbearable after what had nearly been.

Roman looked at her, anguish etched deep. "Forgive me," he whispered. "I cannot..."

Silence hung, fragile and aching. Emmy searched his face, trying to read the storm behind his eyes. And though he had pulled back, she could still feel the ghost of his touch at her cheek, her hand, her very skin.

She swallowed hard, her voice quiet but steady. "I'm not going anywhere, Roman."

He closed his eyes briefly, as though the words both steadied and tormented him. Then he released her hand, slowly, gently, as if letting go of something too precious to keep — but too dangerous to hold.

The fire crackled louder, filling the silence, as both of them sat in the long shadow of what almost happened.

# Chapter 29

The fire settled into a steady roar, the kind that holds a room together. Emmy sat where she'd been all along, one knee tucked beneath her, hands laced so tightly her knuckles had blanched. Roman had drawn back only a breath since that almost-moment, as if proximity itself were dangerous. Between them, a low table and the pooled glow of the hearth; behind them, the house listening.

They didn't speak at first. Silence had a texture now—soft, heavy, threaded with everything he'd told her and everything he'd chosen not to. Emmy watched the flames run their fingers up the logs and tried to name the feeling in her chest. It wasn't fear. It wasn't exactly calm. It was like standing in the doorway of a new room, one she'd walked past for months and only now noticed was open.

"What happens now?" Her voice surprised her by being steady. It dropped into the quiet and lay there, honest.

Roman's gaze lifted from the fire. The green of his eyes looked darker in the hearth light, shadow and embers caught together. "Now," he said slowly, "you decide if you can bear knowing what you know. And I decide if I can bear… letting you."

Her fingers tightened again. "You've already let me."

A breath that might have been a laugh tugged at one corner of his mouth. "Against my better judgement."

"Against your habits," she corrected gently.

He inclined his head, conceding the point. For a moment they watched each other as if they were both learning the other's face anew—hers, pale with the night and the hospital; his, carved with the weight of years that didn't show on skin.

A shiver ran down her arms then, involuntary and obvious. The room was warm, but the day and the confession had left a chill she couldn't shake. Roman noticed before she could pretend otherwise. He rose without comment, crossed to a chest set beneath one of the tall windows, and took out a folded wool blanket the colour of old moss.

"Here." He shook it loose and settled it around her shoulders with a careful thoroughness that made her throat tighten. His hand, in the last moment, brushed the side of her neck; the touch was light, almost incidental, and yet she felt it everywhere.

"Thank you," she managed.

"Tea?" he asked, as if this were a perfectly ordinary morning and not one that had upended her understanding of the world. When she nodded, he disappeared through an inner door. She heard the familiar small music of a kitchen—water, cups, the simple rhythm of a man who had made himself at home inside his solitude for a very long time.

Emmy let her eyes travel the room while he was gone. The lounge revealed itself in layers: the high panelling; a tall clock with a face the colour of cream and numbers painted by a careful hand; a long, low cabinet with glass doors that held a regiment of old books and stranger items—an astrolabe dulled by time, a brass weight on a string, a vial with a stopper clouded by age. Each object felt less like decoration than evidence. Someone had been here long enough to gather a life's worth of small certainties and keep them dusted.

Roman returned with two cups on a tray, a small pot and a jar of honey. "I don't have milk in just now," he said, almost apologetic. "I forgot to fetch more after the storm."

"It's fine." She took the cup, grateful for something to hold. The porcelain surprised her—thin, light, a hairline crack running from rim to handle that only made it more precious. Steam curled against her face. She breathed it in and felt herself settle by inches.

He didn't sit immediately. He stood at the mantel, one shoulder lightly resting against the carved stone, eyes on her over the rim of his cup. "There's a part that's yours to choose," he said at last. "What you tell. Who you trust. I have... survived, in part, by being careful. Those I've let close are few."

She thought of June, of the way her friend read the world with a steady teacher's sense and a soft heart, and felt the temptation to say a name. But the vision of Roman in a glass room—his own words—rose up and stopped her. She set the cup down, folded her hands under the blanket.

"I won't tell anyone," she said quietly. "Not because I'm afraid for myself. Because I'm afraid for you."

He exhaled a breath that wasn't quite relief. "Caution is not cowardice," he murmured. "It's what keeps ordinary days possible." He nodded toward the tray. "And I would like... ordinary days. With you. If you want them. We can go on as we have. Walks. Work. Kittens and bread. No grand declarations. Just—time."

Time. The word felt strange between them, a thing that had treated them so differently. She looked up and met his eyes. "I want that," she said, and knew she meant it. "I want to try."

Something eased in his face then, subtle but real. He came back to his chair and sat opposite, mirroring her posture without seeming to intend it, his hands linked loosely like a man holding a rope he has finally stopped tugging against.

"I have to ask something," she went on before courage could ebb. "You said... it was an accident. Not fate." She watched a flicker cross his features; he looked at the fire. "You don't have to tell me the story," she added quickly. "Not now.

513

I'm not asking for all of it. But—does it have an end? Your curse?"

His jaw worked. For a heartbeat she thought he wouldn't answer at all. "If it does," he said softly, "I've never found it."

The honey in her tea had gone cool. She set the cup aside and drew the blanket closer. "Then we won't look for endings today."

It made him huff a sound that might have been amusement. "No. Today we look for beginnings."

They let that rest between them, the smallest smile finding its way to her mouth. She hadn't realised until this moment how tired she was—how the hospital lights and the ambulance's cold vinyl and the taste of fear had worked into her bones. The fire and the tea and the simple act of being seen had begun to undo that.

"You should sleep," Roman said, as if reading the downward pull in her eyelids. "There's a guest room made up, if you'd rather not walk back yet."

The offer startled her—not for its kindness but because of what it implied: trust. Safety. For a second she pictured it— a bed with linen that smelt faintly of lavender and woodsmoke, sunlight sneaking past a curtain in a pattern she hadn't learned yet. The house felt different now that the truth had changed the air inside it. More itself.

"I… think I should go home," she said carefully. "I need my own walls around me while my brain catches up."

He nodded, unoffended. "I'll walk you."

"You don't have to."

"I know."

They stood at the same time. The blanket slid from her shoulders and he caught it, folding it loosely and laying it along the back of the chair with the ease of a man whose hands prefer doing to thinking. She picked up her coat and he helped her into it without ceremony, as if he had always done such things.

They went out through the hall, the echo of their steps softened by runner rugs. In the entry, he lifted a lantern from a hook; its glass had been polished until it carried a faintly warped reflection of the world. He lit the wick with a match from a small tin, sheltered the flame with his palm until it steadied, then opened the door.

The morning had moved on while they spoke. Light lay thin and honest over the lawn. The edges of the grass still wore dew, and the hedges along the drive shivered when the wind combed them. They walked without hurry. Gravel whispered underfoot. Once, a robin burst up from the low yew and landed ahead of them as if to inspect their progress, body tilting with each tiny step.

"Does it hurt?" Emmy asked after a while, surprising herself. "When you're… hurt. Do you feel it?"

515

"Yes." He didn't pretend otherwise. "Pain is a language the body always understands. I feel it. It simply... doesn't end me."

"I saw the rod," she said, because saying the thing out loud made it less like a dream set loose in her. "I saw it in you."

He kept his eyes on the drive. "So did I."

"And you were calm."

"I was afraid," he corrected softly. "But not of dying." He glanced at her then, quick and real. "Of losing you."

She didn't trust herself to speak after that. They finished the remainder of the walk in a quiet that had grown companionable, the kind born of two people who have stopped pretending. At the gates he set the lantern on the low stone pillar and turned the iron latch. It gave with a familiar clack.

They took the side path down toward the village, the one that slid between hawthorn and old brick. The square had begun to stir—an elderly man sweeping his step, the smell of fresh bread pushing out of the bakery's back door, a post van shouldering into its day. Emmy felt the world adjust around her the way a coat settles on shoulders.

Outside the bookshop's separate door, they paused. The sign above it creaked once in the light breeze, a sound she'd learned to love. Roman looked up at the window with its thin white curtains as if memorising it, then back at her.

516

"Thank you for coming," he said. It was an odd sentence, and exactly right.

"I don't know what I'll think later," she admitted. "Or tomorrow. I don't know if I'll wake up and feel like I dreamt all this. But right now…" She let herself smile. "Right now I'm glad I came."

"Me too." The words were simple. He made them feel wide.

He didn't reach for her again, and she didn't close the space either. That restraint felt like respect. He took a half step back, as if to turn away, then stopped. "The kittens," he said, unexpected as a petal falling. "Will you come by later to see them?"

"Yes," she said at once, surprised by how much she wanted that sentence to be true. "After I've had a nap. And something that isn't hospital tea."

A ghost of a smile touched his mouth. "I can manage eggs."

"You always can." The fondness in her voice came out before she could stop it. It didn't feel like a mistake.

He picked up the lantern again, more out of habit than need now that the daylight had found its confidence. For a second longer they looked at one another, the quiet running between them like a seam. Then Emmy slid her key into the lock and felt the tumblers yield. She glanced back. "Later," she said.

"Later," he echoed.

She stepped into the narrow stairwell, the familiar smell of old paper and polish rising to meet her. The door clicked shut behind her with its usual small authority. She stood there for a moment, leaning against the cool wall, and listened. The sounds of the morning moved through the building—the shop below settling into itself though it was closed, a pigeon landing on the sill and moving on, the hush of her own breath. Somewhere outside, Roman's footsteps receded, steady and unhurried.

Upstairs, the flat waited exactly as she had left it: mug on the counter, the view from the window holding to its square of sky. She put the kettle on without quite meaning to, turned it off again before it boiled. The hospital wristband still circled her arm; she slid a finger beneath it and paused, then left it on, a small proof that the day had happened.

On the table, the stack of exercise books sat where she'd dropped them the previous day, a green pen lying at a diagonal. She touched the top cover and felt the steady thread of ordinary life run beneath her fingers. It didn't make the extraordinary smaller. It made it bearable.

When she finally lay down, the sleep she fell into was immediate and clean, as if her body had been waiting for permission. She dreamed in fragments: firelight on carved wood; the particular green of his eyes; four small shapes kneading at straw; the sound of scaffolding and a hand closing around her, pulling her into shelter. When she woke, it was early afternoon and sunlight had shifted to the other side of the square. For a heartbeat she lay still, counting all the things that were the same—the ceiling's hairline crack, the hum of the fridge, the scuff in the skirting board—and then the one thing that wasn't.

A knock sounded, soft as a question. She sat up too quickly, then laughed at herself and went to the door. When she opened it, there was no one there except for a small wrapped bundle on the mat: a brown paper parcel tied with twine. On top, a note in precise, old-fashioned script.

Rest. Then come when you're ready. The small ones are loud with opinions. — R.

She pressed the paper to her mouth and smiled into it. The parcel held still-warm scones—plain, no lemon at all— and a tiny jar of strawberry jam. It was an ordinary kindness. It felt like a promise.

Emmy ate half a scone at the counter, jam bright on her tongue, and stared out at a sky that was trying on blue. She thought about the way Roman had said ordinary days, as if the phrase were something rare. She thought about the fire licking up the grate and the way his hand had tightened over hers when she'd said she wasn't going anywhere. She thought about time, not as a wall but as a path she could walk at her own human pace, with a man who had been forced to walk it differently and might—if she chose—let her set a rhythm he could bear.

She washed her plate, left it to dry. She pulled on her boots, tied her hair back under a satin scarf because the afternoon still had a wind to it, and stood with her hand on the latch. She didn't owe the empty room an answer, but she said one out loud anyway.

"Later," she repeated, smiling, and stepped back into the day.

# Chapter 30

The late afternoon light clung to the rooftops of the village, burnishing them in bronze as Emmy stepped out of her flat. The bookshop's bell jangled faintly behind her as she pulled the door closed, the sound swallowed quickly by the quiet of the street. It wasn't busy — just a couple of shoppers with bags, a boy balancing on the curb, the distant rumble of a lorry on the main road. Ordinary, almost comforting. And yet her chest carried none of that ease.

Her feet moved of their own accord, turning toward the path that wound up to Roman's estate. The same path she'd taken before, and yet today it seemed different — heavier somehow, weighted with all she now knew, all she wasn't sure she was ready to know.

She told herself she was only going to see the kittens. That the promise of their small, mewling lives was reason enough. But the truth thrummed deeper: she wanted to see him. To look at him without chaos closing in, without stone and scaffolding and bloodless wounds between them. She needed to know if he would let her.

The fields opened up, the long grass shifting in waves as the wind bent it low. The manor's silhouette rose against the fading light, sharp and steady as if time itself had never laid a hand on it.

The late afternoon had thinned to gold by the time Emmy reached the gate. Iron met her palm with its small, familiar resistance; beyond, the drive unrolled in a pale ribbon toward the house. She stepped through. A breeze pressed the hedges into a soft, one-sided bow and let them spring back. Somewhere a woodpigeon worked at its two-note hymn. Ordinary sounds, ordinary light. The shape of an unordinary day.

Roman met her halfway, as if he'd known the exact moment she would appear. He wasn't carrying a lantern now; the sky did the work. He had his sleeves rolled again, and the line between his brows—habit rather than worry—smoothed when he saw her.

"You came," he said.

"You asked." She lifted the brown paper parcel in her hand—its twine already undone and re-wrapped. "And you fed me."

"Bribery," he said gravely. "Effective on schoolteachers and kittens alike."

He didn't reach for her, and she didn't step in. It felt right to let the space be what it was—a seam rather than a gap. But when he gestured toward the side path, she fell into step beside him without thinking, the quiet between them a new kind of ease.

"They've found their voices," he warned as they walked past the kitchen garden. Bean poles made a jagged picket against the sky, their twine ladders slick with light. "Small opinions. Loud insistence."

"I've taught Year Four," she said. "I'm trained for this."

He let out a low sound—not quite laughter, the shape of it. The outbuilding door stood open a hand's width. Inside, straw and old wood and the particular warm, milky smell of animals braided together. Roman eased the door wider and stood aside.

The nest was exactly where it had been before: a low box tucked near the wall, hay tucked in a messy wreath, an old wool blanket folded beneath. The mother cat lifted her head when they entered, ears pricking, amber eyes bright and untroubled. She made a small questioning sound that softened as soon as Roman knelt.

"There," he said, voice dropping as though they'd stepped into a chapel. "We're only visitors."

The kittens were a handful of moving commas. One was dark as soot, a little smudge with a pink mouth; another a classic tabby, stripes like careful script; the third wore white socks and a half-mask, as if he'd fallen asleep during painting;

the fourth was pale with ginger ghosting his back, sleepily determined. Their eyes were beginning to crack open, opal-slit and uncertain. Emmy crouched, the hem of her coat settling around her boots, and felt her chest loosen in that way new life always undid her.

"Hello," she whispered, because anything louder would have been an intrusion. "You've grown."

"They're convinced they've invented living," Roman murmured. He held out his hand, palm up. The soot-dark one nosed his thumb with surprising purpose, then latched onto the side of his hand as if he were a cliff. Roman didn't move until the kitten worked out that the cliff wasn't edible and slid backwards in baffled dignity.

Emmy laughed before she could swallow the sound. It rung lightly against the beams and did nothing at all to disturb the mother cat, who, with the long-suffering air of new mothers everywhere, lay her head back down and allowed the world to go on.

"May I?" Emmy asked, and waited for Roman's nod before offering a single finger. The white-socked kitten patted at her, claws no more than suggestions. "You are ferocious," she told him solemnly.

"Utterly," Roman agreed.

She stayed like that a long time—knees objecting, heart behaving itself by beating in something like contentment—

until pins and needles made themselves known and she rocked back onto her heels. Roman rose first and offered her a hand. She took it. Warmth drew through her in a line from palm to shoulder, nothing romantic about it, and entirely so.

"Tea?" he asked.

"Please."

They didn't go to the great room this time. He led her through the side door straight into the kitchen: a generous space that looked as if it had been added and mended and added again over years, not designed in one go. Wide flagstones. A table scrubbed pale with use. A deep sink with a single porcelain chip in its rim. Potted herbs lined the sill, their green clean and particular—thyme, basil, something she couldn't name. The window opened onto the interior courtyard, and through it she could see the tiny tree that anchored the space, leaves bright as if lit from within.

Roman set the kettle on the hob and lifted a basket from the counter. "Eggs?" he asked without looking round. "They're on strike sometimes after a storm. Today they were generous."

"Eggs would be perfect."

He moved with that economy she'd noticed before—no wasted motions, no clatter. Two shallow bowls came down from a shelf, butter softened, a heel of bread cut on the bias and dropped into the iron pan. He cracked the eggs one-handed with the absolute lack of showmanship that marks long practice. Emmy, who had eaten a scone and jam and called it lunch, found her hunger arriving all at once.

"What is it," she said, "about eggs and bread that makes a day feel solvable?"

"Ancient magics," he said dryly. "The reliable kind."

They ate at the table with the window unlatched, the courtyard's quiet poured in—the intermittent trickle of water from the little rill that slid into the pool, the soft fret of leaves. Swallows arrowed overhead, stitching shadows across stone. Emmy watched him cut his toast into precise corners and felt herself ease further, moment by moment, into this small plain grace.

"Thank you," she said after the second mouthful. "For… all of it." It meant the eggs and the scones and the note in the neat, old-fashioned hand; it meant the firelight and the truth he'd given her and the restraint afterward.

He didn't pretend to misunderstand. "You're welcome."

"I meant what I said earlier," she went on, because silence could invite doubt. "I won't tell anyone. Not June. Not anyone."

A small muscle worked in his cheek, and then was still. "I know."

That surprised her. "Do you?"

"I know what you are," he said, and the sentence could have been a trap in other mouths. In his, it sounded like a fact that asked nothing more of her than to keep being it. "You hold what is given. You don't spend it to make a story."

She looked down at her plate, suddenly shy of tears over something as simple as being seen. "I don't promise to be unafraid," she said after a breath. "I promise not to run on fear alone."

"That's braver than you think," he replied.

When they'd finished and Roman had set the plates in the sink, he reached for a cloth, dipped it, and wiped the table in slow, absent circles. Emmy drifted to the window. The courtyard had its own temperature, its own weather; sunlight collected there even when the rest of the world decided to be stingy. The tree's leaves caught and kept the light, and a bee busied itself in something pale and fragrant near the wall.

"You made this," she said, not a question.

"My mother loved it," he answered simply. "It did what it was meant to do."

Emmy turned that over. She didn't need the rest of the sentence to hear the whole of it.

He opened the door and they stepped out. The flagstones still held warmth from earlier, late sun folded along the walls. Doors opened from three sides into the space—kitchen, a passage to the hall, another to somewhere she hadn't been yet.

Roman left them closed. The court felt like a small, inward-facing world, everything else set at a kind distance.

They didn't talk much there. A kind of wordless drift took over—Roman refilling the little pool from a half-hidden tap, Emmy picking windfall petals from the path and collecting them in her palm without really meaning to. He sat for a while on the low stone bench and sketched quick, loose lines in a small notebook, glancing up as if catching something that moved too fast for words. When she leaned closer, he angled the page so she could see: the mother cat, in two strokes and a suggestion; a tiny flurry of kitten-scramble; her own hand on the sill, the curve of her wrist, the edge of a sleeve. He didn't say anything when she realised. He didn't need to.

"Will you show me the orangery again another day?" she asked finally, remembering the first time she'd stepped into its candle-light and green.

"Another day," he agreed. "When evenings are cool enough to make it necessary."

She nodded. Ordinary plans. A quiet draft for a future she hadn't known to imagine last week.

When the light slipped toward evening properly, they went to check the kittens once more. The mother lifted her head again, untroubled; one of the pale ones had rolled onto his back and was testing the usefulness of his legs with all the finesse of a drunkard. Roman righted him with two fingers.

"That way," he advised, and the kitten, affronted by physics, huffed soundlessly and nosed into a sibling's ear.

They shut the outbuilding door to its usual hand's width and started back along the path. The house looked larger in this light—not forbidding, exactly, but full of more corners than a single day could contain. Through one ground-floor window Emmy caught the angled glint of glass in a case, the flash of something gilded and delicate—a pocket watch, perhaps, or a compass whose face had gone opaline with age. She didn't ask. She would have a lifetime to ask and then some, if she wanted it, and today was not for that. They continued to walk down heading towards the end of the wood.

At the gate, Roman paused and checked the latch as if it were a ritual. They took the track down into the village as the street began to gather its evening—someone drawing in washing; the pub chalking up the day's pie; a child calling for a ball and being told to use his inside voice though he was outside and thrilled with the fact of it. Emmy saw all of it and felt the rightness of the ordinary running out to meet her.

At her door they stopped again. The bookshop below would open tomorrow; the blackboard leaned against the inside of the glass, waiting for chalk. Roman's eyes went to the window as they always did. His hand rested lightly against the jamb, as if memorising the grain.

"Will you be all right?" he asked.

"I will." She tugged the satin scarf at her nape where the breeze had teased it loose. "Will you?"

A wryness flickered at the edge of his mouth. "I've had practice."

"Practice," she echoed, and shook her head. "I'm going to bring you something tomorrow. Something aggressively ordinary. A casserole, probably. You can pretend to be impressed."

"I won't have to pretend."

"Don't start thinking you can get out of this with flattery," she said, and then, softer, "Thank you. For today. For the small things."

"They're the real ones," he said. "The small ones."

She put her key to the lock but didn't turn it yet. "We're... all right?"

He took a fraction of a step—not closing the space, only narrowing it enough that she could see the fine lines that appeared at the corner of his eye when he smiled, lines time hadn't bothered to give him but tenderness had. "We're not at the end of a road," he said. "We're at the start of one."

It wasn't a declaration. It was better. It was a promise that didn't need either of them to be more than what they were.

She nodded. "Later," she said, the word having decided itself between them and finding its way back.

"Later," he returned.

This time she did turn the key. The door yielded, and the stairwell held its familiar cool. She stepped inside and looked back once. Roman had already turned away, not out of haste but because some moments are gentler when they're not looked at too hard. He lifted a hand in a small salute and headed down the lane, his figure lengthening in the low sun.

Upstairs, Emmy set her scarf on the back of a chair and leaned her forehead for a second against the window. The square went about its knitting. A couple strolled arm in arm. A dog paused to decide whether to bark at a pigeon. The evening put its hand on the shoulder of the day and said, kindly, enough.

Emmy touched the hospital wristband still circling her arm and left it there, not because she needed reminding of hurt but because it had started to mean something else. Proof that a life could veer and not break. Proof that she had walked through a door and found a room where the air was different.

She made tea without thinking. She set a second cup beside her own on the counter and laughed softly at herself and left it there anyway. When she sat, it was with a pen and one of the books from the pile she had been avoiding. In the margin of an especially brave story problem she wrote, in green ink, Excellent work. Keep going. She closed the book and put her hand flat on it for a breath, as if the encouragement were for her as much as for the small person who would read it Monday.

Outside, the light went slowly. The colour pulled down, leaving the edges blue. Emmy stood, turned off the lamp, and watched the last brightness settle itself on the rooftops. She didn't know what Book Two of her life with Roman would ask of her—what old stories would come walking, what truths would ask to be carried. But she knew this: she had chosen not to run.

Down the lane, a fox stepped out, looked around as if he owned the place, and went about his business.

"Ordinary days," Emmy said into the quiet, and smiled at the way the words fit in her mouth. Not ordinary like before, no. Ordinary like a heartbeat—constant, steady, miraculous only if you remembered to notice.

She turned from the window, carried her empty cup to the sink, and let the evening close behind her like a soft, good door.

# About the Author

Lucy Novacek has always loved creating stories filled with quiet beauty and deep emotion.

For years, she jotted down ideas and fragments — little pieces of characters, moments, and dreams that stayed with her.

Her debut novel, Eyes of Green, has been close to her heart for over a decade.

Lucy's writing is inspired by her love of cosy English villages, nature, and history — settings where time seems to slow and small details come alive.

When she isn't writing, she enjoys spending time outdoors with her young son, exploring woods and gardens that often find their way into her pages.

Follow Lucy on Instagram for updates and behind-the-scenes glimpses: @Lucy.Novacek

# Coming Soon

The story continues…

A new dawn awaits in Book Two of the

Eyes of Green saga

Printed in Dunstable, United Kingdom